Keep
Calm
and
Carry a
Big Drink

ALSO BY KIM GRUENENFELDER

There's Cake in My Future

Misery Loves Cabernet

A Total Waste of Makeup

Keep Calm and Carry a Big Drink

KIM GRUENENFELDER

ST. MARTIN'S GRIFFIN
NEW YORK

This is a work of fiction. All of the characters, organizations, and events portrayed in this novel are either products of the author's imagination or are used fictitiously.

KEEP CALM AND CARRY A BIG DRINK. Copyright © 2013 by Kim Gruenenfelder. All rights reserved. Printed in the United States of America. For information, address St. Martin's Press, 175 Fifth Avenue, New York, N.Y. 10010.

www.stmartins.com

Library of Congress Cataloging-in-Publication Data

Gruenenfelder-Smith, Kim.
    Keep calm and carry a big drink / Kim Gruenenfelder. — 1st. ed.
        p. cm
    ISBN 978-1-250-00504-5 (trade paperback)
    ISBN 978-1-250-02491-6 (e-book)
    1. Female friendship—Fiction.   2. Magic—Fiction.   I. Title.
    PS3607.R72K44 2013
    813'.6—dc23   2013026246

St. Martin's Griffin books may be purchased for educational, business, or promotional use. For information on bulk purchases, please contact Macmillan Corporate and Premium Sales Department at 1-800-221-7945, extension 5442, or write specialmarkets@macmillan.com.

First Edition: December 2013

10 9 8 7 6 5 4 3 2 1

To my favorite men:

MY SON, ALEX,

MY HUSBAND, BRIAN,

and my father,

EDMOND J. GRUENENFELDER

(1946–2013)

Acknowledgments

Thank you as always to my wonderful editor, Jennifer Weis, and my brilliant agent, Kim Whalen, for continuing to allow me to work in my pajamas. And thank you to my publisher, Matthew Shear.

Thank you to Janet DiVincenzo and Kim Whalen, for coming up with my title. I raise a big drink to you both.

Thanks to Bindu Balaji and Seema Bardwaj, for helping me with the Indian wedding details. I hope I didn't screw anything up too badly.

Thank you to Jeff Greco, for letting me base a character on you. I love you very much. And to his partner, Brian Gordon, whom I hope doesn't mind being called "Clark Kent without the glasses" in the book.

Thank you to Dorothy Kozak, Gaylyn Fraiche, and Brian Smith, for reading. And reading. And reading. And giving notes. Then defending your notes. I mean, what could be more fun than hearing me answer, "I don't know why she does that. She just does!" You know how important it is, what you do for me.

Thanks to my wonderful family: Brian, Alex, Mom (Carol),

Dad (Ed), Bonus Mom (Janis), Jenn, Rob, Haley, Declan, Maibre, Caryol, and Walter. To: Laurie, Patrick, Carolyn, Cormac, Bob, Suzi, Michele, Missy, Nancy, Jen, Christie, Dorothy, and Gaylyn. It's the friends you can call up at 4 A.M. who matter.

And to my fellow writer friends Quinn Cummings, Nancy Redd, Jennifer Coburn, Anita Hughes, and Joe Keenan: thank you for listening to me when I complain about writing, giving me encouragement when I need it, and reminding me (also when I need it) that I must quit bitching and be grateful that I can get away with not having a real job.

A final thank-you to my father, Edmond Gruenenfelder, who passed away suddenly and never got to read this book. You taught me self-worth, the importance of hard work, and to love the English language. I miss you every day and the world is a slightly colder place without you in it.

Keep
Calm
and
Carry a
Big Drink

ONE

I can think of several things a bride does not want to hear on her wedding day: The orchids being flown in from Ecuador have frozen. Her future mother-in-law is already tanked on vodka gimlets in the lobby bar—and hitting on the bride's father. The caterer is out of Yukon Golds and is wondering if he can replace the garlic mashed potatoes with Tater Tots.

But perhaps the worst thing a bride can hear on her wedding day just came from me, her maid of honor: "Okay, I need to tell you something. But you have to promise me you won't freak out."

Seema, the bride, radiant in a bright red silk sari with sparkling beading, Swarovski crystals, and heavy gold embroidery, keeps her eyes fastened on me as she turns her head sideways. "Has there ever been a good conversation that started with that statement?"

"Um . . . well . . . ," I begin, looking up at the ceiling as I struggle to find some comforting words. "There have been some productive ones."

Nicole (Nic), Seema's bridesmaid, elbows me hard in the ribs, then bulges her eyes out at me.

"Ow!" I yell, doubling over and nearly dropping on the carpet. "How is that helping?"

Nic chastises me. "Mel, I told you not to say anything yet."

I rub my belly and struggle to breathe. Yeah, this whole "maid of honor" thing is going splendidly. "Uh-huh. So we're going with the 'utter denial' card? You think that's going to work better?"

"We played that card all the time when Seema was dating," Nic reminds me. "What's it going to hurt for a few more minutes?"

Seema juts out her lip at us, but stays calm. "I'm going to pretend I didn't hear that," Seema tells Nic with preternatural calm. Then she turns to me. "What's going on?"

I look down at my beautifully beaded, royal-blue, short-sleeved Indian choli top and matching royal-blue lehenga skirt and try to find a way to let Seema down easy. "There is the remotest possibility that your groom is MIA."

Nic shoots up her arm to elbow me again, but I instinctively jump back and point my finger at her. "You are eight months pregnant. I could totally take you."

This is true. Nic is so huge, her taut belly looks as if it's trying to smash through her beaded, gold lehenga and matching choli. Nic narrows her eyes and cocks her head at me ever so slightly to indicate, *Oh, you think so?*

I step another foot back. No, actually I do not think so. I think I am the weakest woman here, both physically and emotionally.

Which is okay, actually. Being the beta dog is highly underrated. Sure, you don't get the first bite of the buffalo. But then again, you're free to just sort of let things happen to you, which requires much less energy than the uphill battle most women call "life." Plus, the alpha bitches inevitably waste their time on—

Seema snaps her fingers in front of me, breaking my train of thought. "Mel, eyes on me. What do you mean MIA?"

"Missing in action."

Seema raises her eyes to the ceiling. "I know what *MIA* means," she tells me with excruciating patience. "What happened?"

Nic's cell phone beeps a text. She quickly starts reading, then typing back, as I tell Seema, "Apparently, everyone on Scott's side gathered to start the baraat . . ."

For those of you who, like me, are clueless about Indian weddings, the baraat is the first part of an Indian wedding ceremony—where the groom's family and friends, in our case assembled in front of a hotel a block away, dance in a parade toward the bride's family and friends. The two groups greet each other during what's called a milni, then we all dance toward the mandap (basically a canopy for the wedding), set up in the courtyard of a trendy downtown LA hotel, and begin the wedding ceremony. It's all wonderfully festive and colorful.

Except when the groom gets cold feet.

I continue, "Then Scott walked out of the lobby, got on his horse, and promptly galloped away."

Did I mention the groom leads his group to his bride by riding a white horse down the street? This initially struck me as incredibly romantic, and very Prince Charming. Of course, right now, not so much. I don't remember Prince Charming charging down Figueroa Street on a trusty steed named Deathray, trying to get the hell out of town. But maybe that's how Snow White's or Cinderella's wedding began, and they just left that part out when they told the children the story about how Mommy married Daddy.

Seema's eyes widen. "I have a runaway groom?"

"Now, we don't know that . . . ," I try to reassure her.

Nic reads the text from her phone. "He's been spotted racing down Olympic Boulevard, heading toward Staples Center."

"Are they sure it's him?" I ask.

Nic looks up from her phone. "How many thirty-three-year-old men wearing white sherwanis and riding white stallions do you think are in downtown today?" Nic's phone rings, and she picks up immediately. "Talk to me."

Seema grabs her chest and begins to hyperventilate. "Oh my God. I'm being left at the altar. Who does that actually happen to? I've never heard of someone really having that happen to them."

"Okay, calm down. This is not the time to panic," I try to reassure her.

"Are you crazy? This is the *perfect* time to panic!" she snaps at me. "It's one of those FOAF stories you hear: the Mexican rat, and the friend of a friend who gets left at the altar after her groom leaves her for her slutty maid of honor."

"Well, obviously, that didn't happen. Your slutty maid of honor is still here," Nic chimes in.

I turn to Nic and put my hands palms up. "Really? Now?"

Nic waves me off. "What? I meant that as a good thing."

Seema continues to monologue, in her own world. "And the bride ends up marrying the geek who loved her in high school, who she wouldn't even give the time of day to back then, because what other options does she have so late in life?"

Nic covers her phone. "You've just described Ross and Rachel. That never happened to anyone in real life."

"It's happening to me now!" Seema exclaims. "Oh my God. I'm going to end up spending the rest of my life with a Milton or a Leonard." She collapses onto an overstuffed, white satin chair. "I can feel my gut clenching." Seema grabs her stomach. "Oh, God, please don't let me throw up all over my wedding sari."

Nic covers her phone. "The cops tried to pull him over, but he galloped onto the sidewalk, then escaped diagonally through the square in L.A. Live's courtyard."

I rush up to Seema and put my arm around her. "Everything's going to be fine. Scott loves you. This is just some horrible misunderstanding."

Seema starts gasping for air like a trout just yanked from a river. While listening to more groom updates, Nic absentmindedly hands Seema a white paper lunch bag. She immediately grabs the bag and breathes. The bag puffs up, contracts, puffs up, contracts . . .

"Okay, the cops have him down," Nic declares triumphantly, giving us a thumbs-up.

"Down?!" Seema exclaims just as her iPhone plays "Highway to Hell." Scott's ringtone. And a joke she's probably regretting right now.

Seema keeps exhaling and inhaling into her paper bag while I rifle through her purse, grab her phone, and pick up. "Hey," I say, attempting to be casual and breezy with Scott. "So what's going on?"

Scott sounds worried. "How's Seema doing?"

I watch Seema continue to hyperventilate into the bag. My voice is squeaky as I eke out, "Well . . . you know . . . every wedding has its little glitches."

I'm hoping I've given Scott a great lead-in for a joke, followed by an apology, and a new estimated time for his arrival. Instead, Scott says the absolute worst thing a bride could hear on her wedding day. "She is going to hate me for this. I have fucked everything up. I tried, but I just couldn't do it."

Little did I know that a few hours later, I would decide that it was time for me to stop being the beta dog. That I would be tired of letting life happen to me. That it would be time to be active in my life choices, maybe even aggressive, and get the life I wanted, not the life I thought I was supposed to lead. And who knows— maybe that first bite of buffalo would be the best buffalo I'd ever eaten.

But that realization didn't happen for a few hours, and first I have to go back a week. . . .

Two

Okay, kids, put away your books, eyes on your own paper, and number two pencils only.

My fingers fly over the keyboard of my notebook computer while I recline on Nic's guest bed on this quiet Saturday morning. I am mid-rant:

What is a cake pull?
(A) A traditional bridal shower party game originating in Victorian England, now inflicted . . . Did I say *inflicted*? I'm so sorry. I meant *celebrated!* As in "We're *celebrating* that yet another friend is getting married before me. We're *celebrating* that a woman has taken yet another eligible bachelor out of the rotation. We're *celebrating* that retail establishments have managed to trick a bunch of hopelessly romantic, unmarried women into wasting hundreds of dollars on yet another ceremony designed to lead us to the open bar and into some man's hideously inappropriate arms for the evening."

I hit send and then begin to type (B).

My friend Jeff IMs me back, interrupting my rant:

As long as the hideously inappropriate arms are not attached to the groom's father, I think that could be fun.

He's such a guy. I can type a hundred words before I even start to make my point, and he can counter me in one sentence.

I continue to type my point anyway:

(B) A bridal shower game that, with the clever use of sterling silver charms that are supposed to serve as little fortune-tellers, can manage to make any woman question any and all of her choices in life, be it in romance, career path, or whether she should have Thai food for dinner.

Jeff IMs:

Honey, all I asked was "What is a cake pull?" Please stop typing a thesis paper on the subject.

I hit send, then keep writing:

(C) A bridal shower game

But before I can finish typing, Jeff writes back:

If you're going to bitch for this long, can't you at least pick up the phone?

I immediately type back—

No.

I hit send, then begin typing an explanation:

I spent the night at Nic's house getting Seema's bridal shower ready. I don't want to wake anybody.

But before I can hit send, my Skype rings. I click the green button on the first ring to see a video pop up of a gorgeous dark-haired gentleman standing in the middle of an empty tropical bar. He is a thing of beauty—slightly tanned, glowing skin, pecs to make a girl swoon, beautiful white (but not too white) smile. Needless to say, such a vision inspires great passion in me. "I told you not to call!"

"Yeah, well, you told me that before our first date," Jeff (aka the gorgeous gentleman) tells me. "But look at how well that turned out."

He's being sarcastic. We broke up more than twelve years ago.

"Besides, I'm not calling. I'm skyping," Jeff argues. He lifts a beer pint into view and takes a healthy gulp. "And you need to calm down before you give yourself a stroke."

"Sorry. I'm in a mood," I admit, grabbing a shower favor wrapped in white mesh and tying a red ribbon around it.

Jeff leans into his screen to get a better look at what I'm doing. "I'm seeing white tulle, red ribbons, and . . ." He looks farther into his computer's camera to decipher what I'm wrapping. "What is that? An elephant?"

"It's a tealight holder," I tell him as I finish tying a perfect bow and toss it into a pile of favors on the other side of the guest bed.

"It looks like an elephant."

"It's an elephant-shaped tealight holder."

Jeff shakes his head. "I stand corrected. The point is, I'm not seeing a cocktail glass."

My eyes widen. "It's seven o'clock in the morning here."

He narrows his eyes and shakes his head slowly to show a lack of comprehension. "And your point is . . . ?"

I can't help but laugh. Jeff has many great features: good-looking, loving, smart. But mostly, he cracks me up. "God, I miss you. Promise me you're still going to be my date for the wedding."

"I'm shutting down the bar for four days just to come to LA. Be very flattered."

"I am."

"Good, because my boss was pissed."

I roll my eyes at his lame joke. "You *are* the boss."

"I know, which means I know how lazy I can be." Jeff takes another drink of his beer. "And I totally didn't buy my excuse that I was going to my great-aunt's funeral."

There's an urgent knock on my bedroom door. "Mel," Nic whispers, "I hear voices. Are you up?"

"Hold on," I say to Jeff, then I yell through the door, "Nic, it's seven o'clock in the morning. Shouldn't you be resting in your condition?"

Nic bursts into my room, her swollen belly coming in a good two seconds before the rest of her. "Please. I'm almost eight months pregnant. I get up every twenty minutes to pee. I'm rethinking a few of the shower games. What do you think of the needle-and-thread game?"

"The what?"

Nic lifts up a glossy bridal magazine to read to me. "Tell the bride to leave the room. Ask a guest to hold a needle, then have the bride come in and try to thread the needle. Make sure the guest slightly moves the needle so the bride can't thread it."

"What could be more fun than that?" Jeff says dryly. He downs the remainder of his pint. "And speaking of thread, my drink is empty."

Nic walks around me to view my computer screen. Her eyes and mouth burst open. "Jeff! OMG!"

Jeff's eyes widen too, and he imitates her sorority-girl voice exactly as he says, "Nic! WTF?"

Nic laughs. "I'm sorry. I have kids now. I meant, 'Oh my God!' " Her voice goes up two octaves. "You look fan-fucking-tastic! Super-handsome as always. I hate you!"

"And you're so tiny," he lies. "Be honest, is there really a baby coming? Because I want a DNA test."

"I . . . *love* you!" Nic exclaims. "Now, what do you guys think of the game?" Nic begins reading from her magazine again. "Tell your guests that the conversation the bride is having with her friend while threading the needle is the same conversation Seema and Scott will have on their wedding night. You know, 'I can't get it in. Quit moving.' "

" 'Why can't you just throw away the sock that has a hole in it, you cheap bastard,' " Jeff continues.

We both look at him on my screen. "Just me, then?" he says, drawing himself another beer from a tap behind his bar.

Nic turns to me. "What do you think?"

I think, *Ick!*—but I'm not going to say that out loud and hurt her feelings. "Well, it's not as bad as the guess-the-baby-poop game," I say weakly.

Nic looks up from her magazine. "Word."

Jeff actually spit-takes his beer, then begs, "Please be kidding."

"It's not as bad as it sounds," Nic states.

"Honey, it couldn't *possibly* be as bad as it sounds," Jeff retorts.

"You microwave different kinds of chocolate bars into diapers, and your guests are supposed to look inside the diaper and guess the candy," I tell him.

Jeff looks as if he might hurl. "So Nic's the one who's pregnant, but I may be the one to throw up. That's probably the most disgusting party game I've ever heard of. And I'm a gay man."

"Which is why no one did it at my baby shower," Nic assures him. "Jeff, do you have any suggestions?"

"Skip the party games, get a male stripper and a lot of booze, and call it a day."

"Personally, I would love that," Nic tells him. "But, unfortunately, it doesn't fit in with the theme of Seema's wedding."

"Which is?"

Nic and I repeat the mantra in unison, "Don't piss anyone off."

Lately, there seems to be a trend going on in themed weddings. The Monopoly wedding, the Enchanted Forest wedding; I've even seen a Star Wars wedding (and all I can say to that is, wow, the bride must really have wanted to close the deal with that guy!).

The official theme for Scott and Seema's wedding is, and I quote, "Let's try not to piss anyone off too badly." I suspect other couples, particularly those where the fiancés are from different cultures or observe different religious traditions, have been in their position.

Scott comes from a nonpracticing Protestant family. You know, they celebrate Christmas, but not so much that they trek out to midnight mass in Connecticut in the middle of a snowstorm in December. Their Easter has to do more with a candy-bearing lagomorph than an everlasting deity. The only wings associated with Sundays are chicken and made to be eaten while watching football. We all know the type. Personally, I am the type.

Naturally, Scott's mother insisted on a full-blown Christian wedding, complete with a minister, a white dress, and a sermon.

Seema is a third-generation American of Indian descent who

was raised Hindu, and in her family's case that just means that she has a few Ganesha and tealights in her kitchen for a small shrine, and that she celebrates holidays such as Diwali (Indian New Year). But I don't remember her ever going to temple. Plus she gets to eat meat. (Her dad is Punjabi, and they eat meat.) She grew up in Arizona, puts up a Christmas tree every year, and has attended more than her share of Easters, Passovers, and Hanukkahs.

Since both of Seema's parents were born and raised in the States, and since they don't go to temple either, naturally Seema is having a full-blown Indian wedding that's going to include a henna ceremony, a one-hour ceremony in Sanskrit, several bridal dresses that were made in India, a mandap (the wedding canopy), and a white horse.

This has been fine with me, as I actually get to wear a cool maid-of-honor dress, as opposed to some of the hideous bridesmaid's frocks I've been forced to wear in the past. I mean, what is it with brides and colors like Spam Pink or Sea World Aqua, not to mention the fixation on satin or tulle? Who was the first bride who passive-aggressively hated her maid of honor so much that she decided to wrap her in an explosion of taffeta?

My outfit is a beautiful blue silk, hand-beaded choli (which is a midriff-baring top), and matching lehenga (a free-flowing skirt) that she had made for me in Mumbai. Nic gets to wear a gold silk choli and lehenga with gold embroidery and beading and looks like motherhood personified with her eight-month-pregnant belly ever-so-slightly peeking out of the ensemble.

Their wedding has gone from a small affair for close friends and family to a three-day celebration featuring two different ceremonies—an Indian one during the daytime on Saturday, followed by a Christian one Saturday evening, a rehearsal dinner/henna ceremony the Friday before, and a brunch on Sunday at which they will serve everything from eggs Benedict, bacon, and sausage to Pongal, vada, dosa, aloo sabzi, and nan.

For the most part, people are getting along pretty well, and the wedding is going to be exquisite. I've never seen two people so happy while planning their wedding and I'm sure it will go off without a hitch.

But their theme still means that we have to be extrasensitive about Seema's bridal shower.

"Unfortunately, Seema's Aunt Hema is coming, so we have to be G-rated," Nic explains to Jeff.

"And yet thread-the-needle seems like a good idea," Jeff reminds her.

"The shower's in less than six hours, and I'm clutching at straws," Nic admits defensively. "Other than the cake pull, Mel has nixed all of my other ideas."

"I never agreed to the cake pull," I remind Nic. "Not after what happened last time."

Nic waves me off. "Right. Like you've ever said no to something that involves cake."

Her statement sounds insulting, but since it's spot-on, I'm gonna let it go.

"Nic, can you explain the cake pull to me in a hundred words or less?" Jeff asks.

"It's a bridal-shower game with silver charms buried inside the frosting of a two-layer cake and pulled out by a ribbon. Each guest pulls one ribbon from the cake, and the charm that is attached to that ribbon is supposed to determine the guest's future. So, for example, the girl who pulls the engagement-ring charm from the cake would be the next to get engaged, the girl who pulls the baby carriage will be the next to get pregnant, etc."

"Is there a charm to get Mel to come visit me in Hawaii?" Jeff asks.

"The passport," Nic answers. "But she's already asked for the antique phone, which means good news is coming her way."

"Hmm," I say, thinking aloud. "Maybe I would like the passport. My last day of school was Friday, and I have tons of time to kill. Maybe I should go abroad this summer. I've always wanted to see Paris."

"Or Hawaii," Jeff suggests.

"Hawaii doesn't need a passport," I tell him.

"And Paris doesn't have a free guest room for you to stay in for as long as you want."

Jeff makes a fine point. Those student loans are not going to pay themselves down, and a free place to stay would keep expenses more reasonable. But mostly, it would be wonderful to see Jeff. Since he completely reinvented his life and moved to Maui two and a half years ago, there's been a hole in my heart I haven't quite been able to fill.

"Oh, my date's here!" Jeff says cheerfully, hopping off his bar seat. "Gotta go!"

"Isn't it four in the morning where you are?" Nic asks.

"I'm a guy. We live to start dates at four in the morning. Love you both. Bye!" And he flickers off.

Speaking of flickering, I have a flickering of jealousy pass through me. Not because he's my ex-boyfriend, but because I can't even remember the last time I liked a guy enough to see him at four in the morning. Or even at 8:00 p.m. on a Saturday night.

"What do you think about toilet-paper bride?" Nic asks.

I turn to look at her. "I don't think it would be one of your best looks."

THREE

At noon, I'm all dressed up in my favorite purple Suzi Chin dress (which expertly hides my recent increase in girth) and some modest beige pumps. I sit at Nic's nicely appointed granite kitchen island, stabbing large cooked shrimp with multicolored cellophane-tipped toothpicks and placing them on a decorative serving tray while Nic places a pile of bingo cards next to me.

"I've been inspired!" she tells me proudly. "Bridal bingo!"

Nic trots over to her refrigerator and pulls out two bottles of champagne while I read the squares on the bingo card at the top of the pile. "On this card the *eternal* and *bridesmaid* squares are right next to each other."

Nic pushes the champagne bottles into a giant stainless steel bucket filled with crushed ice, then turns back to get more bubbly. "Fine. I'll take that card."

I flip to the next card. "On this one, the *mother-in-law* square is next to the *groom* square, with the *bride* square three spaces away diagonally."

Nic shoves two more bottles into the big bucket, then pulls the cards away from me to put them back on the counter. "You're overthinking this."

"I'm just saying, have you even looked at where they put the word *sex*? Because if it's near a space marked 'free' . . ."

"I'm begging you not to finish that thought."

I shrug, then go back to my toothpicking. Nic pops open a bottle of champagne. My face lights up. I happily grab a champagne flute, then wave the glass in front of her, a gleeful, oversize grin on my face.

Nic laughs and pours me a glass.

The doorbell rings. "I'll get it," I say, nabbing a large shrimp for myself to accompany my champagne. I walk through Nic's marble foyer, with a glass of champagne in one hand and a now-empty toothpick in the other, and open the door to Seema.

"Why do women get married?" she asks me irritably.

I look up to the ceiling to think. "Um . . . so they can feel morally superior to the rest of us?"

Seema takes my glass of champagne, takes a very healthy sip, and marches in without giving me my glass back. "Scott and I just had the biggest fight."

As she heads toward the kitchen, I close the door then quickly follow. "I'm sorry. What happened?"

"I don't want to talk about it," Seema says angrily, then sighs. "I just want to get drunk, get presents, and revel in the mockery that is the supposed bliss of the engagement."

Okey-dokey.

"There's our blushing bride!" Nic gushes happily.

"Shyeah, right," Seema responds.

"Trouble in paradise?" Nic pats her hand on a barstool by the kitchen island, inviting Seema to sit. "What is it? Did he ask for a prenup? Has he not written his vows yet? Do you want a nice ginger martini for your signature cocktail at the reception, but he's going all hoppy and IPA beer on you?"

"I don't want to talk about it." Seema sighs, then downs the rest of the champagne from my flute. She grabs the open bottle of champagne from the stainless steel bucket and refills my glass.

Oh, dear. It's a little too early to be one of those kinds of days. "We have mixers to go with that," I hint to Seema. "And not just orange juice." I point to several pitchers of mixers in a rainbow of colors. "I also made fresh peach purée, not to mention strawberries mixed with muddled basil, plus the purple one is a reduced Concord-grape juice mixed with orange zest, orange bitters, and rosemary—"

"Stop," Seema interrupts, furrowing her brow. "You have *met* me, right?"

I take a deep breath, then say to her diplomatically, "I'm just suggesting that you might want to take it easy on the champagne. You don't want your Auntie Hema seeing you loaded."

Seema takes another gulp of champagne. "First off, don't say *auntie*. You sound like you're being condescending. Second, not to worry, in the last ten years she's never seen me sober."

Aunties are the older Indian women who help the bride with her wedding, both with the henna ceremony the day before, and then with putting on her sari the day of the wedding (a several-hours-long process). Seema only has a couple of aunts: Hema and Neya. Personally, I think they're charming and lovely women. They drive Seema crazy. Which is fair, because she adores both my aunt Jacqui and my aunt Kris, and they are both nuts and a total embarrassment, so we break even.

Hema came into town a week before the wedding just to be at the shower today, so we're conscientious about everything' being perfect.

Nic promptly walks over to Seema, takes the glass out of her hand, and gives it back to me. "Hey! That's mine!" Seema protests.

"Oh, no," Nic says. "You are *so* cut off for now. And your guests will be here any minute expecting a happy bride. So vent before they get here."

Seema only pouts for a moment before unloading. "Scott doesn't want to give up his loft after we're married. He is paying almost three *thousand* dollars a month on rent. That's money that could be going toward our retirement fund, toward buying a bigger house. . . . Hell, at this point, I'd agree to use the money to go on a camping trip to Mount Rushmore."

I furrow my brow. "Why Mount . . . ?"

"I just *really* hate Mount Rushmore!" Seema whines. "That's not the point. The point is, he already has an exit strategy. While I'm planning our wedding, he's planning our divorce. So why am I bothering to marry him in the first place?"

"My advice?" Nic says calmly. "Let it go."

"Let it *go*?" Seema shrieks in disbelief.

"Let it go," Nic repeats. "Men need time to adjust to the idea of 'forever.' You need to see your future together sort of like a great-white-shark attack. Just keep him in the water, swimming happily, and eventually it'll sneak up on him and strike."

"She says that in such a soothing voice," I say to Seema, a little disturbed.

Seema grabs my flute out of my hand for the second time. I let her.

"I thought I said you were cut off," Nic tells her sternly.

"And I thought you saw marriage in a more favorable light than the opening scene from *Jaws*," Seema retorts, then drains half a glass in one gulp. "Anyway, I had Scott drop me off specifically so I could imbibe. Mel's driving me home."

"*I am?*" I ask, surprised.

"You're not?" Seema asks me.

Rats. "No, I guess I am," I say, letting my shoulders slump. Damn, no champs for me.

Seema grabs a large shrimp from the platter I'm assembling, takes a bite, then says to Nic through a full mouth, "I cannot believe you're taking his side."

"There are no sides. It's marriage. You're a team now."

Seema glares at Nic disbelievingly. I probably just look confused. Nic rolls her eyes. "Okay, fine. There are always two sides. Sometimes three or four. My point is, just take a few days to meditate over this before you go off. Scott having his own apartment doesn't mean he's planning to do anything stupid. He's not the type to divorce, nor is he the type to have an affair. Frankly, he's too lazy."

Seema's eyes nearly burst out of their sockets. "Who said anything about an affair?!"

"Oh," Nic says. "Ignore me. I'm the wife of an NBA coach. That's where my head naturally goes. My bad."

Seema nervously starts to lift my glass to her lips again, but I lower her hand. "Ignore her," I tell Seema. "Isn't this the guy who doesn't want to go to his own bachelor party tonight?"

"Yes."

"Well, then."

I hear Seema's phone beep in her purse. Seema opens her purse and reads a text.

A smile creeps onto her face, and she quickly texts something back.

"Is everything better?" I ask as I move on to prepping cheese and crackers, and Nic begins putting out bottles of soda.

"I don't know, maybe." Seema is still smiling. "He is being

pretty cute though." She puts her phone down next to her purse, walks over to grab another shrimp, and, before popping it into her mouth, asks, "So, what do you guys have planned for me today?"

Nic's eyes light up with pride. "What do you think about bridal bingo?"

"I think it's a bad idea to squeal 'Oh–sixty-nine!' in front of my aunt," Seema retorts.

"Then again, it would be nice to be able to say 'I–twenty-seven' without lying," I point out.

"No, no," Nic says, handing Seema the pile of bingo cards. "It's bridal bingo. See? The squares say things like *romance* and *intimacy.*"

Seema sighs deeply. "Why on earth would I want my aunts and friends ruminating over my intimacy?"

Nic, trying to stay upbeat, takes back the cards and makes a show of throwing them away over her shoulder. "Not a problem. They're history. What about the game we played at my shower? Fantasy date/date from hell?"

Seema squints her eyes at Nic. "Walk me through this. I finally get the man of my dreams, and I'm already supposed to be fantasizing about another guy?"

"If we play, do we know a celebrity who does dishes?" I wonder aloud as I pick up the bridal cards from the floor to throw them away.

"Fortune-cookie game?" Nic suggests weakly.

Seema's face drops, and she looks over at me for clarification.

"Be afraid," I say to her, shaking my head slowly. "Be very afraid."

Nic continues, "Each guest pulls a fortune cookie out of a bag, then breaks the fortune cookie open and reads it. Only they have to end their fortune with 'in bed with Scott.'"

Seema puts out the palm of her hand. "In front of my seventy-two-year-old aunt?"

Nic gives up and crosses her arms. "Fine. But, other than toilet-paper bride, all we have is the cake pull."

"When did you agree to a cake pull?" I ask Seema.

She shrugs. "I figured the last time it brought me good luck. Not that I believe in it. But, you know . . ."

"I really don't think it's a good idea to test our luck again," I whine to Nicole. "What if something goes wrong?"

"What could possibly go wrong?" Nic asks me huffily.

"Okay, I can think of, like, five bad romantic comedies off the top of my head whose trailers all started with that statement."

"Not to worry." Nic pulls a two-layer cake from a pink cardboard box on the counter. "This time, I figured out how to rig the cake correctly."

Seema and I exchange cautious looks. "I'm pretty sure I can name at least one bad romantic comedy that started with that statement," Seema whispers to me.

I put up the peace sign with my index and middle fingers and silently mouth, "Two."

I'll admit, the cake does look amazing. A two-layered confection covered in white buttercream frosting. White satin ribbons spoke out of the middle of the cake, and on top sits a giant porcelain topper in the shape of a heart. Nic takes a small bowl of white frosting out of her refrigerator and adds a little frosting here and there to make the cake look perfect.

I begin to question her. "Are you sure you can—"

Nic quickly drops her frosting knife. *"Ow! Owwwwww!"* she howls, then quickly grabs a chair with one hand and clutches her stomach with the other. "Ow, ow, ow, sweet mother of holy fuck!"

Seema and I both rush to her. I quickly ask, "Is it time?"

Seema asks if she should call the doctor.

Nic makes a show of waving us off with her hands, but she's doubled over in pain and can't speak.

"What can we do? What do you need?" I ask Nic.

"I'm fine." Nic takes a deep breath and consciously releases the tension in her body.

"I knew this was too close to your due date. You should not be throwing a party in your condition," I say to Nic, who goes back to frosting the cake with more buttercream as if nothing ever happened.

Nic waves me off. "Women have been in my condition since . . . well, since there were women. I'm fine. I'm just in false labor."

Seema and I exchange pained looks. Seema asks first, "What the hell is false labor? Is that a thing?"

"Yes. Although I'm pretty sure the term was coined by a man. Nowadays they call it Braxton Hicks contractions. I'm fine. I don't want to talk about it. More fun things to think about, such as . . . ta da!" Nic does her best impression of a knocked-up *Price Is Right* model as she presents the cake to us.

It does look good, and I'll bet she's got dark-chocolate layers in there. But I've been burned by cake before.

"You've got it straight this time, right?" Seema asks Nic dubiously as she takes a sip of champagne from my flute.

"I have it straight," Nic tells her irritably. "Mel, you wanted the antique phone, it's right here. Pull."

"No, I didn't want the antique phone," I insist to Nic as I tug on a white satin ribbon and pull out a sterling-silver phone charm. "I wanted the passport."

"But the phone means good news is coming your way," Nic tells me.

"Not specific enough. I want the passport."

Nic makes a show of rolling her eyes. "Fine." She points to a different ribbon. "Passport's right there."

I yank out the ribbon and grin from ear to ear as I admire the silver passport.

"Pull gently!" Nic lectures me. "You're going to get the cake all messy."

"Better the cake look messy than I get the wrong fortune again!" I tell her.

"Was it really such a bad fortune?" Seema asks me.

I turn away from her ever so slightly. I kind of don't know how to respond to her question. Was the charm I pulled a year ago really such a bad fortune? Maybe not, but I want a better one this time.

Last time Nic tried to rig a cake, it was for her bridal shower, and she attempted to give me the engagement-ring charm. I had been with my boyfriend, Fred (now known officially as Fuckhead), for six years, and I desperately wanted to marry him. But instead of the ring, I pulled the chili-pepper charm, which was supposed to symbolize a red-hot sex life in my immediate future. At the time, sex with Fred had dwindled to nearly nonexistent, and I hated that damn cake. But the nine-inch disks of baked chocolate batter turned out to be right. I soon learned Fred was cheating on me, and I kicked him to the curb.

The next few weeks after the breakup were hideous. We got back together, he proposed, I said yes, but I soon realized he was still cheating. I did what any smart woman would—I got the hell out.

Then I made the mistake of trying to date again. How the hell do people do it in this day and age?! I tried to tackle dating the way I do everything else in my life: find out the requirements to attain your goal and work like crazy to fulfill the requirements.

Buy cute new underwear: check. Run every day for a cute body: check. Let all of your friends know you're looking: check-minus. Horribly bad idea in retrospect. I did the blind dating thing, the online thing, I tried speed dating, I perused "target-rich environments" (the target being a nice single man) such as sports bars, hardware stores, and one spectacularly craptastic deep-sea fishing trip.

I might as well have slept until noon, then stayed on the couch in my pajamas guzzling mai tais all afternoon while watching Food Network for all the good it did me. The results would have been almost the same, except with the PJ/mai tai/TV option I might have finally mastered the art of making the perfect crêpe suzette or roasting and deboning a whole chicken.

The rewards for all of my hard work included a guy throwing up on my shoes after I kissed him, going out to dinner with a man whose fiancée showed up halfway through the date (although technically she wasn't his fiancée when she first got to the restaurant, since he didn't propose to her until the end of dinner, sooo . . . yeah), getting propositioned for a threeway by a dentist, and having a pimply teenager at Home Depot generously offer to sleep with me. If my dating life had been a rocket, it would have leaked fuel all over Cape Canaveral, then accidentally blown up Florida.

And then I met Danny. Beautiful, perfect-bodied Danny. He was smart, nice, funny. He had a good job, genuinely liked me, and told me constantly that he was in love with me. And the cake nailed it in terms of the red hot chili pepper, for that man had a knack for making a woman . . .

TMI. Let's just say our sex life wasn't the problem.

The problem was I wasn't in love with him. Maybe because he was the first guy I dated after a serious relationship; I don't know. For months I kept trying to force myself to feel that . . . spark.

I was thirty-two and desperately wanted kids. But every time he brought up marriage, I got nauseous. Like a genuine, sick-to-my-stomach, "What is wrong with me?" pukey feeling. No matter how hard I tried, it never felt right. And I had compromised on so many other aspects of my life, I couldn't compromise on whom I was going to hold hands with in fifty years.

So we broke up.

If you ask my friends, they would tell you that it was completely amicable. They were wrong. The only time breakups are amicable is when no one cares enough to be hurt. That was not the case for either of us.

I turn back to Seema and shrug. "Fair enough. But I still want the passport this time."

As I carefully push the passport charm back into the cake, Nic points to Seema. "Seema, you want the baby charm, right?"

"Yes!" she says excitedly, which is rather uncharacteristic for her.

"It's right here, under the four o'clock position from the heart cake topper," Nic tells her.

As Seema pulls out the baby-carriage charm (just to be sure), I ask Nic, "Why do we need a cake topper?"

"It's just another insurance policy against getting the wrong charms," Nic assures me. "Not that we got the wrong charms last time, but this time I want to control my destiny a bit more. Based on the angle of the topper, I can point to each ribbon around the cake and know exactly what charm is hidden inside. Check out this ribbon. That's mine."

I pull out a square charm. Nic smiles, clearly pleased with herself.

Seema leans into Nic to get a better look. "What is that? An earring?"

Nic is clearly offended. "No, it's not an earring. It's a picture frame. It means a future with a happy family."

Some days I swear these jewelers just make this shit up.

The doorbell rings. "Your guests are here," Nic chirps excitedly to Seema. "Can you guys go greet them while I finish tucking these charms back in?"

"Okay," I say, hopping off my seat to go greet the guests in the front hallway. "Just remember the passport . . ."

"One o'clock position, after I place the topper directly in front of Seema. You can't miss it!" Nic assures me. "Seema, you're midnight."

Seema and I head over to the front door, and I begin the long-standing single-gal tradition of trying to be happy for yet another friend who got to a major milestone first.

Actually, I *am* happy for her; I just wish that I didn't have to participate in the following conversations over and over:

Happy Guest: "So are you and Danny thinking about tying the knot?"

This question should be followed by a swig of peach Bellini, followed by my upbeat, though not too cheerful, answer that we broke up months ago. (Instead, since I am driving, I drink Diet Dr Pepper. It is not the same.)

My answer is always incredibly well received, with said guest looking embarrassed and grief stricken for me, patting me on the shoulder, and telling me I'm still young, I'll find someone even better. Or that she never really liked him. (Say what now?) Or that ubiquitous assurance that, and I quote, "Everything happens for a reason." A statement that people only use when your news is so hideously awful, they can't think of anything comforting or useful to say.

But the romance question isn't nearly as bad as the questions about my pink slip.

Guest (looking at me with a mixture of concern and pity): "Have you any more news about your job next year?"

I teach calculus at a public school in Los Angeles, and unfortunately, because of state budget cuts, this year they're going to have to lay off a bunch of teachers. Because my union insists on "last in, first out," I may not have enough seniority to stay. So last March, I received a "possible layoff" slip from my high school, and it's been weighing heavily on my soul ever since.

What is a "possible layoff" slip? Government bureaucracy at its finest. Basically it's a sheet of paper that tells me that it is possible that my employer won't be needing my services next year, but that I shouldn't make any plans to do anything else because they'll probably need me. This is the fourth one I've received in as many years.

My perpetual job insecurity is probably the last thing I want to talk about at a party. (Though why I'm not married yet is definitely running a close second.)

Since I'm driving Seema later, I continue to console myself with more Diet Dr Pepper, then give my pat answer: No, I have not heard anything yet, but pink slips are common in the Los Angeles Unified School District, and they happen every year. I am always hired back, I will be fine.

Grief stricken and/or embarrassed look by guest, followed by comments ranging from "I'm sure it'll all be fine—you're so good at what you do" to "Everything happens for a reason" to "You still get unemployment and some pension though, right?"

And finally, there are the conversations of where I will be living next month. You see, Seema owns her house; I am just renting a room from her. I have agreed to move out when Scott moves in. And the rental market in Los Angeles is everything you'd think it would be in terms of both affordability and quality—meaning it lacks either one or both of those features, depending on where you look.

By the fifth time I am asked, "How is the apartment hunt going?" and "Are you excited to finally get to live alone?" I have switched to full-sugar Coke and begun counting down the minutes before we start the opening of the presents (Ooh . . . Aah . . .), the pulling of the charms from the cake (Yikes! Really?), and the hugging good-bye of the guests, followed by the postgame gossip session ("She's back together with that loser?" "I swear to God if I had those Miss Piggy legs, I would never wear that skirt").

An hour later, we have all stuffed ourselves with mini quiches, mini arugula-and-shrimp pizzas, melon balls with prosciutto, and bowls of namkeens (a sort of spicy, salty snack mix) and samosas (Indian potato pastries). The food is amazing, Nic's place is beautiful, it's a great opportunity to see my friends—and yet I just want to curl up in a ball and cry.

At some point, I wander into the empty kitchen, ostensibly to get more food, but really to take a time-out. I walk over to Nic's sink and admire her backsplash.

Nic has two stepdaughters (bonus daughters, she calls them), Megan and Malika, who are ten and six. They're constantly drawing pictures, so last year she had her favorites turned into kitchen tiles, which she has turned into a backsplash above her counter. The pictures show the kids' versions of a perfect family. One was made by Malika when she was five and is a line drawing that looks like four little snowmen in the family: big snow-daddy Jason, slightly smaller snow-stepmommy Nic, an even smaller Megan, and the smallest, Malika. Next to that is a much more artistically advanced Christmas tree; a heart tile made by a smaller child with *I Love You* written in the middle, an arrow going through it diagonally; and about a gazillion tiles showing stick figures, hearts, and *I Love Yous* in various combinations.

A long line of pictures representing nothing but peace, tranquility, and love. Not to mention knowing what your life's passion truly is, and that you're fulfilling it daily.

I'm horribly jealous of Nic for a moment. I wish I knew what my life's passion was. I wish I had something in my life I was motivated to work on every day.

I hear the kitchen doors swing open, and turn around to see Nic. "You okay?" she asks quietly.

"Never better," I lie, smiling and holding up my flute of Coke for a toast.

The two vertical lines between her brows shows me she doesn't believe me. "You missing Danny right now?"

"Not exactly," I tell her truthfully. Though I do wonder why I'm feeling such sadness in my gut right now, almost like a weight that's pulling me down. I absentmindedly play with a white doily on her shiny granite counter. "I think I miss what I thought he'd be. Or I miss knowing what I thought my future was going to look like. Or . . . I don't know . . ." My voice peters out.

Nic sits down on a chair at her kitchen island. "None of us ever really know—"

"—what our future is. Yeah, I know, I get that. But you know you're going to be a mom, Seema knows she's going to be a wife. I just . . . I guess I just wish I knew what I was going to be. Like, if I knew I would always be single . . . okay, fine. Maybe I'd be okay with that. Maybe I wouldn't keep hoping for something that doesn't exist."

Nic's stares at me, clearly studying me. "What *are* you hoping for?"

I think about her question for ten seconds, then twenty. It's a good question. Finally, I shrug. "I don't know. Maybe that's part of the problem."

Nic considers my answer. "For the cake, you wanted the passport charm. Where do you want to go?"

I can think of twelve places off the top of my head. But only one really stands out in my mind: "Hawaii."

"Well, there you go. School is over, get on a plane."

"I don't want to go to Hawaii alone. How depressing."

"You're not alone. Jeff lives there these days."

"Yeah, running a bar for honeymooners. Hawaii's the place you go to when you're in love. Not run away to because you can't find love. I want to see it when I can share it with someone."

"Go anyway."

Before I can answer, Seema pushes through the doorway. "I need cake."

"Why? What happened?" I ask.

"Nothing happened. I just need cake."

Nic picks up the cake and heads for the kitchen door. "Your wish is my command. Mel, can you grab the cake knife and pie server?"

As I grab Nic's superfancy sterling-silver serving pieces, Seema puts her hand on Nic's chest to stop her. "You're sure you did this right?"

"I'm sure," Nic insists, a bit insulted.

"Because I don't want to pick a Winnebago charm," Seema warns her.

"First of all, it's not really a Winnebago. Symbolically, it's a travel charm—"

Seema puts her hand to her chest. "Nic, try to understand that in my mind, if there is a hell, I won't spend eternity in a fiery abyss filled with sinners. I'll be stuck in a Winnebago for all of time, driving around North Dakota in February with Karl Rove and Kim Kardashian."

Nic shakes her head slowly. "That's *oddly* specific."

"I have nightmares. Let's go."

Seema opens the kitchen door to let Nic through with her cake, and me to follow closely behind with the serving pieces.

Earlier, Nic promised us up and down that she would put the cake topper in front of Seema, we would pick the charms in the midnight and one o'clock positions, and we'd live happily ever after.

Now, as a math teacher, I could have told Nic the problem with using a cake topper as a marker for a circular cake. If you turn the cake 180 degrees, the cake topper looks exactly the same. Which means the midnight position is now in the six o'clock position, and my one o'clock position is really seven o'clock. Etc. So when we all grab our white satin loops and pull out our charms . . .

While other guests squeal in delight, let's just say I am not as enthusiastic. "What the hell?" I blurt out after seeing my charm.

"No . . . ," Nic groans as she sees hers for the first time.

"Okay," I ask, showing mine to Nic, "can we trade this time?"

"What did you get?"

"The money tree," I say sadly, tossing it on the table.

"Oh," Nic says, confused. "Well, at least that's not a bad one. It means a lifetime of financial security."

Right. That's not so bad. Maybe I'll just spend the rest of my life worrying about making money, and waking up every morning to go to a job that I hate just to have more of it. Fan-fucking-tastic.

"I got the moon," Nic says, holding up her charm for me to see. "Trade?"

It doesn't look too ominous, her cute little half-moon charm. But, then again, I've been to this fire before. "Depends. What does it mean?"

Nic can't suppress an eye roll. "An adventurous nightlife."

I look down at her belly. "How are you . . . ?"

"I know, right? Trade?"

As I try to decide if I even want an adventurous nightlife, we hear from a girl in the group. "Ooohhhh, I got the wedding cake!" she giggles. "Does that mean I'm the next one to get married?"

"It does indeed," Nic says, immediately plastering on her happy-hostess face. "The yellow sheet of paper in front of each of you is a list explaining what each charm means."

While all of the guests read their charts to foresee their futures, I watch Seema's jaw tighten. She leans toward Nic and whispers, "I thought you had this rigged."

"I did," Nic whispers back defensively, frowning at her charm.

"What did *you* get?" one of Seema's friends asks her excitedly.

"The snake," she says, reluctantly showing it to the bevy of giggling women at the table.

And that's when the gasping begins. "Oh my God!" Seema's auntie Hema exclaims. "It's a curse!"

Seema sighs loudly, having clearly anticipated this reaction. "It's only a curse if you kill it," Seema tells Hema calmly.

"No, it's a curse," Hema insists, throwing her left hand in the air. "The wedding will be cursed."

"No, no, Mrs. Suresh." Nic points to Hema's sheet of paper and moves her finger down the list. "A snake means 'slow, steady progress and extreme good fortune.'" Nic taps a particular line on Hema's chart. "See, it says so right here."

"Not in Indian culture!" Hema tells her authoritatively. "In our culture, a snake is bad luck."

Seema takes a deep breath and tries to calm her down. "Auntie Hema—with all due respect, just because you have a fear of snakes does not mean that an entire country—"

"I'm telling you it's bad luck."

I'm already on my iPhone, looking up alternatives for all of our charms. "According to this article I googled, it's only several generations of bad luck if you kill the snake—but I don't see anything about pulling it out of a cake."

Hema's jaw sets as she glares at me. "Are you going to tell me about my own people's traditions?"

Oops. "No, ma'am," I say, looking down sheepishly.

"Do you see me telling you how Norwegians celebrate Christmas?" Hema asks me.

I can feel myself squinting. "Um . . . actually I'm sort of an Irish/German mutt more than . . ."

I'm pretty sure Seema's aunt begins chanting a prayer under her breath.

Seema leans into me. "Suddenly, the Winnebago isn't seeming so bad."

Four

An hour or so later, we have piled Seema's gifts into my car and made it home relatively unscathed.

"I always pictured my bridal shower going differently than that," Seema says to me slightly slurrily as we get out of the car and I hand her a giant box of towels from Bloomingdale's.

"What? You didn't think it would include your aunt calling your mother in a panic so that they could recheck your horoscope for next week?" I say as I pull out several boxes from Target and slam my trunk shut.

"That, and I didn't think I'd ever open a gift in front of my seventy-two-year-old aunt only to see that it was a vibrator."

"It was kinda cool that she knew what one was though," I suggest weakly to Seema.

"You know, it really wasn't."

We walk up Seema's flagstone walkway to the front door. I unlock it, and the two of us step in.

"You're home early!" Scott yells from the bedroom, maybe a little nervously.

"I wanted to say good-bye before your bachelor party starts,"

Seema yells to him, putting down the towels, tossing her purse down on the coffee table, and walking across our living room toward her bedroom.

"Give me a minute!" Scott says. "I wasn't expecting you for another hour."

Uh-oh.

Seema walks to the bedroom, unfazed. "Don't worry. I just want to take off my bra, slip into some yoga pants, and—"

Scott slams the door shut before she can walk into their room.

Seema jolts her head back in surprise. She turns to me, then looks back toward her door. She shakes her head. "Okay, I know you don't have a woman in there," she yells through the door. "So what's the deal? Did you buy a snake?"

Scott opens the door and pops his head through the doorway. He is wearing a red-and-gold turban. "Was I supposed to buy a snake for the ceremony?"

"Well, look at you!" Seema exclaims. Then she smiles and flirtatiously asks, "Are you gettin' all groomlike?"

Scott grins. "I am," he says proudly, making a show out of walking out of her bedroom. He is wearing a cream-colored dupion-silk sherwani (a groom's overcoat) that is heavily embellished with intricate Zardozi, maroon embroidery and beading. He also sports matching maroon silk kurta pajamas, dark red beaded pointy slippers, and the red-and-gold turban.

Scott does a spin. "So, can I rock a sherwani or what?"

Seema continues to grin at him, almost blushing. "Wow . . . you look amazing."

"I do, don't I?" Scott says happily, then leans in for a kiss.

She smiles even more brightly as she kisses him back.

All is well in the kingdom once again.

And I, despite myself, feel a twinge of jealousy.

My friend is totally and completely, butterflies still in her stomach, madly in love. And she gets to marry the man she aches for. After thirty-two years of waiting, fretting, bad dating, bad hair, bad outfits, and pretending to care about football scores, she finally gets her happy ending.

And as much as I'm mad at myself for feeling this way, I'm a little saddened by that.

Stop it Mel, I think to myself. *You're letting the lack of momentum in your own life get the best of you. People's lives are like fields— there are times of rapid growth, and times when the soil is fallow. There is nothing wrong with taking a little time to figure out what's next in your life. If people were constantly moving to the next phase of their lives as quickly as possible, we'd all be grandparents by thirty-six, and dead by forty. There's nothing wrong with a little boredom.*

The two are giving each other bedroom eyes, so I decide to give them a little privacy. "I'm gonna go unload the car."

Scott offers to help, but I insist it's one of my maid-of-honor duties, and I shall go it alone.

By the time I get back, they're locked in their room.

And I decide it's time to finally drink some champagne.

FIVE

Who's the love of your life?

Who's the guy who just popped into your head?

Who's the man you would spend the rest of your life with, if it were totally under your control?

I stare at the yellow legal pad I just wrote on.

It's ten in the evening and, boy, am I having a "glass half-empty" kind of night. Actually, I'm having more of a "glass completely shattered because I threw it against the wall" kind of night.

But I'm trying to snap myself out of it. I'm trying to figure out what I really want in my life, so that I can go after it, full speed ahead.

I look at my nightstand, where my money-tree charm sits, mocking me.

Damn it, I hate that charm.

I refill a champagne flute from IKEA that Seema received today from a bottle of champagne left over from the shower.

It's pink. It's yummy. It's expensive. And it's not making me feel any better.

I begin writing on the legal pad again.

If you can't face your job another day, what do you want to do instead?

What makes you happy? It can be anything—biking near a beach in the Maldives, taking black-and-white photos in Chicago, throwing a great dinner party here in Hollywood. What is it? And why aren't you doing it?

Many women my age can answer that question with "Because I have children to take care of. And a husband, a dog, a job that pays the bills, an aging parent. I have responsibilities." But I can't say that. I don't have any major responsibilities. So why don't I get off my butt and start doing something to make my life better? . . . Anything!

I toss the notepad onto my bed dejectedly, walk across my bedroom, open my top desk drawer, and rifle through the debris of old receipts and Post-its for a candy bar. I usually have a candy bar hidden in here somewhere. I find a Twix. A "fun-size" Twix, but a Twix nonetheless.

Normally candy makes me very happy. I have a thing about candy; it's one reason I used to regularly run five miles a day: so I can always eat candy.

But tonight I am more relieved to see it than happy. The truth is, I'm never really "happy" anymore. Sometimes I'm "content," I guess, but even that feeling is fleeting lately.

Fleeting contentment. I suppose if one were honest with oneself, one might say that's depression.

Ick. *Depression.* That's an ugly word. A serious word. One that implies doctors and medication. I'm not that bad. Or am I? Is how I'm feeling normal? And what is normal anyway?

I pop the little chocolate bar into my mouth, stare at my wall, and think.

I think one reason depression (if I should call it that) can be so insidious is because usually it just creeps up on you. Frequently, it's not one really catastrophic event that brings on a bout of depression—a breakup, a death, a job loss. It's more like a small snowball rolling downhill, getting bigger and bigger as it descends, until it becomes so gigantic you don't even know how to get a melt-down started.

Right now, nothing is wrong in my life. I'm just not . . . happy. And I haven't been for quite some time.

I go back to my bed, sit down cross-legged, and silently stare at the money tree.

Something must really be wrong with me if I am depressed over getting a money tree. Who wouldn't want more money?

Easy. Someone who's stuck in her job and wants out, but knows that in this economy there is no better job out there, and that she has no other options.

Okay, maybe I'm in a mild depression. I can snap out of it. It's nothing that requires medication, just a general lethargic feeling and a sneaking suspicion that there's more out there in life and I'm missing it.

I've never been to Paris. I've always desperately wanted to go, but it's never been a good time. First, I had college, and college loans. Then graduate school, and more loans. By the time I got my first job as a public-school teacher, I was so in debt that I couldn't imagine traveling anywhere farther than Fresno.

I was just starting to see the end of my debt. Was finally put-ting away a little every month to use toward travel. Finally ready to move on to the next adventure in my life.

And then I got the pink slip, along with a hint from my princi-pal that this year might be different: this year I may really be let go.

But here's my dirty little secret—I kind of hope they do fire me. Then I'll be forced to try something different. Right now, I'm just stuck.

It's weird to feel stuck on the path you worked your ass off to take. I have wanted to be a math teacher since I was in third grade. My parents thought I'd grow out of it, but no. The older I got, the more I wanted to teach children. I wanted to surround myself with their optimism, their zest for life. With the added bonus of having two months off in summer and three weeks off at Christmas. Plus I wanted to be surrounded by math, which is (well, used to be) my version of *The New York Times* crossword puzzle. Challenging, yet inherently logical.

I followed my bliss, worked like a madwoman to get what I wanted, and found myself pretty happy with my job and my life for several years.

And then . . . I don't know, my job's just not doing it for me anymore. I loved it for a really long time, and now I don't, and I don't know what to do.

Then there's my love life.

I remember the butterflies I got in college when I met the man of my dreams. (Even if the man was only eighteen.) Mark. Before Jeff, I dated Mark. And for six blissful months we made out every free second we had, slept on top of each other on his couch so we could get alone time away from all of our roommates. Talked on the phone all night during the few hours when we weren't in the same room with each other. We actually did the "You hang up first" thing on more than one occasion. But then I didn't want to have sex with him, and we broke up, and I found Jeff (who had no problem not having sex with me), and back then I figured I'd find dozens of men in my future who would make me feel that way again.

Now, I'm closing in on my thirty-third birthday. There are no butterflies for thirty-three-year-olds. There's lust, there's guarded hope for the future, but there's no feeling as if you're going to throw up in the time between when he rings your doorbell and when you open the door.

In some ways, that's actually a good thing. (Vomiting can be so off-putting.) But right now, that lack of excitement is probably contributing to my depression.

Adding to my romantic and career problems is the fact that I have to move out of Seema's house soon. I have never lived alone, and the fear of that could be causing some of my late-night ice cream binges and might be a plausible excuse for why I've been missing my five-mile runs lately.

But deep down, I know it's none of these things. My depression is so insidious because there is no real reason for me to be depressed. There's nothing seriously wrong with my life, nothing to fix that I have the power to fix. I just have nothing I'm looking forward to. I have no passion. I believe the French call it ennui. I have nothing I'm dying to accomplish, no finish line to push myself to cross. These days are just about getting through the days—there's no going forward. For someone as goal oriented as me, that's depressing.

I have put on ten pounds in the past six months. No one has actually commented on my rapid increase in size, but let's face it, when friends gain that much weight that quickly, we all wait until they're out of the room before tsk-tsking, "She looks awful. What happened to her?"

What happened in my case was simple: I just quit running every day. It wasn't something I intended to quit—just one day I didn't feel like doing it, so I didn't. Then the next day I didn't run either. And I happily discovered that it was nice having an extra hour in my day, every day, to lie on the couch and leaf through the latest *Cosmo* or bridal magazine (Seema's been leaving a lot of those around lately). Want to read twenty-seven different descriptions of the Hawaiian islands? Pick up three bridal magazines and let the dreaming begin. Not to mention Paris, London, Florence . . . Hell, at this point, I'd settle for a trip to the Poconos.

Then on the nights when I didn't feel like dreaming about travel, I'd turn on the TV and spend hours watching mindless sitcoms or reality shows. Usually with my trusty Häagen-Dazs or Ben & Jerry's sitting loyally by my side.

It was way more fun than pushing through pains in the backs of my thighs while I ran uphill—the same hill I've been running up for eight years.

Soon, I replaced my evening jog with a few glasses of wine at night. And that previously mentioned Twix bar. Some nights a slice of cake to cheer me up, or a trip to Pinkberry for a large chocolate yogurt, and instead of fruit toppings I now added Oreos.

Oreos instead of fruit. *The Real Housewives* instead of running. A little wine to reward myself for a day of hard work. Nothing tragic—much of it quite pleasant. New activities to distract me from the ennui.

But then my mind takes over again, and I go back to being me, and no amount of ice cream or cookies or wine can distract me from that. I wonder if this is what a midlife crisis looks like. I'm only thirty-two though. Do I plan to die young?

I wash down the candy with champagne, pick up my money-tree charm from my nightstand, and stare at it. What if I do die young? What if I work my ass off for a retirement I never see? What if I spend my whole life preparing for the life I'm going to lead, then never get around to living it?

There's a sudden pounding at our front door, which scares the crap out of me. It's after eleven, so I'm kind of spooked out.

I freeze in my bed, careful not to make a sound.

A few moments later there's another knock, and a deeply

masculine (albeit slightly slurring) voice booms from outside, "Seema, I've got the chauffeur standing here with my bags, I'm drunk, and I know there's a key under one of these rocks, but I'll be damned if I can find it in my compromised condition."

What drunken ex-boyfriend has decided to pull a Dustin Hoffman in The Graduate *at this late hour?* I think to myself as I tiptoe out into the living room nervously and silently lean toward the door to try to secure the dead bolt.

I hear a key go into our front lock before I can get to the bolt.

The door creaks open, and a mysterious man walks in.

I scream and jump the guy.

He screams too, grabs me by the waist, throws me onto the couch, and pins me down.

It's at this point that I realize that, on top of me, is one of the best-looking men I've ever seen.

Lucky for me, he's happy to see me. "Mel!" He beams. "Damn, woman, you get sexier every time I see you."

My eyes bug open. "Jay! What are you doing here?"

Vijay, Seema's smoking-hot older brother, slowly climbs off of me. (Rats.) "Visiting my sister. Who thoughtlessly forgot to pick me up from the airport tonight." He gives me a kiss on each cheek and sits down next to me. (That's not as cheesy as it sounds—he lives in Paris.)

"That's because we didn't think you were coming until next Thursday."

Jay smiles. "Oh, I'm not."

I should really get Botox or Dysport—it would keep me from furrowing my brow in confusion so often. "What do you mean you're not?"

"I told my *family* I wasn't flying in until Thursday. I have to fly to San Francisco Monday for a big meeting, so I thought I'd head to LA a couple of days early and see friends before the wedding craziness begins." He leans in to me, inhales my scent, then grins. "You smell like a combination of champagne, chocolate, and Chanel No. 5."

"Thank you," I say brightly. Wait, is he flirting with me? "I've had a bit too much champagne tonight. Chocolate too. There was a lot of both left over from Seema's shower today."

"Too much champagne? That's a shame. Because I have a lovely Bordeaux I brought all the way from Paris, and I could use someone to share it with." Jay leans toward to me seductively, and I wonder if he's going to kiss me. Instead, he looks over my shoulder and raises his hand "hello" to someone behind me. "Andre. The eagle has landed. You can toss the bags anywhere."

I turn around to see Andre, his chauffeur, standing by my door with a black bag in each hand, smiling (possibly in amusement) at Jay. "Yes, Mr. Singh," Andre says, then puts Jay's bags down next to the couch. "And it's good to have you back in town."

"Happy to see you too." Jay stands and pulls Andre into a sloppy "I love you, man" hug. "Sorry you have to get up so early Monday to pick me up."

"Not a problem," Andre says, hugging him back, then nodding to me. "You have a good evening, ma'am."

"Thank you. You too," I say. Andre closes the door behind him, and I stand up and walk over to the door to lock the bottom lock, then the dead bolt.

Then I turn to Jay.

Wow—he is still so beautiful. A perfect six feet tall, glowing bronze skin, eyes you could lose yourself in for days. It's been a while since I looked at a man and got all googly-eyed—and I'm liking that feeling.

The first time I ever met Seema's older brother was back when I was rooming with her in our freshman dorm in college. He was two years older, a junior at Stanford majoring in French literature (apparently much to the chagrin of their parents). I thought he was the most sophisticated and intelligent man I had ever met. Not to mention so breathtakingly handsome that the first time I met him I actually giggled. Then I stared at the floor, the wall, the ceiling, and anywhere else I could find that was not him for at least an hour.

He stayed on our couch for a long weekend, and during the seventy-two hours that he was there, he slept with not one but two women, both of whom bugged Seema for months asking about him. His James Bond–worthy success with the ladies sort of cured me of my crush. But I am embarrassed to admit—only sort of. One could say, "The heart wants what it wants." But I think it was other parts of my anatomy that craved his attention.

Nonetheless, I was a virgin then and never got together with him. He lived his life as a bon vivant, and bon vivants are scary when you're of a certain age—that age ranging anywhere from eighteen to, say, thirty-two.

"How have I not hit this?" Jay says cheerfully yet seductively as he makes a show of waving his hands around my body. "I swear, you could be a Frenchwoman: you get better and better with age."

I shake my head and smile. "You know, if that came from anyone but you, it would be horribly cheesy. Yet, somehow when you say it, you're charming as always."

"I'll bet you look even better when you're not wearing Eeyore slippers," he says playfully.

I look down and am immediately mortified. Indeed, I am in Eeyore slippers, which match my fetching Eeyore shorty pajamas. I smile and shrug. "Well, maybe if you had told us you were coming a few days early, I could have worn something more Victoria's Secret and less Disney Store," I flirt.

"A powerful incentive to do so next time," Jay flirts right back.

"So, do you have any interest in sharing a Château Calon-Ségur Saint-Estèphe with me? Or are you off to bed?"

"Yes, and no," I answer, having never heard of a Château blah-blah-blah, nuh-nuh-nuh, but figuring a handsome man bringing me French wine can only be a good thing.

Jay unzips his suitcase. "So, how's Seema doing? She seemed pretty stressed the last time I talked to her."

"She's fine. I think she'll be better once this is all over and they head to Kenya. Did you pack your sherwani?"

"Yeesss . . . ," he says, dragging out the word to two syllables and sighing. "And my turban. And my tuxedo. The way she nagged me, you'd think I was planning to go to her wedding in beachwear and flip-flops."

"In fairness, that was your signature look back in college." I want to add that it was a fantastic look on him, but I don't have the nerve to say that aloud.

Jay pulls out a bottle of red wine. The label has a heart on it. "Back in college I also thought wine coolers and Budweiser were acceptable forms of libation." He holds up the bottle. "Trust me— I've upgraded."

Jay smiles at me warmly. I know this is wrong, but after all these years I still want to kiss him. Actually, I want to climb on top of him like a kitten on a scratching post.

My cooler head soon prevails, and I break eye contact. Getting together with Jay would be a complete disaster for a variety of reasons: First, he's Seema's brother. Next, he's thirty-five and has never been married. Plus, he lives on the other side of the planet. And finally, he's slept with enough women to make Hugh Hefner blush and give an STD lecture.

"Let me get you a corkscrew," I say, grateful for the excuse to escape to the kitchen.

"Seema tells me you're single again," Jay says casually as he follows me to the kitchen. "So now that you're a free woman, when are you coming to Paris to stay with me?"

The question takes me completely off guard and makes me think of my missed passport charm from earlier today. "School's finished, and I've got nothing to do besides watch summer reruns and eat. How's your Bastille Day looking?" I joke as I pull a cork-screw from a drawer.

Jay puts the bottle on the counter and leans into me. I can smell his breath. It's a combination of red wine and mint, and all I can think about is how it would feel on my neck.

"Let me check." He pulls away from me and quickly checks his iPhone. "I can make myself free every night that week." He tells me as he reads his screen. "I'll probably have to go in to work a few of the weekdays, but I can play hooky a bit, and we can always send you off to the Louvre or Notre Dame on the days that I'm busy."

"Wait . . . you're serious?" I ask, allowing myself to get the tiniest bit excited. "Could I really come stay with you in Paris?"

"Of course. I'm staying with you these next few days, why shouldn't I return the favor?"

Technically, he's staying with his sister, not me, I think to myself as I hand Jay the corkscrew and watch him open the bottle effort-lessly (everything he does seems effortless).

Then again: a free place to stay in Paris. Hard to resist.

I pull out two wineglasses. "I'll think about it."

"Let me tempt you further." He pours our wine. "I live in Mont-martre, right in the middle of the eighteenth arrondissement," he says in such lilting French, I want to grab him by his loosened silk tie, pull him to my room, and have my way with him immediately. "On your first day, we could hit the French market in the late morning, I'll make us some *jambon blanc et fromage* sandwiches, and we'll do a picnic at the Parc du Champ de Mars, next to the Eiffel Tower. Then we'll head to the Musée d'Orsay, which if you ask me is even better than the Louvre, and check out the Monets, the Manets, and the Gauguins. I remember years ago you had this coffee mug of Monet's *Water Lilies* painting. You should see it in person. It's incredibly soothing. I could stand there and stare at it for hours."

He remembered that mug? I loved that mug. Whatever happened to that mug? "Ummm . . . Well, I . . ."

Jay continues to entice me in more ways than one. "For dinner, we have an abundance of choices. After all, it's Paris. There's this wonderful little place I go to called L'Escargot Montorgueil, obviously in Montorgueil, that, yes, has the best snails you've ever eaten, but also a beef fillet you would love. Or if you like chateaubriand, we could go to Le Tastevin. Or there's an amazing little boîte in the Latin Quarter—"

"Have you ever been to the restaurant in the Eiffel Tower?" I ask him excitedly.

Jay pauses for a second, which makes me self-conscious.

I quickly backtrack. "I just . . . I know it's lame, but I've always wanted to eat at the Eiffel Tower. It's sort of a bucket-list thing."

"You mean the one on the first floor, or the Jules Verne?"

"Um . . . the Jules Verne?" I guess, not having any idea which one I mean.

Jay hands me my glass of red. "I have not, but it sounds perfect. Then we end the night with drinks and a cheese course at the bar at George V, then go back to my apartment, where we'll split a bottle of your favorite something in front of the fireplace. And that's just day one."

Shit, I could never afford all of that, I think to myself. But instead

I say, "Don't you have a girlfriend who would be mad if I was there?"

Jay cocks his head, confused. "Does Seema think I have a girlfriend?"

"Oh. No, I just . . . I mean, looking at you, I kind of always assume you have a girlfriend."

"No," Jay promises me, furrowing his brow as though trying to decipher how I could have come up with such an odd conclusion. "When our parents came out last fall, I did introduce them to Jacqueline. But we weren't a real item or anything. She was mostly doing me a favor. You know how moms get when you're in your midthirties and there are no grandchildren on the horizon."

I do indeed. Something tells me that for men it's more of an annoyance. With women, we take it to heart, decide there must be something inherently wrong with us, then get even more depressed than our mothers.

Jay swirls the wine in his glass, leans in to sniff it, then takes a sip. "Not bad, but I think we should give it ten minutes to open up." He gently takes my hand and cheerfully pulls me toward the living room. "Let's go make out on the couch for a while."

I grab my glass and allow myself to be pulled to the couch, knowing he's not the least bit serious. Jay has had opportunities to have his way with me since we were young, and other than a kiss hello in college on the lips (which has, sadly, turned into a kiss on each cheek since he moved to Europe), I am chaste in his eyes.

Jay leads me to the couch, and we both take a seat. Instead of leaning in toward me, he leans back against the corner of the sofa and lounges his right arm out as if to invite me in for a hug. "So, what is going on in your life? Tell me everything. How's school treating you?"

Ugh. I don't know exactly what Jay does for a living, but I do know it makes a healthy six figures. In euros. So anytime we talk about work, I feel like a Vegas lounge singer talking to Beyoncé. "Oh, you know, same old, same old," I answer nervously.

Why am I so nervous? It's not as if I've never been on a sofa with this man before. It's not as if I haven't known him for a million years. And, yes, okay, I still think he's hot, but after this many years knowing a person . . .

"And your cousin Julie?" he asks, killing the mood completely.

Julie and he had a brief fling back in college when, granted, I had a boyfriend. Then they hooked up a few years ago when he came to Los Angeles, when I, once again, had a boyfriend.

Naturally, I was jealous as hell both times.

"Julie's good," I tell him, my voice cracking. "She's married now, so she has a date to the wedding." Good God, why do I say things like that out loud?

Jay nods. "Husbands are good for that—built-in dates."

"Yeah," I say awkwardly, nodding as well. Then I take a nervous sip of wine and blurt out, "Guess you're gonna have to find someone else to dance with to Eric Clapton that night."

He smiles at me, shakes his head slowly, and asks in confusion, "Eric Clapton?"

"Yeah. Remember, sophomore year our dorm had this dance, and you were flirting with Julie, and then "Wonderful Tonight" came on, and you were talking about how he first released it in 1977, but it didn't really take off until more than ten years later, and she grabbed you and you guys danced, and then . . . well . . . um, you know." I dart my eyes around the room, unable to make eye contact any longer.

Jay cocks his head. "Wow. I vaguely remember that. I'm surprised you do."

"Three point one four one five nine two six five." Butterflies are doing cartwheels in my stomach. "Those are the first nine digits of pi. I have a good memory."

Why did I say that? Did that even make sense? What is wrong with me? And how quickly can I get to my bedroom, slam my door, jump into bed, and throw the covers over my head, scared of this ghost of crushes past?

Jay stares at me as if he's trying to figure me out. (Good luck with that—I've been trying for thirty-two years to no avail.) I try to make eye contact with him again, but I once again get so nervous, I turn away. "Can you quit doing that?"

"What?"

"Looking at me like you're studying me. I hate that."

"Sorry," he apologizes, unruffled. He takes a sip of his wine, then puts it on the coffee table and watches me again.

Dude, thanks for listening.

"You know, I actually was kind of trying to get you to dance with me that night," Jay confesses.

"You were?"

"Mm-hmm. You asked me to dance to Ricky Martin's 'La Vida Loca,' and I said no. Then at some point a slow song came on, but it was really lame. I can't remember why I didn't—"

"Spice Girls. 'Two Become One,'" I interrupt, nearly yelling out the answer.

Jay appears startled by my outburst, but quickly shrugs it off. "I'm sure you're right. Anyway, then some slow Clapton came on . . . which was more my speed . . . but you had a boyfriend then, so . . ."

His voice trails off, and I let silence fill the room.

"I had kind of a crush on you back then," Jay admits.

I turn to him, eyes wide. "You did? Seriously?"

"Why do you think I came to visit Seema so often?" he asks, chuckling a little.

Jay Singh—THE Jay Singh—had a crush on me once? Me? Wow. Wow. Wow. Say something clever. Prove to him you're worthy. I finally come up with "I had a little bit of a crush on you back then too."

He seems surprised. "Yeah?"

"Yeah," I reiterate nervously. "I mean, I always had a boyfriend, so there was nothing I could do about it back then."

"You shouldn't have let that stop you," he says jokingly (half-jokingly?). "You'd be amazed how many girls I've dated who've had boyfriends at the time."

Okey-dokey. Now what? I put the wineglass back up to my lips, then decide to put it back down. I want to be clearheaded (or relatively clearheaded) for this.

Well, let's see . . . Choice number one: slowly stand up from the couch and head to my bedroom, careful to turn around and eye him seductively right before disappearing into my boudoir.

In Eeyore pajamas? Difficult to pull off.

Choice number two: look at him coquettishly while I sip my wine and hope he thinks to make a move on his own?

I've spent more than a decade waiting for him to make a move. Once, when I tried to eye him coquettishly, he asked if I had something in my eye.

Choice number three: skip the wine, the coquettish look, and the trip to the boudoir, and pounce on him like a poodle on her favorite chew toy!

"So, do you have a date to the wedding?" Jay asks me, interrupting my internal debate.

"Huh? Oh. Not really," I say a bit too quickly. "I mean, kind of . . ."

But before I can explain the Jeff situation, Jay leans in and kisses me.

It's a soft kiss. No tongue, no expectation. Just a very nice, sweet kiss.

I have no idea what to make of it.

So I do what most women do in this situation—I fill the room with lots of unnecessary words. "Jeff's my date. Remember my old boyfriend from my sophomore year?"

Jay looks disappointed, and I quickly try to think of a way to backtrack. But before I can explain further, we hear Seema and Scott walk up the front walkway.

We both immediately retract to opposite sides of the three-cushion couch.

"I'm just saying, it was a little strange to walk in on, that's all," I hear Seema argue to Scott as we hear the key going into the lock.

As the key unlocks the dead bolt, I can hear Scott continue the heated discussion. "So you're mad because I was *talking* to the stripper, instead of letting her grind me?"

"I'm not mad you were talking to her!" Seema says, clearly mad. "I just don't understand why you needed to talk to her about where our future children are going to elementary school."

"The LA public school system is *very* complicated," Scott points out as Seema opens the door. "You've got your magnets, your charters, plus open-enrollment options. And that's not even taking into account looking for a house near a good neighborhood school."

Jay jumps off the couch (so quickly as to almost be insulting) and jokes, "And then there's preschool. You've got your blocks, your colors, should you focus more on letters and numbers, or sandbox time?"

"Jay!" Seema practically squeals. "What are you doing here?"

"Apparently missing the weirdest bachelor party on record," Jay says, pulling her into a huge hug.

"I thought you weren't coming until Thursday," Seema tells him as Jay and Scott shake hands.

"When is the rest of the family coming?" Jay asks.

"Monday. Well, except Auntie Hema, she's already here."

"Then I'm not coming until Thursday."

Seema shakes her head at his answer, then jumps up a bit and gives him another hug. "Oh, I'm so excited to see you! Let me go put on my pajamas, and we'll stay up all night catching up."

Seema trots over to her bedroom, and Jay and I exchange a disappointed look.

Which Scott notices. "Um, Seema, maybe we should just go back to my place and let Jay get some rest. I'm sure he's had a long flight and would like to catch his breath."

"Don't be silly," she yells from her room. "I only see my big brother twice a year! I wanna make the most of it!"

Scott glances knowingly back and forth between Jay and me. "Seema, you might not be the only person making the most of his visit."

Seema pops out of her room wearing an adorable pair of red silk pj's. "What are you talking about?"

Scott points to our glasses of wine on the table. "I think we may have been intruding."

Seema bursts out laughing. "On them? Please. Mel would never have him." She points to my wine. "I'm gonna grab a glass of that, and I'll be right back."

Seema heads to the kitchen to get herself a glass of red and get Scott a pint of IPA, and I spend the next hour sneaking flirtatious glances and smiles back and forth with Jay while listening to Seema monologue about her wedding.

I have a brief moment of hope when Scott announces he's calling it a night and heads to bed, but this is quickly dashed when I hear Seema uncork another bottle of wine in the kitchen. Half an hour after that, I concede that she has outlasted me and announce that I'm going to bed.

Once in my bedroom, I change into a pretty silk robe, a pretty lace camisole, and nonperiod underwear. I brush my teeth and spritz both my neck and my bed with Chanel No. 5.

Then I wait for Seema to go to bed so I can sneak back out to see Jay and finish that kiss.

As I wait, I accidentally glance at my silver money-tree charm, and for the first time in my life I seriously consider going to Paris. Okay, so it's not a passport. Maybe it's not supposed to be. Maybe there is a giant sculpture of a money tree in some small avant-garde gallery in the middle of the Latin Quarter. I mean, the last time Nic did a cake pull, I had wanted the engagement-ring charm. Instead, I got the red-hot chili pepper, which was supposed to represent a red-hot sex life. Since I desperately wanted the man I was living with to propose, the charm made no sense to me at the time. But then I realized my boyfriend was cheating on me, and I broke up with him and met another guy, who gave me red-hot sex, and it all made sense. Maybe this charm will make sense too—I just need to help it along a bit.

My hint of retiring early didn't do any good. All I heard from my room was an excited Seema babbling to her brother until 3:14 A.M., at which time my eyes got too heavy to stay awake any longer, and I drifted off.

And just before I fell asleep, while I was in that hypnagogic state when you're neither asleep nor awake, I thought about Paris. And the charm. And the charming man in the other room.

And my future started to make a little more sense.

Six

I was hoping my going to bed last night would inspire Jay to encourage Seema to go to sleep, then engage in a little silent nocturnal traffic. True to my usual run of luck in the romance department, this never happened.

I wake up at 6:15 in the morning, alone in my bed.

This will not do. I have a charm to live up to.

I tiptoe out of my bedroom and into our living room to see Jay asleep on the couch.

He must be dreaming because he looks dreamy. His bare chest peeks out from under the light pink covers Seema loans out to guests.

"Jay," I whisper.

With his eyes still closed, he moans ever so slightly, puckers his lips a bit, then rolls over to face me. It's a coincidence—he's still out cold.

I tiptoe to the couch and sit down quietly next to him. Then I lean toward his ear and whisper louder, "Jay."

He effortlessly (there's that word again) wraps his arm around my waist and whispers back in a sleepy voice, "I'm up. One more minute."

The he pulls me into a spooning position.

Hmm. On the one hand, yummy. On the other hand—does he have any idea he's just pulled *me* into a spooning position? Or does he think I'm a Yvette or a Laura or some other French girl?

I let his warm breath caress my neck for a while and dream of a life with him near the Seine. Without thinking, I take his hand, bring it to my mouth, and lightly kiss it. Then I rest my head onto his chest, grin like a Cheshire cat, and fall into a comfortable sleep.

I wake up a while later to a soft kiss on my cheek. I can feel the warmth of Jay's body, and his arms wrapped around me. I turn to him, and he smiles.

"Good morning," he says to me in the most romantic way.

"Good morning."

"I missed you," he says softly, then leans in to kiss me.

And we kiss. And it is amazing. His tongue is playful, but not trying to give me a tonsillectomy. His breath is slightly minty, yet not yet Colgated beyond recognition. His lips are soft and warm.

I have thought about this moment since my freshman year of college. It is at once totally different from I thought it would be, yet amazingly perfect.

We kiss for a while. Ten minutes, an hour, who can say?

At some point, he pulls away from me, smiling. "I'm sorry to wake you," he whispers softly.

I can feel myself smirk as I lean in to continue kissing him. "No, you're not."

He's not. And neither am I. Until he moves his hand up to my bra area.

As I have no bra on, I jump a foot.

"Do you want coffee?!" I ask, jumping off the couch as if it were on fire. "Or mimosas? We still have a lot of champagne left from yesterday."

Jay sits up. Seema's pink blanket drops down to reveal he has pajama bottoms on, but from the waist up he is naked and exquisite. He puts out his hand to me. "No, I'm good. Come back."

I do, and we kiss some more. "What if Seema wakes up?" I whisper.

"Then you'll just have to defend my honor."

"I'm serious."

"So am I."

Despite my fear of getting caught, we continue our makeout session. Every few minutes, his hand moves up toward my chest. I push it down, then he moves down to my underwear. Where I push his hand back up.

"What? Are we in college?" I ask, laughing a little.

"I hope not. In college, you would have never let me get to third."

"Third? You're not even at second."

"I know. But I have my sights on third." Once again he moves his hand to my chest, over my camisole, but this time something in my little brain decides it's okay.

It's fantastic, as a matter of fact.

"Do you want to move into my room?" I whisper.

Jay smiles, wordlessly stands up, takes my hand, and leads me to my room.

We begin kissing again before we even get to my doorway. "You're not getting to third," I assure him.

He moves his hand toward my left breast. "Isn't Jeff gay?" Jay asks, as his hand and mine meet and wrestle for the umpteenth time.

"Wait. What?" Where did that come from?

Jay kisses my neck, licks my neck, then stares into my eyes seductively. "Your date for the wedding—your old boyfriend. Isn't he gay?"

"He might be. Why do you ask?"

"Just making sure he'll be okay with you having your way with me all weekend."

I'm torn between giggling and slapping him. "What makes you think I'm interested in having my way with—"

Jay breaks my concentration with another fiery kiss. How did he get his hand under my clothes that quickly? "And that he'll be okay with you coming out to Paris to see me."

I halfheartedly push Jay's hand away. "Okay, just because you're being really cute right now . . ."

Jay pushes me farther into my room. "Shut up," he flirtatiously commands.

"Shut up?"

"Yeah. Shut up."

"I'm not—"

I am silenced by his kiss again.

It's a *really* good kiss. One that lasts for several hours.

And, no, I did not have sex with him.

But I sure thought about it. Every minute for several hours.

SEVEN

The time flew by. If it hadn't, we might have thought through a few things.

Such as avoiding a pounding on my door by Seema around 10:00 A.M.

"Jay, you better not fucking be in there!" she yells through the door.

"I think you may have switched your infinitive and verb there!" Jay yells back jokingly.

Fortunately, we are both still fully clothed (well, relatively) when she bursts in.

"Oh, *hell* no!" Seema says at the sight of Jay jumping off of me, then quickly trotting to the other side of the room.

He puts his palm up to his sister. "Before you overreact . . ."

Seema ignores him completely, setting her sights on me. "He has a girlfriend."

"I do not," Jay insists, grabbing one of my shirts to try to cover himself. "Why does everyone keep assuming that?"

Seema's eyes bug out at him. "I don't know. Maybe because Mom and Dad *met* her last year."

Jay looks relieved. "Oh. That." He turns to me. "That's just Jacqueline."

Ah . . . the French pronunciation. *Zhah-ke-leen*. It's a wonder French people ever get anything done with that accent—you'd think they'd just die happily in bed.

"Seriously, with my roommate?" Seema angrily whines at him, walking over to Jay and smacking his arm. "You're really going to take advantage of a girl who's depressed about not being married this week?"

Wait—whoa!

I want to yell that aloud, but Jay and his sister are in midfight, and I learned long ago not to try to break up two dogs when they're snarling at each other.

"Do you *really* think if I had a girlfriend I'd be sleeping with your best friend?" Jay asks his sister self-righteously.

"We didn't sleep together," I quietly assure Seema.

Nobody hears me. Instead, Jay continues to make his point, "Don't you think if I had a girlfriend, she'd be here with me this week? I mean, do you really think I'm such an asshole I'd cheat on my girlfriend? What kind of a guy would that make me?"

"Pretty much any guy she's dated in the last ten years," Seema answers.

"Hey!" I exclaim.

Seema turns to me. "I'm just trying to protect you." Then she turns to Jay, still not buying what he's selling. "So who is Jacqueline then?"

"It's pronounced Jacqueline," Jay corrects her with his French accent.

Seema crosses her arms, not dissuaded.

Jay rolls his eyes. "She's just a friend I had come to dinner a few times last fall so Mom and Dad would get off my back." He turns to me. "I swear."

Good. I feel better, but Seema still eyes him suspiciously.

He continues to make his point. "She's a lesbian. Her girlfriend's Genevieve." He turns back to me. "I promise, I'm telling the truth. If you come to Paris, I'll invite them out to dinner the first night you're there. We'll make it a foursome."

Seema opens her mouth, but Jay points his index finger at her before she can respond. "I heard it as soon as you did. That is not what I meant."

Seema stares him down. "So did you sleep with her?"

Jay doesn't answer for a moment, then rolls his eyes, a presidential candidate not wanting to dignify the question. "Like, a million years ago," he says offhandedly.

"I think she meant me," I tell him.

"Oh, " Jay says, relieved. "Then, no. Not yet."

"Not yet?" Seema and I ask in unison.

Jay shrugs. "Oh, come on. I'm a guy. Do you ask Colin Kaepernick if he plans to score a touchdown?"

Seema squints her eyes and puts out the palms of her hands. "What does that even mean? It's like you're just saying random words now."

Scott appears in the doorway, wearing Seema's purple bathrobe. "Honey, I'm really hungover. Let's go out for breakfast."

"Can't you see I'm in the middle of something?" Seema tells him.

"Yes. I'm hungover, not blind," he tells her patiently. "And this is really none of your business."

"Says the man without any siblings or roommates," Seema snaps at him. "I'm sorry you don't get it, but this most certainly is my business."

Scott turns to Jay. "Dude. You gonna be a dick after the wedding's over?"

"Of course not. I've already invited her to stay with me in Paris for her birthday."

"Oh," Scott says, a bit surprised. He visibly relaxes as he says to Seema, "Well, there you go." Then he disappears from my doorway. "I need bacon."

"I'm not done here," Seema yells toward him.

"I'll let you make another case against my loft," Scott tempts her from the other room.

Seema clenches her jaw, torn. Finally, she walks up to Jay and wags her finger in his face. "I swear to God, if you hurt her, I will break you like a twig."

"That's exactly what I just told him," I hear Scott call calmly from their room. "I just said it in guyspeak."

Seema turns to leave. "Yeah, but I actually meant it!" Seema yells to Scott as she walks to the doorway. She turns back around to Jay. "I will be back at two, and then I'm taking you shopping."

"Yes, ma'am," Jay says a little mockingly.

Seema puts her hands on her hips. "Do you even know what I'm taking you shopping for?"

"Nope. Don't care. I promise I'll go wherever you want and do whatever you say at two o'clock. For now, I'm half-naked and in a pretty girl's bedroom, so go away."

Seema opens her mouth to speak. Then for some reason she takes a moment before saying sternly, "I'm not kidding. Two o'clock. . . ." Then she warns "And she better still be intact when I get back."

"Dude!" I yell at her.

"Sorry," Seema quickly apologizes to me. "I'm backing off."

Seema makes a show of putting her left index and middle fingers up to each eye, flipping them toward Jay's eyes, then back to hers as she slowly backs out of my room and walks away.

The second she's out of view, Jay races over to the door and closes it silently.

I am still in bed. "How did you know my birthday was on Bastille Day?"

He smiles sexily as he strolls back to bed. Before he kisses me he says, "I think the more important question is . . . does that get me to third base?"

EIGHT

Seema took Jay out all afternoon, ostensibly to return some wedding gifts, show him her wedding venues, and have a nice, quiet lunch, just the two of them. I totally understood, she wanted and deserved to spend time with him. But I was disappointed anyway. Jay did text me around five o'clock to ask if I wanted to join them for dinner, and I said yes.

Texting. Man, do I hate texting. I know it makes me old, but I feel so disconnected from someone whose voice I can't hear. You're not talking, you're typing. As if men weren't uncommunicative enough before, now they've invented something that allows them to have entire relationships without ever having to speak to you. (What do you bet texting was invented by a group of guys? I'm just sayin' . . .)

Scott was still at the house, so at some point I meandered into the kitchen to hang out with him. I watched him as he sketched on a white pad.

"What'cha working on?"

He seems startled. "Hey, didn't hear you. You want me to get out of your hair?"

"No, no. This is your house in a week. I'm the one who should be leaving."

Scott raises his eyebrows. "Yeah, well . . ."

What I want to say is *Yeah, well . . . what?* But instead, I head for the coffeemaker. "You want some coffee?"

"I'd love some. Thanks."

I grab two blue mugs Scott and Seema just received as wedding gifts from the cabinet, pour us some French roast. "Do you take anything in your coffee?"

"Nope. Just black."

I bring his coffee to the kitchen table, place his mug down, then grab an ice cube from the freezer, throw it in my cup, and take a seat. I crane my neck a bit to see what Scott is working on.

On his sketch pad I see a graphite-pencil drawing of a thin, yet curvy, woman dressed in an early-1960s swimsuit. Very *Mad Men,* very cool. Next to her, written in bright red, are the words *I Love Her More Than Anything.* "Wow. That's amazing."

"Thanks. This is for my next series of pieces. It's loosely based on the *Six-Word Memoirs* books. Each piece will be titled with six words."

The more I look at the picture, the more I realize the girl looks as if the weight of the world is on her shoulders. Yes, she looks great, lounging on a beach chair with a martini glass in her hand, and donning a fabulously stylish hat. But . . .

"Her eyes look so sad," I almost whimper.

"They're supposed to. The person looking at this will hopefully have a whole group of questions in his or her head: Why is she unhappy? Is she a mistress? Is she a beautiful woman who won't let anyone in? Is she unable to have children? Secretly in love with another? What is it?"

"It's really good," I tell him, haunted by her green eyes. I wish

I had his passion and talent. I'd love to be able to communicate with people with nothing more than a picture. "What are the *Six-Word Memoirs*?"

"You've never heard of the *Six-Word Memoirs*?" Scott says, visibly surprised. "Seems like the kind of book you would have bought. Huh. Well, anyway, these editors at *Smith* magazine, Larry Smith and Rachel Fershleiser, asked people to write their lives in exactly six words. They put the best six-word sentences into a book called *Not Quite What I Was Planning*. It was on *The New York Times* bestseller list for a while."

"Hmm," I say, still looking at the girl. "So why is she so unhappy?"

Scott looks at his picture, purses his lips, thinking. "Not sure. I suppose that's up to the person looking at her."

He slowly closes his pad, looks up at me, and forces a smile.

"Are you unhappy?" I finally ask him.

"No," he says immediately. Then he's quiet for a while. "I'll admit, this whole 'combining of our lives' thing has been way more stressful than I thought it would be. Seema has so many ideas of what she wants, and sometimes I feel like I'm getting a little lost among the details. But it's fine. I can ride the wave for a few more weeks."

"Have you told her how you're feeling?"

He lets out a mild chuckle. "Yeah, the groom's feelings? Not something a bride really wants to hear about right before her wedding. Trust me. We've been mildly fighting since I put the ring on her finger. Not *fighting,* that's the wrong word. It's just—you know— she knew what cake she wanted, she knew what she wanted the invitations to look like, she knows exactly how her mehndi ceremony is going to go . . ."

"So you're just fighting about wedding stuff," I say, relieved.

"Well, it's a little more than that. It's little things. Like, she knows I hate going to Burbank because I don't trust the cops there, but she books our tickets through the Burbank airport anyway just to save money. Or I really didn't want the sheets that we registered for. But we looked at so many sheets. I mean, seriously, we looked at literally a wall of sheets at the store where we registered. And then she picked, like, the third ones from the top, which were beige, and I wasn't crazy about them. But she seemed to care so much about those sheets, and I wasn't willing to die on the hill over linens, so we picked the ones she wanted."

It doesn't feel as if we're just talking about sheets, so I say nothing and wait for him to continue. Scott takes a moment to have a sip of his coffee, then gets into the deeper issues. "And I want kids. Soon even. Like, maybe start trying in a year, give us a little time to be Mr. and Mrs. James before jumping into 'Mommy' and "Daddy.' But she wants to start trying the minute we get married. And . . . I guess that's fine. But it's like, wow, okay, I guess we're jumping right in. And then we had this huge fight about my loft. . . ."

"I heard."

"And I'm sure I came off as an asshole."

"No," I quickly assure him.

"Yeah, I'm sure I did. Because Seema has no problem telling people what's bothering her. But I don't like doing that—I like to be a little more chill, a little more private. But then people hear about our fight from her point of view, so she looks good, and I'm the thoughtless jerk. But just because I don't get riled up about every little thing doesn't mean I don't have opinions. And just because I'm not telling all of my friends we had a fight doesn't mean I'm wrong."

"No one thinks you're a jerk. You're one of the nicest guys I've ever met."

Scott clearly doesn't believe me, but he gives me a sincere

"Thanks." He takes another sip of his coffee, deep in thought. "You know what happened when I tried to stand up for myself about my work space? Instead of discussing it like rational adults, she accused me of keeping it because I was planning on having an affair. Then she got it into her head that if I wanted to keep the place, this was my safety hatch and represented a subconscious need to stay a bachelor, so maybe she should do me a favor and not marry me."

I cringe and shake my head slowly. "Sorry. Believe me, she does *not* mean that. You're her dream guy. You're the man she pined over and bored all of us about every day for a year before you finally kissed her. 'What's he mean by this text?' 'He kissed me hello—do you think that means anything?' 'If I wore a mask to the Halloween party, do you think I could kiss him without him knowing it was me?'"

Scott rolls his eyes self-consciously at my compliment, but grins. "Really? A mask?"

"I never told you that—" I warn him.

Scott shakes his head, clearly amused. "Did she really think that would work?"

I shrug. "Desperate times, desperate measures."

Scott, still smiling, nods. "Wow." He blurts out in amusement, "She is *such* a geek!"

"Such a geek," I concur.

Scott continues to smile, looking up at the ceiling a moment. "I love that. Thank you. I needed to hear that."

"Anytime you need stories for how ridiculously in love your wife is, come to me. So are you guys okay?"

"We're good."

"Excellent." I stand up. "Okay, this coffee isn't working for me. I have *got* to take a nap if we're seeing Nic and Jason tonight."

Scott smiles and wags his eyebrows up and down. "Did ya get any?"

"Shut up! No."

"But you're gonna get some?"

I might have taken a little too long to respond to his question. I shrug. "I don't know. It's complicated."

"Relationships always are, darlin'."

"If things are bothering you, talk to her."

Scott keeps smiling as he waves his hand back and forth in a mezzo mezzo fashion. "Maybe after the wedding, once things have calmed down. In the meantime, do you think maybe I could do some of my work in the living room if I get inspired? Sort of a trial run?"

"Go for it." Then I add awkwardly, "You know, you'll have my bedroom to work in soon. I promise I'll be gone by the time you guys get back from safari."

"Don't rush. We have time."

"Thanks. But I don't want to be in the middle of that loft fight."

"It's not a fight. It's just . . ." Scott shrugs. "Life. It's fine."

"Okay." I take my coffee to the sink, rinse it out, then putter out of the kitchen. I stop and turn around. "By the way, don't be mad at me."

His eyes widen as if to ask, *About what?*

I'm embarrassed to have to tell him. "I bought you guys those sheets."

Scott nods and smiles. "Well, when you get married, I'll return the favor and buy you an Xbox."

A minute later, I am back in my room and climbing under my covers. As I drift off to sleep, my thoughts soon drift away from premarital drama, and over to predating temptation.

NINE

After Seema and Jay spent the afternoon together, they and Scott and I meet up with Jason and Nic at a local Thai restaurant to enjoy one last relaxed meal before all the wedding insanity begins.

As we stuff ourselves with piles of pad see ew, garlic-and-pepper shrimp, sweet-and-sour pork, and eight other specialties of the house, Nic and Jason compete with Seema and Scott in a home-made version of *The Newlywed Game*. Fortunately, since Jay and I have been dating for all of about six hours, we get to be the moderators.

" 'Strangest gift you've received so far?' " Jay reads from a light blue index card while I use a large serving fork to transfer a piece of deep-fried quail in curry sauce from a large plate in the center of our table onto my smaller plate.

Scott and Seema look at each other knowingly. "Your call. What do you think?" Scott asks her. "That ugly pendant, or the hideous blood thing?"

"Wait, there's a hideous blood thing?" I ask, intrigued.

Seema closes her eyes and shakes her head slowly. "The problem with being friends with artists. One of them gave us two tiny crystal tubes, two syringes, and two needles for a gift. We're supposed to take each other's blood, put it in vials, and wear it around our necks."

"Ugh," Jason groans. "Shades of Angelina Jolie. Shudder. Shudder . . ."

"Cringe, cringe . . . ," Nic finishes his thought. Then she asks Seema, "So what is the pendant?"

"No, wait," Jay says quickly, pointing at Seema. "Let me guess. The pendant is gold, hideous, and from Uncle Ravi."

Seema's eyes light up as she shakes her head, "How did you know? The latest hideous pendant also has an uncut emerald in it that looks like—and I swear to God I'm not exaggerating—it looks like it's staring at me. I have already put it in my safety-deposit box to collect dust as I will never wear it and can't sell it."

As Seema describes the pendant to Nic, I lean in to Jay to whisper /ask, "If she will never wear it, why can't she sell it?"

Off my look, Jay explains, "Traditional Indians give jewels, cash, or gold. You know how some women have expensive china and crystal they never use packed up in a hutch? Seema has the ugliest gold jewelry you've ever seen securely tucked away in a safety-deposit box in downtown LA."

"True dat," Seema exclaims, wonderfully out of character for her.

Nic shakes her head and tells Seema, "See, this is why you register. For us, it was an ugly green-and-bright-yellow ceramic monstrosity that we have to take out and display every time Jason's aunt Josephine comes into town."

"I thought you liked that thing!" Jason exclaims to her.

"Tell me what it is, and I'll tell you I like it."

"It's a . . ." Jason struggles for an answer, then gives up, shrugging. "Giant asterisk maybe?"

"Okay, next *Newlywed Game* question," I say, flipping over a pink index card and reading, " 'First date you ever had?' "

Seema confidently answers, "Dinner at Café Beaujolais," while Scott simultaneously says, "Our first coffee at the museum."

Seema turns to him. "You geek. That was not a date."

"Just because you didn't know it was a date doesn't mean it wasn't."

She shakes her head, "That might be the sweetest thing you've ever said."

Scott smiles, then corrects her, "Oh, no. The sweetest thing I ever said was 'Met a goddess. Became a family.' "

This is followed by three *Awww*s and one "Aw, crap, I can't top that," from Jason.

"Your turn." I ask Nic and Jason, "First date?"

Nic goes with "A very romantic dinner at Mélisse." At the same time Jason answers, "A very strange funeral."

Jay's eyes widen. "You took Nic to a funeral for your first date?"

Jason bites his tongue ever so slightly in amusement as he nods his head. "No. She took me. It was a cat's funeral. Mr. Whiskers."

"That is so weird," Jay says, turning to Nic. "For some reason, I thought you were allergic to cats."

"Oh, I am. Deathly. But in all fairness, it was *my* cat's funeral."

Jason and Nic explain to Jay that they first met at a party. Jason spent the next week calling her and asking her out. She kept saying no, and as the week went on, her reasons became more and more ridiculous. Finally, she declined dinner to go to her "cat's funeral." She figured she'd look like a crazy cat woman and finally scare Jason away. No such luck. He sent flowers, then attended the service. "Or tried to, anyway," Nic finishes the story. "Since there was no cat, services were tricky."

"Wow," Jay says, and turns to me. "What's the weirdest thing you've ever done to get a date?"

I wave my hand in protest. "I plead the Fifth." Then I look down at the next index card. "Men, what is the one thing you would say most freaked out your wife while planning the wedding?"

Scott flashes Seema a big ole grin. "Oh, *wife*! I like the sound of that."

"I got this one," Jason says. "The baby-carriage cake charm Nic pulled at her wedding shower."

Scott points to Jason. "Cake charm. You nailed it. For Seema, it was the snake she got yesterday. Totally freaked her out."

"I was not freaked out," Seema corrects. "I was annoyed. Now, Auntie Hema: she was freaked-out."

"You got a snake at your bridal shower?" Jay asks Seema. "Isn't that bad luck or something?"

"Only if you kill it," Seema insists. "Anyway, I didn't get a snake, I got a snake charm."

"Whoa, hope that doesn't mean you're marrying a snake charmer," Jay jokes.

Nic turns to me. "How come neither of us thought to make that joke?"

I shrug.

Jay reads the next index card. "Okay, next question: 'Boxers or briefs?' "

"For which one of us?" Seema and Scott joke in unison.

Ten

After dinner, I drove Jay home in my car, and Scott dragged Seema back to his place downtown. (I owe you one, Scott!)

The moment we are in the car and out of sight from everyone, the drive becomes deliciously flirtatious. I had forgotten what it was like to still be in the chase part of the relationship (if I could call it a relationship). You know, the part where you're not sure if you're going to have sex or not. The part where you're both still tentative, and each kiss sets off a spark to your lips or your neck or your . . . well, any part he has not yet kissed.

My last boyfriend was a one-night stand that lasted about three months. I had picked him up at a bar (very retro of me, in this era of online dating), during my "slut on the rebound" phase. He was nice, and we certainly went on dates. But I knew I'd "get some" at the end of each date because I "got some" the first night. So the seduction part was off the table. Before him, I was with a boyfriend for over six years. That seduction had been shoved off the table, into the trash, and out to the curb for pickup.

So it had been a long time since I had had a man eye me as completely and seductively as Jay was doing right now.

I turn to Jay, who is lounging back against the passenger seat, making a show of ogling me lasciviously. "So, where to?"

Jay smiles as he puts his hand on my knee. "Wherever you want."

"There's a place called Yamashiro up in the hills that has the most amazing view of the city."

Jay moves his index finger to push my skirt up ever so slightly. "I like the view from here."

I make a show of rolling my eyes and easing my skirt back down. "Don't distract me. This is Hollywood. There are cops everywhere."

Jay slowly puts up both palms in surrender and leans back in his seat. But he never takes his eyes off me.

I feel uncomfortable as hell. But in a good way. "Or we could go dancing. There's an amazing jazz place downtown not far from where your sister is getting married." I turn to him and smile nervously. "I know you're an amazing dancer."

Jay puckers his lips, "As much as I love the idea of an activity where you have to do whatever I want, and in heels, I have some other thoughts about how we could accomplish that."

I turn to him in mock irritation. "Does everything that comes out of your mouth have to be a double entendre?"

He smirks at me. "It doesn't have to be, it just sort of works out that way. So, you do know we're gonna have sex tonight, right?"

My jaw drops and Jay laughs. "Figured I'd go with a single entendre."

I shake my head. "We are *not* having sex tonight."

"How can you know that for sure?" he asks me lightly.

I slow down and stop for a red light. "I can know that for sure because I love kissing you, and I'm having a lot of fun with you. But you leave in a few days, and I'm not that kind of girl."

Jay nods his head to concede my point. "Fair enough." Then he leans in and kisses me.

We make out until the light turns green and the SUV behind me starts honking angrily.

I begin driving again. "I have an idea. There's this great wine bar in Los Feliz . . ."

"Do you have wine at home?"

"Pretty sure you're leading the witness here."

"Plus you have that view I like at home," Jay continues.

"View? We live in the flats. There's no . . ."

"I meant you."

I nod. "Oh. Got it."

"And we could turn on music, if you really want to dance."

I smile bashfully and make a left onto the street that goes back toward my place.

ELEVEN

Jay and I get home about ten minutes later, and he holds my hand as we walk up the flagstone pathway to the door. "Do you think Seema has any of those formal crystal wineglasses she registered for?" he asks, as though an idea has suddenly occurred to him.

"She's has eight of them so far. Why?"

He looks up and toward his left as he cocks his head, an idea percolating. "I think you should go to your kitchen, find whatever bottle will make you happy, and borrow a few of the glasses. I'm going to get my iPad and do a quick playlist for us to dance to."

"Um . . . okay," I say, wondering what he's up to.

We go inside, and I head to the kitchen while he rifles through his suitcase.

I quickly text Seema:

Can we use your new wineglasses?

I then walk over to the wine refrigerator and debate which bottle to pull. "You're not going to play striptease songs or anything, are you?" I yell to the other room.

"Good Lord, what is wrong with you, woman?" he yells back from the living room.

I decide to splurge and pull out a bottle of Zinnia Pinot Noir Reserve that I have been saving. "It's just that I remember back in college, you once took your shirt off to Aerosmith on the radio, and you gyrated your hips in a way that—"

"Christ, was I ever so young and stupid that I thought *that* would work as a form of seduction?" Jay asks as he appears in the doorway. "Where would I find matches?"

I pull a matchbook from a pile by Seema's mini-shrine and throw them to him.

He catches them in one hand and smiles. "Thanks." Then he disappears.

My iPhone beeps. I check the text:

Of course on the glasses.

Don't sleep with him.

With a little luck neither of us will sleep, I think to myself.

I notice the living-room light go out as I grab two glasses from our cupboard. They're by Waterford, and the pattern is this crisscross of lines that make the glasses look like a bowl of diamonds ready to surround our wine.

I carefully place the glasses next to the wine and twist the corkscrew into the cork just as I hear the soulful guitar playing of Eric Clapton's "Wonderful Tonight" waft into the kitchen.

Wow. He remembered. . . .

I smile, and my breath catches a little.

"What do you think of the selection?" I hear Jay ask from the living room.

"I think that'll work!" I yell back jokingly. I pull down the corkscrew arms and pull out the cork. Then I look up and ever so quietly and shyly whisper-sing along with Clapton.

Jay walks in, leans against the doorway, and says to me, "You have a pretty voice."

I stop singing immediately, smile and turn away shyly. Jay offers his hand to pull me into a dance. Still blushing, I tuck my right hand into his left, and my left hand onto his shoulder.

And the two of us sway to Clapton, right in the middle of the kitchen.

This is the dance I've been dreaming about for more than ten years. I can't believe he's really here—holding me. Dancing with me. Wanting me.

Jay. THE Jay Singh.

What on earth did I do to deserve this?

And there we dance, and my heart is beating so loudly that I can feel it in my throat. His cologne smells almost spicy. It's subtle, and warm, and mixes with the clean scent of his recently shampooed hair. And as silly as I know it is to feel this way, I want to inhale his scent forever.

After a few more minutes the song begins to end. Jay pulls away from me ever so slightly and exquisitely sings the last line along with Clapton:

"Oh, my darling, you are wonderful tonight."

He leans in and softly kisses me on the lips, and I already know that I will go back and replay this memory over and over in my head for the next few months like a high school girl obsessing over her first crush.

At this point, I also know he's right—we are totally sleeping together tonight. This was even more romantic than attending a cat funeral.

TWELVE

After several hours of him playing offense, and me playing defense, eventually I scored. Well, I'm choosing to see it that way anyway.

The sex is amazing. So perfect that in a way I almost wish it hadn't been, because he leaves tomorrow morning, and now I'm going to miss him even more than I would have before.

Afterward, Jay gently puts his arm around me, I lean into that sweet spot between his chest and his arm, and we cuddle.

It's one of those rare moments in life when everything is perfect, and you want for nothing.

Meaning the moment when my brain starts racing.

I shouldn't have done this! In effect, we just started dating yesterday. Plus, isn't there some long-standing tradition about men trying to land a bridesmaid at a wedding? So, like an idiot I just played into that one. Plus, how can we forge a relationship if he lives on the other side of the planet? Sure, I can fantasize about quitting my job and packing up my whole life and moving to Paris, but I would never really do it. All of my friends are here. I don't even speak French. Plus, I am now one of those women who jumps ahead in the relationship the minute she jumps ahead in the boudoir. (Did I just think the word *boudoir*?) Plus . . .

"What are you thinking about?" Jay whispers to me softly.

I smile and sort of flirt as I say, "That I'm a slut."

Jay pulls his head away from me slightly to get a better look at me. "Really? So am I. What a coincidence." He smiles and gives me a soft kiss on my cheek.

"Also that I wish you could stay longer," I admit.

Why did I say that? Guys already want to leave the minute sex is over. They're already scared of commitment. Why give him another reason to hightail it out of here?

"Me too," Jay says quietly. "But I'll be back Thursday."

"Yeah, but you'll be with your family, and I have friends coming into town, and by Thursday, things'll be different, you know?"

He strokes my arm softly. "In what way will things be different?"

I interlace his fingers in mine, bring his hand up to my lips, and kiss it lightly. "I don't know. They just will. Once a man sleeps with a woman, the chase is over, and he looks at her differently."

Jay gives me a hug and whispers, "You're overthinking this. Let your brain calm down and go to sleep." Then he pulls me into spooning position and closes his eyes.

Which of course is my cue for my brain to start racing again: What did *that* mean? *Go to sleep?* How was I supposed to interpret his tone? Sweet? Or was I being chastised? Is this a onetime thing, similar to what happened to those girls back in college, when he'd have two in a weekend? Or do I get to at least look forward to next weekend? Will there be another woman in San Francisco, then another at the wedding? Do we have any shot at a meaningful relationship, or did I just set myself up to start crying sometime in the next few weeks. . . .

"Your brain is still going a mile a minute, isn't it?" Jay asks knowingly with his eyes still closed.

"Yes," I say sheepishly.

"So does that mean you won't be my date to the wedding?"

I sit up and turn to him. "Do you really want me to be?"

He opens his eyes. "Ye-es. I really want you to be," he says in a tone that lets me know that I should have assumed that. "In case I've been too subtle, I like you. I like you a lot."

"I . . . I like you too." I pause. "Very much."

"So, you ready to go to sleep now?"

He likes me. He really likes me. I lie back down, grinning from ear to ear, and close my eyes. "Uh-huh."

About a minute later, I pop my eyes back open. "Can we have sex in the morning before you leave?"

Jay gives my belly a little squeeze with his arm. "I'm a guy. As such, I refuse to dignify that question with a response."

Thirteen

Monday morning, I dropped Jay off at the airport. We made out at every red light on the way over there. We made out at the curb for so long, a TSA agent told me to move my car. The moment I pulled my car away, my phone beeped that I had a text.

Miss you already.

Life was good. So good that instead of a morning doughnut, I had a black coffee, then went home and got in my first run in weeks. (Okay, months. Shut up.)

That afternoon, Nic and I are sitting in a posh Beverly Hills bridal salon, wearing our red velvet bridesmaid's dresses, sipping complimentary champagne and bubbly water (although, at these prices, I can't say the word *complimentary* with a straight face) and waiting for Seema to emerge from her dressing room, wearing the gown she'll be dressed in for the Western ceremony. This is her final fitting, and things are not going as planned.

"It doesn't fit!" Seema yells from her dressing room.

"Of course it doesn't fit!" Nic yells back. "You're the one who insisted they take it in another inch at the waist. Dirty little bridal secret: no one loses weight right before their wedding—we all gain. The seating chart alone can send you to a bag of Oreos before breakfast. You should have the seamstress let it back out."

"No!" Seema insists. "I spent over four hundred dollars on a custom-fitted lace bustier just to get into this dress, and I will be damned if I'm not going to fit into it on Saturday."

"Seema, there is nothing wrong with being curvy," I say to her. "Men love Beyoncé, and she's—"

"If you mention Beyoncé one more time, I swear to God, I'm going to come out there and eat you," Seema threatens. Then she makes a grunting sound that I'm pretty sure I've only heard in national parks.

"Sweetheart, is there anything I can do to help?" Sandra, the matronly bridal saleswoman, asks her pleasantly.

"No. Go away," Seema snaps at her.

"I think I know a little trick—"

"I'm not wearing the girdle!"

"It's not a girdle," Sandra assures Seema. "It's Spanx. Those are totally different."

We all know what Spanx are. Who is this woman kidding?

Sandra continues, "You could wear it to the ceremony, then change into your honeymoon ensemble later that evening, in the privacy of your hotel suite."

There's silence in the dressing room. Seema's at least considering the idea.

"Nic, did you change into your wedding-night ensemble after your wedding?" Seema asks through the dressing-room door.

"You're talking to the wrong girl. After my wedding, I was on a red-eye with my new husband and two new stepdaughters en route to Disney World. Changing into a skanky bit of red lace and matching thong might have seemed inappropriate."

"Hey!" Seema shouts. "My outfit is not skanky."

"What? I meant that in a good way."

We hear some quiet crinkling in the other room.

Nic makes a show of raising her tiny nose in the air and taking a good whiff. "Did you sneak Milanos in there?"

Seema opens her door and tosses a half-eaten bag out to me.

I catch it and open the bag. Then Nic and I share what's left of the cookies as Sandra gently continues to make her case: "If you could just try the Spanx on, ma'am."

"Oh, fine," Seema says. "But can you bring me some champagne to dull the pain?"

Sandra smiles. "Of course."

Sandra pulls a pair of nude-colored Spanx from a drawer, then pours a glass of champagne from a bottle in a silver bucket and brings it to Seema's fitting room. Seema reluctantly opens her door to let the woman in.

Champagne at work. That doesn't sound too bad. Maybe I could become a wedding-gown salesperson. I do like reality shows with weddings—particularly the ones that show gowns. I wonder, are there any money trees in this store? I glance around the store just as Sandra shuts Seema's door.

The moment we're alone, Nic turns to me, and her face lights up. "So how was he?" she whispers.

My index finger shoots up to my lips. "Shh!" Then I lean in. "I didn't sleep with him."

"Why not?"

"Why not?! Um, because I've been dating him for all of thirty-six hours."

"You're not *dating* him at all. And you've known him almost half your life. It's time to close the deal."

"First of all, you're being crass. Secondly, I have not known him half of my life, you're making me sound ancient."

Nic crosses her arms. "How old are you now?"

"Thirty-two."

"And what's half of thirty-two?"

"I don't like where this is headed."

"Sixteen. You met him when you were eighteen. Close enough."

Shit. I *have* known him for almost half of my life. Well, that's just creepy.

"Time to"—Nic pumps her fist—"rock . . . his . . . world."

"Okay. . . . First off, blondes should never say 'Rock his world' unless they're playing Sleazy Party Guest Number Two in a raunchy sex comedy from the nineties!" Seema yells from her dressing room. "And secondly, for God's sakes, that's my idiot brother you're talking about. Obviously, she did him, but have a little discretion."

Nic turns to shut the door. "What?" Then back to me. "Really?"

Oh, shit. "Did he tell you I slept with him?" I yell toward Seema's door.

"No. He swore up and down that you didn't. Which means you did. Don't lie to us. One, it's unbecoming, and two, you suck at it, so knock it off."

I involuntarily look at the ground sheepishly. Nic observes me. "You totally nailed it," Nic yells toward Seema. "And she totally nailed him."

"Did it ever occur to you that I didn't nail him, he nailed me!" I blurt out defensively. "Wait, that didn't sound right."

"Ladies, take a look at our beautiful bride!" Sandra chirps cheerfully from the dressing room.

Sandra opens the door, and Seema walks out. I smile and cover my mouth with my hands. Happy tears begin to well up in my eyes. "Oh, my God. You are gorgeous."

And she is. The ivory, V-neck, floor-length sheath gown by Allure Couture is covered in tiny Swarovski crystals, so she literally sparkles as she walks out to us. "You don't think it makes me look fat?" Seema asks me.

"You're being ridiculous," Nic tells her at the same time as I assure her, "You're stunning."

Worried, Seema turns to see her backside in one of the many full-length mirrors in the salon. Rather than admiring how perfect she looks with the sparkly sweep train, she says, "I think I may have to take up smoking for the next few days."

"Seema . . . ," Nic admonishes.

"Or Dexedrine. How hard do you think it is to get Dexedrine if you order it online from Canada?"

Sandra makes an adjustment to the back of the dress. "The Spanx work like a charm. You're perfect."

Seema sighs nervously at her reflection, then turns to us. "Okay, girls, come stand next to me. I want to see how we look together."

Nic places both hands on her overstuffed armchair and pushes herself up and off in a practiced pregnant woman's move, then moseys her way over to Seema. I also walk over. Nic stands on Seema's right, while I stand to her left.

And there the three of us are. Grown-ups. One about to be married, and another already married, with a baby on the way. Back when we were in college, during those middle-of-the-night conversations when we should have been studying for finals, we would talk about boys, weddings, babies, and careers. Futures that, back then, always seemed like a lifetime away. Futures that on alternate nights (sometimes alternate hours) thrilled us, worried us, and occasionally scared the hell out of us.

And here we are now. The future's here.

Seema silently scrutinizes our reflections, deep in thought.

"Well," I ask her, "what do you think?"

She puckers up her lips, then slowly nods her head. "I'd do us."

Fourteen

The next several hours are spent with Seema and me doing wedding-y stuff: picking up the dresses, walking through the hotel venue one more time, confirming details for the outdoor Indian ceremony in the morning, the late-afternoon, indoor Western ceremony, and the lavish reception that evening. Finally, we headed out to Big Sugar Bakeshop.

No—not to confirm the wedding cake—to get cupcakes. It's been a stressful day, and nothing releases stress quite like a cupcake. Well, okay, yes—sex. But it's easier to procure a cupcake on short notice.

Speaking of sex, throughout the day, Jay has been texting me. Oddly enough, as much as I hate texting, in his case I am pleased. Because this way, Seema doesn't know whom I'm "on the phone" with. And I can check my texts whenever she isn't paying attention to me (and with it being her wedding week, that's pretty much anytime). So I've been getting everything from sweet texts such as *Miss u. Can't wait 4 Thursday!* and *You were so cute this morning* to ones that I am torn between finding exciting and wanting to delete immediately. (If texting makes me nervous, one can imagine how I feel about sexting.)

> So, are you out buying sexy new underwear?
>
> You're a pig.
>
> But if a woman really likes a guy, doesn't she go out and buy new underwear?
>
> Who told you that?
>
> My sixty-year-old boss—but she's French, so somehow it sounds charming when she says it.
>
> Well, it doesn't sound charming when you say it.
>
> I'll bet you look good in red lace.
>
> I'm hanging up now.

"Are you texting him *again*?" Seema asks me as she parks her car in our driveway.

"No," I say as my fingers race around the keyboard.

Seema turns off her car and begins to gather up her purse, the box with her veil, and the box with the rest of the cupcakes. "You know, if you write back to him immediately, the chase is over."

"The chase went on for over ten years," I say as I hit send. I look up at her and smile. "I like it better now."

"Just be careful." She opens her car door. "Can you bring in my dress with yours? I have too much to carry."

"Done." I grab both her wedding gown and my maid-of-honor dress from the rack in the backseat.

I take our gowns out of her car and we head into the house. As we walk up the flagstone pathway, Seema asks, "Do you want me to ask him what his intentions are?"

"Yeah, that would be perfect," I say, trying to make my voice drip with sarcasm. "And while you're at it, why don't you ask him how many children we're going to have, and if he sees himself having a summer or winter wedding?"

Seema gives me an amused look. "Point taken." She looks down at her stomach and sighs. "Man, I'm huge. I should not have had that second cupcake."

"And to think you were only going to order one?" I mock. "I knew it wouldn't get out of the car alive."

Seema points to me. "You are a bad influence."

She puts her key in the lock, and we open the door to find a stunningly beautiful redheaded woman posing on a stool, naked, in the middle of our living room. To her right is Scott, covered in red paint, an easel with canvas in front of him. Scott, paintbrush in hand, lights up when he sees Seema. "Hey, you're home early."

"Yeah, I am," she nearly spits as she storms in, crazed, and heads right to him. "Are you out of your fucking mind?"

I keep the door open and try to neutralize the situation. "Clearly you're working," I say, even though I'm not even sure he is. "We can come back."

Scott ignores me, instead giving Seema an exasperated look. "Honey, you said you wanted me to give up the loft. If you want me to work from home, you have to be ready to see stuff like this, and not freak out."

"Oh, I am going to freak out all right," Seema challenges. "I am going to freak *the fuck* out! Seriously, what the hell were you thinking?"

The model instinctively tries to cover up her privates with her hands. "I thought your wife was cool with all this," she says to Scott as she walks over to our white chair and grabs a button-up shirt.

"Oh, I'm so *not* cool with all this!" Seema bellows at the model. Then she turns her anger back to Scott. "You got paint all over my hand-knotted wool rug."

"Wait," I say, a bit confused. "You're mad about the mess? You're not mad that he has a naked woman in the middle of the room?"

"I would be if he covered her in paint and let her roll all over my rug," Seema yells, then grabs a wet rag, drops to the floor, and tries to clean up a giant red splotch in the middle of the floor. "Seriously, the rug's black-and-white. You're covered in red paint. What is your next piece called? *Newlywed Murder*?"

I silently close the front door as the model quickly buttons up her shirt and shimmies into a pair of underwear.

"That's it! I give up!" Scott exclaims, looking as if his head is about to explode. "You want me to give up my loft, but you don't want me to actually do my work here. How the hell am I supposed to win, Seema? Huh?" He looks up at me, takes a millisecond to calm down, then turns to Seema to assert himself. "And by the way—I hate the sheets."

Seema, now resembling Cinderella scrubbing the floor so she can go to the ball, looks up from the smeared mess. "What are you talking about?"

"The sheets you wanted to register for?" Scott begins, a teakettle about to blow. "I hate them. They're beige."

Seema stands up, ready for a fight. "They're off-white."

"Which means they're beige!" Scott shouts. "And by the way, no sheet color should be called *linen*. You know what linen is? It's a sheet!"

I turn to the model, now squeezing into a size-zero pair of jeans. "Would you like some coffee?"

"I'd love some," she says nervously, and the two of us skedaddle to the kitchen to give them privacy while the fight continues.

"Are you really trying to turn a fight about your sloppiness into a fight about what we registered for?" Seema challenges.

"It's beige! Which is brown, and I hate brown with the fire of a thousand suns!"

"Oh my God. 'The fire of . . .' Who actually says that?"

"You know I hate beige! You don't care! You know I don't go to Burbank! You don't care!" Scott yells over her. "And listen, lady, if you can't deal with the mess, maybe I should keep my loft!"

Model girl and I stare at each other in the kitchen while the living room goes dead silent. I try to lean around the doorway to see what's going on. But before I can, I hear a door slam.

I peek through the doorway. Scott is standing by himself in the middle of the room, trying to figure out what to do next. He takes his palette and throws it down in frustration, but on a drop cloth. I see him walk over to Seema's door. "Okay, I didn't mean that. I'm willing to get rid of the loft. But you can't complain when I make a mess. You're marrying an artist. I'm not gonna change, and I'm not gonna suddenly like brown. This is who you're marrying. For better or worse."

Silence from the other side of the door.

Eventually, Seema slowly opens her door. "I'm sorry," she says quietly, almost timidly. "You're completely right, and I totally overreacted."

She pulls him into a hug, and the two hug in silence for a bit.

"I'm really sorry," Seema repeats. "Planning this wedding and dealing with our families has been way more stressful than I thought it would be, and I've been taking it out on you and I'm sorry."

I watch Scott kiss her forehead. "Well, you're pretty cute, so I guess you're forgiven."

Seema smiles, looks at her ring finger, and twirls around her engagement ring nervously. "So you wanna get the eggplant sheets instead?"

"The dark purple ones? God, yes," Scott says, his shoulders visibly relaxing.

And the two of them get back to their Happily Ever After.

Which, overall, is a very good thing.

I just wish I hadn't bought them those beige sheets. Now I have to go back to the store.

FIFTEEN

It's three o'clock in the morning, and I'm now officially in my clingy phase. Some women deny the clingy phase—insisting that it turns men off. Yes, well, of course it does. So does nipple hair—which is why we do our best to try to hide it from them at all costs. But that doesn't mean it doesn't exist. Any woman who says she hasn't gone through the clingy phase is either lying through her teeth or completely delusional. For me, the phase starts the second a guy doesn't respond to my phone calls, texts, or e-mails fast enough. The phase is an inescapable step in the natural progression of dating for me, and it took me all of two days to become a freakin' lunatic over Jay.

Monday went great. We texted each other throughout the day. He called me from his hotel room before bed that night, we talked until both of our eyes were heavy, and I nodded off to sleep feeling wildly content and wanted.

Then Tuesday hit. Tuesday morning, before I even brushed my teeth, I texted him a quick *Good morning!*. Two minutes later, I regretted writing it, as I didn't want to look too available.

Then again, I reasoned, didn't I clue him in that I'm available the minute I got naked with him?

I checked my iPhone and e-mails compulsively all morning. All for naught. He finally wrote back around lunchtime, but then only to say:

SF beautiful. Wish you were here.

A nice sentiment, to be sure, but that's it??? All that talking back and forth yesterday, and now I'm downgraded to a sentence? My local bakery sent me a longer text this morning, *and* they offered me a dollar off cupcakes.

I spent an hour constantly checking my phone screen for more, and worrying about what to write back to his one sentence. I debated: I couldn't write too much, as that would show too much interest. But if I wrote nothing, would that imply I'm not really interested and encourage him to go find another girl to write texts to? One sentence back was probably my best bet.

After a mental debate that proved to me that I need a job without so much summer vacation, I settled on the following:

Me too. ☺

Then I waited five more hours for a response.

At six, I shot him another text:

Off to dinner. Are you around later so I can whisper sweet nothings . . .

Delete, delete, delete.

So we can have phone sex?

Ugh—no. Delete. I settle on:

Are you around later?

Two hours later (!) I get this back from him:

I don't know. Let me call you later. Work not going
   well—been tied up in stressful meetings all day, now
   off to a stressful dinner, followed by stressful drinks.
   I'm exhausted, and wish I could just climb into bed
   with you and sleep.

And sleep? What on earth did I say in my texts that ever im-
plied sleep?

So that was at eight. It is now five hours, three glasses of wine,
two red-velvet cupcakes, a bag of M&M's, and one personal pan
pizza with pepperoni and extra cheese later.

And I am in my room, staring at his last message on my phone.

Damn it! I played it wrong again. I have been dating for almost
two decades, and I'm still just as clueless as when I asked Kent
Rogers out to the Sadie Hawkins dance via a note confiscated by
my English teacher, who then read it aloud to the class.

I hear the TV go on in the living room. I tiptoe over to see if it's
Scott or Seema watching.

I push my door open slightly to see Seema, curled up on the
couch dressed in Grinch pajama bottoms and a matching Grinch
T-shirt. I can't help but notice the box of Entenmann's cheesecake
on the coffee table in front of her. No plate for a slice, just a box

full of cake and her fork. I open my door completely. "Whatcha watching?"

She presses the buttons on the remote control. "I have no idea."

I walk out and take a seat next to her. "Is that Entenmann's up for grabs?"

She hands me her fork. "Go for it."

As I dig in for a giant forkful, Seema asks, "So, are you obsessing over my brother?"

"No!" I say immediately, trying to sound insulted. She hikes one eyebrow up at me. "Yes," I admit, deflating my shoulders. "But I know I shouldn't." I stuff a chunk of cheesecake into my mouth, then say through the midnight snack, "Speaking of family, how did the big dinner with both sets of parents go tonight?"

Seema squints her eyes, thinking. "Mom asked Scott when they'd be hearing news about the annaprashana."

I can tell from her tone of voice, she's irked. But for the life of me, I have no idea why. I can't remember what an annaprashana is. "Which would be the . . . ?"

"It's the ceremony when a baby eats his first rice. Sort of like a christening or a bris in terms of inviting everyone to welcome the baby into the world. You light incense, say a prayer to the gods, the baby eats a little rice pudding, and you do this thing where he or she picks from a variety of objects to determine his or her future. It's basically a big party. It's pretty cool actually."

"Oh," I say. "Well, if it's fun, then why are you upset?"

"Because I'm not actually pregnant yet, so my mother's comment was annoying as shit. Heaven forbid she just get excited about the wedding. Nope. Instead, let's jump ahead and make her daughter feel bad about not giving her grandchildren yet."

I rub Seema's shoulder sympathetically. "Parents do that. They don't mean to."

"I know," Seema says, rolling her eyes. "Also, she's hideously worried about the snake charm I pulled and assured me in front of the entire table that if anything goes wrong with the wedding, she'll smother Nic with a pillow."

"So, at least everyone's staying calm," I say dryly.

"Yeah. Oh, and after she explained what an annaprashana was to Scott's mother, Janet, Janet decided to smile exuberantly and declare how wonderful it was to be in LA, where everyone's so exotic."

"Well, that doesn't sound—"

"*Exotic* seems to be Protestant code for 'weird.'"

"Ah. See, I did not know that."

"Then she announces that she"—with this, Seema's voice changes, going up two octaves while her face lights up with false cheer—"absolutely insists that before we do the first rice, we go back to the church where Scott was christened after we have each baby. Oh, it will be such fun."

I wince in sympathy. "Each?"

"Each," Seema repeats in her normal voice. "At which time Scott's father bellows and says we need to have at least one boy, hopefully three, to carry on the James name. Because you know that name will die out if we don't breed immediately. Just ask Etta James, Henry James, Harry James . . ."

"Who?"

"Bandleader. Married to Betty Grable. Jesse James, LeBron James."

"Okay, I get it," I say, shaking my head. I hand the fork back to Seema. "You need this more than me."

Seema takes the fork from me, breaks off a big piece of cheesecake, and eats it. "Enough about me. What's going on with my idiot brother?"

Gulp. "Oh, I don't want to bore you," I say nervously. "This is your week."

She tells me through a mouthful of cheesecake, "I can't tell if you're saying that because you're still all sexed up and happy, or you're entering stage one of the clingy phase. Spill."

Seema eyes me knowingly. *Damn, am I that transparent?* Finally I confess, "He didn't call or e-mail me tonight."

I figure that is enough sharing, but Seema looks at me expectantly, waiting for more.

So I continue, "And now I'm getting all weird. And I shouldn't, and I promise not to mess up your wedding in any way. I just wish . . . I wish I knew where I stood with him."

"You want me to call him?"

"God, no! Then he'll know I'm getting obsessed."

"Good point. You want to show me what you last wrote?"

"God, yes!" I say in the exact same tone.

By the time Seema blinks, I am already in my room, grabbing my phone.

I return to the couch and show her my last text, and his last response. Seema thinks for a moment. "Knowing Jay, he's been burning the candle on both ends since the night before he left Paris, hasn't slept in days, got back to the hotel after a work dinner, in his mind thought he'd 'lie down for a minute,' then promptly passed out."

"You think?" I ask hopefully.

"I know. That boy could sleep through incoming. But just to make sure, write to him, saying you're going to bed. If he's with a woman, he'll quickly text you back something noncommittal. If he's awake and by himself, he'll call. If he's passed out, you won't hear from him."

I stare at my phone, then look up at Seema. "Have you always been able to read men so well?"

"What? No. God, no. Just my brother. But seriously, give me your phone."

Seema yanks the phone out of my hand. She types on the keypad, then shows me the screen:

Don't want to call, since it's so late. Just going to bed—
    your mom made Seema a little nuts this evening,
    so I was a dutiful maid of honor and provided
    champagne, Entenmann's, and her favorite Cary
    Grant movie. XOXO

"This okay?" Seema asks me.

Just as I start to say "I'm not sure I would use the word—," Seema has already hit the send button. My shoulders slump, "Why did you even ask?"

"It was just a courtesy. I didn't mean it," she tells me, then tosses my phone on the coffee table. "Now, about that Cary Grant movie you just texted him about? Do we have *An Affair to Remember*?"

"Are you mental, woman? I'm in clingy mode—the last thing I need is a super-romantic movie. How about *Mr. Blandings Builds His Dream House* or *I Was a Male War Bride*?"

"Both comedies. *Charade*?"

"You want to show me Paris right now?"

"*North by Northwest*?"

"Done." I pop off the couch to get the Blu-ray.

"And about that champagne you texted him . . . ?"

I laugh, head to the kitchen, and get us our millionth bottle of champagne for the week, two flutes, and another fork.

We spend the next ten or twenty minutes inhaling cake and champagne, watching the Sexiest Man Dead get framed as a CIA agent and waiting for a text or call from one of the Sexiest Men Alive. Nothing from Jay. Seema smiles at me. "See?"

I smile and tell her she made me feel much better. Which is a lie, of course. She did make me a feel a little better, yes. But, sometimes hanging out with your best girlfriend watching old movies is merely a place marker to kill time until a girl can speak to *him* again.

Or as I like to call it, the clingy phase, stage two.

The following morning put my mind at ease. Around 6:00 A.M., my phone begins ringing its newest ringtone—Eric Clapton.

I pull the phone from my nightstand and answer groggily, "Hello?"

"Did I wake you?" Jay asks me softly.

"No, I always sound like Elmer Fudd after two packs of ciga-rettes," I joke. I sit up in bed and try to wake up. "How are you?"

"Good." He sounds sleepy. "Tired. I miss you."

"I miss you too."

"We went to this restaurant last night, and it had an amazing view of the city. I wish you could be up here with me—you'd have loved it."

I smile. "I'm sure I would have." Then I ask awkwardly, "So how late were you up?"

"Not sure. I got here and thought I'd rest for a minute before I took a shower, and then I just zonked out." I smile wider. Seema was right. "Anyway, I better get to that shower and start my day. Just wanted to say good morning."

"Good morning," I repeat, more brightly now.

His voice sounds brighter too as he says, "All right. I'll call you later."

"Great."

"Great."

Neither of us gets off the phone.

"We're not going to be one of those couples who . . ."

"No, I'm going. Bye," I blather, then practically slam down the phone.

Then I snuggle back into my covers, grinning like a teenage girl.

Sixteen

That afternoon, I am waiting in the luggage area, my knees bouncing slightly up and down, thinking, *He's here! He's here! He's here! I can see him walking down the LAX people mover.* I stand at the glass revolving doors keeping out the riffraff like me from the people with airline tickets. I'm so excited, I continue to bounce up and down ever so slightly.

No, I'm not waiting for Jay (although he might inspire such a reaction from me too). I am waiting for Jeff. My college sweetheart. Up until a few days ago, the best-looking man I ever dated (Jay might be able to give him a run for his money, not sure). Definitely the nicest, most loving man I ever dated. When Jeff sees me, his face lights up and he picks up his pace. He pushes his way through the revolving doors, holds up a beautiful lei of purple and white flowers, and brightly says to me, "Aloha!"

I burst into a giant smile as I run into his arms. "Aloha!" I yell, wrapping my arms around him, then jumping up to wrap my legs around him too. "My God! You look fantastic."

"Oh, please, sweetie," Jeff retorts. "I've gained at least ten pounds since I moved to Maui, and my hairline's receding so quickly you'd think it was Napoléon's army at Waterloo."

I make a show of rolling my eyes as I jump off him. "Shut up. Your hair's perfect, your eyes are still as electric blue as a Siberian husky's, and you look exactly the same as you did in college. Which I hate you for, by the way. I'm the one with gray hairs and a food-baby belly that looks like I'm three months along."

Jeff steps back to give me the once-over with his eyes. "Please. You're perfect. If anything, you need a sandwich." He puts the lei over my head, then kisses me once on each cheek. I pull the lei up to my nose and inhale. "That smells amazing. What kinds of flowers are these?"

"Orchids."

I'm so touched. Why can't I find a straight man who treats me so nicely? "You brought orchids all the way from Hawaii?"

He smiles. "I want to take credit for being awesome, but the truth is I bought them at the Costco near the airport. Now, tell me about the guy."

I give him a look. "What guy? There's no guy."

He smirks. "Wow. Coy. That means you've had sex."

My jaw drops. "How did you . . ."

"Ha! I totally didn't!" he exclaims, proud of himself for psyching me out. "But you did! You did have sex!" He grabs my hand, kisses it quickly, then asks, "So who is he? And do we hear wedding bells?"

"Do you remember Jay? Seema's brother?"

"The guy I had a crush on in college?"

Cue another jaw drop.

Jeff puts up his left palm. "I've said too much. Sorry. Go on . . ."

"Seriously?" I whine. "You had a crush on him *while* we were dating?"

"Sweetie, in the first five minutes you met me, I raved about George Clooney *and* Rosemary Clooney. Not my fault you didn't read the signs. Now tell me about the Jay hookup."

We get Jeff's bags, then spend the next fifty-five minutes creeping along through horrible LA traffic. But time flew as the two of us talked a mile a minute and spoke in shorthand about everything from our dating exploits of late, to our jobs, to what numbers we picked in the Mega lottery, to whether *People*'s Sexiest Man Alive deserved to have been picked that year. (Jeff said he was too old, but that a man who can provide a baby with six zeros attached clearly has some value to women.)

I have not seen Jeff in almost three years, yet we are talking as if we just saw each other yesterday.

When we get to Seema's and my place, I park the car, and Jeff and I get his luggage. As we approach the house, Jeff asks the million-dollar question. "So, he invited you to Paris. You never answered me—are you going?"

I shrug. "I don't know. Probably not. But it's nice to think the opportunity is there."

"What is with you? Just go!"

"I'm not even sure if it's a serious invite."

"Are you having sex with the man?" Jeff asks, leading the witness.

I shrug self-consciously. "We might be having 'met at a wedding' sex. I'm not sure that counts.'"

"All sex counts. Don't you keep a list?"

"A list of what?"

"Of all the men you've slept with."

"I don't need a list."

"Oh, that's so sad," Jeff deadpans.

"No, it's not sad. I've haven't been with that many men. If I had a dime for every man I've had sex with . . ."

"You still couldn't use a parking meter for more than twenty minutes. Oh, remind me, I owe you a dime," Jeff jokes.

I make a show of glaring at him before I unlock the door. As we walk into the house, I see Scott sitting crisscross applesauce on the carpet in the middle of our living room, surrounded by white poster-board circles. He looks . . . *pained* is the only word that pops to mind. Seema stands nears him, in front of a big, purple poster board placed on an easel. She holds a black Sharpie up to a white circle with the number 3 scrolled on it. "I don't think having a singles' table is bad if it's close to the dance floor," she assures Scott.

Scott holds in a sigh. "I will give you a hundred dollars right now if you can name one person, ever, in the history of weddings, who was happy to be put at the singles' table." Upon seeing us, Scott's face lights up. "Oh, company. Thank God. Break time!"

"Jeff!" Seema practically screams, running up to him and hugging him (the man inspires such enthused reactions in women). "Oh my God! You're here!"

"Seema," he says, giving her a bear hug. "You're even more gorgeous than last time. Engagements clearly agree with you." After the hug, Jeff walks over to Scott, who stands to shake his hand. "I'm Jeff."

"Scott."

As they shake hands, Jeff turns to Seema. "You didn't tell me how gorgeous your soon-to-be-husband is."

"I most certainly did," Seema insists.

He turns back to Scott and says to him in all seriousness, "If you ever hurt her, I'll hunt you down and kill you."

Scott smiles. "I would have it no other way."

We have the standard chitchat (How was the flight? What's the weather been like in LA?), but soon Seema cuts to the chase, asking Jeff, "How do you feel about helping us with the seating chart?"

Jeff feigns insult. "You assume that just because I'm gay I instinctively know how to make a seating chart?"

She looks at him as if that were the stupidest question in the world. "Um . . . duh."

"Set me up with someone cute and single?"

Seema looks over at me. "Don?"

My eyes light up and I nod. "Yeah. Don's good."

Jeff eyes widen. "Oh, Don. I am loving Don. Now tell me, who's Don?"

"He's the principal at my school," I tell him. "Insanely hot, age appropriate, and recently out of a long-term relationship."

Jeff immediately scribbles his name and Don's onto table six. "We have a winner."

"Wait, why did you put yourself at table six?" Seema asks.

"Not too close to the dance floor and its booming speakers. Not too close to the bar and its booming drunks." Jeff tapes circle six to the middle-left part of the chart. "Who's next?"

Seema scrunches her lips as she examines the chart. "What if we put your aunts Beth, Jane, and Nancy with your uncle Sam?" she suggests to her fiancée.

"Sam's fine," Scott tells her as he picks up a circle from the floor, stands up, and hands it to her. "Just don't sit Aunt Beth next to Uncle Solomon."

While Jeff sticks the white circle onto the poster-board seating chart, Seema turns to Scott. "Do you *have* an Uncle Solomon?"

"I do. And I'm pretty sure he hates Aunt Beth."

"Have I met this uncle?" Seema asks.

"Probably not. I haven't seen him since I was five."

"So naturally we invited him," Seema says sarcastically.

"He's also my godfather."

Seema turns to Scott. "Wait, you have a Christian godfather named Solomon?"

"Yeah. Why?"

Seema won't take the bait. "No reason. Why doesn't he like Aunt Beth?"

"She left him for Aunt Jane."

Jeff leans in. "Let's put Aunt Beth at table six. She sounds fun."

Jeff takes the names Aunt Beth and Aunt Jane and tapes them onto table six as Seema scrutinizes the board again. "Do you want your uncle Solomon at table thirteen or fifteen?"

"Whichever's farthest from table six," Scott reasons.

Seema writes *Solomon* in red pen on table fifteen.

"What does the red pen mean?" I ask.

"Danger, danger, Will Robinson. If this person sits next to the wrong person, all hell will break loose, and someone might not enjoy his chicken tikka masala," Seema says dryly.

"Have you considered Vegas?" Jeff asks Scott.

Scott leans in to Jeff and says quietly, "I suggest it daily."

"I heard that," Seema says to Scott.

Scott puts out his hands. "Did I stutter?"

Something tells me a lot of prewedding conversations contain those words verbatim.

Seventeen

That night, Jeff and I decide to take a cab over to central Holly-wood and go on a "cocktail crawl." Jeff calls it "research"—he needs to observe how the décor of the hot new clubs has changed over the past few years, what new drinks are in, what the happy hours are like, etc. He even asked one bartender to get the man-ager so they could discuss lighting.

It's now around midnight, and I am lounging on a sofa/mat-tress at bar number four doing another quick round of texts with Jay:

So . . . going out with another man already? I'm hurt.

Not just another man—a ridiculously handsome one plying me with booze.

I guess in 21 hours, I am going to have to fight him for your honor.

Oooooohhhhh. I hope so.

Have you bought something in red lace yet?

No.

I immediately type this and send. Then I reconsider and type:

Maybe.

Ooohhhhh—send me a sexy pic when you get home.

I most certainly will not.

All right, I'll just have to get one of you myself tomorrow.

The hell you . . .

I see Jeff snaking through the crowd, lightly pushing people out of the way as he carries a tray with six martini glasses in a rainbow of colors: green, purple, pink, blue, orange, and one that has layers of yellow and red. I quickly type:

I gotta go. Leave me a sexy voice mail before you go to
   bed.

Actual talking? I must really like you. Good night.

Good night.

xoxo

xoxo

I smile as I look at our conversation on my screen one more time. *Xoxo.* Life is good.

Jeff arrives at my couch and hands me the tray of martinis, which I place on the club's version of a nightstand. Jeff is on the phone, calmly making a point to the person on the other end. "Because he's an asshole. . . . Because he's an asshole. . . . I don't know. . . . Okay, did you sleep with him? . . . Well, there you go. . . ." I watch him shake his head and wince. "Because we're men!" he says in a *Duh!* voice. "We are not only able to have sex with you even if we don't like you, sometimes we prefer it that way." He hands me the blue martini as he listens on the other end. "That is not sexist! There are scads of men I'd sleep with who I don't like. Do I have to remind you about Schrödinger's blow job?" Jeff looks up at me and puts up his index finger to tell me one more minute. He says into his phone, "Sweetie, I'm out with friends, and I have to go. . . . I love you too. . . . Okay, good-bye." He hangs up the phone and shakes his head. "I swear, I wonder how any of you ever breed." Then he breaks into a smile and motions to the blue drink. "What do you think?"

I make a face. "What is it this time?"

"Something with blue curaçao and ginger. We have a blue drink at Male 'Ana, but I think I could improve on it."

I take a sip and wince. "Blech! Too spicy."

"Fair enough." Jeff hops onto the mattress with me. "Speaking of spicy, who here is cute?"

"Everyone. But we're too old to talk to any of them."

"Well, that's just limited thinking." Jeff takes the yellow-and-red martini drink from the tray and samples a bit.

"Really? And what would you suggest we talk with them about?"

Jeff shrugs. "Prom, Chutes and Ladders, One Direction . . ."

I look around the room at all the beautiful twenty-two-year-old girls in miniskirts and sky-high heels, and I can't help but whine, "This is depressing. Why aren't we at a gay bar?"

"Because I know it doesn't look like it, but I'm actually working." Jeff hands me his drink to sample. "Besides, I'll go to one tomorrow night, when you're with your loo-oove-ah."

I try to suppress an embarrassed smile as I take the cocktail. "He's not my lover."

"Did you make love to him?"

I shrug and turn away from Jeff sheepishly. "Maybe."

"Then let's hope he's your lover. Otherwise, he's a one-night stand, and you're a slut."

Jeff's phone rings again. He answers without so much as a hello, saying instead, "I don't even know how I got designated the gay best friend who can give advice in the first place. God knows, I can't keep a man." He listens to the voice on the other end for a good thirty seconds before putting his thumb and index finger to each eye, and squeezing his eyes shut. Another good thirty seconds pass before he pops his eyes back open. "Schrödinger's blow job." He repeats for the second time in less than five minutes. "Now go have fun." Then he presses the button to hang up. Jeff points to an orange drink. "Taste that, and tell me what you think."

I take a sip. "Ick. What is that? Gin?"

"I thought it was a misstep myself when I watched him make it." Jeff picks up the glass and holds it up to examine the color. "Although maybe with a coconut rum . . ."

As Jeff takes a sip of the gin drink and swishes it around in his mouth, I say, "Okay, I have to ask—what is Schrödinger's blow job? And what does it have to do with dating?"

Jeff reaches over to the nightstand to pick up a pink drink in a martini glass and hands it to me. "Do you know what Schrödinger's cat is?"

"Of course I do," I say, vaguely insulted. "In the 1930s, Erwin Schrödinger came up with his theorem—"

Jeff nearly does a spit-take. "Theorem? Good Lord. When you get drunk, you become even more of a geek. Okay, so you know there's a cat in a box with a flask of poison that has been opened, and the cat might be dead from said poison. Or not. And until you open the box, you don't know whether the cat is alive or dead. Which means until you open it, the cat is both and neither, all at once."

"I fail to see what a dead cat has to do with sex."

"Really? You've exhausted all the possibilities for the word *pussy?*"

Without wanting to, I begin racking my brain, trying to come up with different wordplays.

"I'm kidding," Jeff says, then taps my forehead with his index finger and smiles. "But I love to watch that little mind race. Anyway, in the gay community, some of us, on occasion, have dated men who think they're straight because there are certain things they won't do with us. But no matter who the guy is or what his hang-ups are, he usually will be willing to get a blow job."

"Do I want to hear the rest of this?" I take a sip of the pink drink.

"Knowledge is power. Anyway, basically the theory from some of these men goes like this: If a man puts on a blindfold and gets a blow job, it doesn't really matter if he's getting it from a man or a woman, because he can't see who is giving him the blow job. Therefore, if he happens to be getting a blow job from a man, that doesn't make him gay."

"Meaning the blow job is like the cat in the box, in that it could be either from a man or a woman until you take off the blindfold."

"Exactly."

"First off, obviously, these men are gay."

"Honey, you say 'tomato' . . ."

"And second, so what does this have to do with dating?"

"Single, straight men, for the most part, will let any woman blow them or have sex with them. But they might as well have a blindfold on. Getting sex doesn't mean they're in a relationship with the woman. And just because the poison is out of the bottle doesn't mean your pussy is dead yet. You have to open the box to know for sure."

I glare at him. "A dead pussy being one that is in a relationship?"

"You look offended."

"Why can't you say the cat is still alive if you're in the relationship?"

"Because the cat was alive, then is dead. You are single, then in a relationship. My point is, just because a woman is sleeping with a guy, that doesn't mean he thinks they're in a relationship. He needs to take off his blindfold first."

I blink several times while I absorb Jeff's theory. I take another sip of the pink drink, which seems to be mostly vodka. "That actually kind of makes sense," I am forced to admit. Then I shake my head slowly. "I still can't believe you killed yourself to get a PhD in theoretical physics only to wind up opening a bar."

"The two are completely intertwined. I'm trying to solve the problem of cold fusion by using the ideal combination of ice, rum, and a blender."

I furrow my brows at him. "Have you been working on that joke long?"

"Not too long. Oh, I got another joke for you. A neutron walks into my bar and orders a beer. When he asks for the check, I tell him, 'For you, no charge.'"

I shake my head slightly and chuckle as I grab the green drink. "You are such a geek."

"So the neutron says to me, 'Are you sure?' And I say, 'I'm a proton—I'm positive.'" Jeff opens his mouth wide like Fozzie Bear right after a terrible joke.

I shake my head again. "I'll admit, that's kind of funny."

"Thanks. I got a charge out of it myself."

"Do you get a lot of men with these jokes?"

"No, but I screen a lot of men. If they don't get it, they're out."

"Unless they can loan you a blindfold."

"Well, I wouldn't want to be a snob about it."

The rest of the night was spent talking about men, about college, about everything from Hawaii to physics to backgammon. I was having a great time.

And I was really happy. Unlike the bevy of women who seemed to call Jeff every five minutes to ask him to translate what the men in their lives were doing, I did not ask him one question about Jay.

Because in the back of my mind, all I could think about was the *xoxo* I got.

I was one dead cat.

Eighteen

Thursday, Jeff had to spend the afternoon visiting family, so I had the whole day to get ready for my reunion with Jay.

I do all of the things an obsessed girl with too much time on her hands does to get ready: I buy new bubble bath and spend twenty minutes debating which scent to choose. What makes a guy want a girl more—if she smells like a rose or a cucumber? I also go to Bloomingdale's to buy not one but two new matching bra-and-underwear sets. One in red lace, as requested. The other in black satin. (The satin one makes me look good, but not as if I were trying. Because God forbid a man knows you're trying.) As long as I'm there, I buy a new set of sheets with a thread count so high, it resembles the winning numbers of this week's lottery.

Which is fine—I feel as if maybe I won the lottery with Jay—we shall see.

That afternoon, I pick up Jay from the airport.

His look is casual, yet flawlessly put together. Wearing a dark blue, tailored suit, no tie, the top button of his shirt unbuttoned, he looks like a model in *Esquire* magazine.

Of course, he's speaking (and laughing) in French with a

gorgeous redhead in a low-cut dress, which makes him a little less appealing.

Cue the insecurity. . . .

Fortunately, his face lights up when he sees me. "Mel!" he says, beaming. He trots up to me quickly, kisses me hello on the lips, then pulls me into a hug.

Ahhhhhh . . . Life is perfect. My shoulders slump and I ooze into him, inhaling the scent of his hotel travel soap. I could stay in these arms forever.

I hear a woman's lilting French behind me. I pull away and turn to see the woman he was speaking with waiting politely to be introduced.

All I catch from Jay is *excusez-moi* and some other French words and phrases (including the words *mon amour*? Or did I imagine that?) before he says, "Mel, this Colette, a friend of mine from a rival agency. Colette, c'est Melissa."

Colette smiles (although it is not a warm smile) and puts out her hand. "Je suis très heureux de faire votre connaissance."

Jay shakes his head. "Melissa ne parle français," he says to Colette sweetly.

"It's okay," I begin quickly "I can parle. I took high school—"

"Oh, sorry," Colette says in a thick accent. "A *plaisir* to meet you."

I take her hand and shake it. "A pleasure to meet you as well."

"So, someone has finally caught ze playboy."

I turn to Jay to see his eyes bulge out slightly at her. Then he forces a smile.

She notices his reaction and apologizes to me. "Sorry. My English is bad." But then she turns to Jay and almost smirks as she asks him, "Un play-boy jouisseur?"

"Colette . . . ," he begins rather tersely.

She ignores him, turning to me. "I have tried to entice Jay to spend ze evening with me, but he says he has a girlfriend he sees this weekend. She is his love. I assume that is you?"

Girlfriend? His love? Wait, what? Je suis intrigued.

Jay emits a nervous laugh as he puts his arm around me. "Okay. Great to see you, Colette. We should do it again soon." He kisses her once on each cheek, then drags me by the hand over to Baggage Claim.

"Isn't she just going to follow us?" I ask, turning around to see Colette's eyes darken as she watches us leave.

"No. She's on the next plane back to Paris. She followed me out just to meet you. Now she'll have to go through security again, which is going to take at least an hour." Then he mutters something in French under his breath.

"You know I did take high school French. You can say stuff out loud."

"Not what I just said."

We quickly walk through the sliding glass doors and into Baggage Claim. The moment we are lost in the crowd and away from Colette, Jay turns me around and his smile returns. "I missed you," he almost whispers, then pulls me into a long kiss.

After the kiss is over, I murmur, "I missed you too." Then I kiss him again.

As much as I'm loving this kiss, that incident with Colette was weird. When we stop kissing long enough to come up for air, I ask, "Is she, like, an old girlfriend or something?"

Jay shakes his head and exhales a loud breath. "Or 'something'—yes. I slept with her a few times a few years ago. Total bunny boiler. I don't want to talk about it."

I knew it! "Oh. Okay," I say to him nonjudgmentally (or at least with as little judgment as I can muster). Then I try to casually ask, "So what happened?"

Jay looks confused. "I just said . . ."

I shrug. "Yeah, I know but . . . here's the thing: we just started sleeping together. So when you say, 'I don't want to talk about' what happened with a girl, I cannot help but get obsessed. So you might as well just tell me now before I start getting all girlie and tense while you're trying to be all cute with me later this evening."

Jay leans in. "So you think I'm cute?"

"Don't change the subject. Just tell me what happened. I'm sure it's not nearly as bad as whatever I will conjure up in my pretty little double-X-chromosome head."

Jay debates for a moment, then shrugs. "Okay. Well, she was engaged when we met, and it was supposed to be a fling. But then a few weeks in, she started talking about how she loves me and has to break off her engagement, and I knew she didn't mean it. But *then* she met this other girl I was dating, and she totally freaked out in the middle of the Saturday farmers' market. I don't judge—you and your fiancée have an open relationship, that's cool. But don't expect me to be exclusive when you're going home every night to another guy. You know what I mean?"

He slept with an engaged person? Definitely sorry I asked. But instead of showing any emotion, I answer, "Perfectly."

Jay smiles a relieved smile. "Good. And I'm sorry about the playboy thing, and telling her you were my girlfriend. I just needed an escape—I didn't think she'd follow me out to meet you."

Rats. I was kind of digging the girlfriend part. But again, I don't give anything away. Instead I smile and say, "No problem."

Jay rubs my shoulders. "Excellent. Now let's get my luggage, and the massage oils I bought for you when I was in San Francisco, and see where the afternoon leads us."

We spend the next ten minutes kissing, then getting luggage, kissing, then finding my car, stealing kisses at every light on the way home, and finally kissing as we walk up the pathway to my door.

And I know this afternoon is going to be perfect.

Until I unlock the door.

I should have known my luck would run out. After all, this is my life we're talking about.

Nic sits on the couch, her pregnant hugeness leaning back on several pillows. She has a notebook in hand. Seema, wearing a giant Native American headdress, complete with multicolored layers of feathers, sits on the floor, surrounded by gifts, some wrapped in silver paper, some wrapped in white paper, and some unwrapped and pulled from their boxes. "A five-piece place setting of our stainless, plus a silver nut bowl," Seema tells Nic.

Nic gives an approving nod. "Nice." She writes it down in her notebook, then looks up and smiles. "Hey, guys! You're just in time for final wedding preparations. Today we're doing thank-you notes! You can never thank too early."

Jay makes a show of turning around to leave, but I stop him. As he drags his luggage in, I take a seat on our couch arm, the only free space in the room. "Have you had a good haul?" I ask Seema.

"Embarrassingly good, actually. A lot of my family sent checks."

"Always in season," Nic chimes in.

"And I always know just what to wear it with," Seema jokes. She looks up to Jay as he kisses her on the cheek. "How was San Francisco?"

"Exhausting, but not nearly as much as spending the weekend

with the family will be. And now I must ask: What the hell are you wearing?"

"It's a Native American headdress."

"Oh, God!" I spit out, shocked.

"I'm trying not to be offended," Seema says, clearly offended. "Scott's great-great-aunt, who as far as I can tell is a million and two, was apparently confused over which kind of Indian I was. Not to mention what I might want to wear . . . ever."

"Good Lord," Jay says, shaking his head slowly.

"Surprisingly, this is not the worst gift I have received. Or the strangest for that matter."

"What was the strangest gift?" I'm almost afraid to ask.

Seema hands me a white envelope. Inside is a $200 gift card for the Burj Al Arab hotel. "What's the Burj . . ."

"It's the world's only six-star hotel."

"Oh. Cool."

"It's in Dubai."

"Wait. Are you going . . ."

She shakes her head no.

"Then why . . ."

"I have no idea."

"Does that one count as worst or strangest?" Jay asks.

"It's in the running for strangest—although the earthquake kit was a bit odd. Nic, show them the worst."

Nic reaches down next to the couch and pulls up two fairly large clay jars: one purple, one red, both with black squares pasted to the front. The purple one's black square has Seema's name engraved in gold, with her birth year underneath and slightly to the left, and the red one's black square has Scott's name engraved with his birth year underneath. Nic sets them down on the table. Jay and I exchange a look.

I shrug, "Well, it's a little odd, but . . ."

"Urns for our ashes—one for each of us. That black plate is engravable for the years of our deaths."

"Oh, yuck!" I blurt out.

"Creepiest bookends ever," Jay elaborates.

Seema shoots a pleading look to Jay. "Please tell me you brought wine."

"I did. But it's for Mel and me."

"Have I shown you the painting of Elvis yet?" Seema asks Jay.

"Because nothing says class like crushed velvet," Nic says.

"So, three glasses then," Jay says, heading for the kitchen.

NINETEEN

I'd say, overall, Seema got a pretty good haul: lots of checks, plenty of silverware they'll never use to complement towering stacks of china they won't use, some nice nonbeige towels (from me), and a Wii game system (which Scott registered for, and Jay bought).

Jay and I spent the evening with the bridal party and their families at an understated Italian restaurant with an incredible view of the Pacific Ocean. I divided my time between reminiscing with the girls about our single days (okay, for them it was reminiscing, for me it was more like reliving a horror movie), talking to the older people about their weddings, and trying to keep Jay's hand from going too far up my skirt underneath the table.

We left the restaurant by nine, as Seema pointed out that we all needed to go to bed early in preparation for the Christian-wedding rehearsal at "nine o'clock in the fucking morning" (Seema's words, not mine).

I had no problem going to bed early. She didn't say anything about sleep.

While Jay went to the kitchen to uncork a second Napa red he'd bought (and give a little to his sister—I could hear their mumbled talking), I raced around my room lighting scented candles, rinsing my mouth out with mouthwash, reapplying powder, squirting myself with a bit more perfume, squirting Jay's pillow with a mist of perfume, throwing off my dress and tossing it into the closet, and putting on a black, satin, short robe that matched the bra and underwear I bought earlier today.

I wasn't going for the red lace tonight. That would go under my bridesmaid's dress on Saturday. After all, part of the fun of the beginning of the relationship is the chase and the buildup, right?

I wonder if men spend half as much time thinking about this stuff as we women do.

My iPhone rings: Jeff. I pick up immediately. "Don't come home yet."

"Don't be silly. It's not even ten. I'm still getting ready to go out. But don't wait up for me. I'm just going to crash at Paul's place."

"No, no . . . ," I practically whine. "You're only here for a few days. Come home, just not until . . . saaaayyyy . . . one?"

"Please. Go bag the best man. I'll see you in the morning, after the rehearsal."

Jay chooses this moment to make his entrance. He looks so effortlessly hot: his hair is lightly tousled from the Pacific air from earlier, his shirt cuffs are rolled up, his tie is gone and replaced with two unbuttoned top buttons.

Yum.

Carrying the wine bottle and two empty wineglasses intertwined in his fingers, he looks so polished, suave, and debonair. "Hey," he says quietly in his sexiest voice, "you look phenomenal."

"Sssshhhhh!!!!" I blurt out loudly, quickly raising my index finger to my mouth.

"Did you just shush the man you plan to have sex with to talk to the man you'll never have sex with?" Jeff asks me over the phone.

"Come home," I tell him sternly as Jay sets the bottle down on my desk and begins pouring. Then I whisper into the phone, "Just not until one."

"How is theoretical physics like leftover wine?" Jeff asks (knowing I have the answer).

I roll my eyes. "Because, while the concept makes sense to some people, it is totally lost on me."

"Exactly. Much like begging a gay man to come to your house to cockblock a hot straight man makes no sense to me. So how does he look?"

Jay hands me my wine. "Perfection," I grudgingly admit to Jeff.

"Have fun. Oh—final joke of the night. A neutrino walks into my bar—"

"Congratulations. You just found a way to make me hang up."

"Love you," Jeff says to me with a smile in his voice.

"Love you too."

And he's gone.

As I hang up the phone, Jay begins lightly kissing my neck. "Have I mentioned how gorgeous you look tonight?"

"I suck," I say, staring at my phone guiltily. "He invites me to visit him in Hawaii all the time. The one time he comes here, I'm pawning him off on a friend."

Jay continues to kiss my neck. "I doubt he cares."

"I'm still feeling guilty."

"Why? I haven't asked you to do anything weird yet," Jay jokes. (Well, I hope he jokes.) He lifts up his wineglass for a toast. "Here's to being pawned off on a friend. I'm hoping Seema does it for the rest of my trip."

I smile, and we toast. I taste the wine. "This is . . . exquisite. What's it called?"

"Opus One. An exquisite wine for an exquisite woman."

"Opus One?! Holy crap! You must really like me!" The words rushed out of my mouth before I could hustle them back in. Seriously, why do I say things like that? Am I just determined to ruin everything?

"I do really like you," Jay assures me in a matter-of-fact tone that makes it sound as if we've been dating for years. "So, when are you coming to visit me in Paris?"

I take another glorious sip of my wine as I take his hand and walk him to my freshly made and freshly perfumed bed. "Oh, I don't know. Someday."

"*Someday?*" He sits on the bed. "One of the most insidious words in the English language. Someday we will be dead. For now we live. Come next weekend."

"Next weekend?!" I blurt out. Then I decide not to have this conversation. Not right now. Not with a gorgeous man in my bed whom I've spent years dreaming about. "Okay, I'll think about it."

"Maybe this will convince you," Jay says gently, putting down his wineglass, then taking my face in his hands and giving me a kiss that makes my knees buckle. Actually buckle.

And (lucky for me!) that wasn't the only thing he did that night to convince me to visit.

TWENTY

Sex is confusing.

Well, the act itself isn't confusing. Or at least it hasn't been since that guy . . . Why am I thinking about *that* guy? Oh, yeah, because he was the first person to make me wonder, *What the hell just happened here?* I suppose that's one advantage of being in your thirties: at least you no longer stare at a dark ceiling in silence, or worse yet snoring, and wonder, *Did I do something wrong?*

On the flip side, perfect, multiple-orgasm sex that literally shows up at your doorstep can be confusing too. Particularly when you know it's going away in a few days.

I don't react well to things going away. No one does, but I'm obsessed with worries of loss. I bought twenty boxes of Twinkies after Hostess declared bankruptcy, and I hadn't had a Twinkie since I was twelve. (Side note: any cream filling whose name begins with a *k* should be sucked out with a straw, spit into the trash, then replaced with Reddi-wip. If you use the nozzle properly, it will blow your Twinkie up to twice its normal size and be almost palatable.)

Back to sex being confusing. What am I going to do? I don't

know if I'm feeling love or lust, or just a rush of pride at having finally conquered my crush after all these years. But I do know I don't want to say good-bye.

It's now about 2:00 A.M., and I am in my living room, finishing off a pint of Ben and Jerry's AmeriCone Dream, and surfing the net on my notebook computer.

Jay putters out of my bedroom, wearing only pajama bottoms, and looking so perfect that I want to lock him in my bedroom and keep him here forever. "Hey," he whispers, "Are you okay?"

I quickly close my computer window and shut the notebook. "I'm fine," I whisper back. "I couldn't sleep. Sorry to wake you."

Jay smiles sleepily and quietly takes a seat next to me. "It's okay. You can make it up to me later. So . . . talking to an old boyfriend online?"

"What? No. Why would you think that?"

"You could *not* have closed your computer fast enough. And I think I know you well enough to know it's not porn. Although if it were, I think I just found the perfect woman."

Without thinking, I glance at my computer, then awkwardly say, "It's not a big deal. I was just looking up . . ."

And then I stop talking. Shit. I turn to Jay, who waits for me to finish my sentence.

Which I do not want to do.

I shake my head. "It's silly. I was just looking up this restaurant in Paris called L'Arbre d'Argent," I admit sheepishly.

I can tell from Jay's look that I have surprised him. "You mean La Tour d'Argent? Wow, you've got good taste. But we can go there if you want."

"No. Not La Tour d'Argent, L'Arbre d'Argent. It means 'money tree' in French and . . . wait, is that La Tour place, like, a really nice restaurant or something?"

He chuckles to himself. "Yeah, you could say that."

My curiosity gets the best of me, so I flip open my computer and type in *La Tour d'Argent*.

Jay stands up and heads to the kitchen. "I'm peckish. Can I go forage around your kitchen for snacks?"

My fingers are racing around the keyboard madly. "Go for it. There's ice cream in the freezer hidden behind the Lean Cuisines, and a bag of M&M's hidden behind the low-fat popcorn." Then I see La Tour's website. "Holy Mother of God! Look at this view!"

I hear Jay open the refrigerator as he calls out, "It's pretty spectacular, isn't it? Hey, are there Chee•tos up for grabs?"

"Sure. Bring them out. Oh my God, they have pictures of the plates!" I say, staring at a different kind of Internet porn—food porn! (aka porn for women!) "Look at these crêpes! And the meat! Is that duck? *Canard* means 'duck' right?"

Jay emerges from the kitchen with a bottle of champagne, two flutes, and a family-size bag of Chee•tos. "They are known for their duck. And lobster and, you know, pretty much everything. It's a Michelin-starred restaurant."

As I drool over the restaurant's website, Jay pops the cork of the bubbly. "Ah, one of my favorite sounds in the world." He pours me a glass. "So, does that mean you're thinking about visiting?"

I sheepishly look at him. "Kinda. Maybe?"

Jay hands me the filled flute. "What would make that a 'Yes. Definitely?'"

I take the glass as I tell him nervously, "I don't want to be a bother."

He pours himself a glass. "If you were going to be a bother, I wouldn't keep inviting you."

Exit "clingy phase" to make room for "insecure fourteen-year-old with a crush on the prom king" phase. I take a sip of champagne, then ask him in all seriousness, "Why me? I'm sure there are a lot of women in Paris who would love to go to La Tour d'Argent with you."

Jay considers my question for a moment. "You do realize there is no right answer to that question."

"Sure there is," I say as I dig into the bag of Chee•tos. (The answer is obviously *Because I am truly, madly, deeply, in love with you and have longed for you for so many years, and even though I know everything about you, you are perfect . . . for me. Run away with me! Have my babies!* Not a lot of men give this answer, but that doesn't stop us women from asking them the question.)

"No. There isn't." Almost amused, Jay elaborates, "If I say, 'No, there are no women who would want to go with me to a decadent five-star restaurant for a romantic night,' I sound like a loser. On the other hand, if I say, 'Well, yes, of course there are women. Scads. I'm practically Hugh Hefner back in 1950!'—then I'm an asshole."

"Scads?"

"That's a word, isn't it? *Scads*?" Jay asks as he helps himself to some Chee•tos.

"And why would you want to be Hugh Hefner in 1950? He was married then, and the first issue of *Playboy* wouldn't be published for another three years."

Jay tilts his head to the side, his face rendered a little blank by my knowledge of useless trivia.

I point to his face and wave my index finger around. "That's what I mean. Why do you want me hanging around your pied-à-terre, thoughtlessly correcting you all the time?"

"Well, you're pretty cute, even when you're correcting me." He winks at me. "And it's not a pied-à-terre. I only have one. It's an apartment." He says "apartment" with an accent that is so sexy, I want to pin him to the couch and have my way with him for the third time this evening.

I say nothing for a while. At least twenty seconds. Which, when you've been with someone for months or years, is not only *not* a long time, it's usually a welcome respite. But when you're both nervously chomping on chips and wondering what the other person is thinking, it's an eternity.

"Hey, I got a quote for you to *not* correct me on," Jay says, taking the big bag of Chee•tos. "'It's better to be absolutely ridiculous than absolutely boring.'"

"Albert Einstein. But what does that mean?"

"Just come to Paris. Don't give it too much thought—better to be ridiculous than boring." Jay smiles with rather smug satisfaction. "And it's not Albert Einstein."

It is too. But it is more important to be adored than right. I shake my head. "Oh, you're right, it's . . ."

"Marilyn Monroe."

"Right," I say, as though I just remembered who said it. (Not!) "Great quote."

Jay starts laughing. "Oh my God—you don't believe me."

"What? Of course I do."

"No, you don't. You are actively fighting the urge to look it up online right now and see if I'm right."

"No!" I deny, feigning offense. A few seconds later . . . "Okay, yes. A little in my head. But I love the sentiment, and it's a great quote."

Jay puts out the bag for me to grab another handful. "I'll make you a deal. If you look it up, and I'm right, you come to Paris. Next week."

I take some and pop a few in my mouth. "I won't make that deal since I'm sure you're right."

Jay, still smiling, shakes his head. "You do know that now I can't fall asleep before you. I'm not going to give you the satisfaction of looking it up without me there."

"Oh, I can think of a few ways to put you to sleep," I flirt.

"Round three?"

"Race ya!"

And we make a joke of racing each other back to bed.

He did fall asleep before me. Once challenged, I could not resist the urge to tiptoe out to the living room, open my computer, and google the quote:

Imperfection is beauty, madness is genius, and it's better to be absolutely ridiculous than absolutely boring. —Marilyn Monroe

Well, I'll be damned.

I google the words *money tree* along with *Marilyn Monroe*. Sadly, nothing. But I did find this quote from her:

We should all start to live before we get too old. Fear is stupid. So are regrets.

Hmm. I wish she had gotten old—I'll bet she would have said even more cool things.

TWENTY-ONE

Friday was busy. We had the Christian-wedding rehearsal in the morning, which went off without a hitch. Well, okay, other than a passive-aggressive future mother-in-law loudly asking why the ceremony couldn't be held "in a real church." And a future father-in-law showing up with a hooker. Or maybe she's his third wife—I wasn't really clear.

Note to self—make sure those two are nowhere near each other, or the bar, or the fire pit during the Indian ceremony.

The rehearsal was to be followed by Seema's mehndi ceremony in the early afternoon. Which seemed like a good idea at the time.

For those of you who, like me until a few weeks ago, have no idea of what exactly a mehndi is, allow me to explain. You know those temporary henna tattoos you had painted on in your teens to drive your mom nuts, or had done during a wild weekend in Vegas because even loaded on tequila shots and rum drinks you still couldn't face a needle without fainting at the sight of it? (Show of hands? No? Just me?)

Well, that's sort of a Westernized version of what a mehndi is. Anyway, a mehndi is a temporary tattoo made from applying turmeric paste in various patterns and designs to the bride's face, hands, and feet, and sometimes her legs and arms. And the mehndi ceremony is what's held during the time artists are applying the paste to the bride.

It's basically a big party traditionally held at the bride's house (meaning our place) at which the women in the bride's life (including her mom, aunts, cousins, and friends) come to sing, dance, drink, and help the bride move around after all of the paste is applied.

In other words: Seema's mom is coming over.

Meaning Jay's mom is coming over.

A fact I really didn't think through until the middle of the rehearsal that morning.

We are now thirty minutes from thirty women coming over, and while we should be worried putting out cheese, crackers, nan, chicken, olives, etc., instead Seema and I are racing from my bedroom to hers, trying to move all of Jay's stuff out of my den of iniquity.

I race into Seema's room, tugging along his half-zipped suitcase. "Okay, hide this."

"I don't need to hide it," Seema insists. "Mom knows he's staying here."

"Yes! But she doesn't know he's staying there!" I say, pointing toward my room in a fierce gesture. "And I would prefer she not see me as the slut her son is bagging for the next three days."

We hear the loud splashing of vomit into the toilet in the bathroom. Afterward, an out-of-breath Nic yells through the closed door, "Don't forget to do a mommy check!"

Seema and exchange glances. "What's a mommy check?" I yell to Nic through the door.

"Also called an idiot check," Nic yells back. "It's the last look you give your hotel room even if you're absolutely sure you packed everything. So named because kids leave their glasses in hotel rooms, and their bathing suits, iPods, textbooks."

"Good idea!" I yell to her. "It's possible I—"

And then I hear *bwah!* Again in the bathroom.

Yuck.

Seema and I both scrunch up our noses, grossed out. Seema whispers, "I thought morning sickness was supposed to be over by six months."

I whisper back, "I thought it only happened when you were pregnant with a girl."

"It can happen anytime, no matter what sex the baby is," Nic yells through the door. "And by the way, I'm pregnant, not deaf!"

Then we hear *bwah!* again.

"Just try to feel better," Seema says in a falsely cheerful voice. Then whispers to me, "She's got the hearing of a tiger moth."

A thought occurs to me. "Oh, God. I'm pretty sure he left his red boxers under my desk."

I race back to my room, where I find said boxers, an empty wine bottle, and two dirty glasses. Plus some sundry items in my trash that I decide to take right out to the big black can outside.

For the next twenty minutes, I cleaned, then put out food, like a hurricane. And by the time the party started, Nic wasn't the only one out of breath and ready to throw up.

TWENTY-TWO

The mehndi ceremony is turning out to be a blast. There is food and singing. Dancing and champagne. A man who is texting me frequently.

Granted some of the texts were a bit mundane:

> At Bloomingdale's now. Can you subtly find out if Seema really wants a $400 ice bucket?

I look up at Seema, being painted by two craggy, old women who specialize in this art. "Jay wants to know how much you want the ice bucket."

"Eh." She shrugs. Then she gets excited. "Tell him I want the cheese tray!"

I quickly type back:

> She says she wants the cheese tray.
>
> Done. Thanks, love.

And he's off. But before I can think of what he means by "love," Kamala, Seema's mom, grabs my phone and stares at my screen. "Is that Jay? I need to tell him to buy me bunion cream while he's out."

"Ma!" Seema exclaims. "Did you just pull that out of Mel's hand?"

"Oh, it's okay," I begin sheepishly. "I didn't really need—"

"To talk to my son!" Kamala snaps at her daughter self-righteously.

"What if they were having a private conversation?!" Seema barks back.

Oh, shit. Jay, please don't write back something slutty. Please don't write back something slutty. . . .

"What would they possibly be having a private conversation about?" Then Kamala turns to me. "Mel, honey, can you show me how to type back to him?"

"Um . . . sure," I say nervously. "You just click on this keypad right here . . ."

"Mom. Give Mel back the phone, and get Dad to buy the cream," Seema says a little too sternly.

"He never buys the right kind," Kamala says offhandedly while beginning to type. She stops and looks up at Seema. "What's *Vamehndied*?"

Shit. Not that I know what that means, but it just sounds like a *Kama Sutra* term to me. "Ummmm," I begin sheepishly, "could I just take a look at that?"

I cautiously take my phone out of Kamala's hand, using only two fingers. Then I read the screen . . .

Are you getting Vamehndied?

I don't know what that means.

I made it up. You know what Vajazzling is?

His mom wrote the first response, but clearly he thought it was me. So I quickly write back:

Your mother's reading this. She's the one who doesn't
    know what it means.

Oh. Hi, Mom.

Kamala reads over my shoulder. "You're dating him, aren't you?"

I don't detect any judgment in her tone. It's as if she just figured it and doesn't know what to do with the information yet.

Before I can answer, Seema's phone rings. As both of her hands are being worked on by the artists, she asks, "Nic, can you answer my phone and put it up to my ear?"

"It's your brother, isn't it?" Kamala asks knowingly.

"No!" Seema blurts out, clearly offended. "It's Scott. He probably just has a few questions about the sangeet tonight." Nic presses a button and puts the phone up to Seema's ear. "Hi Sweetie," Seema says.

I can hear Jay ask with concern, "How much did Mom read?"

"I would absolutely go with a nice filet," Seema answers, then says in a voice that sounds like code, *"Rare . . ."*

"Sweetie, I can hear him," Nic says under her breath to Seema.

Seema covers the phone and tells Nic sotto voce, "You could hear a pizza box being opened from across the room."

I start to tell Seema, "Actually we can all hear . . . ," just as Jay says over the phone, "Shit. Does she know I slept with her?"

"He's sleeping with her?!" Kamala exclaims. Then she looks at me. "He just got here yesterday!"

"Actually, he got here Saturday," I say in my defense.

Kamala repeats, "Saturday!?"—as Seema and Nic both yell, "Mel!"

Then I hear Jay mutter, "Oh, crap."

Then Kamala turns to me. "What about Jacqueline?"

"Lesbian," Seema says matter-of-factly to her mother.

"What?!" Kamala cries. She walks up to Seema while muttering to herself, "Why is that boy always introducing us to lesbians?" Then she puts out her hand and orders, "Give me the phone."

Seema tries not to. "Mom, I . . ."

Her mother starts squeezing the palm of Seema's hand over and over quickly to let her daughter know she's not playing. "Phone, young lady. Now."

Sighing, Seema resignedly hands over her cell.

Kamala begins speaking rapidly in French.

Rats. Other than hearing *nous* and *vous* a couple of times, I'm lost. I can tell from the tone of her voice she is not pleased and is lecturing him.

How is it all moms have that same tone of voice when they're lecturing?

Eventually, I hear something I do understand, a quick "Je t'aime, mon choux" (I love you . . . cream puff?), and Kamala clicks off the phone and hands it back to her daughter.

Kamala then looks around the room purposefully. "Have any of you ladies come here this weekend with the hopes of bedding my son?"

We hear a smattering of weak *No, ma'am*'s and *Uh-uh*'s that I'm not quite buying, so I doubt she is. Kamala continues, "Has anyone here slept with my son in the past and come here this week-end hoping to rekindle the friendship?"

Considering Seema has an assortment of friends here who go back fifteen or twenty years, I guess I shouldn't be surprised by the show of hands.

I'm still surprised by the show of hands.

Kamala makes a quick count, sighs to herself, then announces, "Apparently, for this weekend, Jay and Melissa are an item. If any of you is even remotely thinking about making a scene at the wedding over this recent bit of news, as a few of you did at Seema's cousin Vyshali's wedding last year, I suggest you rethink that. Her father and I just cashed in part of our 401(k) to pay for this, and I will break you like a twig."

TWENTY-THREE

It took several hours for all of Seema's artwork to be done, but by the end of the day she was festooned with a combination of birds, leaves, and other patterns covering her hands, arms, and feet. When the artists were done, she looked exotic and stunningly beautiful.

The rest of us had smaller patterns painted on our hands. I had a peacock painted on each hand, which is India's national bird and represents grace and beauty. Nic opted for flower buds and leaves painted on her belly, which symbolize new life and fertility.

Seema's mother spent much of the rest of the day neither avoiding me nor seeking me out. I didn't know what to make of it.

That night, Seema and Scott hosted a combination rehearsal dinner/sangeet.

The sangeet is a traditional music-and-dance ceremony that happens before the wedding in India. In the interest of smushing everything into one weekend, Seema and Scott combined it with a rehearsal dinner to make it a huge party held in a large loft downtown.

I am wearing my favorite purple silk Junim dress, which has been dyed to look like a sunset, a pair of understated diamond stud earrings, and some Jimmy Choo sparkly heels that I will also wear to tomorrow night's wedding. These clothes usually make me feel terrific about myself—I feel like my legs look good, my tummy looks small . . . I even have a great hand tattoo.

But right now I don't feel terrific, I feel wildly stressed out. I'm sitting at a table with Nic, Jason, and Jeff, watching Jay and Seema listening intently to their mother several tables away.

Well, Jay seems to be listening intently. He's not a mama's boy, but he has this pleasant smile and total eye contact with everyone when he listens, and his mother is no exception. Seema—not so much. Every time Kamala turns away from them, Seema lets out a suppressed eye roll. Even when Kamala is looking right at her, I have seen at least one clear sigh from my bride through a forced smile.

God, I wish I knew what they were talking about.

"What about him?" Nic says to Jeff. "He's pretty cute."

Jeff looks across the room and shakes his head. "Too much product in his hair. Next!"

"Since when does a gay man hate hair product?" Nic asks Jeff.

"Careful. That stereotyping makes your butt look big."

Nic's husband, Jason, tries next, pointing to a different male guest, "What about him?"

Jeff is visibly horrified. "Yuck! The guy couldn't even be bothered to iron his shirt tonight!"

"You know, shirts can come off," Nic points out.

"Not in his case, they can't. I haven't even met the guy, and I can already see myself doing light housework for him? No. Next!"

"What do you think they're talking about over there?" I ask the group nervously.

"Barcelona's soccer team," Jeff says. "That and the foolproof way to cook a lobster."

I try to give Jeff my most irritated glare. He puts his arm around me and gives me a half hug. "Honey, I'm sure it's not about you. This is the first time she's seen her kids together in ages. Let her have her moment with them."

I continue looking toward their table. "She completely avoided me after she found out today."

"What?" Nic snorts. "No, she didn't. You're being ridiculous."

I turn to Nic. "Am I?" I retort. Then I put my focus back on Seema's table. "Nic, you have great hearing. What are they saying?"

Nic squints at me. "I have good hearing, not bionic hearing." She turns to Jason. "Honey, I'm so big, getting out of this chair is going to require a forklift. Can you go to the bar and get us a bottle of champagne?"

Jason smiles warmly at the mother-to-be. "Of course." He rubs her belly, gives her a quick kiss, and heads out to hunt down bubbly.

"Is it okay to drink champagne when you're pregnant?" I ask Nic delicately.

"Of course not. It's for you."

"I've already had champagne."

"And I've already had sex. What's your point?"

"Wait," I say, surprised. "Today?"

"You're not the only one dating a hottie."

"Speaking of hotties." Jeff motions to a group of men, all in suits, sitting three tables down. "What about him? Do any of us know him?"

Our entire table makes a show of looking toward that table. "The one who looks like he was an extra in *The Godfather*?" Nic asks, lifting her upper lip in disgust like Lucille Ball in *I Love Lucy*.

"Okay, if it was him, it's not anymore," Jeff says. "No. The distinguished gentleman with the slightly graying hair."

"Oh!" I recognize the guy immediately. "That's Seema's boss. Reese."

"Hellllooooo, Reese!" Jeff practically purrs. "Gay, right?"

I nod. "Good eye."

"Fab. So what do we know? Married? Serious relationship?"

Nic shakes her head. "I know he used to date this guy named Kevin."

"They broke up," I tell Nic.

"Awwww . . . ," Nic says, her shoulders drooping. "That's a shame. I liked him. They made such a nice couple."

"Not to me they didn't," Jeff snaps at Nic, glaring at her. "Whose side are you on?"

Nic puts out the palms of her hands in surrender. Then Jeff turns to me. "How long were they dating?"

"I don't know," I say, trying to remember. "At least a few years."

"Excellent. When did they break up?"

I look up to the ceiling, trying to recall. "Maybe a month ago?"

Jeff nods. "All right. I can be rebound guy."

"Or was it six months?" I say to myself, still trying to remember.

"Even better. I can be fiancée guy." Jeff turns to Jason, now walking back to us with a bottle of Moët, which he places right in front of me. "Jason—wingman me?"

Jason turns to survey the room. "Sure. Which one?"

"Graying hair in the Prada."

A clearly confused Jason looks over to Nic for clarification.

She smiles. "The expensive black suit and ridiculously over-priced purple tie," she translates.

"Oh." Jason checks out the table. "Yeah, all right. Think any of them are into basketball?"

"God, I hope so," Jeff says as he grabs his beer and jumps out of his seat. "That way I won't have any competition."

"How come you're allowed to stereotype, but I'm not?" Nic asks.

Jeff's already halfway to Reese's table as he turns to her and quips, "For the same reason you can make blond jokes and I can't. Wish me luck."

For a moment Nic and I watch in silence as the boys flirt with the other boys. Then I turn back to obsess over Jay and Seema, who are now talking with both parents at the table. I manage to make eye contact with Jay for a brief second. He smiles and winks at me.

"What do you think of Jay?" I ask Nic as I pour myself a glass of champagne.

"What do *you* think of Jay?"

"You're a reporter, not a psychiatrist."

"Both ask a lot of questions," Nic assures me. "And both know when their subject's avoiding answering a question."

I look back over at Jay and feel a slight tightening of my gut. "I have had a crush on him for over ten years. I'd give anything to be able to throw caution to the wind and love him totally and completely without worrying about getting hurt. But I know I can't."

Nic lets out a deep breath of relief. "Oh my God, I'm *so* glad you said that."

I am a little flummoxed by her reaction. "You know, it's kind of insulting to hear my best friend happy that I won't go after my dreams."

"No, no . . . I swear that's *not* what I meant at all. But come on, your job's here, your friends are here. What are you going to do, buy a one-way ticket to Paris and just cross your fingers and hope for the best?"

It takes me a minute to respond to that. What I *want* to say is, *You quit your job to be with the man you're in love with. The man whose baby you're about to have. And here I was thinking I was ad-*

mitting to being a putz who never throws caution to the wind. But, apparently, I am just a putz. Because I have found someone who I've wanted forever, who is available, who seems to like me, and who is inviting me to Paris to be with him. That doesn't happen to a lot of women—and certainly not at our age! And I'm tired of being an also-ran. I'm going!

Instead, I sheepishly look at the tablecloth and say, "Yeah."

Nic's attempt to backtrack is so obvious, you could hear a truck beep in warning. "I mean, you know what an amazing life you have here. And you know that in the real world, people get hurt in relationships all the time. Relationships end every day. You know in your gut that you could be setting yourself up for a big fall."

I cross my arms, refuse to look at her, and instead look over at Jay. Once again, I've got a doozy of a comeback in my head: *To hell with it! I've got two months until my job starts again—if it starts again. I'm gonna take my silver cake charm with me and go find a money tree in Paris.*

Then out of my mouth comes "So you don't think there's even a chance Jay's the one?"

"You're upset."

"No," I insist, shaking my head and acting as if her observation were absurd. "I was just asking your opinion."

"My opinion isn't important. Do you think he is?"

I know if I answer anything in the affirmative, she'll think I'm an idiot, so I slowly and begrudgingly I shake my head no.

Just then, Scott, Seema, and Jay stand up to take their leave, with Seema's parents staying seated at their table to talk to other relatives. As the three head toward our table, I see Seema and Jay are both carrying manila envelopes. Jay is his usual suave, un-ruffled self, Scott is suppressing a laugh, and Seema looks as if she were about to have a stroke. As they get to the table, Seema seethes at her brother, "Seriously, how can you say nothing the entire time?"

"There's a time to throw yourself on the sword, and a time to let things go," Jay responds calmly. "Check your watch."

"Oh, my *watch*?" she snaps at him sarcastically, "Maybe I'll have a nice mother-encrusted *watch* to check."

Scott bursts out laughing. Seema points to him. "You think that's funny? Maybe we should go over to your parents' table and see what they—"

Scott waves his hands back and forth horizontally as he snorts one more time. "No, no. I'll stop," he promises.

"What were you guys talking about?" I ask nervously as I look over at their mother. "She hates me, doesn't she?" I ask Jay. Then I turn to Seema. "It was about my being a slut, wasn't it?"

"It had nothing to do with you," Jay assures me, sitting down next to me and rubbing my knee warmly.

"What's a mother-encrusted watch?" Nic asks Seema.

Seema slams her manila envelope into Nic's chest and shakes her head as she sits down. "Seriously, how are brides expected to get through a weekend of current family and future in-laws without the generous and constant application of booze?"

Nic pulls a thick, pink, eight-and-a-half-by-eleven-inch piece of paper from the envelope while asking, "Which brides do we know who do that?"

Seema shrugs. Jay says to me, "Our mother gave us each a diamond, and Seema is a bit unenthused."

"Is it encased in an ugly setting?" I ask Seema knowingly (she has a bunch of those).

"You could say that," Seema says, turning to Nic. "Read."

Nic reads from the pink piece of paper, "'This certificate entitles the bearer to a one-half-carat diamond made of the loved one's ashes." She looks up at Seema. "I don't understand."

Jay smiles. "After they're cremated, Mom is going to have some of both her ashes and my dad's turned into diamonds, which we get to keep for eternity."

"She wants me to turn mine into a necklace," Seema says, stealing my champagne flute and taking a healthy swig. "I don't want my mother around my neck forever!"

Jay turns to me. "I'm thinking of having mine turned into a dog collar."

"If you make a joke about two bitches getting Mom around their necks, I will bite you," Seema threatens. She flags down a waiter for more champagne. He appears with a tray full of flutes, which Seema quickly places two by two on our table. "Honestly, I'm not sure this wedding can get any more stressful."

"Scott, dear," Scott's mother says from behind them, "I've just talked to your aunt Debbie, and she wants to sing at the real wedding."

Real wedding?

"We're thinking 'You Light Up My Life' by Debby Boone," Scott's mother informs him, beaming at the brilliance of her suggestion.

Scott's eyes widen, but he smiles pleasantly and says nothing. Instead, without looking at Seema, he instinctually grabs her arm as she tries to lift her glass to down more bubbly.

Note to self: during one's wedding weekend, never dare the Gods by asking if the wedding can get more stressful.

TWENTY-FOUR

Around midnight, Jay and I retire to my bedroom, where we start making out, begin the dance of shedding our clothes, and try not to listen to Seema and Scott fight in the next room.

"Why didn't you just tell her your aunt is *not* singing?" Seema asks him loudly.

"Because it's not that big of a deal," Scott insists. "It's three minutes out of your life. We'll get through it."

"We'll get *through* it?! When did it get to the point where we had to get through this wedding?"

"Um . . . the minute we told our parents?" Scott responds as though the answer were brutally obvious.

I stop kissing Jay and whisper, "Should we go do something?"

"Nah, this is normal," he whispers back. "I went through this the night before I was supposed to get married."

He leans in to kiss me again, but I jut my head back away from him. "I'm sorry. Say what, now?"

Scott opens my door without knocking, causing both of us to cover ourselves up. "Guys, don't get too comfortable. We're going to Vegas."

"The wedding's tomorrow. We can't go to Vegas," Seema tells him, also appearing uninvited in our doorway.

"Why not?" Scott asks her.

"Why not?" Seema repeats as if it were the stupidest question she's ever heard. "How about because hundreds of people have already driven in, flown in, booked hotel rooms, and bought presents. We have a responsibility to them."

I turn to Jay and whisper, "Now when exactly did you get married?"

"Oh, I didn't," he whispers back.

"So we have to go through an entire day of wedding craziness just for our guests?" Scott asks Seema.

"Yes."

"But we can't go through three extra minutes for my aging aunt?"

Seema is about to respond, but she realizes she's been out-debated. She sighs, then apologetically says, "You're right. You're absolutely right."

Scott smiles and opens his arms. She walks into his hug, then asks, "When is this not going to seem so awful anymore?"

"Sunday, after brunch, when we stop being Seema and Scott and start being the Jameses."

Seema smiles. "Mrs. Seema James. I do like the sound of that."

Scott smiles back, takes her hand, and gently kisses it. "Has a nice ring to it, doesn't it?"

She's almost blushing as she grins wider and nods her head. Scott turns to us. "Sorry for the intrusion. As you were." Then he silently pulls my door shut.

"No problem," I yell through the door.

A few seconds later, once we know the coast is clear, Jay and I begin kissing again.

Okay, as hot as he is, there's no way I can let this go for more than thirty seconds. I pull away from him abruptly to ask, "When did you not get married?"

"Oh, Seema never told you about that?"

I shake my head.

"Huh. I swore her to secrecy, but mostly I meant don't tell Mom and Dad. Remember when Seema came out to Paris to see me two falls ago? I was eloping. She was going to be my best woman."

I'm stunned. Seema traveled halfway around the world to secretly support her brother, and she never even told her best friends? I mean, wow—that's loyalty. But I'm a little hurt that even when I started dating her brother, she didn't give me a heads-up.

"So what happened?"

"She left me at the altar," Jay says a little uncomfortably.

I wonder if, in the dark, he can see my eyes bug out and my jaw drop. I quickly sit up. "What idiot would leave you at the altar?"

Jay seems uncharacteristically ruffled. "Um . . . well, her name was Tatiana, she was Italian . . . she realized she loved another guy, and that was it."

"How long were you dating?"

"Not long. Almost six months. When he found out she was engaged, that motivated him to declare his undying love, blah, blah, blah . . ." Jay's voice just got a little shaky there.

I shake my head in disbelief. "What an idiot!"

He seems surprised by my outburst. "I know. We got engaged pretty early on. But I really wanted to get married and become a dad and—"

"Not you! Her! Who leaves the best-looking man on the planet? The best kisser on the planet! Jeez, the rest of us are fighting over hamburger, and she's throwing away filet mignon. It's appalling!"

That was probably a stupid way to say it. But Jay just looks at me with amusement and smiles.

"What?" I ask insecurely.

"Nothing. You're just very sweet." He takes my chin in his hand and kisses me lightly on the lips. "Where did you come from?"

"Um, Arizona?"

We kiss for a bit before I ask my next question. "So, has what she's done totally soured you to marriage, or do you still think about it?"

"Not at all. I'm dying to get married. I mean, I'm not getting any younger. And I want kids, so . . ." He shrugs. "I don't know." He puts his hand on my bra. "Do we have to talk about this now?"

I look down at his hand over my lingerie. "Well, when you put it that way . . ."

Once again, everything is amazing. A girl could get used to this.

But the best part is afterward, after he falls asleep, as I lay in his arms and listen to his gentle breathing. For the first time in a long time, I'm not in clingy phase. Or desperately-looking phase. Or wondering-if-I'll-ever-get-married phase, or wondering-where-this-is-leading phase.

Nope. For the first time in years, I am at peace and not worried about what is next.

What a wedding gift.

Twenty-five

The following morning is not so peaceful. First, Jay and I are awakened rather brutally as Seema bursts into my room at six to gleefully scream, "Wake up! Wake up! Wake up! I'm getting married today!"

The next few hours are a blur. The four of us pack up our various wedding attires for the day and take a limousine to downtown, where Seema and I are dropped off at one five-star hotel, then Jay goes with Scott to the five-star hotel down the street. Nic meets up with us, sending Jason to Scott, and the three of us spend the next few hours getting ready in the sumptuous honeymoon suite. Seema's mother and aunts take at least an hour to help Seema into her sari, a sumptuous red silk dress dripping in sparkling beads, lush gold embroidery, and Swarovski crystals, while Nic and I easily change into our lehengas and cholis (gold silk with gold embroidery for her, royal-blue silk with silver embroidery for me) and nosh on room-service pastries. Then hair and makeup people come to work on all of us until they make us glow.

About five minutes before the baraat is set to begin, Seema asks her mom and her family to go down to the lobby and tell everyone that we will meet them down there in a few minutes.

The moment Seema shuts the door behind them, she slouches over, instantly changing from a statuesque model into a camel with five too many straws on her back. "God, this dress weighs a ton. I need to lay down for a second," Seema says as she nearly falls into the plush white sofa next to her.

"Are you all right?" I ask, a little alarmed.

"I'm fine, just physically worn-out already. Seriously, with all of the crystals and beads on this thing, you might as well spend your day sporting a suit of armor. Why has no bride ever mentioned that?"

"It's probably like telling pregnant women what's really going to happen," Nic guesses. "Why ruin the dream?"

Seema doesn't move from the couch. "I have something for you guys. Mel, can you go to my suitcase and check the left front pocket? There should be two black velvet boxes in there."

I walk over to the suitcase and unzip the pouch. Inside are two black velvet, rectangular boxes. I pull them out and hold them up. "These?"

"Yup," Seema says as she struggles to sit up.

Nic grimaces a little. "Is the dress really that heavy?"

"Honestly, I don't know how Miss America contestants wear stuff like this." Seema's face lights up as I hand her the boxes. "Thank you." She flips each one open, confirms what's inside, then shuts them, handing each of us a specific box. "You're either going to think this is really cool, or really stupid. Okay, so last year, when Nic was getting married, we did that cake pull. And I got the shovel, which I thought meant a lifetime of hard work. But it actually meant nurturing and caring. And then Scott got the heart charm accidentally, and the rest, as they say, is magic."

"I think it's 'the rest is history,' " Nic corrects.

"You know, I'm trying to have a *moment* here . . ."

"Sorry," Nic says quickly.

"Anyhoo . . . open your boxes."

I open my box to see a silver bracelet tucked into black velvet. As I pull the bracelet out, Seema explains, "I made a charm bracelet for each of you. Nic, yours has a baby charm, like the one you pulled at your wedding shower, and your moon charm from my shower. Mel, yours has a chili pepper, and a money tree. And I also included a shovel on both of yours, to remind you of how much I care about you both.

"Here's to many more celebrations with many more charms."

Nic and I gush thank-you's and admire our new jewelry. As Seema helps Nic put on her bracelet, I look at my charms and smile. There's a chili pepper, a money tree, a shovel, and . . . wait . . . "There's an extra charm on mine." I look at a gleaming-silver Eiffel Tower.

"Oh, I loved that one," Seema says, finishing Nic's bracelet, then turning to me to help me with mine. "According to the chart, that's supposed to symbolize a honeymoon is in your future. But I figure in your case, this is not the universe talking. It's just your nosy roommate telling you to go to Paris and see what happens."

I smile blushingly, touched by Seema's approval. I nod slowly. "You know, I just might do that."

Seema clicks the clasp of my bracelet shut, and we both hear Nic start crying.

We turn to see her waving her hands over her face. "I'm sorry. It's pregnancy tears. Even the lame stuff is so sweet."

As Seema gives Nic a hug, my phone rings. I look at the screen to see it is Jay, who should now be in the baraat, dancing toward us. I pick up immediately. "Sorry. We were just having a girl moment."

"Scott may be making a run for it," Jay says to me under his breath.

"Shit!" I overhear a surprised Nic say.

Her damn hearing. I turn to her and glare.

I don't take my eyes off her and Seema as I say into the phone, "You know what? She looks stunning."

Without missing a beat, Nic turns to Seema and says, "I just realized your mother's probably waiting right outside your door, and she should be downstairs with the rest of your family so we can get that milni started! Mel and I are going to get her out of here."

"That's not necessary," Seema says calmly, unaware of the tornado about to hit. "We'll all go."

"No, no, *you*"—Nic points at Seema—"need to make an entrance. And we are going to make that happen." Nic grabs her phone from her purse, takes my hand, and drags me out of Seema's suite.

I continue talking to Jay very quietly. "Does your mom know yet?"

"No. The wedding planner called the bride's side to say we had a glitch, and we're coming soon. I'm going to get into a cab and track him down. Just don't let Seema know what's going on."

"Okay. Keep me posted." I hit end-call on my phone.

Nic is texting something on her phone and says, "He's not answering his cell."

"Of course he's not answering," I say a little too harshly to Nic. "Grooms don't carry cell phones!"

"They do if they're running," Nic argues.

I shake my head, as I turn to walk back into Seema's suite. "I cannot believe this is the second time in a year I am dealing with a wedding runaway."

"Excuse me," huffs Nic, offended, "I was *not* a runaway bride."

I try to give her my best sarcastic look. "How do you figure?"

"I locked myself in the bathroom. You knew where I was the whole time," she tells me self-righteously.

Yeah . . . that's much better, I think to myself. I wonder, what would it be like to be in a normal wedding? Seriously, I have to think about finding some new friends.

As I reach for the doorknob to the honeymoon suite, Nic grabs my wrist. "Don't tell her anything yet. Just stall."

I nod, unsure of the best course of action.

Nic and I walk back into the bridal suite, where Seema takes one look at us and says, "Shit. What's wrong?"

Nic and I exchange a look. Nic shakes her head no at me.

I force a smile. "Nothing."

Seema has the same look on her face that my mother used to get when she knew I was lying.

"Okay," I begin, "I need to tell you something. But you have to promise me you won't freak out."

"Has there ever been a good conversation that started with that statement?" Seema asks.

"Um, well . . ." I begin, looking up at the ceiling. "There have been some productive ones."

Nic elbows me hard in the ribs, then bulges her eyes out at me.

"Ow!" I yell, doubling over. "How is that helping?"

Nic chastises me. "Mel, I told you not to say anything yet."

I rub my belly and struggle to breathe. "Uh-huh. So we're going with the 'utter denial' card? You think that's going to work better?"

"We played that card all the time when Seema was dating," Nic reminds me. "What's it going to hurt for a few more minutes?"

Seema juts out her lip at us, but stays calm. "I'm going to pretend I didn't hear that," she tells Nic. Then she turns to me. "What's going on?"

I look down, trying to find a way to let Seema down easy. "There is the remotest possibility that your groom is MIA."

Nic shoots up her arm to elbow me again, but I instinctively jump back and point my finger at her. "You are eight months pregnant. I could totally take you."

Nic narrows her eyes and cocks her head at me ever so slightly to indicate, *Oh, you think so?*

I step another foot back. No, actually I do not think so.

Seema snaps her fingers in front of me. "Mel, eyes on me. What do you mean MIA?"

"Missing in action."

Seema raises her eyes to the ceiling. "I know what *MIA* means," she tells me with excruciating patience. "What happened?"

Nic's cell phone beeps a text. She quickly starts reading and typing back as I tell Seema, "Apparently, everyone on Scott's side gathered to start the baraat. Then Scott walked out of the lobby, got on his horse, and promptly galloped away."

Seema's eyes widen. "I have a runaway groom?"

"Now, we don't know that." I try my best to sound reassuring.

Nic reads the text from her phone. "He's been spotted racing down Olympic Boulevard, heading towards Staples Center."

"Are they sure it's him?" I ask.

Nic looks up from her phone. "How many thirty-three-year-old men wearing white sherwanis and riding white stallions do you think are in downtown today?" Nic's phone rings, and she picks up. "Talk to me."

Seema grabs her chest and begins to hyperventilate. "Oh my God. I'm being left at the altar. Who does that actually happen to? I've never heard of someone having that happen to them."

Well, that's a lie—it happened to her brother. I mean, how could she not have told me.

Wait—bad Maid of Honor! Back to the subject at hand. I try to sound soothing. "Okay, calm down. This is not the time to panic."

"Are you crazy? This is the *perfect* time to panic!" she snaps at me. "It's one of those FOAF stories you hear: the Mexican rat, and the friend of a friend who gets left at the altar after her groom leaves her for her slutty maid of honor."

"Well, obviously, that didn't happen. Your slutty maid of honor is still here," Nic chimes in.

I turn to Nic and put my hands palms up. "Really? Now?"

Nic waves me off. "What? I meant that as a good thing."

Seema continues to monologue. "And the bride ends up marrying the geek who loved her in high school, who she wouldn't even give the time of day to back then, because what other options does she have so late in life?"

Nic covers her phone. "You've just described Ross and Rachel. That never happened to anyone in real life."

"It's happening to me now!" Seema exclaims. "Oh my God. I'm going to end up spending the rest of my life with a Milton or a Leonard."

She collapses onto an overstuffed, white satin chair. "I can feel my gut clenching." Seema grabs her stomach. "Oh, God, please don't let me throw up all over my wedding sari."

Nic covers her phone. "The cops tried to pull him over, but he galloped onto the sidewalk, then escaped diagonally through the square in L.A. Live's courtyard."

I rush up to Seema and put my arm around her. "Everything's going to be fine. Scott loves you. This is just some horrible misunderstanding."

Seema starts gasping for air like a trout just yanked from the river. Nic absentmindedly hands her a paper lunch bag while she listens to more groom updates. Seema immediately grabs the bag and breathes. The bag puffs up, then contracts, puffs up, contracts . . .

"Okay, the cops have him down," Nic declares triumphantly, giving us a thumbs-up.

"Down?!" Seema exclaims just as her iPhone plays "Highway to Hell." Scott's ringtone. And a joke she's probably regretting right now.

Seema keeps exhaling and inhaling into her paper bag while I rifle through her purse, grab her phone, and pick up. "Hey," I say, attempting to be casual and breezy with Scott. "So what's going on?"

Scott sounds worried. "How's Seema doing?"

I watch Seema continue to hyperventilate into the bag. My voice is squeaky as I eke out, "Well . . . you know . . . every wedding has its little glitches."

Then Scott says the absolute worst thing a bride could hear on her wedding day. "She is going to hate me for this. I have fucked everything up. I tried, but I just couldn't do it."

I take a deep breath and quietly plan his death.

"Can you hand Seema the phone please?" Scott asks.

Seema puts down the paper bag, and I hand her the phone. I can overhear Scott on his end say, "Okay, don't hate me."

"You don't have to give up your loft," she says to him as quickly as she can, her tone desperate. "You don't have to give up your loft, and we don't have to go out to dinner on Sunday nights, and I don't need kids right away, and we can go camping in Kenya, I don't need room service, and we never have to go to Burbank again, you were right, I was wrong, the police in Burbank can be real jerks—"

Nic and I can hear Scott interrupt. "Speaking of police, I'm about to be arrested."

Seema stops talking. Pauses a moment. "I'm sorry. Say what now?"

"Turns out you need a permit to ride a white stallion through the streets of downtown Los Angeles on a crowded Saturday afternoon. Which is kind of secondary to my other offense: you're also not supposed to actually ride your horse in the streets, as it blocks traffic."

A look of understanding crosses Seema's face. "Oh my God. You can't ride a horse, can you?"

"Technically, I can. If by *ride* you mean not falling off the horse. He and I just had a little disagreement about where we were going."

Apparently, when Scott got on his horse, he spooked it, and it started running in the wrong direction from the rest of the groom's party. Scott quickly galloped past a police car, and the cop inside started his siren and told Scott to pull over. This spooked the horse even more, so it pretended to be a quarter horse and ran even faster. Soon, the horse had run off the road, and into the middle of the L.A. Live courtyard, a crowded tourist spot in front of the Nokia Center in downtown. Scott was eventually pulled over by a policewoman on her own horse, who calmed down Scott's horse and got it to stop. As soon as he got off his high horse, so to speak, he called Seema.

Within minutes, Nic is in the lobby stalling the wedding guests, and I am in a cab, racing to Olympic Boulevard and Flower Street. Soon, my taxi has pulled up next to two police cars, a chestnut-colored police horse, several police officers, Prince Charming, dressed in his white sherwani and turban, and his trusty white steed, who from here on out will be known as Soon to Be Glue Stick.

I tell the driver to keep the meter running and climb out of the cab in my full-on royal-blue silk regalia, which inspires a few tourists (and possibly some locals) to start snapping pictures with their cell phones.

I walk over to Scott, who sits at the curb, deep in thought.

I ask the policewoman if we can have a moment (we can), so I gingerly sit down next to him.

"Hey," I say softly.

Scott forces a smile. "Hey."

"The trainer is coming now. She took off for lunch, thought you had it under control. She's also bringing the permits, so I don't think you're getting arrested." Scott just stares back in response—says nothing.

So, there on the curb, the two of us sit in silence. With all my heart I want to believe that Scott is still a decent guy and that he's going to say something profound—something about romance or love, I don't know. But something that will inspire me.

However, I've been around enough guys to know they do stupid, cowardly things, and he might very well say he can't go through with it, then become a douche right in front of my eyes by waiting just long enough to indelibly humiliate my best friend in front of the people she loves most in the world.

He continues to say nothing. How the hell are men capable of saying nothing?

Finally I sigh. "Okay, so how are we going to play this?"

"I'm not getting back on that thing!" Scott exclaims with that tone of panic men get when they don't want to admit they're scared.

"You don't have to," I say, handling him in the calmest manner possible. "The trainer will take her back."

"I *do* have to. That's the problem."

"You don't have to. You don't know how."

Scott's voice starts to rise. "Don't tell me I don't know how to do something. Men have been leading baraats for thousands of years."

"Yes. Men who have ridden horses. What if the ceremony had involved flying a plane? Would you have just climbed into the cockpit without lessons?"

Scott thinks about that, sighs. He makes a growling sound that doesn't quite sound human, followed by "Fuck! So how am I supposed to lead the baraat to marry my wife?"

"I don't know. Walk?"

"I can't walk. I need to be on the horse."

"Why?"

Scott sort of blows up at me. "Why? Because otherwise I am showing my future wife that I can't do yet another thing she thought her husband would be able to do when she was a little girl playing bride. She's already learned that I can't cook, that I can't wake up in the morning on my own, that she hates my clothes, and that, yes, I watch football, and, yes, I even have a team. Do I really need to add *can't ride a horse* to that list?"

I'm not sure how to answer that. I assure him, "No one ever broke up with a guy because he couldn't ride a horse."

"But they do break up with men for ruining their wedding," Scott agrues. "Do you know what I miss about dating? All the women I went out with thought I was perfect. Whatever they thought I should be, I'd just let them think that's the guy I was. A month or two in, the cracks would start to show, I'd break up and move on."

"Yeah, and have the girl think you're a dick!" I blurt out.

"Not all women think—"

"Yes. All women. All women you break up with think you're a dick for at least the first month afterwards. We may still want to get back together, we may still want to sleep with you, but we think you're a big, fat . . . meanie!"

Scott gives me a face. "Meanie?"

For that, I shove him. "Do you have *any* idea how lucky you are that someone knows everything about you and still wants you?" I yell at him. "Do you know how many of us are still searching for that, dreaming of it, worried it may never happen for us, and you're going to throw that all away just because you can't ride a fucking horse. Get over yourself!"

I stand up and angrily say, "You're, like, really fucking awesome usually, and even if you don't see it, someone else does. So you're going to stand up, you're going to follow me into my cab, and you're going to marry that woman, quickly, before she has time to realize what a putz you're being right now. Let's go!"

I determinedly march over to the cab. Scott slowly stands up and follows me.

Huh. It worked. Note to self: being a raging lecturing bitch works.

A few minutes later, the Singh-Jameses begin a new tradition: Rather than the groom leading his family and friends to the wedding on his trusty white steed, this one rode in the backseat of a yellow Prius taxi and slowly led his party to Seema's hotel, where his bride and her group happily waited.

I have never—never—seen anyone as happy as Seema looks when Scott emerges from the cab. I watch him get out of the car, kiss her on the cheek, and whisper something in her ear.

She bursts out laughing.

Then she looks at me, standing by the cab to pay the driver, and mouths, *Thank you.*

I must be grinning from ear to ear, and I nod my head slightly and watch the two of them as they lead both families to the first ceremony of the day.

And there was much rejoicing.

Oh, except Seema's future mother-in-law was already tanked on vodka gimlets and had been hitting on Seema's dad in the lobby while I was gone. But what family can't say that?

TWENTY-SIX

The first wedding ceremony of the day was beautiful, colorful, exotic, and romantic. After Scott led the groom's party to the bride's group, we all danced over to the ceremony site.

I have never been to such a colorful wedding. Many of the female wedding guests are dressed in saris and lehengas in vibrant hues of all sorts of colors: pink, purple, green, blue, every shade of the rainbow, and many wear bangle bracelets in gold and other colors.

I've also never heard a wedding so loud. But in a good way.

At the site, the mandap has been built as a stage over the hotel pool, which also had a makeshift fire pit in the middle of it. The best of fire and water.

Seema stops at the deep end of the pool, near the stage. Scott walks up to her, and she hands him a coconut and a bright yellow garland.

Scott's bridal party (Jay and two friends) gather around him, then he is officially received by Kamala. She applies a red powder called kumkum to his forehead. I can see her whisper in his ear, "Glad you made it."

Scott smiles, bows, and leans in to her to whisper, "You and me both—Mom."

Kamala smiles as he hands her the coconut (a ceremonial gift for the new mother-in-law).

Seema's parents then escort Scott and his best man, Joe, to the mandap, where they are seated on colorful cushions near the fire pit. Jay and the other man from the bridal party then sit nearby.

Next, Seema walks over, carrying a red garland and escorted by her uncle Ravi. She is seated facing Scott, and the two prepare for the ceremony to begin.

The rest of the crowd have already gathered and take this time to remove their shoes and find seats.

I'm sort of surprised by how chaotic and loud everything is. Children are running around, including in and out of the mandap, while the ceremony goes on. Apparently, this is a good thing, as children are considered a good omen. Everyone in the audience is talking. This is nothing like the weddings I'm used to, usually solemn, almost silent ceremonies in a house of worship.

I lean over to Jay and whisper, "Hasn't this officially started? When is everyone supposed to quit talking?"

"Indian tradition," he tells me in a normal voice. "This is a celebration. People are allowed to talk, dance, even drink if they want to." He looks down at my toes. "Cute nail polish."

I want to tell him to shush but I also don't want to be disrespectful. Instead, I whisper, "Thanks."

The Hindu priest begins to address the crowd, "We have come together to wed Seema, daughter of Kamala and Mohinder, to Scott, son of Thomas and Janet. Today they build together the foundation of their marriage upon the earth, in the presence of the sacred fire and the radiant sun, among their family and friends."

The smoke from the sacred fire blows into Nic's and my faces.

We cough and shut our eyes tight. Once the smoke smells as if it's dissipating, we both open our eyes again to refocus on the ceremony.

A small choir group sings what are called slokas. Their voices are melodic as they begin, "Vignesh varaia varadaia . . ."

I lean in to Jay and whisper, "Which song is this? Whisper back."

He seems annoyed by my request to lower his voice, but whispers, "They are invoking Lord Ganesha."

"That's the elephant, right?"

"He's not an elephant—he's a deity. But he does have an elephant head. And a human body."

Fortunately for Nic and me, Jay talks us through the whole ceremony: the invocation of Saraswati, then the prayer for harmony.

The choir is soon seated, at which time Seema begins the jaimala, which the priest explains to the audience is the exchange of garlands used to symbolize the acceptance of the bride and the groom by one another. She puts her garland around Scott, and he returns the favor. Then they recite vows, pledging to respect one another as partners.

As they do this, my mind wanders to a daydream about my wedding with Jay. I know—it's stupid, and wayyyyy too fast. But what woman hasn't had at least a fleeting thought of what a handsome third date would look like in a tuxedo? It's just a harmless fantasy about placing a red, white, and yellow garland around his neck—I know I'm being silly. But I also dream of what I would do if I won the lottery, and I've never bought a ticket. Odds-wise, this dream is almost as realistic.

Next, Seema's parents ceremonially wash Seema's and Scott's feet and give the bride and groom flowers. The priest then says to

Kamala and Mohinder, "Do you, Kamala and Mohinder, approve the wedding of your daughter Seema, to Scott?"

"We do," they say, and take a seat. Scott knows this is his cue to hold Seema's hand, which he does. Then he declares, "I, Scott, take you, Seema, into my heart as my wife."

Aw . . .

She smiles. "I, Seema, take you, Scott, into my heart as my husband."

The priest once again addresses his audience. "A circle is the symbol of the sun, the earth, and the universe. It represents holiness, perfection, and peace. Do you have the rings?"

Seema and Scott, all smiles, each hold out a ring.

The priest continues, "These rings are a symbol of unity, that your lives are now an unbroken circle, and that wherever you go in the world, you will always return to one another. Please exchange your rings."

As Scott and Seema wordlessly put the rings on each other's left hand, I glance over at Jay, who gives me a smile and a friendly wink.

The priest proclaims, "And now, Seema and Scott, you are married."

And the crowd goes wild.

The couple, who had been sitting facing each other, now move to be side by side. Seema's father puts Seema's hand in Scott's. Her cousin Bindu then sings a mangalashtak, a song she composed just for Seema's wedding, with the choir.

The priest then continues, "The couple will now give rajaham, which is a sacrifice to the sacred fire."

Thank goodness someone is explaining all of this to me.

The priest turns to Jay, who stands up as Seema cups her hands and places them in Scott's cupped hands. Jay takes some rice from a bowl and puts the rice in her hands, which Seema and Scott then throw into the fire. Then they stand up.

As the two walk around the fire pit four times, chanting, their priest explains to us, "This is the mangal phera—or walk around the fire. Seema and Scott pray for happiness, long life, and good health."

Seema and Scott sit down again. Seema's quick to sit first. Several members of the audience laugh. The priest chuckles and explains to us Westerners, "It is tradition that whoever sits down first will be the boss of the marriage." He leans in to Scott and jokes, "Bet she didn't tell you that part, huh?" The audience laughs again. Then the priest continues, "Now is the time to confirm the marriage with the seven final steps, known as the saptapadi. Seema and Scott, will you please rise?"

As Seema and Scott rise and take the seven steps, the priest asks that the couple be blessed with food, strength, prosperity, happiness, and children, and that they live in harmony and be the best of friends.

Then he eyes the audience, as if they're all in on a private joke. "Scott, you may sneak a kiss to your bride."

Their kiss is chaste, but causes the crowd to erupt into joyous applause.

Seema and Scott feed each other sweets four times. Seema's mother gives Scott a gift. Scott's mother walks up to the mandap and puts a gold pendant hung on a yellow string, known as a mangalsutra, around her daughter-in-law's neck.

There's another reading and song, and we're done.

Magic.

The guests cheer and throw flower petals on Scott and Seema as the two walk offstage and into their new lives.

And that—as they say in show business—is a wrap. Well, until the next ceremony anyway.

Time to break for lunch!

Jay stands up, puts out his elbow for me to take, and leads me to party number one.

TWENTY-SEVEN

The next hour was spent taking pictures with the bridal party and their families. Jeff showed up with a tray full of Indian hors d'oeuvres for us to nosh on while we waited for the next photo setup, and two waiters took drink orders and got us anything else we needed.

(By the way—isn't that amazing? Someone who could have just enjoyed being a wedding guest not only thinking about the bride's needs, but taking the time to make sure she's taken care of? Why is it always the gay men who do that for us? Maybe wanting sex from us isn't the big behavioral motivation for men that we are told it is.)

After the pics, Seema and her cousins performed a traditional wedding dance that the bride does for her groom, then they spent time chatting with wedding guests for the next hour.

Then, while guests continued to party downstairs, Seema, Nic, and I began preparing for the craziness of wedding ceremony number two.

But not before Jay and I snuck off for a little private time.

"That was *amazing*!" I say to Jay, leaping around and practically dancing as he and I walk hand in hand through the hotel hallway toward the room he has reserved for the night. "The fire, the water, all of the color everywhere, the beautiful singing. I have never been so inspired in my life!"

"Indian weddings are pretty great," Jay agrees. "And the pulao was off the hook."

We stop at one of the doors, and Jay puts his hand on my cheek and pulls me in to kiss him.

We kiss for a few moments at the doorway, acting like teen-agers alone together for the first time.

I break away from the kiss. "I better go. Seema is expecting me. And you're supposed to be getting ready with Scott and the other boys."

"One more minute." Jay leans in and kisses me lightly on the lips. Then he takes my hands, lifts them to his lips, and gives them a gentle kiss. "I want you to see our room before you go."

Jay pulls a card key out of his pocket and slips it into the door. The green light buzzes on, and he opens the door to reveal his room, a six-hundred-square-foot confection with a white sofa, white chairs, and a king-size bed complete with luxurious white linens.

"Holy crap," I say as I walk in. There is a floor-to-ceiling win-dow showing us Southern California in all of its summer glory from twenty-five floors up. I walk up to the window to check out the view. The day is so clear, you can see the ocean all the way from downtown. "This view is spectacular."

"The view is pretty spectacular from here too."

I turn around to see Jay eyeing me lasciviously. I make a show of rolling my eyes at his compliment. Then I glance over at the front door to see that my black overnight bag has magically ap-peared in the room. "When did you have time . . ."

"Oh, I'm full of surprises," Jay promises. He takes my hand and leads me to the bed.

We begin to make out again, although every time his hand goes under my lehenga, I move it away. "We can't. Not right now."

"No one will miss us."

"The brother of the bride and the maid of honor. I'm going to guess they are."

"Seema won't mind if you're a few minutes late," he whispers, trying once again to get under my lehenga.

As if on cue, Christina Aguilera, Pink, Mya, and Lil' Kim begin belting out on his phone, "Hey sista, go sista, soul sista, go sista."

Seema's ring.

I give him a look to show I've made my point. "What? That could be anyone," Jay says jokingly.

Jay moves in for another kiss. But before we can get too far, my iPhone beep chimes in. I pull away to get my purse and answer it, "Hello."

"My mother won't go back downstairs until my bridal party is here," Seema whispers. "Where are you? Where's Nic?"

"I don't know where Nic is, but I'm—"

"She's having relations with your brother!" Jay says loudly into the phone as he doughnuts his arm around my waist playfully.

"I am not!" I vehemently deny, pushing him away and quickly getting off the bed. Then I say into the phone, "Seriously, I'm not. I'm coming right up."

"Good. Because Mom is with me, and it might be considered bad form to keep us waiting."

Yikes. "Good point, Mrs. James."

"Mrs. James," Seema repeats. "That has a nice ring to it, don't you think?"

"It does indeed. I'll be right up." I end the call.

Jay stares at the ceiling. "I think it sounds a little"—he makes up a stuffy East Coast accent—"'Muffy and my great-great-grandparents met on the *Mayflower*.' But don't quote me."

Jay crawls over to me and puts one arm around my waist, trying to pull me into bed. "You can be a few minutes late."

I lean in to kiss him again.

"No, she can't," I hear Seema say firmly on my phone. "And by the way, I'll get even with you for that *Mayflower* quip."

I stop midpucker, startled, and pick up my phone. "Did I not hang up?"

"You have to press the red end-call button, you dork," Seema tells me.

"I'm coming up now." I press the red button. Twice.

And I bolt out of the room.

I open the door to leave, but turn around in the doorway before I leave to ask, "Are you serious about me coming to Paris to see you?"

"Of course."

"I want to go," I say, then surprise myself by rephrasing that. "I mean . . . I'm going to go. I'm going."

Jay's smile gets even wider. "Perfect."

I grin, blow Jay a kiss, then practically levitate up to Seema's suite.

Twenty-eight

I race up one floor, tear down the hallway, and see Nic, sitting against the wall, doubled over in pain. "Jesus!" I run over to her and kneel down to her level. "What happened?"

"Braxton Hicks contractions happened," she says through clenched teeth. She grabs the lower part of her stomach and mutters, "Son of a fucking goddamn bitch motherfucker!"

That's succinct. "You're having contractions," I say, trying to sound calm.

"No." Nic breathes out a "Hee. Hee. Hee," as if she were doing yoga. "I'm having Braxton Hicks is all. It's false labor." She puts out her hand so I can help her up.

"Are you sure this is false labor?" I ask, as I take her hand with my left hand and put my right under her arm to help lift her up. "It sure looks real to me."

"I'm not due for another week, and no one delivers their first child early. I'm fine."

She stands up, inhales a normal breath, then smiles, back to her normal self. "See, I'm good. Just need a few Tylenol, and I'm ready to boogie."

I eye her suspiciously. "Should I call Jason?"

"Absolutely not. I'm fine."

"But he's just downstairs at the midwedding cocktail party with the girls. I could run down—"

"I said I'm fine," Nic insists, her voice seeming to issue a warning. "We have had enough drama at this wedding today. There's no reason to send a bridesmaid to the hospital just so she can be told to go home."

"Okay," I tell her, but I secretly turn on the stopwatch function on my iPhone.

The next twenty minutes are spent racing to get into our next set of bridesmaid dresses, helping Seema out of her Indian ensemble, helping her into her bridal gown and veil, and walking down to Ballroom B. Also known for the day as the Western Wedding Chapel.

As the three of us stand in the plush hallway outside the ballroom, waiting for guests to take their seats, Seema whispers to me, "How's he look?"

I peek through the golden double doors to see Scott, Scott's best man, and Jay standing at the front of the altar, waiting for the bride to make her grand entrance. Jay is gorgeous—the tuxedo makes him look so sexy, it makes me swoon.

"Awesome," I say, then turn around and announce, "And I'm going to Paris to see him!"

"Okay, I was talking about my groom," Seema points out, "but good for you."

"Are we ready for wedding number two?" the wedding planner asks as she hands Seema a massive bouquet of deep red roses interspersed with white lilies.

"We are." Seema's voice is confident and relaxed. She turns to me. "How do I look?"

"The most beautiful I've ever seen you."

And she is. She is exquisite in her ivory, floor-length bridal gown. And the V-neck of the gown perfectly frames the large raindrop-shaped ruby brooch surrounded by small white diamonds that she wears around her neck. Her shiny black hair is up in a chignon, and she wears a beautiful veil with a tiny tiara in the front made of small rubies and diamonds.

"Bridesmaid number one!" the wedding planner whispers, putting up her arms like Natalie Wood starting the race in *Rebel Without a Cause*. Nic takes her bouquet of white orchids from the planner and prepares to make her entrance.

"And . . . go!" the planner yells/whispers.

Nic doesn't move. Or I should say, only her upper body moves— forward, then bent over. I left my iPhone upstairs, but it's obvious: she's having another contraction.

A pregnant pause, so to speak. Nic gently puts her hand over her belly.

"Nic?" Seema begins.

"I'm fine." Nic tells her through a strained breath.

"Goooo . . . ," the wedding planner repeats.

Nic takes a deep cleansing breath, then forces herself down the aisle with her pregnant-woman waddle.

Seema turns to me, "Is she . . ."

"Nope," I say confidently.

"And maid of honor," the planner whispers, putting her arms up again.

I start to go, but Seema grabs my arm and asks nervously, "You would tell me the truth if she was in labor, right?"

"And maid of honor . . . go!" whispers the wedding planner, throwing her arms down.

"Of course I would," I lie.

"Because if she needs to be at a hospital . . ."

"Seema," I say, putting up the palm of my hand to stop her, "we don't get a lot of perfect moments in life. Go enjoy this one."

I then take my all-white peony bouquet from the planner and make my grand appearance in the doorway.

All eyes are on me. Ick. I hate this part. Remembering what the wedding planner instructed, I step forward with my right foot, then bring my left foot together. Right foot out, left foot together. As I take my first steps down the aisle, I slip into a bit of a daydream. One might think I would fantasize about Jay standing at the altar, excited to marry me in front of our dearest friends and family.

But, no. Actually my dream is to be allowed to run up the aisle and get my part of the procession over with. There is something sort of ridiculous about taking two and a half minutes to walk less than fifty feet. Right foot forward, left foot to close, and right foot forward, left foot to close.

My mind is racing. All I can think is *Today everything changes.* By tonight, I'll be the last of my single friends. The three of us will never have an impromptu slumber party ever again. We won't spend an hour getting ready for a fraternity party, me sneaking the Spice Girls onto the iPod, Seema changing it to AC/DC (the old stuff, with Bon Scott). We'll never talk about first dates again, or what we want in a boyfriend, or what we want to do when we grow up.

We are grown-up. For better or worse.

As I pass row five, I make eye contact with Jeff, who blows me a kiss. I smile at him and give a little wave as I walk past. Then I look over at Jay, standing with the other groomsman, looking polished, yet approachable. He smiles and gives me a wink. I smile and blush.

I take my place at the front of the altar, and the double doors close.

Silence. Ladies and gentleman—the show is about to begin.

A few seconds later, we hear the familiar first few bars of "The Bridal Chorus" from Wagner's opera *Lohengrin*. In my mind, I sing along, *Here's comes the bride, here comes the bride, here comes the bri-ide, here comes the bride.* (Okay, so I don't know the words. Wagner's German anyway.)

The golden doors open, and Seema stands there, looking resplendent. Her father links his arm into hers, then slowly walks her down the aisle. She is all smiles, glowing as she takes it all in. She makes eye contact with guests, greets them with smiles and winks, and, in the most gracious way, works the room.

When Seema finally makes her way to Scott, I see him mouth the words, *You look beautiful.* And I realize his eyes are wet.

Then I realize, so are mine.

Their ceremony is actually quite short, less than fifteen minutes. At one point Nic looks pained, but I think that may have had less to do with Braxton Hicks and more with the wincing we all tried to stifle at Scott's aunt Debbie's rendition of "You Light Up My Life."

When the first few bars of "Wedding March" by Felix Mendelssohn begins, Scott takes Seema's hand, and the two walk down the aisle as man and wife. Again.

I follow a few moments later with Scott's best man. Then Jay puts out his arm for Nic to take, and the two of them walk down the aisle.

And let the party begin!

TWENTY-NINE

Nic managed to get through another set of photo ops without anyone's suspecting a thing. Now, while Jay, Seema, and Scott pose for photos with immediate family, Nic, Jason, and I are able to hang out during the last part of the cocktail hour, which is being held in the funky gold lobby just outside the ballroom. The gold perfectly accents Seema's bridal palette of dark red, which includes dark red tablecloths, maroon cocktail napkins, and deep red roses in red vases. The bartenders and servers even serve a signature drink that looks like a bloodred martini. Dracula would be impressed.

Nic, Jason, and I stand at a small cocktail table covered in a dark red silk tablecloth with a ruby-jeweled overlay. Jason and I try the red martinis while Nic nurses her club soda. I take my first sip, then nearly do a spit-take, "Ewww . . . What do you think is in this?"

Jason sniffs his drink, takes a cautious sip, then tries to suppress his gag reflex. "I don't know. Blood sausage maybe?"

Nic turns to him. "Is that a thing?' "

"In LA, you never know," he says, sniffing his cocktail again. "Maybe it's an acquired taste."

"It's weird," I say, but try another taste. I shake my head quickly. "No. It's even worse the second time. Which is strange, because Seema hasn't had a misstep at either of her weddings."

"You mean other than putting her groom on a horse?" Nic reminds me.

"Could happen to anyone," I joke.

Jeff walks up to our table, looking handsome and flawlessly put together in a Prada tuxedo. He is peeved. "Do you know what's wrong with men?"

"They fall all over themselves to court you until they've slept with you, then quit calling?" I guess.

"They love sports," Nic guesses.

"Hey now," Jason, the basketball coach, jokingly warns her.

I excitedly put up my hand. "Oh! Oh! I know. They text instead of calling." Then I rethink it and come up with an even better answer. "Wait, no! They're slobs!"

"They don't know how to dress!" Nic speculates.

"Oh—they're sluts!" I continue.

"They actually say what they mean instead of what you want to hear!" Jason answers.

Nic turns to Jason. "Yeah. We hate that."

"You do," Jason assures her. "You say you don't, but you do."

Jeff rolls his eyes. "Okay, the question was mostly rhetorical. Although, Mel, I like your answer about them being slobs. No, it turns out Christophe has a boyfriend."

Oops. "Well," I try to reason, "does it matter? You were only seeing him for the weekend."

"Whom he brought to the wedding," Jeff elaborates.

Nic and I both cringe.

"*And* who just asked me if I wanted to have a threeway."

That pretty much gets a "Eeewww" from everyone at the table.

Jeff turns to Jason. "Why are men such pigs?"

Before Jason can answer, Nic blurts out, "Oh, I love this game! Shorter chromosome!"

"Rhetorical!" Jeff interrupts.

I raise my hand. "But I have a good one."

"No," Jeff says firmly. "I was just saying men are pigs"—he points toward Christophe and his (rather large) boyfriend—"and that one's got to be at least a three-hundred-pounder hog." He takes a sip of my drink and makes a face. "Ugh. Saffron?! Honestly, when did people start believing they could put whatever they want into a martini glass and it was art? The only thing worse than signature drinks at weddings is people writing their own vows. I need a beer. What can I get everyone?"

"Anything to wash the taste out," I say.

"Story of my twenties." He pats Nic on the belly. "Mama, are you good? Should I track down some mini lamb chops from a passing waiter?"

"I'm fine. And always," Nic answers.

"Then I will be right back."

Nic turns to Jason. "I do not hate it when you say what you really mean."

He tilts his head, accepting her challenge. "I want to watch golf and baseball all day tomorrow."

Nic shakes her head. "That is so not happening. But I'm glad you were honest about it."

"And I never, ever, want to watch another romantic comedy that stars Meg Ryan, Channing Tatum, Robert Pattinson, or any leading lady whose first name is Jennifer."

Nic rolls her eyes. "Fine."

"Plus I don't really care if the baby's new sheets have the elephant print or the ducks."

Nic's jaw drops. "How can you like the ducks? Seriously—dude!"

A waiter walks up to us, carrying a silver tray of lamb chops. "Would anyone care for a lamb chop?"

Nic turns to me. "He's fast."

I sigh. "I know. I should have married him when I had the chance." I watch Nic's jaw clench, and her hand slowly close into a fist. I roll my eyes. "Oh, for God's sakes! Just go to the damn hospital!"

Nic's jaw is still clenched. "And miss filet mignon with peppercorn sauce and twice-baked au gratin potatoes? No, I don't think so."

Jason turns to her. "Wait. Are you in labor?"

"No. I'm having Braxton Hicks."

"Which are now about ten minutes apart," I tell Jason.

"That's not true," Nic tells Jason.

I hand Jason my iPhone with the stopwatch function. "I've been recording her for over an hour."

He reads my recorded times and looks up at Nic with concern. "Don't you think . . ."

She puts up her index finger as if to signal, *Hold that thought.* "Holy. Fucking. Shit," she says, leaning onto the table and holding her breath.

Jason calmly suggests, "Honey, we need to get you to the hospital."

"I'm not missing this wedding. I'm fine."

"You're not fine. You're having our baby. And I would prefer that you do it in a hospital. With a doctor, and sterile equipment, and drugs."

Nic shakes her head. "We're not doing drugs."

I can tell from the look on Jason's face, they've been having this argument for a while. "Baby, would you do a root canal without drugs?"

"If I was pregnant, yes."

"No!" I blurt out.

"A little more support . . ."

"Remember that time in Santa Barbara when you needed a Vicodin?"

"I was twenty," Nic counters.

"It was an ingrown toenail," I remind her.

Nic takes a deep breath and says through gritted teeth. "It was a painful toenail. And . . . again . . . I was twenty!"

Jason calmly helps his wife stand up and looks deep into her eyes. "Honey, if I'm wrong and it's not labor, I will spend the rest of my life apologizing. But, please, just for my sake, can we go to the hospital, just to make sure you're okay?"

Nic considers his request, then shakes her head. "I'm sure I'll be fine."

"Just . . . for me then? Please?"

Nic sighs as she stares at her husband. "How can I resist that face?" She turns to me. "Text me later?"

I smile and give her a hug. "Of course."

"You don't think Seema will be mad that I'm leaving?"

"I think she'd be more mad if your water broke all over the plush hotel carpet."

The next time I saw Nic, she was introducing me to her new baby boy.

THIRTY

The wedding reception continued the magic until midnight. The food was amazing, the drinks top-notch, and the best part? I did not once have to dance Gangnam style, point to my ring finger to Beyoncé, or try to get through the Electric Slide.

At one point, Jay requested "Wonderful Tonight," which became our last slow dance of the night. But even that could not compete with the joy of watching Seema dance the samba with Jeff. Halfway through the song, she pulled off her strappy heels and tossed them to me, then danced with abandon.

I think at least once in every wedding, the bride should dance with abandon. There are so many wonderful yet solemn moments: the first dance, the father-daughter dance, sometimes a mother-son dance. Sometimes you need a little Santana and that Matchbox Twenty guy, whose name escapes me, to really let loose.

Seema and I madly texted Nic back and forth all night, but unfortunately she was still in early labor, so we had no news.

Those of us who know how to close a party (and Seema knows how to close a party) had a final toast of champagne about midnight, then retired to our rooms to launch a few intimate soirées of our own.

Which Jay and I did for quite a romantic while.

The room is now silent, millions of floors away from the Sturm und Drang of the city below. I rest in Jay's arms and stare out the window overlooking the glittering lights of Los Angeles.

Jay whispers in my ear, "Penny for your thoughts?"

I could have gone romantic. Or sexy. Maybe even playful. Instead, I went with the truth. "I'm just wondering where the expression *hit that* came from."

Jay doesn't answer, so I sit up and turn around to face him. "You know, like, when guys point to a girl and ask their buddy, 'Did you hit that?' 'Would you hit that?' 'Are you gonna hit that?' Who was the first douche bag to come up with that? It's such a violent way to express what can be a very tender and spiritual act."

Jay sits up. He looks sleepily at me in the dark. "Is that really what you're thinking about right now?"

"Yes," I say to him with some urgency. "Now the expression *bagging a bridesmaid*—that kind of makes sense. One could argue that if you seduce the woman between two sheets, it's sort of a makeshift bag. And while the idiom *tapping that ass* is crude, it could be construed as being akin to tapping a maple tree for syrup, or a keg for beer: one is extracting a kind of nectar, if you will. Graphic, but descriptive."

"Is my jaw dropped?" Jay asks quietly, then says almost to himself, "I feel like my jaw should be dropped."

"*Bone* obviously refers to the—"

Jay interrupts me by gently putting his hands up to my cheeks and giving me a kiss. It is a nice kiss, soft and romantic. I allow

my thoughts to take five while I breathe in the scent of his cologne and enjoy the warmth of his body.

When we stop kissing, Jay answers, "*Hit that* is probably just a
mindlessly insulting continuation of the expression *hitting on.* As
in to *hit on* a young lady. Nothing violent or insulting intended.
Now let's get some sleep."

"Okay," I say, smiling. We both lie back down. I nestle into the
spot between his chest and his arm and close my eyes to settle in
for the night.

About thirty seconds later, I pop my eyes back open. "You're
probably right," I blurt out. Then I push myself to continue the
conversation. "Well, I mean, about it not being intended to be violent. But I think it *is* intended to be insulting. I mean, really: *hit
on, bag, bone, tap, nail.* They're all expressions men use to let us
know the act meant nothing to them. We're just antlers on the
wall, a tapped-out tree, a dead cat."

Jay opens his eyes, confused. "A dead . . . ? Does this have something to do with the fake cat funeral Jason went to in order to woo
Nic?" Jay asks in a sleepy, now weary, voice.

"No, it has to do with Schrödinger's blow job." My voice is
fully awake.

"Wait . . . The piano player from Charlie Brown who Lucy has
a crush on?"

"Oh my God! That's Schroeder. Ew!"

"Okay, stop," Jay tells me firmly. "Your brain is going a mile a
minute. What's up?"

As I face him, I debate how to tell him what I'm dying to say,
I love you. I want you. I ache for you. Instead all I come up with is
"I wish you weren't leaving tomorrow."

"Honey, I wish I wasn't leaving either. But I keep inviting you to Paris. You can come see me whenever you want. What happens next is totally up to you."

"So you didn't just bag a bridesmaid because it's tradition?" I ask, my voice dripping insecurity.

Jay laughs lightly. "No." He looks deep into my eyes and jokes, "I bagged a bridesmaid because after more than ten years, she finally didn't have a boyfriend."

I laugh and give him a hug. "Thank you."

"You're welcome," he says as he lightly strokes my back.

I pull back to face him. "You know, I *could* turn this around and say I bagged a groomsman."

"I can handle that. I like the sound of that."

"I nailed him. He was bagged and tagged. Locked and unloaded. I was the one in control."

"Well, I wouldn't go that far," Jay jokes.

I point to him. "You know how else I am going to be in control?"

"How?"

Okay, Mel, are you really going to do this? If you're really going to do this, now is your moment. You'll never have the guts to tell him this once he leaves. I take a deep breath.and declare "I'm accepting your offer. I'm coming to see you in Paris."

Judging from his smile, he seems genuinely delighted. "Great. When do you want to come?"

I decide to go for broke. "How about next week?"

Aw, why did I do that? Now I am going to completely freak him out.

He seems surprised, but unfazed. "Great. Can we please make it any day after Tuesday?"

"Sure." Then I can't help myself and ask suspiciously. "Why Tuesday?"

"Have to get the Swedish twins out of my house." Re: my jaw involuntarily dropping, "I'm kidding! I swear, I'm kidding. I just want the maid to come before you get there. That's all."

"So I really can come?"

"Over and over again."

"That's not what I meant."

"Well, six of one . . ."

Thirty-one

Five days later, everything was different. Seema and Scott were on a safari in Tanzania, Jay was back in Paris, Jeff was back in Maui, Nic was at home with her new baby, and I was wondering if I was out of my goddamn mind.

"What the hell am I doing in New York?" I exclaim to Nic over the phone from a bar at Kennedy airport. "I am out of my goddamn mind!"

The cheapest fare I could get to Paris for that Thursday had a connecting flight through JFK. Which wouldn't be so bad, except that I'm here for four and a half hours. Just enough time to have nothing to do in the airport, but not enough time to grab a taxi, see the city for a few hours, go back through security, and be at my gate in time for the next flight.

I've decided to use this time productively, and by that I mean completely freak myself out.

"Okay, so I got laid at a wedding," I continue, taking a healthy sip of a glass of wine. "Big deal—happens to maids of honor all the time. They don't go half-cocked to the other side of the planet for a booty call!"

I see a nice-looking man a few seats away crack up a little as he reads his book. Pretty sure he's laughing at me.

"Okay, I wouldn't normally say this a few hours before a man is seeing you naked, but are you anywhere near a box of doughnuts?" Nic asks.

"I also should have taken business class. There were some nice business seats for only twenty-two hundred dollars more each way."

"Do you have twenty-two hundred dollars more each way?"

"Of course not. My God, do you realize I am literally traveling halfway around the world for sex? How pathetic is that?"

It takes me a minute to notice Nic hasn't responded. "You're not saying anything. Is it that pathetic?"

"Huh," Nic spurts out, sounding startled. "Sorry. I think I fell asleep for a second there. What did you say?"

"I said I'm out of my mind," I repeat calmly. "What was I thinking?"

"You're thinking a handsome man who lives in Paris invited you there, and that it was time to use your damn passport."

"I should have just married Fred when I had the chance. Gotten it over with."

"Now you are out of your fucking mind. He cheated on you every chance he got."

I shrug. "Every relationship has its issues."

"And what does that even mean? 'Gotten it over with'? What exactly are you getting over?"

"Dating. If I had just gotten married when the opportunity presented itself, I'd be done now. No flying to the other side of the planet for sex. If I wanted sex, I'd just roll over and tap someone."

The good-looking man near me tries to suppress a laugh. Since he's reading a book, I hope he's laughing at the book and not me.

"Yeah. That's why we get married," Nic says, yawning, as she rocks her new baby softly. "All the easy sex."

"And the being done."

"Yes. It's just one giant finish line over here." She yawns again and closes her eyes.

"Maybe I should quit my job."

"In this economy?" Nic asks with closed eyes.

"Okay, I have to move. Maybe I should move to the Westside. Or maybe I should run for political office. Or take up knitting. Or rescue a dog. I don't know—something."

"You're going to France for sex. That's something."

"It's crazy."

"True. But it's something."

I shake my head. "It's not enough, and it's temporary, a few weeks at the most. I need to make a change. A concrete, long-lasting change." I take a moment before I say the next words out loud. "What I'm doing day to day is not how I want to spend the rest of my life. You have the baby and your family, Seema has Scott. I don't have any responsibilities yet. And if I don't do something different now, I don't think I ever will."

Nic opens her eyes. She seems to have really heard me. She nods. "Okay. So what should be different? How do you want to spend the rest of your life?"

I sigh. "I have no idea. According to the charm I pulled, I'm gonna make a lot of money. Maybe I should start by playing the lottery?"

"I wouldn't read too much into that charm. My experience with those charms is that they're never what they appear to be. I think my charm was right—I am leading a wild nightlife. Meaning I no longer sleep at night."

"You're only in day four."

"Don't remind me. I didn't sleep during the month leading up to when he was born because I got up every twenty minutes to pee. So I was ridiculously overtired before I even started day one. I promise you—God is a man with a twisted sense of humor. No woman would do this to her bitches."

"Do you want me to come home and help?"

"Absolutely not. Jason's mom is here now, and my mom's coming next week. You go have your sex. I do think I better get the baby into bed though. He'll be up in less than three hours for the next round of breast-feeding."

I smile and say softly, "He's a really cute baby."

I can hear the smile in her voice when she says, "Yeah, he is. Thanks."

There are so many things I want to say: how terribly lucky she is. How desperately I want what she has. How much I admire her for always having her life so together. Instead I just say, "Promise you'll call me if you need anything."

"With the eight-hour time difference, you'll be the perfect person to call during the two A.M. feeding. Love you."

"Love you too."

"Now go have sex with someone while you still have a taut tummy."

I laugh. "Will do."

And she's off.

I click off my phone and kill time by checking for texts, phone messages, and e-mails.

The cute blondish dude a few seats away from me looks up from his book. "If it's any consolation, I've flown across the country for sex."

I think about that for a minute. "Not quite as crazy, since it doesn't require a passport. Plus, you're a guy. It's different."

"In what way?"

"You are the man—you are the aggressor. Society decided a long time ago that your team makes the passes and rushes yards to get a touchdown. My team, on the other hand, plays defense."

He nods, smiling at my wording. "I do make a lot of passes."

"Therefore, it's way more pathetic as a girl."

The guy laughs and points to the empty seat next to me. "May I?"

"Sure," I say, moving my purse over.

He closes his book and takes the seat beside me. I jut my chin toward the book. "What are you reading? Is it any good?"

"Something called *Six-Word Memoirs*. My mom gave it to me for the plane."

"Ahhh, your mom. That explains why it's an actual book, you know with paper and binding."

He laughs again. He laughs easily, I like that. "Indeed. After finishing it, I plan to listen to a mix tape on my Walkman."

I look at the cover of his book. "I've heard about *Six-Words*. My friend is doing an ar—" I stop myself. Although I love Scott, and I know he's successful at his job, somehow saying *My friend is doing an art installation based on its premise* sounds pretentious as hell to me. So I bend the truth a bit. "My friend was teaching my class about it for a project."

Handsome dude rests his face on his left hand and focuses all of his attention on me. "Cool. Are you a writer?"

"Teacher." I think about that and awkwardly correct myself. "Or at least I was until this past June. I taught math."

He nods. "And what do you do now?"

Crap. I have just discovered a more diabolical question to have to answer than *Why is a girl like you still single?* "It's a long story," I evade.

He checks his watch. "Well, I've got about an hour. And you, from what I understand, have about four and a half hours until you're off to Paris."

My eyes widen. "Were you eavesdropping?"

"We're the only two people in the bar, and I'm reading a book my mother gave me. Of course I was eavesdropping." His eyes twinkle. "You're very fun to listen to, you know."

I smile and look away from him shyly for a moment. "Why is it the charming ones are always only around for an hour?"

"Because it's easy to be charming when you're only on deck for an hour." He points to my wineglass. "What are you drinking?"

"Wow. Okay, *that* is charming."

"What is?"

" 'What are you drinking?' Not 'Can I buy you a drink?' More of an observation: 'I have noticed that your glass is getting empty, and I would like to take care of you.' "

Blondie smiles and looks up at the ceiling for a moment. "Thanks. I think. So what are you drinking?"

"Cabernet."

He looks at the bartender. "Kyle, can you get us a bottle of your best cabernet and two glasses?"

I point to his pint, now empty, save the beer foam. "Oh, but you're drinking beer. I don't want to—"

"Nonsense. I get to be charming for an hour. What man can resist that opportunity? So, you wanna tell me about the guy?"

"Yes. But first, can I ask you a personal question?"

"When I was sixteen," he answers immediately.

I laugh a little. "No. What's your name?"

"Ben."

As Kyle the bartender uncorks our cabernet, I put out my hand. "Hi, Ben, I'm Mel."

He shakes my hand. "Mel. Short for . . . ?"

"Not telling. Too much fun to be a woman of mystery—if only for an hour. So, you want to tell me about the girl?"

Ben looks confused. "What girl?"

"The girl you flew across the country to have sex with."

"Oh, her! Nothing to tell," he says, shrugging. "College sweet-heart. We ran into each other at a reunion. She invited me to visit her, I flew out, disaster ensued. You?"

"I've had a crush on him since I was eighteen. Saw him at a wedding last weekend, he invited me to Paris, so I'm going. Do you think I'm crazy?"

"You know, I might not be your best judge. I wish you luck though."

"Thanks."

Kyle finishes filling our glasses and places the bottle between us. Ben raises his glass for a toast. "Here's to doing crazy things in our youth in search of love, and even crazier things in our old age once we've found it."

I smile, and we toast.

"Do you believe in fate, Ben?"

"I'm gonna go with no."

I nod slowly. Right. He's right—I knew that.

Ben points to me. "I'm assuming you're going somewhere with this though, so continue."

"I went to this bridal shower for my friend—"

"And you got depressed because it wasn't you."

"Why does everyone assume a single woman can't be happy for her engaged friend?"

"For the same reason I couldn't be happy for my college room-mate making five million dollars before he turned twenty-eight."

"Software?"

"What else could have made that kind of money so quickly? Seriously, he had been out of school for less than six years. Who does that?"

"I hear that. But in the case of *my* friend, I am actually very happy for her. That wasn't my point."

Ben gives me a doubting look. I make a show of rolling my eyes. "Okay, I wasn't as happy for her as I should have been, but that's still not my point. My point is we did this cake thing at the party, and this charm told me I was going to make a lot of money."

He furrows his brow, confused. "I'm sorry, wait. It *told* you?"

"Yeah . . . Well, it's kind of like the charm you pull is supposed to symbolize your fate."

He nods slowly, still not getting it, but continuing to be charming for my hour. "Okay, so it's like an augury?"

"Yes!" I say, raising up my hand and pointing to him excitedly. "It's like an augury. Do you believe in auguries?"

"No."

I wave him off quickly. "You're a guy, of course you don't. Anyway, my *augury* didn't tell me anything about love or happiness, it just said I was going to make a lot of money. And I shouldn't be depressed about it, but I am. I don't want money—I want romance, love, adventure, a reason to want to go to work every day. And then I started to wonder—are we all fated to our destiny, does everything happen despite ourselves? Or, if we make enough of an effort, can we change things? I mean, a planet naturally goes around in space over and over again, but if you use enough energy to push, it *can* leave its orbit. I mean, that's just physics, right? So there might be a L'Arbre d'Argent in Paris. Maybe it's a restaurant, and maybe the charm wasn't dooming me to have money instead of love. Maybe it's just trying to tell me that I need to go to Paris."

"L'Arbre d'Argent?"

"It's French for 'money tree,' Do you want to see my money tree?"

He opens his mouth, but I shut him down. "It's not a sexual thing, if that was your joke."

Ben shrugs. "Honey, you threw that right down the middle for me, I had to swing."

He called me honey. Why am I just a little bit happy that he called me honey? I put out my wrist and show him the money-tree charm on my bracelet. "What do you think?"

He gently takes my wrist and gives the bracelet a good, long look. Finally he says, "I don't know what I'm looking at."

Embarrassed, I pull my hand away. "Never mind. Maybe this is a girl thing. Girls are superstitious about psychics and charms and fate. Men don't understand."

"No, no. I think I get what you're saying. And men can be superstitious. There are a bunch of athletes who have lucky charms of some sort or another: a pair of socks, lucky numbers on their jerseys, maybe a routine they do right before the game. So why not have a charm that means something to you?"

"Thanks," I say, self-consciously glancing at my charm before returning my gaze into his green eyes. "I know logically it's stupid, but I still keep trying to find meaning in the damn thing."

"I think I know what it means."

He's patronizing me. I roll my eyes playfully. "No, you don't!"

"Sure I do. Your life was okay, and going along pretty much as you planned it. But it wasn't great—and you weren't excited about anything anymore. So, no matter what that charm ended up being—an airplane, a heart, a puppy, whatever—you had already decided that that charm was telling you that you needed to change. And now you're changing."

I suddenly feel a little sick, and totally exposed. He may have a point. Shit! Am I that much of a basket case?

We hear a woman announce over the loudspeaker in Bronx English, "Flight Eighty-Six to Los Angeles International Airport will begin boarding in five minutes."

"Whoa. It must be later than I thought," Ben says, pulling out his wallet. "Kyle, can I get the check?"

Kyle immediately places the bill on the counter. I reach to pick it up, but Ben gets to it first, throwing down a credit card before I can even see the bill. "No, no. It's on me."

"But you barely had anything. And most of the bottle's still left."

"And you have four more hours until Paris. Enjoy. And enjoy Paris."

He smiles at me, and for one silly moment I don't want him to go. Something about him makes me feel relaxed and okay with the world. So I hint, "Do you live in LA?"

"Nope. Doing a big seeing-the-family run. Saw my parents in New York, now I'm going to see my sister and her kids."

"Oh," I say, disappointed.

Kyle gives Ben his card back with a receipt. Ben signs it quickly, takes his book and his carry-on, and stands up. He puts out his hand. "I had a lovely time, Mel . . ."

"Melissa," I say, taking his hand to shake it. "Good luck, Ben."

"Benoit."

"Benoit? Is that French?"

"Oui." He gives me a flirtatious smile. "My mom's family is from there. See why I don't believe in fate? All the times I went to Paris in my childhood, not once did I meet a vision of loveliness going there in the hopes of finding sex. I can't catch a break."

I smile. "Vision of loveliness, huh?"

"Too much?"

"No, no. Gotta say, you pulled it off. Charming as hell."

He shrugs, still smiling. "Turned out I only had to be for less than an hour."

Ben starts to walk away, then stops. He turns around and walks back to me, puts down his carry-on, takes my hand, and kisses it. "I really wish I hadn't met you in an airport."

I blush. I am speechless. He smiles, picks up his carry-on, and turns to leave. As I watch him walk away, I call out, "Hey! Your last name wouldn't happen to be Arbredargent, would it?"

Ben turns back to me, smiles, and yells back, "Honey, if it had been, we'd already be on our way to city hall to get married."

I laugh. "So what would your six-word memoir of our time together be?"

Ben gets this almost wicked look in his eyes. " 'Fell in love for an hour.' You?"

" 'Saw change. It didn't scare me.' "

He nods his head at me approvingly, then turns around and walks out of my life.

I sure liked the way he called me honey.

I sip my wine and check my e-mails. One from Seema just came in:

Scott was bitten by a green mamba snake before the safari even started. He's fine, and in recovery. But we are soooooo never doing another cake pull.

THIRTY-TWO

I managed to get a few hours of sleep on the flight from New York to Paris, which was good because we landed around eight in the morning, Paris time, and I had no idea what to expect of the day ahead.

The view from my window before we landed was nothing like what I thought it would be. Instead of a huge cityscape, with the Eiffel Tower in plain view, the scenery was incredibly green and farmlike. It looked more like what Scotland looks like in my head. Not bad by any means—just totally different from how I pictured it.

Soon my plane lands at Charles de Gaulle Airport, taxies on the runway for a rather lengthy time (Are we going to that gate? No. That gate? No. How may fucking gates are in this terminal?), then finally parks at Terminal 2 (Deux).

I'm officially in Paris!

Okay, well, an airport outside Paris, which basically looks like every other airport I've been to. As I walk out of my gate and trudge toward customs, it occurs to me that I could have accidentally jetted into Detroit or Chicago. Other than the "Je vous blah,

blah, blah" lilting over the loudspeaker system, and everyone's dressed much better. Very few T-shirts and sneakers here.

Customs takes awhile, which gives me time to freak out again. I haven't booked my return flight yet. Will that make me look stalkery, or will Jay think it's a good thing? Spontaneous, whimsical. Although I have Jay's phone number in Paris, I don't know how to use the French phones yet, and I turned off my phone before we left New York. What if he isn't here waiting for me? What if I can't find him?

I'm next in line, and other than for the tightening of my gut that I feel every time I face police, I am fine. I show my passport, they ask me a few questions, and I am on my way. I wheel my old, black suitcase through the arrivals exit, and there he is.

I catch my breath. Everything is going to be perfect.

Jay's dressed more formally than in Los Angeles, with a freshly ironed button-up shirt that shows off his buff chest and small waist, a pair of dark blue jeans, and black Mephisto loafers. His face lights up when he sees me, and he puts out his arms and pulls me into a bear hug. "Hey, kiddo! You made it!"

Kiddo?

I hug him back, and being in his arms again feels so good that I forget all about kiddo.

We begin kissing, making out for so long that I'm positive people are telling us to get a *chambre*.

Finally, the two of us come up for air, just long enough for me to see an older, blond woman glaring at us. "Oops," I say to Jay, blushing a little, "I think maybe we overdid it. People are staring."

He glances around to see whom I'm looking at, and his eyes make contact with the blonde. He leans in to me and whispers, "Oops is right. Let me introduce you."

Jay takes me by the hand and walks us over to the woman. He

brightly says, "Bonjour," gives her a kiss on each cheek, tries to introduce me—

And then gets slapped.

Uh-oh. I think I've seen this episode before.

Jay doesn't miss a beat. He puts his hand over his cheek, smiles at the blonde, and begins speaking to her in rapid French. His voice is warm and conciliatory, though his words are mostly gibberish to me. Apart from the occasional *elle* and *je suis,* I am completely lost.

The blonde yells in French, then switches to . . . Italian, maybe?

His French then sounds placating. When I hear him say the name Melissa, I smile and wave to the woman. She returns my smile with a glare as Jay keeps talking.

About a minute later, Jay once again kisses her on each cheek, only this time she kisses back, placated, and utters a crisp "Au revoir."

And she walks away.

What the hell was that all about?

Jay smiles at me warmly, takes my wheeled luggage, puts his arm around me, and brightly says, "We could take the train in, but I'm thinking a taxi. Are you hungry?"

"Wait. Who was that?"

"Oh, that was Simone. She's very high maintenance. Forget about her."

"But she slapped you."

"Oh," he says, as though he had already forgotten that part, "well, I probably deserved it. Let's get you some crêpes."

"Okaaaayyyy," I say, dragging out the words in the hopes I get more of an explanation.

Jay turns to me, kisses me lightly on the forehead, then leans in to almost whisper, "I'm so glad you're here."

"Me too." Though my Spidey sense is up.

Jay looks me in the eye mischievously, then proposes, "You know, instead of crêpes, we could go straight to my place and get you settled in."

Who could resist such a suggestive suggestion?

We take a cab to his apartment in the eighteenth arrondisse-ment (a French word that basically just means "section of the city") and settle in.

We settle in for several hours.

Thirty-three

Around noon, I awake from a catnap in the nicest sheets I think I've ever slept on in my life, and with an afterglow that could last until Christmas. A note is on Jay's pillow:

I went out to get picnic supplies. Was going to wake you, but you looked so cute. Back in a bit.

I sigh contentedly and lie back down in the bed.

I'm in Paris, and for the first time in a long time I feel excited about the day and the future.

I look over at the light streaming through Jay's bedroom windows. The sunlight feels different from home—brighter. I know Paris isn't called the City of Light because of the sun, but today it sure feels like it could be.

And it's not just the sun. *Everything* here feels different. More romantic. Better.

I stare out of Jay's window at the stone buildings across the street, with their bow windows sticking out from well-preserved grayish-white rock, and their ornate cast-iron balconies. What an insane view. And this isn't some hotel where you pay through the nose for a view for one night; this is just Jay's day-to-day Paris view. It's like nothing I've ever seen. Breathtaking.

I watch a woman in an apartment across the way watching TV in her robe and slippers. How can anyone here ever have time for television when there's nothing but amazing things to look at everywhere you turn? I mean, she could be getting groceries right now! Doesn't she know that?

Jay lives in a two-bedroom apartment in Montmartre, near the trendy Abbesses area, and near the Sacré-Coeur. The apartment was built well over a hundred years ago, but it has clearly been restored: all of his floors are dark, shiny hardwood, set in a diagonal pattern, and no cracks anywhere in the walls. (I live in Los Angeles—earthquake territory. If you don't have cracks in your walls, your house was just built last Tuesday.)

I ease out of the million-thread-count white sheets to grab my black J.Crew dress from the floor. I slip it on and make my way into the living room to get my luggage.

While his living room still has the slight feel of a bachelor pad (what is it with men and giant flatscreen TVs that take up an entire wall?), it looks like something out of a men's magazine that would be entitled "How to Lull Your Women into a False Sense of Security." He has tastefully decorated in earth tones and reds, and the couch and matching chairs are overstuffed and comfy. Coffee-table books are set out on his dark wood coffee table—one of Paris at night, and one of Paris in the day, plus an assortment of glossy art books from museums around the world.

In our haste to get to the bedroom, I left my suitcase on the floor by his front door. I wheel my suitcase into his bedroom, open it to find my makeup bag, and head into his bathroom.

The bathroom has stone tiles of various shades of green, and a green, stand-alone tub with gold claws. You know those gold talons at the bottom of bathtubs that look ridiculous in the middle of the suburbs of America? Those same feet look completely appropriate here, and positively decadent.

I peruse his shower caddy, which only holds basic shampoo and soap. How on earth can someone own a tub like this and possibly use the shower? Then I notice that he has three bottles of bubble bath in a basket on a wooden stand near the sink.

Nice.

I open the first bubble bath, a clear bottle with purple liquid inside and the word *Lavande* scrolled on the label. I sniff—*lavande* must mean "lavender." The next bottle says *Rose* in purple calligraphy on its pastel pink label. One sniff brings me back to New Year's Eve, when Seema and I regularly check out the rose floats that will be in the Tournament of Roses parade the next day. The third bottle says *Satsuma*, which I already know is orange.

Gotta love European men. The only American men I know who have bubble bath have girlfriends or wives to go with . . .

Wait a minute.

I can't help myself. I slam his bathroom door shut, then quickly open his medicine cabinet, to look for . . .

Again, wait a minute. What am I doing? This poor man is letting me stay in his home alone, and I'm rewarding his trust by rifling through his things? At what point in my life did I get so suspicious that I have to paw through a man's medicine cabinet in search of . . .

I knew it!

I pick up a pink toothbrush. Hah! No man uses a pink toothbrush! Not even a metrosexual from Paris. (Or at least I don't think so. Of course, I may have read once that in France the baby boys' rooms can be decorated in pink and the baby girls' rooms can be in blue. Or was that Sweden? Brazil maybe?) Wait, he also has condoms in here. Which he must be using with . . . Oh, right. Me. Okay, so he gets a pass on those.

Here's a big bottle of moisturizer. Do men use moisturizer? Is a big bottle a good thing? I read the label, but of course it's all in French and it neither says *homme* or *femme* anywhere, so I don't know if it's for men or women.

I pop the cap open to sniff. Smells like cucumber. Crap—is cucumber masculine or feminine?

"I'm home!" I hear from the living room.

Shit. I quickly, yet silently, close the medicine cabinet and feel complete embarrassment and shame wash over me.

"I'm in here!" I yell, then take a moment to flush the toilet and wash my hands.

I walk out to meet Jay in the kitchen, where he unloads groceries and wine from reusable canvas bags. "Wow. Look at all this!" I say, taking a baguette and holding it up. "They actually have baguettes in France."

"*Boules* too," Jay says cheerfully. "But I figure we'll start you off with the classics." He takes the baguette from me and places it on a wooden cutting board. He leans in to give me a quick kiss. "How did you sleep?"

"Like a rock," I say as I watch him pull a bread knife from his knife block and begin slicing the baguette. "Sorry to conk out like that. I was tired."

"No worries. You stayed awake for the really important part," he jokes, wagging his eyebrows up and down.

I blush. Yes, I did. I did indeed.

"Can I help?"

"I'm good," he says as he finishes slicing the baguette into sandwich-size rolls, "although if you want to grab a bottle of white from the fridge, that would be great. Do you like a little ham or a lot of ham on your sandwich?"

"I like a lot of everything on my sandwich."

"My kind of girl," he says, all smiles as he unwraps the ham he just bought. "I got this from the local charcuterie, along with Brie from the cheese shop, of course, and a ripe tomato. I figure we can go to the Champ de Mars park, have a picnic near the Eiffel Tower, then head to the Musée d'Orsay, which is open until six today. Does that work?"

"C'est parfait," I tell him, trying to show off what little French I've learned in the past few days.

"Great," he says, continuing to assemble the sandwiches. "I couldn't get reservations for that restaurant you wanted until Sunday night, so I figured tonight we'll either head to the Latin Quarter for dinner or hit L'Escargot Montorgueil. What do you think?"

"Whatever you want," I say, snagging a thin slice of ham from his pile. "They both sound amazing."

"We'll play it by ear. I definitely want to hit Chartres and Notre Dame tomorrow. We'll want to avoid it Sunday, unless you want to go to mass. Wait—do you go to mass?"

"Usually just at Christmas."

"Great. Then we'll do the Louvre Sunday. So how long do I have you for? When's your return flight?"

I was dreading this question. I didn't know how long he wanted me to stay when he invited me out, and I was too shy to ask him at the time. I was worried that I'd scare him off if I stayed too long, but that I wouldn't have any shot at a relationship if I left too quickly. So I just didn't book a ticket back.

Plus, as usual, I am broke, and I figured the longer I can leave that charge off my credit card, the better.

"I booked an open ticket," I tell him, careful to watch his response and see if he gets weird. "I wasn't sure how long I'd hang out with you, and I didn't know if I would feel like taking the Chunnel to London or a train to Barcelona or Venice or . . . wherever the wind takes me."

That sounded noncommittal and unstalkerlike, I proudly think to myself.

Jay nods. "Cool," he says, finishing up his sandwich. "I say Latin Quarter tonight. Snails later in the weekend."

Cool. He said *cool.* We're all cool. Okay then. I was worried for no reason.

His doorbell buzzes a few moments later. Jay wipes his hands clean with a dishtowel. "Can you pick out a wine and pack it and the sandwiches in the canvas bag? I'll go see who that is."

"Sure." I go to his fridge.

"Oh, and the corkscrew is in the left drawer!" Jay yells from his living room.

I hear him open the door, then a woman's voice speaking quietly in French, and him responding by whispering.

Suddenly, everything's quiet in the living room.

Shit. I knew it. What is French for Don Juan? I poke my head out of the kitchen doorway to ask, bracing for the next attack of a woman spurned. "Which is the left drawer?"

Jay turns to me and says in a normal voice, "Sorry. Left of the sink."

I watch as a young woman, who could be Audrey Hepburn's grand-daughter with her flawless ivory skin and dark pixie cut (and no one should look that good in jeans. I'm just saying), sees me for the first time.

Here we go . . .

Halle's face lights up. She speed-walks in, gives me a huge hug, then kisses me once on each cheek. "[Something-something-something] Los Angeles!" the girl declares with glee. Then she continues talking excitedly to me. I nod several times, pretending I have any sort of clue what she's saying to me. I'm pretty sure at one point she asks me, "Oui?" So I answer her in the affirmative. (Oui. Sure. Why not?)

At this, she lifts her arms joyously, gives me another kiss on each cheek, then turns to leave, speaking a mile a minute at Jay, giving him a quick kiss good-bye as well, then walking out into the hallway with an "Au revoir!"

Jay laughs to himself, returning her "Au revoir!" and closing the door behind her.

I laugh. "Okay, what was that?"

"That was Justine. And she loves you."

"Good to know. And why exactly does she love me?"

"Because you're American, as is her boyfriend. Plus, you didn't leave me at the altar. So you get points from her for that." He passes me to return to the kitchen. "Let me get the corkscrew."

"Boyfriend? So you never dated her?"

Jay seems startled. "Justine? God, no. She's nineteen. Let me get us some plastic cups, and we're outta here."

Just me being paranoid. Whew.

Thirty-four

Within minutes, we are out of the apartment and strolling hand in hand down Rue des Abbesses. He tells me about his neighborhood, which is apparently a pretty hip spot, and swarming with artists. He shows me the house where Picasso lived, then we take *le métro* over to the Champ de Mars for a lovely picnic with lots of wine, and even more kissing.

The Champ de Mars is a park in the seventh arrondissement that surrounds the Eiffel Tower. It's sort of like Paris's version of Central Park and takes up about sixty acres, right in the middle of the city, which ends on one side with the Seine River flowing past. Like the rest of Paris, it is insanely beautiful, filled with bursts of colorful flowers, greenery, and views of the buildings in the city.

Again, how does this city stay in business? How can people ever go to work or get anything done when there is so much beauty to drink in?

We find a spot on a lawn near some flower beds with an incredible view of the Eiffel Tower. "How about here?" Jay asks.

"Amazing," I say, pulling out my phone and snapping a picture of the tower as Jay pulls out a small plaid blanket and lays it out for us.

"Smile!" I say, pointing my phone at him.

He does, and he looks great. "Let me get one of you," he tells me after I click the photo.

"No. I hate pictures of me."

Jay purses his lips, confused. "Huh. You didn't seem to mind the video camera in my room this morning."

My eyes bulge out. "What?!"

"I'm kidding." He pulls out his cell phone, puts his arm around me, aims the phone at us, and commands, "Say *fromage*."

Just as I start to say *Fromage!* he leans over and kisses my open mouth.

He snaps the pick, then turns the phone around to show me. "A French kiss in Paris."

I take his phone and grimace. "Ew. I look awful."

"You do not. You never look awful." He says this as though it's a fact, not an opinion.

A girl could get used to that.

I have a seat as Jay pulls out the bottle of wine and the corkscrew. "This is a Chablis I like, and by that I mean it is a chardonnay from Chablis, France, not that hideous white wine I used to buy by the jug and serve you back in college."

"You mean, back when I thought anyone who gave me anything other than Jell-O shots was a class act?" I ask him jokingly.

"Indeed." He pulls out the cork and pours me a glass. "Ma lady." He hands me the glass, sneaking in a quick kiss along the way.

I take a sip as he pours a glass for himself. "Wow, this is good. Kind of minerally—not sweet in that cloying way."

"You have a good palette. I visited the village of Chablis last year. The town looks like a postcard, all green, with old-fashioned churches and stone buildings. Amazing people, and dying to get rid of the bastardized version of their name." He takes a sip, swishes it around in his mouth, then swallows. "This bottle is supposed to have an aftertaste of 'wet rock.'"

"You seem to say that with your tongue firmly planted in your cheek," I say, sticking my nose into the glass and taking a whiff.

"Well, I just remember at the time thinking, 'Wet rock?' What's that a euphemism for? Used Kitty Litter?"

I laugh. "So why did you buy it then?"

Jay laughs. "Truthfully, the woman pouring the tasters was cute, and I was tipsy, so I bought a case." He takes another sip. "It is good though. Even if my palette can't detect notes of meow."

As Jay pulls our sandwiches and some apples from his bag, I people-watch. Because we got here around the tail end of lunchtime, hundreds of office workers are still sitting around, eating their lunch outside. Well-dressed men and women, chatting, laughing, some reading a book quietly, others checking their phone or working on their notebook computer.

I shake my head slowly at the scene. "Man, people are just . . . sitting here . . . like it's a normal day."

Jay turns to see what I'm looking at. "What do you mean?"

"I mean, like, that guy over there in the suit could be an architect, checking his phone to find out what his wife wants him to bring home for dinner. But he gets to do it in this exquisitely perfect place. Maybe to him the Eiffel Tower is what the Hollywood sign is to me—something you see around, but never think about." I point to a twentysomething woman in dark blue, skinny jeans. "And that girl over there with the computer could be a writer, not even noticing how spectacular these flowers are because she's too busy worrying about her deadline."

I take the first bite of my ham-and-cheese sandwich. "Wow," I say with a full mouth. "This is insane."

Jay smiles, pleased with my reaction. "The trick is to get the Brie so warm, it's almost runny. That and, my little secret, get your ham flown in from Spain. You might want to think about going there. It's only a little over an hour's flight."

"Mmm . . . being able to fly to Barcelona at the drop of a hat. Another way Parisians are lucky and don't even know it."

A sad smile seems to creep over Jay's face.

"What?"

"Oh, nothing. It's just . . . I'm probably leaving Paris soon. I put in for a transfer to New York. That's why I went to San Francisco last week. I needed to have the finishing touches put in my new contract over at my company's headquarters."

"Really?" I say, trying to hide my disappointment.

"Yeah. I'm kind of done with this city. At least for now."

"Wow. Done." I look over at the Eiffel Tower, majestic and iconic. "I can't imagine ever being done here."

"Neither could I a few years ago. When I was a kid, I dreamed of living here, and then I worked my ass off to make it happen, and then . . . I don't know. It wasn't what I thought it was going to be." He turns to look at my reaction. "I know—that's coming off as really spoiled, isn't it?"

"No, I get it."

"No, you don't, and that's cool. One of my friends keeps joking, 'Show me a beautiful city, and I'll show you a man who's tired of fucking in it.' "

I stare at him, a bit puzzled.

Jay shrugs. "That might sound funnier in French."

"Probably. But I do know what you mean. I passionately wanted to teach my whole life, but now I'm bored with it. I desperately wanted to marry the guy I dated for years. Now I can't imagine what I ever saw in him. I used to love running, now I don't see the point. It's like none of the things that used to make me happy still do." I rethink what I just said. "You know what? Let me rephrase that. It's more like different things are making me happy now than when I was younger. Like I have to go after some new dreams. Maybe it's time for you to go after some new dreams too."

"You might be right," Jay says, noticeably pensive. He makes a show of shaking his head as if he were shaking out the cobwebs. "Okay, enough serious talk. You didn't fly all the way out here to become my therapist. What do you say we finish our picnic, head to the Musée d'Orsay, then make out under the Eiffel Tower at sunset?"

"I say perfect," I declare through a mouthful of sandwich.

"Excellent," he says, scooting over to me and putting his arm around me. Then he does something I don't think he's done since college—he gives me a gentle kiss on my cheek. "I'm really glad you're here," he says softly.

I smile. "Me too."

We hold hands, and for a while we eat and drink contentedly and people-watch.

"Do you think anyone here desperately dreams of going to America?" Jay eventually asks me.

I have to give it a moment's thought as right now I can't imagine being anywhere else. But I finally conclude, "Probably."

Jay's brow furrows. "Like maybe that girl with the computer over there dreams of getting a PhD at Stanford and is working on her application right now. Or maybe that guy to our right is in love with a girl who lives in Cleveland and is doing everything he can to be with her."

I nod. "I hope so. It's easier to get through life when you have something to work toward."

"I don't know if it's easier, but it's better."

Jay and I watch the French girl flip her notebook shut and begin to pack up. "It's definitely better," he repeats, a bit lost in thought.

Thirty-five

The Musée d'Orsay is actually a restored rail station on the bank of the Seine known mostly for its impressionist art. (Jay told me some of the impressionist paintings are actually castoffs from the Louvre. Who knew?)

Jay knew to buy our tickets on the museum's website, so we managed to escape the long lines of sweaty tourists waiting to buy a ticket to see the dancers of Degas, the Tahitian scenes of Paul Gauguin, the dance scenes of Renoir, and the landscapes of Monet.

My favorite painting is a blue one Monet painted called *Nymphéas bleus* (Blue Water Lilies). It's feminine—white water lilies floating in a blue pond. For whatever reason, I couldn't take my eyes off it. I must have stared at the painting for ten minutes before Jay comes up behind me, doughnuts his arms around my waist, and rests his chin on my shoulder. "Is it as good as the one on your coffee cup?" he asks me in a quiet, museum voice.

"It is," I say, smiling and putting my hands over his. "I love gardens. I love the feel of them. Yet I've never tried to grow anything. That's weird, huh?"

"No. I like Porsches, but that doesn't mean I plan to build one in my spare time."

"True," I agree aloud, though I feel as if I haven't made my point.

I continue to look at the painting and try to guess what Monet must have been feeling when he painted it. The pond was part of a water garden he had installed on his property, so it wasn't an accidental source of happiness, it was intentional. And he didn't paint a sky to go with it, or even land around the pond, he just painted the pond. Nothing to detract from the flowers and the water. Maybe all of his fame and money didn't bring him true happiness. Maybe later in life he realized that something as simple as watching a lily float through water made him happy. So that's what he focused on.

Something as simple as watching a flower float through water is one of those little pleasures in my life. Yet I never think to pick up flowers when I go to my local Trader Joe's. Or go to Home Depot and buy a few flowering plants. It's such a little thing to do for myself. Why don't I ever bother?

I make a resolution right then and there to buy more flowers when I get home, and to try to appreciate the little things I take for granted every day.

I turn to Jay and give him a quick kiss of gratitude. "This was just what I needed. Thank you."

Jay smiles. "No problem. It's a beautiful place. Care to go home and work up an appetite before we head out to dinner?"

I am probably blushing. "That's also just what I need. You read my mind."

"Great." He kisses me lightly on the lips, and we hold hands as we walk through the museum and out the front door and into the sounds of the city.

Jay's cell phone rings, a French chanteuse crooning what I'm pretty sure is the Etta James song "At Last."

I would have found the ringtone charming if the sound of it didn't make Jay slump his shoulders, roll his eyes, and say, "Oh, crap!" He drops my hand, puts up his index finger to signal to me *One second,* and picks up his phone.

"Bonjour," he says, in a businesslike voice.

Okay, Mel, calm down. It's just work. You showed up on a weekday. People on weekdays get calls from work. I decide to pretend the view of the Seine is fascinating as I listen to him get more and more riled up. He's talking a mile a minute, then listening for long stretches. At one point, I think I pick up on a rapid and urgent *Quel le problème?* and a bunch of *nons.*

We appear to be passing a gelato shop, so I signal to ask him whether I should go in there to give him privacy, but he shakes his head no.

Finally, Jay says au revoir to the caller and hangs up. He slowly closes his eyes for a moment, sighs, then opens his eyes to look at me. "I'm so sorry. We've had a problem with one of our accounts. I need to go home and change, then go in to work for a bit. Do you want to come back with me to the apartment, or should I give you a key, and you can sightsee for a while, then find your way back?"

"No, I'll come back with you, if that's okay," I say a little timidly.

I can't explain it, but that call once again pricked up my Spidey sense.

"Okay, it should only take an hour or two," Jay tells me, his mind a thousand miles away. "But I'll be back in plenty of time for dinner."

We get home in what I'm pretty sure is record time. While I

leaf through an art book in his living room and try to stay out of his way, Jay takes a quick shower (which I am not invited to join him in), then dresses in a gray suit, crisp white shirt, and bright red tie. He's barely said five words to me since we got back, and I'm feeling anxious.

"You look very handsome," I say awkwardly as he grabs his briefcase, which rests next to me on the couch.

"Thanks," he says distractedly. "I'll text you when I'm leaving my office. In the meantime"—he reaches into his pocket—"take my key. The gold one's to the building, the silver one works both the top and bottom lock."

I put out my hand, a bit confused by his generosity. "Is this your only key?"

"There's probably another one somewhere in the house. I know Tatiana gave it back to me, but I have no idea where I put it." When he speaks, he doesn't quite sound angry, but he's definitely not friendly either. In the same tone of voice I get, "I'll be home in time for a late dinner. We'll pretend we're from Spain and go at ten." Jay kisses me on the forehead. "Okay, enjoy yourself, whatever you decide to do."

And he's out the door.

What the hell just happened? Is he mad at me? If this had been Seema being dragged into work on a Friday afternoon even though she had guests in town, I would have heard every detail of what was going on, including the client's name, gender, weight, age, and degree of hotness. Plus a flurry of other details she would have vented, hoping for some sympathy.

Her brother, on the other hand, is a clam.

I make a mental note of that. Why didn't he talk to me? What's he hiding?

Okay, and by *mental note*, I mean that after saying good-bye to him at the door, I turn on the TV for ten minutes to watch Sofia Vergara's character in *Modern Family* speak in French, then proceed to ransack his house for clues of another woman.

I do everything from pawing through his sock drawer (nothing but socks), to running my fingers over the top shelf of his closet (nothing but random, old *Sports Illustrated* magazines and some computer cables).

Then I stop.

What the hell am I doing? Okay, so the guy had to go to work. Do I really think this man I trust enough to sleep with would encourage me to fly halfway around the world, only to have him abandon me for a local squeeze? Am I really that messed up about men?

I walk over to his computer, click on Skype, then type in Nic's Skype number.

I know she probably won't pick up, but Seema's still on her honeymoon, and it's the early morning in Maui, so Jeff's asleep. Clearly, I'm desperate. Pick up, pick up, pick up . . .

Nic's video pops on. I see her half-asleep, maternity-blouse flap unbuttoned, and a small person attached to her left breast.

"Boy, am I glad to see you," Nic says, sounding tired, but smiling at me. "How's Paris?"

"I'm insane. Do you have a minute?"

"I have all the minutes you need. Just don't mind my nursing."

"No problem. I've seen your boobs before."

"Not like this you haven't. Cows are fit to pose for *Playboy* more than I am right now. So what's up?"

"I'm the worst girlfriend in the world. No, I'm the worst *person* in the world."

"Nothing like a good hyperbole—"

"I searched his medicine cabinet."

Nic sighs as she looks down at the baby. "Oh, dear," she coos in baby talk. "Auntie Mel's a nut job."

"I know. I'm awful. I am in the most romantic city in the world, eating the most amazing food, drinking the most exquisite wine, and seeing the most beautiful sights with a handsome, charming man who I have had a crush on forever, and I'm determined to ruin it."

"He's latching wrong. Hold that thought." Nic pulls JJ (Jason Jr.) off her breast to readjust him.

"Yikes!" I blurt out.

She looks up at me and shakes her head. "I know. Right?"

I'm stunned. "Women pay thousands of dollars to get boobs like that."

"Please. In a few minutes he will have sucked me dry, and they'll look like deflated balloons. So what event inspired you go through his medicine cabinet?"

"He had lavender bubble bath in his bathroom."

"Bastard," she says sarcastically.

"He also had a pink toothbrush."

Nic's face softens a little. "Hmm. Well . . ."

"No tampons though."

Nic's face perks up. "Well, there you go."

"I'm not done. While he was in the shower, I checked his cell phone for incriminating texts."

She sighs. "You can't do that, Mel. You've only been dating a few weeks."

"It didn't matter. They were all in French."

"Good. Because you—"

"Although I was thinking I could type them into an online French translator and find out what they mean."

"Stop. Let's dial back the insanity here."

"If I could dial back the insanity, I wouldn't be in my midthir-ties, single, and going halfway across the planet for sex. Say some-thing to make me feel better."

"I don't know if I can say anything to make you feel better right now," Nic says apologetically. "I can listen though. Why did you decide to go to Paris? And don't tell me for sex. Because if that's all you wanted, you could have gone to the bar down the street. Or Trader Joe's for that matter."

Nice, uncomplicated question, Nic, thanks. I shrug. "I wanted to see what it was like."

"Okay, what's it like?"

"Devastatingly beautiful and romantic," I say, slightly saddened. "More so than I ever could have imagined. If a city were Cary Grant, this would be it."

"Huh."

"Huh? What's huh?"

"You're not happy when you say that."

"Well, I was happy this morning. But then it . . . I don't know, it kind of faded away."

"Why? What happened?"

"I went back to being me," I say in a resigned tone. "I could say it's because he talked to some other women, but in reality what happened was I started being me again."

"I don't understand. What do you mean by you're 'being you again'?"

I let my eyes flit around the room. Nic doesn't fill up the time with talk; she takes the time to wait for me to answer. Eventually, she looks down at her baby. "He's asleep," she whispers to me, pulling him off her breast, then standing up. "Give me one sec-ond. Don't move." Then she walks out of camera range.

I glance over at Jay's floor-to-ceiling windows to watch the apartments across from me. One woman is in her kitchen, moving bowls around, clearly getting dinner ready. An older couple quietly watches TV together in their living room. A man reads his iPad while his dog lies by his feet. Everyone's life looks so peaceful from across the street.

I focus back at Nic's screen, which shows part of her living room through the doorway of her kitchen (where her computer rests). It looks peaceful too.

Everyone seems to be at peace with his or her life except for me.

I'm not at peace. And that's what I'm yearning for. I don't want excitement in my life, I want contentment. I don't want my brain constantly tormenting me with what-ifs: What if you had become a politician instead of a teacher? What if you had moved to New York when you were twenty-two? What if you had married Danny?

I'm so tired of not being able to turn off my brain. Yet I have this nagging feeling deep inside me that keeps telling me I'm not at peace yet.

The stone of the buildings outside has turned pink from the impending sunset. The scene is idyllic, much better than anything I would have experienced tonight at home, sitting in my bedroom for the millionth time playing solitaire on my computer.

And yet what-if still keeps playing in an infinite loop in my head. Something inside me is still empty, some part of me still needs to be filled.

Nic returns, holding a coffee mug with the painting of Monet's water lilies.

I can feel my eyes bulge out from excitement. "Oh my God. Is that my mug? I saw that painting today!"

She turns the mug inward to get a good look at the picture. "Probably. I don't remember ever buying it. So how was the painting?"

"It was beautiful and tranquil and I stared at it for ten minutes. I'm so glad I got to see it. It was, like, bucket-list good."

"Then why do you sound so miserable?"

"Because it was a temporary distraction. When we left the museum, I was back to being me." I struggle for a moment, trying to figure out how to put it into words. "It's like everything here is gloriously beautiful, but nothing makes me feel like I should be here. This isn't home."

"Honey, it's not supposed to be home. You're on vacation. We take vacations to escape day-to-day life."

"No, that's not what I mean. Or at least that's not why I went on vacation, I guess. Do you know for months leading up to Seema's wedding, I'd been absolutely dreading the changes that were about to happen? You guys have been my family since college. And first you went away and then I knew she was going away, and it's like the hole in my heart kept getting bigger and bigger."

Nic looks pained that I said that, so I quickly tell her, "Don't get me wrong. I love Jason, and I love the baby, and I'm really happy for you. But, sometimes, I miss us. I miss being able to go out with you on a random Tuesday night. And I knew the minute Seema got married, no more random Tuesday nights with her either. Plus I had to move out, so there would also be no more random Sunday-afternoon 'Let's watch reality bride TV all afternoon for no reason' roommate days. And that loss, well . . . it's like it started out as this little snowball: 'Oh, my life isn't quite where I want it.' But over the months the snowball got bigger and bigger, and soon I was running from an avalanche."

Nic nods. "And then Jay showed up, and you were young again."

I laugh uncomfortably. "Yeah. Only this time I got to be with my crush, and he invited me to be with him, and I thought, 'Yup, this is it. This will fill up my hole.'" I shrug. "No pun intended."

I glance back over at the building across the street. In the apartment beneath the older couple, a young mom walks through the door, carrying her baby in one arm, and her diaper bag in the other. "I'm surrounded by perfection, and I still want to jump out of my skin. What's wrong with me?"

Nic shakes her head and juts out her lower lip. "Nothing's wrong with you. You have a big change coming up, and you're getting used to it. For now, just enjoy yourself. Enjoy the moment. No one ever said this guy was the one. And that's okay—he doesn't need to be."

I shake my head. "But if he's not the one, what am I doing here?"

"Seeing Notre Dame and the Louvre, making love to a beautiful man, and enjoying your life. I promise you, the heroine in every story has to take a journey before she gets to where she needs to be. If that doesn't apply to dating, I don't know what does."

"I suppose that makes sense."

"So tell me about the Eiffel Tower. Better than Vegas?" Nic jokes.

I chuckle, then describe everything I've seen so far.

Nic and I talked for a while longer, and she said all the right positive affirmations, and I listened and thanked her. Then I promised not to rummage through Jay's stuff anymore, and to fly back to LA if I was having any more *Lost in Translation* moments.

What I didn't tell her was that I had this nagging feeling that Los Angeles wasn't home anymore either.

And I still had no idea how I would escape that avalanche.

Thirty-six

Jay got home around nine that evening.

I had spent the rest of the day wandering the Montmartre area, walking up the stairs to Sacré-Coeur, taking a lavender bubble bath in his claw tub, and trying not to text him too often. I figure nothing is less attractive than an insecure woman—which is why we women try to hide it so frequently.

I knew I was rewarded when I heard Jay come through the door and cheerfully call out, "Honey, I'm home!"

I appear in his bedroom doorway wearing nothing but his robe and a smile on my face. "I missed you," I say seductively.

Jay's face lights up as he walks up to me. "Wow. You wear my robe well." He puts both hands on my waist and pulls me into a romantic kiss.

"Thank you," I say coyly, "I was just getting ready for dinner. Where are we going?"

"Verjus."

"You know, when you do things like that with your lips, you're just begging to be kissed," I flirt.

"Verjus," he repeats, making a show of puckering up his lips.

He gives me another kiss, and we make out for a minute or two. I try to pull him to the bed, but he stops me. "I made reservations, but we have to get cracking. How quickly can you be ready?"

"Ten minutes?"

"The perfect woman. Let me go change my shirt."

As Jay heads to his closet to pick out a shirt, and I start getting dressed, I ask, "So how did everything go?"

"Oh, awful," he says from inside his closet. "But it's fine now. I just never should have slept with a client."

I freeze as I throw on an elegant, little black dress I picked up from a shop on Montmartre today. "Wait. What?"

Jay walks out of his closet, shirtless. "Women just amaze me. You work closely with someone for a few months, things happen after too much wine in the middle of a business trip in a faraway land, and suddenly you're the bad guy because you didn't make it out to be more than it was."

Wow! I have no idea what to do with that statement.

Jay begins buttoning up his shirt, and despite myself, I hate to say good-bye to that perfect chest, if only for the next few hours.

But back to the matter at hand. Seriously, he just casually tells me he left me today to see a woman whom he has slept with? *What* am I supposed to do with that information?

I finish zipping up my dress as I try to casually ask, "So how long ago was that?"

Jay looks up to the ceiling and squints, trying to remember. "Well, the first time it was . . . let's see, the Christmas decorations were up. Two and a half years ago? Then the time after that was . . ."

After he didn't call her, there was still a time after that?

"Hmm . . . I don't know." Jay continues to think. "Summer. Cannes. Yeah, so that would have been last year. And then . . . I don't know . . . a month or two ago."

If I wasn't dating him, I'd say this guy was a douche.

But that's not a fair accusation. I don't know the whole story. Which I think I convey beautifully when I conclude, "You're kind of a dick to women, aren't you?"

Jay seems unfazed by my observation. "Don't act all insecure. That first time, she had just turned forty and wanted some young guy to play with. But then, you know how some women get the next morning. 'Oh, I don't want my number to go up. This has to be love or it doesn't count.'"

I will be forty in a little over seven years. Was that supposed to make me feel better?

I'm trying not to be mad, but I have to ask, "With all due respect, not being jealous here, but are you leaving Paris for New York because you've slept with all the women on this continent?"

Jay not only doesn't seem angered by my accusation, but his face lights up. "You know? A little bit. I *love* that you get me."

And he walks back into his closet to retrieve a tie.

Seriously—what the fuck?

As we take a cab over to the first arrondissement, I decide not to pursue any further my line of questioning about Jay's harem. Not because I don't care—oh, how I care!—but because I'm not sure I can handle his answers.

I am rewarded for my discretion with Verjus, a lovely restaurant near the Louvre that was actually founded by a few expats from Seattle.

We start in the bar downstairs, splitting a beautiful bottle of Beaujolais. At one point, Jay takes my hand, stares deep into my eyes, and tells me how beautiful I look. Hard to stay frosty after that.

We are soon upstairs, having what is probably the best meal of

my life. We both choose the eight-course tasting menu, which includes foie gras, sea bass, duck, and the most melt-in-your-mouth
beef. By the time we finish the cheese course, I have giggled, flirted,
fed him, and even rubbed his leg occasionally. Between the wine
and his charm, I am slowly relaxing and enjoying the evening.

Famous last words.

"Jay?"

Man, I cannot catch a break here.

Of course. Another gorgeous female voice with a lilting accent
saying his name. I turn around to see . . . Good God, this one's a
model I have actually seen on TV. Six feet tall, maybe twenty-five
(maybe!), flawless mocha skin . . . Are you fucking kidding me?

Okay, well, at least this one is happy to see him. Maybe she's
just a friend. Jay stands, they kiss each other on each cheek, and
then begin rapid French. At some point, he gestures to me. "Chloe,
This is my friend Melissa."

Or maybe *I'm* just a friend.

"It is wonderful to meet you, May-lee-sah." Chloe smiles
brightly and gives me a kiss on each cheek.

"You too Chloe. I've heard—I make a point of looking right at
Jay as I say—"so little about you."

Chloe laughs. "Well, of course not. I was just his en-ess-ah for
a while. Why would he bring me up?"

Jay tries to cover up a wince. He's been foiled again, and he
knows it.

"En-ess-ah?" I repeat to Chloe. "I'm sorry, I don't know that
word."

"Not word," she says in her beautiful lilting voice. "The letters
en, ess, ah. In English, NSA."

She looks at me expectantly, but clearly I'm still confused. Finally she clarifies. "No Strings Attached?"

"Oh . . . NSA," I repeat, as though it suddenly makes sense. I paste an awkward smile on my face.

"Yes, I have a husband, but he is older. And I love him, but sometimes I need to be around someone who is young. Someone who can give me the sex I want, the fun I want, but not the children I want."

I must have looked startled because she quickly backtracks, "Not that he won't make a great father. You will have many beautiful babies, I am sure."

Chloe turns around to scrutinize a table of four across the room. "I must return to my friends. Very nice to meet you. *Bonne chance.*" And with that, she once again kisses me once on each cheek, does the same with Jay, and takes her leave.

The waiter comes to clear our cheese plate, and Jay and I are quiet. Once it is just the two of us, Jay smiles and jokes, "You have to admit, I have had the worst luck keeping my women apart today."

I force a smile. "Indeed."

The waiter brings us our next course, a lovely ganache-filled cake with a paired wine. He describes the dish in both French and English, then disappears.

Once we are alone again, I ask Jay, "So are you not in love with that one either?"

"In love with Chloe? No, she's too young for me, and besides, she never eats. Long term, that would drive me crazy. No, she's like you."

Somehow being compared to a twenty-two-year-old model isn't doing it for me right now. "She's like me how?"

Jay takes a bite of his dessert. "You know, she's great and I adore her. We have fun. Just like you and me."

Oh, shit.

Jeff once told me that contrary to what women want to believe, men always tell the truth. If they say they don't care where we eat tonight, what they really mean is they don't care where we eat tonight. And if they say they're just having fun . . . well, there it is.

"Are you okay?" Jay asks. "You look weird."

"Hmm? Oh, yeah, I'm fine," I assure him in a confident voice. "Just thinking about my flight home."

Get out. Just get through the next twelve hours, don't take anything personally, and get on a plane in the morning. This guy is a bon vivant, and he's not going to change for you, or any other woman for that matter. He loves you, but it's his own weird-ass brand of love, and nothing you do will ever change that. You are old enough to know. . . . Just be happy with what you got, and get the hell out.

"I'm afraid I had to move it up a few days," I say as I take my spoon to enjoy the first bite of cake.

Jay looks genuinely shocked and hurt by this. "What? Why?"

"Oh, um . . ." I put my spoon down and swallow my dessert. "I have this job interview at a charter school that just came up, and they start their year early so . . . I need to go sooner than I thought."

"But you just got here."

"I'm sorry. I got the e-mail earlier today. It's a job I didn't think I had a shot at, and I really need to jump at the chance."

Despite my cool on the outside, my mind is racing on the inside: What is wrong with me? Why doesn't he want me? And if he doesn't want me, why is he being so nice? Even if I'm good in bed, that would be no reason to have me fly all the way out here. Or would it? I mean, it really doesn't require much effort on his part to have a woman just magically show up in his bed. He gets to play Mr. Perfect for a few weeks, knowing that sooner or later I'm going away. Knowing there's nothing to get attached to.

Okay, so I may feel like an idiot, but at least I am an idiot who is almost thirty-three. And that is actually way better than being an idiot who is eighteen and has read too much *Twilight* and listened to too much Maroon 5.

Right now, I want to read *58 Bad Boyfriend Stories* while listening to Pink. It's progress.

"All right. Well, when were you thinking of leaving?"

"Tomorrow."

"Tomorrow?" he repeats, startled.

"I'm sorry to spring this on you. I just . . . I really need to go."

"Can't you at least stay until Monday? You've got to see Notre Dame before you go, and at least a few more museums."

He's right. Yes, I need to leave, but there's no reason not to enjoy the weekend for what it is.

"Okay, Monday," I agree, pleased with myself for keeping in control of the situation.

"Great," he says, pulling out his phone. "Let me change some things around Monday morning so I can take you to the airport."

"No need. I'll take the train."

"No, at least let me take you to the airport."

Proud of myself for getting out of this sticky situation with no drama, I quickly decide to go with the flow. "You know what?" I say, taking a huge spoonful of dessert, "that would be great." I pop the insanely rich confection into my mouth. "So, my only weekend in Paris. What's next?"

Jay pulled out all the stops for my last weekend. After dinner, we walked hand in hand around the city, then stopped at Bar Hemingway in the Ritz Hotel, considered by some to be the best bar in the world. I thought I'd be intimidated by the snooty attitude, but we had a delightful waiter who spoke perfect English and made me feel like a cherished guest. I had a raspberry martini, Jay went with a French 75, and we nursed our drinks and held hands and talked about the good ole days. Then, we headed out to the Eiffel Tower, made out a bit, then went home.

Where we cuddled and did nothing else. Jay made an attempt, but I think we both knew we were kind of done. And that that was okay.

I slept in one of his T-shirts.

THIRTY-SEVEN

Late that night, after Jay falls asleep, I tiptoe into his living room, pull up Skype on the computer, and call Jeff.

He clicks on immediately. "Shouldn't you be having sex right now?"

"Can I come see you?"

Jeff's face falls. "Crap. What happened?"

"Nothing. I am just dating an actual bon vivant from Paris."

Jeff shakes his head sympathetically. "Oh, honey . . ."

"No, it's fine. Really. It was just stupid for me to come out here."

"It wasn't stupid."

"Yes, it was. He was so sweet and said these wonderful things, and . . ." My sentence loses steam, but I don't cry. I don't really feel anything. I throw up my hands to Jeff to signal, *Que sera sera*.

"How soon can you get here?" Jeff says in a voice that is at once authoritative and soothing.

"I don't know," I stutter, fiddling absentmindedly with a piece of paper on Jay's desk. "I told him I was leaving Monday. And I know I should probably really go. But fuck if I don't want to go traipsing around Europe irresponsibly for the next few weeks."

Jeff smiles. "Well, why *can't* you do that?"

"I don't have the money, for one thing. What am I going to do? Blithely run around Europe racking up debt without a thought as to how I'll pay for everything once I get back?"

"Yes," Jeff advises, picking up his iPhone and using his thumbs to click out a text of some sort. "Didn't you say that that cake charm told you that you were going to be rich?"

"I don't believe in that charm anymore. Do you know there is not one L'Arbre d'Argent of any kind here? No trees, no restaurants, not even a nice dessert. . . . Can you please stop texting while I'm talking?"

"Hold on. It's just this guy."

I shake my head and sigh. Then I let my head fall into my left hand as I change the subject. "How did I get myself in this mess? It's like I didn't know what to do with my life, so I hoped some guy would come in and fix it. Haven't I learned my lesson about that enough times? When the hell did I become such a damsel in distress?"

"You're not a damsel in distress," Jeff assures me calmly.

"Am I a damsel?"

"Yes, but—"

"Am I calling you in distress?"

He looks up from his phone. "Go check your e-mail."

"What? Why?"

"Just do it."

"Okay—hold on, I have to shrink you," I say, reducing his image on Skype.

"Wouldn't it be great if we actually could shrink people?" I can hear Jeff say from the shrunken box on the bottom of my screen. "And food. Think of how much we'd save shipping people and food around the world."

I click on my e-mail and see something from American Airlines. "This is why you should have stayed a physicist." Then I open the e-mail. "Oh my God! Jeff—what did you do?"

"That, my darling, is an airline ticket from Paris to Maui, which leaves in two weeks. Don't get too excited. I had to use my miles, so it's coach, and you have, like, seventeen stops in between."

I click on his Skype box and bring him back onto the screen. "Jeff, I can't accept this."

"Of course you can. Happy birthday! Just promise me you'll stop being a damsel in distress and take the time to see anything in Europe you've ever dreamed of seeing. "

"What? I'm going to go by myself?"

"Yes," he says firmly. "For the first time in your life, go do something on your own. Don't think about what anyone else wants to see, think about what you want to see. And wherever you are, stop yourself from worrying about what's coming next. Stop planning. Just promise me for the next two weeks you will just enjoy the moment while it's going on."

I look at the ticket. It is so tempting. "I'd spend my birthday alone."

"That's the whole point. So where would you most want to be on your birthday?"

I look up at Jay's ceiling to consider that. Then I smile wistfully. "Truthfully? Venice."

"Venice? Perfect! I know the concierge at the Gritti Palace. We'll get you a room there and have him plan a whole day for you."

"Okay, I *really* can't afford the Gritti Palace."

"You don't have to. Giovanni will get me some discounts I'm sure, and it's my birthday gift to you."

I'm torn between thinking Jeff is being waaaayyyyy too generous, and being tempted to have an experience I'll never have otherwise. I bite my bottom lip. "I don't know. Seems like a lot to ask. How well do you know him?"

Jeff gives me a look that I can only describe as coy. "Let's just say I know him intimately, but not very well. But I let his sister stay in my guest room last year when she came to Maui, so it'll be nice to allow him to repay the favor. Come on—when are you going to have this opportunity again?"

"Okay, I'll think about it."

"No."

"Maybe if I paid you back in installments . . ."

"No."

"It just seems so irresponsible."

"Says the beta dog."

My jaw drops at the insult. "Okay, now you're just trying to get a reaction out of me!"

"Did it work?"

I cross my arms and pout. He smiles and pumps his fists in the air. "It worked! All right, I'll be in touch. Now go wake your hottie, have sex one more time, and have him take you to the airport Monday. You have an adventure to get to."

I did just that. Bright and early Monday morning I said goodbye to my playboy and began my new adventure.

And for the next two weeks, I toured Europe by myself, yet I was never alone. I met a nice, elderly British couple while I traipsed through Provence, stayed out way too late with some hipsters from Silver Lake (they live ten minutes from my house in Hollywood) while in Lake Como, and hung out with a family of six while touring Rome (it turns out a five-year-old can find better gelato than I can). In Venice, Giovanni took the day off just to spend my birthday with me—and he didn't even know me! And no great surprise, it turns out nothing is more romantic in life than spending twenty-four hours in Italy with a gay man. We rode the canals with a real-life gondolier who sang Italian romance songs (and made fun of his gay friend, whom he had known since elementary school, for being with a girl). We feasted on *vermicelli al nero di seppia,* which are fresh superthin noodles smothered in black squid ink, and the best shrimp scampi I've ever had, and something called sarde in soar, which is an antipasto of sweet-and-sour sardines with onions, pine nuts, and raisins. Sounds hideous—tastes amazing! Particularly when it is being fed to you by a stunning, giggle-inducingly handsome Italian man. We even went shoe shopping. I indulged in my inner female stereotype and bought knee boots with insanely high heels.

Life for those two weeks was nothing short of perfect.

And, yes, I did look for a money tree in every language of every country I went to, and, no, I didn't find an *albero di denaro* in Italy, an *árbol de dinero* in Spain, or an *arbre de diners* in Barcelona.

Instead, I found a feeling of empowerment.

And at thirty-three years old, it was about time I found some of that.

THIRTY-EIGHT

After those glorious two weeks, I spend twenty-eight excruciating hours taking four hundred kazillion planes from Paris, France, through New York and Houston, up to Vancouver, Canada, and back down to the Kahului Airport in Maui. I had a problem with customs, connecting flights were either late or missing completely, I'd barely closed my eyes in the last forty-two hours, hadn't had a shower in forty-eight, and was running several hours late. I had already texted Jeff not to pick me up, and to just go to work because I would hail a cab, and by hour twenty-six, as I looked through my window at the vast expanse of the Pacific Ocean that had been below me for eons, all I could think was *Back to reality*.

Boy, was I ever wrong.

Even before the plane lands, I can see why people call this place paradise. As we are preparing to descend, I look out the window, and the view literally takes my breath away. It was even prettier than I could have imagined—and I have read a *lot* of glossy wedding magazines over the years (and when I say *read*, I mean that in the same way men say they read *Playboy*).

The Pacific Ocean surrounds a towering mountain that I would later find out is called Haleakala. Haleakala is covered in clouds, but below the clouds I can see palm trees that are a shade of green I didn't know was found in nature—although I think I saw it once on a paint square at Home Depot.

We land, and as we taxi to our gate, I see palm trees swaying in the breeze all around the airport. The colors look different here, as though the reds, greens, and blues are on steroids. While in the past two weeks I've seen breathtaking cities, their beauty has come mostly from humans—the architecture of the buildings, the exquisite paintings in the museums, the gold walls and crystal chandeliers in Versailles, the canals and boats in Venice, the castles in Germany. All gorgeous, but all due to the efforts of civilization. Hawaii has an entirely different kind of beauty—it looks effortless, relaxing. Even the vibe on the plane seems more relaxed than when we left.

"Aloha, ladies and gentlemen, and welcome to Maui," the captain says to us in a reassuring voice over the loudspeaker. "Right now we're at seventy-six degrees, and we're looking at some scattered clouds, with a chance of rain later this evening. For those of you who are staying on in Maui, your bags will be at baggage claim one. For others flying on to other destinations . . ."

As the captain tells the other passengers which gates to proceed to for their connecting flights to Oahu, Kauai, and the Big Island, I continue to stare outside the window and wonder how anyone can ever summon up the willpower to leave. There are going to be some serious claw marks on the outside of the plane going back to LA from the flight attendants' having to drag me into the cabin against my will.

We're still just on the tarmac, and already I wonder how things can get any prettier.

Soon, I deplane and walk past the gates. Unlike in Paris or

Houston or Detroit, the interior of this airport is like nothing I've ever been in. Hawaiian music lilts over the speaker system, flowers and plants abound, and instead of a bland, faceless airport bar, there's a tropical-drink bar sporting thatched leaves, a surfboard hanging from the wall, and a sign promising me THE BEST LAVA FLOW ON MAUI.

I take an escalator down to baggage claim, located outside, preparing to grab my suitcase and duffel and grab a cab out to Kihei, where Jeff lives and works. But I emerge from the terminal to see Jeff, holding up a white cardboard sign like a chauffeur. Only instead of my last name written in black Sharpie, his sign reads HE'S AN ASSHOLE.

I giggle and walk into Jeff's arms. "I told you not to come."

He shrugs. "You tell me a lot of silly things that I ignore." He holds up his sign. "Besides, how else would I have discovered this great new way to meet people? Do you know how many people read this and said, 'My ride's here'?"

I laugh. "I'm so sorry I'm so late."

"You should be since you were the one flying the plane and all. Come on, let's get your luggage." He looks over at carousel number one. "What are you carrying these days?"

"What am I *carrying*?" I laugh. "Man, why can't we live in 1961? Then I could just marry you and never have to date again."

"Honey, if you were married to me in 1961, you'd be waiting in breathless anticipation for the key parties to begin in 1968." Jeff looks horrified as my beat-up, old black suitcase (circa 1996) flies down the ramp and onto the conveyor belt. "Please tell me that's not still your bag," Jeff says, pointing at it and sighing.

"I'm a poor teacher with crushing student loans. Louis Vuitton's not exactly in my budget."

Jeff shakes his head. "Colostomy bags have more style." Jeff grabs the handle and tugs the bag off the carousel. "Okay, I have to be at work in an hour. One of my bartenders quit, so I have a little extra work before we open. Let me drop you off at home so you can grab a shower and get some sleep."

I sniff my armpits. "Do I smell that bad?"

"No, but you've been on the road forever, and you can't sleep on planes, so I'm guessing you'd like to wash off the road dust and maybe get in a nap."

"I'm fine. Really. Hey, what's a Lava Flow?"

"Basically it's a piña colada with strawberry purée 'erupting' out of the middle of the glass."

"Do you know how to make Lava Flows at Male 'Ana?"

"I know how to make everything flow at Male 'Ana."

Male 'ana, which is the Hawaiian word for "wedding," is also the name of Jeff's bar. Located near his home in Kihei, he opened the bar to cater specifically to newlywed couples who were staying in the ritzy hotels in nearby Wailea on their honeymoons, places like the Four Seasons, the Fairmont, and the Grand Wailea. Within a few months, he got a bunch of five-star reviews on Yelp, then got mentioned in a few bridal magazines, and now honeymooners come from all over the island, everywhere from Ka'anapali to Hana, to spend the evening listening to romantic wedding music, meet other newleyweds and swap wedding stories, and get hammered on specialty drinks with names like Kipona Aloha and Ho'omaika'i'ana.

"Perfect! Then I'll be your first customer for the night," I chirp happily. "But instead of a Lava Flow, can you make me a money-tree cocktail?"

Jeff narrows his eyes and smirks at me.

I look back at him innocently. "What?"

"Nice try. There is no such thing as a money-tree cocktail."

"Why not?" I ask him without missing a beat.

Jeff bursts out laughing.

"What? I'm serious!"

Jeff puts his arm around me and gives me a big squeeze. "I missed you, geek. Now tell me about Europe. How was Giovanni?"

"Oh . . . my . . . *God* is that man good-looking?!" I practically yell.

Jeff faces lights up. "Isn't he though? *So* good-looking! His lips . . ."

"Gorgeous. I would find myself staring at his lips."

"Fortunately, I found myself doing more than staring at his lips."

We head out past the exhausted families in their Hawaiian shirts and Crocs as well as the deliriously happy new couples waiting for the shuttles to their rental cars, and over to a parking lot surrounded by bright green palm trees in contrast to the black asphalt of the parking lot and streets. Outside, the air feels warm and . . . misty almost. Not humid exactly, just misty. Plus, it smells like flowers. This is, seriously, the strangest airport I've ever been in. Good strange, but strange.

"Do all of the Hawaiian airports look like this?" I ask as we get to Jeff's bright red Mercedes convertible.

"No. They all look different," he tells me as he throws my suitcase into the trunk. "When you land at the Big Island, the airport is built on top of old, black volcanic flows, so it looks like you've landed on the moon. In Honolulu, it looks like San Diego with flowers. Kauai is so green, you'd swear dinosaurs will come up and nuzzle you at baggage claim."

As we climb into our seats, I see a pink bakery box on my passenger seat. "What's this?"

Jeff smiles. "Cupcakes. Open it."

I sit down and put the box on my lap. I open the box to see

two cupcakes: one slathered with white frosting, the other with beige, each with a small, white ribbon poking out. "What did you do?"

"Pull one."

"Which one? Didn't you rig them?"

"Because that's gone so swimmingly when Nic does it?" Jeff asks.

I debate which cupcake to pick. Left? Right? Left? Right? "Are they both the same flavors?"

"No. One's lilikoi with a vanilla frosting, the other's chocolate with a salted caramel frosting."

"Lilikoi?"

"Passion fruit. Local flavor. You'll hate it."

I smile—he totally rigged this. I take the chocolate one, as he knew I would, and pull out my charm. I don't recognize it. I put it in my mouth, lick off the cake, and look again. It's a silver charm of a Hawaiian shirt. "I've never seen this charm before. What does it represent?"

"It means your future is in Hawaii. Wait . . . What a coincidence!" He puts up his hands and makes a show of presenting the area. "And here you are!"

I smile. "You're awesome." I take a bite of my cupcake. "But what if I had chosen the other one?"

"You can pull it and find out if you want to."

"No, I don't want to take your cupcake."

"I didn't say you could have my cupcake," Jeff says immediately, "but you can have the charm."

Curious, I pull the ribbon out of the top of Jeff's cupcake to see a silver charm covered in cake, which I lick off. "Ick."

"I told you, you wouldn't like it."

I look at the charm, which is a Hawaiian flower. "It's beautiful. But what if I had picked this one?"

"Then congratulations! That charm means your future is in Hawaii! Now give me my cupcake."

Jeff winks at me as he puts down the top on his car. Within a few minutes, we have pulled out of the airport and are driving from Kahului Airport down to Kihei, on the southwest side of the island, about half an hour away.

You know that awful drive you have to take from the airport into the city—no matter where the airport is or which city you've traveled to? There's no such thing in Maui. There are no million-lane freeways or highways anywhere on the island, and the drive out of the town of Kahului is stunning.

Soon we are on the Mokulele Highway South, which is all of two lanes, and we are speeding past sugarcane fields on both sides of us, their green stalks swaying in the breeze. Above one sugarcane field is a rainbow that spans a full half circle, from one side of the field to the other. I have never seen a rainbow that complete. If someone had put a picture of this on their Facebook page, I would have assumed it was photoshopped.

And then we get to ocean. Stunningly blue ocean.

I spend most of our journey pretty much repeating different combinations of the same three phrases: "Wow"; "Oh my God"; and "That's beautiful."

When Jeff makes a left onto South Kihei Road, we begin driving through the town of Kihei. On my right side is nothing but ocean. "Do you live close to the beach?" I ask.

"Several blocks up. But I'm on a hill, so there's a nice view of the water from most of the rooms in the house. My bar is about a half mile away from the house, on the bottom of the hill. It's right across the street from the beach, so the views on our lanai are pretty spectacular. Since your plane was so late, I need to drop you off at home, then race over to go open. I can come pick you up in a few hours if you want to see the bar."

"No, no. I want to come with you to Male 'Ana now," I say excitedly, beaming as I grab his shoulder lightly.

"You want to go with me to work? Why? Aren't you exhausted?"

"Nope. Got my fifth wind. I mean, look at this place!" I say, catching the wave of an adrenaline rush from my new adventure. "Plus, your idea of work is my idea of fun. Oh, *and* you've promised me a Lava Flow and a money-tree cocktail!"

"There's no such thing."

"You could just invent one," I point out, having given this a lot of thought.

Because he totally could. Jeff's bar "specializes" in signature honeymoon drinks, each of which supposedly brings good luck to one of seven areas of married life: love, romance, riches, health, luck, happiness, and fertility. I put air quotes around "specialize" because the drinks actually have nothing to do with Hawaiian fortune-telling, divination, or luck of any kind. They are just different concoctions Jeff made up over the years when he bartended to pay his way through college. He took his most popular love potions from that time, dubbed them *lama pa'ipa'i* (which is the Hawaiian word for "cocktail"), put them on his bar menu, then poured them into inexpensive souvenir glasses for newlywed couples to take back to the mainland.

Jeff calls the drinks "a bar version of fortune cookies." I call them marketing genius. Couples bring home the glasses, which not only become sentimental keepsakes from their trip, but conversation pieces with friends, family, and future honeymooners.

The couples happily gush about the place and send their honey-mooning friends, who come to drink and take more glasses home, and the cycle continues on in perpetuity.

"Come on," I badger Jeff. "You invent new drinks all the time. This could be your mai tai. What about something with Midori?"

Jeff furrows his brows at me. "You hate Midori."

"It's taking perfectly good liquor and mucking it up with melon. Can you blame me?" I watch as Jeff makes a left turn into a parking lot surrounding a huge thatched hut. "Wow. Is this it?"

"This is it," he says, slowly passing the bar and parking his car in the back.

"It looks like a tiki lounge," I say, surprised. Which is true—it's basically a giant building made to look like a Pacific-island hut, composed of bamboo, straw, reeds, and dried palm-tree leaves, and dripping with lush tropical greenery and flowers. Replace the parking lot with the Pacific Ocean, and you'd have an overwater bungalow in Bora Bora.

"What did you think it was going to look like? A space station?"

"No, no. It's just, if I were to imagine what the perfect bar in Hawaii would look like, I would pretty much picture this."

"Well, good. If you think that looks tropical, wait until you see the inside."

The two of us head inside, and I feel as if I have died and gone to heaven the moment we walk through the door. The walls are covered in rattan matting and bamboo. The tables and bartop are glass, but under each glass is a thatch table skirt. The stools and chairs are all wicker and painted bright colors. Tiki masks, statues, and totems dot the bar throughout. I pick up a mask that looks sort of like a scary God smiling at me and exclaim, "This is amazing."

"Do you like it?" Jeff asks me proudly. "Every wood piece you

see here is hand-carved by a local artist. And check out this sign."
He walks behind the bar to show me a large sign that says ALOHA!
HERE, YOU'RE OHANA! "This was made of Hawaiian driftwood."

"*Ohana* means 'family,' right?"

"I see you've watched *Lilo and Stitch*. Yes. Three words you
need to know here": *Ohana, aloha,* which means both 'hello' and
'good-bye' and can also mean 'I love you,' and *mahalo,* which means
'thank you.'"

"Mahalo. I can't thank you enough for inviting me."

Jeff smiles. "No mahalo to you. I love having my ohana around."
He then takes my hand and leads me outside. "You have to check
out the lanai."

The outside area, which most Hawaiians call the lanai, is a
dark blue wooden deck surrounded by palm trees, other kinds of
pointy, green trees, and a myriad of colorful flowers. Bordering
the deck in a perfect line every ten feet or so is one of my favorite
things in the world . . .

"You have tiki torches!" I squeal in delight as I run up to one.
"Can we light them?" I put up my hands in prayer. "Please, please,
please."

Jeff seems almost charmed by my reaction. "Most of the restaurants and bars in Hawaii have torches. It's part of daily life
here. And we can, but not until dusk. We actually make a bit of a
ceremony of it here."

"Like a religious ceremony?"

"More like a 'Give everyone in the bar a shot of something
tropical, compliments of the house, pick something fun on the
jukebox, and get the party started' kind of ceremony."

"You have a jukebox?" I ask, amused. "Please tell me there's no
'N Sync or One Direction on your jukebox."

"I'm gay, not a thirteen-year-old girl. Actually, the box has a theme—come see." He takes my hand again and leads me back into the bar.

On one side of the wall is the jukebox, lit up with colored neon lights, and decorated with thatched reeds and tiny, carved tiki gods. Jeff shows me the music choices. "I burned all of the CDs it plays from my computer, and I only give people three choices: romantic first-dance songs to remind them of their wedding; Hawaiian music, because, really, there's no way around that; and every song ever recorded by the Beatles."

"Huh. I never knew the Beatles were known for weddings."

"They're not—they're just awesome."

I look at some of the selections, which include everything from "What a Wonderful World" to Shania Twain's "You're Still the One." I notice song D-4. "Marvin Gaye's 'Let's Get It On' cannot be a first-dance song."

"Actually, it was. I only have songs customers danced their first dance to. But I must admit, several of those songs also fall into a secret last category, which I like to call 'Get the drunk couple to start slow-dancing in my bar while I sell them two more twenty-dollar drinks, then call them a cab.'"

I flip the pages of the songbook and continue perusing. C-1 is a classic. "The acoustic version of 'Layla' by Clapton. Nice . . ." Beneath that, I am surprised by selection C-2. "You have 'Wonderful Tonight' on here?"

"Of course. Classic first dance. But mostly it's a tribute to you. Don't you remember? It was playing during the first slow dance we ever had back in college."

I feel horrible. After everything that had happened with Jay in the past few weeks, I had completely forgotten about that dance with Jeff. We had been dating about a month. He's the reason I didn't make out with Jay that weekend in college—I didn't have time for a fantasy, I was too busy being happy in a real relation-ship. "That's very sweet of you to remember. Thank you," I say, touched. "Hey, you wanna dance?"

"Aw, sweetie, I can't right now. We open in less than an hour, one of my bartenders just quit so I'm down a guy, and I have to start prepping. But we can later tonight."

"I would be honored." I clap my hands once. "So what can I do to help?"

"Nothing. You'd be bored out of your mind. I'm just going to be cutting up fruit, loading up ice, restocking wine bottles—nothing exciting."

"Remember how we always had the rule that if either of us ever came to a party early, we'd put each other to work getting ready?"

"Yeah?"

"Well, I'm here early, aren't I?" I say excitedly.

Jeff considers my point. He shrugs. "If you want to help me, I will always take the help."

And I am excited—this will be fun. I follow Jeff behind the bar. I have not been behind a bar since I was a little sister at Jeff's fraternity in college, helping them serve drinks at their annual Pirate Party.

"Okay, we'll start with the fruit. See these trays?" Jeff asks, point-ing to three plastic fruit trays. "They need to be filled throughout the night with lemons, limes, cherries, and twists of orange. So we need to cut them up and have them ready for opening."

"Cool."

Jeff hands me a sharp eight-inch knife, and I begin slicing limes while he starts working on lemons.

Cut, cut, cut . . . I sure like the sound the knife makes when it hits the plastic cutting board, and the scent of the fresh lime juice smells like a bubble bath. Who knew something as simple as slicing limes could be so relaxing and good for the soul? As I continue to slice, I realize that it's been a long time since I worked with my hands. I normally go from teaching math and grading papers all day to a home of television and microwave dinners at night. I don't cook, I zap. I pretty much stopped cooking after I broke up with my boyfriend. Without an audience to appreciate my efforts, there was no point.

But clearly there was a point. It's a welcome change to be doing something that's brainless, yet gives me immediate, visible results. It's a cheap road to instant happiness. Yay. Maybe when I get home, I'll sign up for a cooking class.

Imagine having to go halfway around the world to figure out that something as simple as cutting fruit could give me so much pleasure.

My zen is interrupted as an exotically beautiful Hawaiian girl in a bright red tropical shirt and short, white miniskirt that shows off her perfect legs bursts through the door and heads right to Jeff.

She's a woman on a mission. "Jeff, I need you to explain men to me. Again," she commands, her tone a combination of anger and frustration. (Been there.)

Jeff, unfazed and clearly used to her outbursts, continues to calmly cut up lemons. "Honey, if I knew anything about men, do you think I'd still be single at my age?"

Pretty girl gets to the bar and sticks her iPhone inches from Jeff's face. "Read this. This is fucked, right?"

Jeff calmly pulls his head back a bit to read the screen. After a moment he surrenders. "I give up. What am I looking at?"

"Remember that guy Billy I told you about?" she asks Jeff, her energy level so high I think she might ping around the room like an old-fashioned silver pinball.

"Not really. You talk about so many men, it's hard to keep track."

"Volleyball guy with the ears."

"Oh, right."

She shakes her phone quickly back and forth in front of Jeff, then says angrily, "He just asked me out."

Jeff reads the screen again, then concludes dryly, "Bastard."

"On Twitter."

Jeff winces. "Oooh."

Leggy-model type notices me for the first time. "Sorry. Hi, I'm Leilani. You must be Melissa."

"Mel. Hi," I say, smiling and wiping my lime-soaked hands on a towel so that I can shake her hand.

Leilani shakes my hand, then wastes no time getting my opinion. "Mel, do you think it's bad if a guy asks you out on Twitter?"

"Depends. Did you meet him in here?"

"Yes."

"Then yes."

"Damn," she exclaims, grabbing a flower-patterned, green-and-white apron from the bar, wrapping it around her waist, and tying it in the front. "Men are so confusing. I'll bet it was so much easier to date at the turn of the century."

"Probably," I say, dreaming of the romance of the good old days. "No phones to wait by, no stupid romantic movies with their unattainable happy endings to watch. A young gentleman coming to your house to court you . . ." I look over at them wistfully.

Leilani stares at me blankly.

Jeff smirks.

"What?" I ask.

"Leilani was born in the nineties," Jeff tells me. "To her the 'turn of the century' was 2000."

"Ah . . . ," I say. Shit. To me, people who were born in the nineties shouldn't even be in high school yet, much less drinking and working at a bar.

Leilani shows me her iPhone screen. "What should I write back?"

I read the screen: *M4C*.

I purse my lips. "Yeah . . . I'm gonna need more. M4C?"

"Meet for coffee," Jeff and Leilani say in unison.

"Oh, never meet a guy for coffee," I advise her with complete authority. "If he's asking you to coffee, he's not all that interested. You might as well have picked him up on OkCupid."

"You're right." Leilani breaks into a naughty smile as she types back, *M4V*.

"M4V?" I ask.

"'Meet for vodka.'" She looks up from her phone to ask Jeff, "Where's Ashley?"

"Who's Ashley?" I ask.

"Our bar back," Jeff tells me. "She's a musician and a part-time student. Plus, she's on Hawaiian time. So, you know, sometimes she oversleeps."

My eyes widen in surprise. "It's four o'clock in the afternoon."

Jeff shrugs, seems resigned to the situation. "Like I said, she's a musician."

"What's a bar back?"

"The bar back is the person who helps me set up the bar, then they restock everything all night, wash glasses, take out trash. You know, scut work."

My face perks up. "I can do that! I'm already helping you set up the bar. And I'm great at scut work."

Jeff shakes his head. "Wrong. You're on vacation. Your job is to be on that side of the bar, drinking Lava Flows until closing, at which time I will drive you home and pour you into the guest room. Besides, Ashley usually—"

Before he can finish his sentence, a beautiful blonde charges through the bar, racing straight to the back room. "I'm sorry I'm late. I totally got stuck in traffic," the blonde says to Jeff as she rushes through the bar. "Hey, Mel."

Hey, Mel? As Ashley disappears into the back room, I wonder why she thinks she knows me.

Leilani follows Ashley toward the back room. "We have no rush hour on this island, and no freeways. How could you *possibly* get stuck in traffic?"

Ashley quickly emerges from the room, carrying a box of cabernet sauvignon bottles. "There were chickens on the road. I had to stop."

"What is it with you and chickens?" Leilani asks, shaking her head. "They're infesting the island. I say run 'em over, fry 'em up."

"That is so mean," Ashley responds as she carries the wine behind the bar. "How can you live on this beautiful island and not want to coexist peacefully with its inhabitants?"

"Because some of its inhabitants taste finger-lickin' good with a little barbecue sauce and a side of fries."

Ashley shakes her head. "You know, you should really think about going vegetarian."

Leilani glares at Ashley, then makes a show of moving her hands from her shoulders down to her hips. "Look at this body. Would you do anything differently?"

Touché. First point, Leilani.

"Uncle Jeff," Ashley begins, "would you please tell Leilani that if she cares at all about heart disease—"

"Wait. Uncle Jeff?" I interrupt. "You're not Ashley as in Ashley his niece, are you?"

Ashley looks at me blankly. "Yeah."

"Shouldn't you be nine?" I ask her accusingly.

Jeff laughs. "Ashley is twenty-two now. Time flies."

Jeff's little niece Ashley, whom I used to buy ice cream, is now a beautiful, busty blonde who has grown up to be my dating competition. How depressing.

Leilani's phone buzzes. She picks it up and reads, *"M4D?"* She looks up. "Anyone know what *D* is supposed to mean?"

" 'Dinner,' " I answer.

" 'Drinks'?" Jeff guesses.

Ashley doesn't say anything aloud. Instead, she walks over to Leilani and whispers in her ear. Leilani's jaw drops, and she grabs her phone and types. "That *better* not be right."

Ashley turns to Jeff. "I see you have the fruit under control. I'll get started on the restocking and the ice."

"Good plan," Jeff tells her as she disappears into the back room. Then he turns to me and smiles. "Which means you're officially off the clock. Let me get that Lava Flow started for you."

"Or you could make me a money tree," I say hopefully.

"That's not the way it works. Besides, don't I get credit for the charm cupcakes?"

"Wait—there are cupcakes?" Leilani asks, putting her phone in her apron pocket.

"There are cupcakes?" we hear Ashley yell from the back.

"No! There are no cupcakes," Jeff says loudly to both of them. Then he looks at me pointedly. "And there are no money-tree drinks either. That's cheating."

"Eeww . . . Don't make drinks out of the money trees. That sounds nasty," Leilani says to Jeff.

"I'm not going to," Jeff assures her.

"Good. Because that would be like when everyone was doing

edible flowers at the five-star restaurants. Why the hell would I want pikake with my ono? You eat your fish, you look at the pretty flowers. You drink your Lava Flow, you look at the pretty money trees."

"Right," Jeff agrees, nodding wholeheartedly and gesturing toward Leilani while he looks at me. "You drink your Lava . . ." He turns to Leilani, confused. "Wait. What are you talking about?"

Leilani continues to make a face. "Money trees are all fibrous. Why would you want to mix them in a drink?" A thought startles her. "Wait. Please don't tell me you're infusing vodka with them, because that is gonna be worse than when you tried infusing vodka with bacon."

I try to quell my urge to get too excited as I ask Jeff, "Is she talking about actual trees?" I snap my head over to her. "You're talking about real trees, aren't you? As in the green things with branches and sap and bark and all that?"

"Kind of, as in the green things. Although some of them are pink and green, and some of them don't exactly have bark. I mean, I guess it's bark. What exactly is bark?"

I smack Jeff on the arm triumphantly. Then I turn to Leilani. "Oh my God, I love you! Where can I find one of these pink-and-green things?"

"Um . . . outside."

"Outside where? Like at an arboretum? Or somewhere in Honolulu?"

"Like outside on the lanai. Jeff has them scattered around the patio."

As I race out to the lanai, I can hear Jeff ask her, "I do?" I look around at all of the flora and fauna. Ready, eager . . .

And having no idea what I'm looking at. There are some tiny trees with spiky, green leaves, and a ton of flowers with greenery around them. But nothing that looks like a Christmas tree, or even a palm tree. I turn to Leilani, who has followed me out. "Show me the money tree!"

"You're standing right in front of one," Leilani says, walking up to me and pointing down at a small bush with long, thin, glossy green leaves that look as if they've been outlined in red.

I smile. "Oh, it looks more like a bush."

"That one does, but we have ones that look like trees too. These things can grow pretty high actually. If you want to go outside, there are some big ones across the street that I can show you." She points again, this time to a taller plant with pinker leaves. "That's one too." She continues to point. "And that one, and that one."

"Those are all money trees?" I hear Jeff say from the doorway.

"Seriously, dude, how long have you been here? They're all over the island."

Mystery solved! The charm wasn't telling me I'd make a lot of money, it was telling me to come here.

But why? Do they need teachers here? Is there a man here? Was it just telling me that I needed to go on vacation to clear my head?

What was the secret message?

And, speaking of messages, Leilani's phone buzzes. She pulls her cell from her apron, reads, and grimaces. "Crap! Ashley was right. And there is no way I'm meeting a guy for D on a first date."

THIRTY-NINE

Gotta love the Internet! I'm fascinated by all I've learned about this plant in only half an hour. When I googled *money tree* the night after Seema's bridal shower, all I found were ads for financial services, articles about saving for retirement, and a few strange personal ads. But tonight, when I added the word *Maui* to *money tree,* I got thousands of hits, including nurseries from all over the island that sell all sorts of different versions and sizes of the shrub.

"*'Dracaena marginata,'*" I read excitedly to Seema from my computer while sipping a Lava Flow in Jeff's back office. "'Also known as the Madagascar dragon tree, the red-edge *Dracaena,* and here in Maui, the money tree. Grows best at temperatures between sixty-five and ninety degrees Fahrenheit in plant hardiness zones ten through eleven.'"

"I can't believe you just moved all of your stuff out without telling me!" Seema exclaims. She just got home from Africa (like, less than an hour ago) and has just skyped me to discuss my surprise wedding gift. Seema continues to fume. "When I got home, I was afraid we had been robbed."

"Don't be silly," I say, still reading. "If you had been robbed, they would have taken the headdress. What do you think a 'plant hardiness zone' is?"

"I can assure you, no one will ever take the headdress," Seema snaps. "Then I call my brother and he says you left weeks ago. What the hell is going on with you lately? You are not acting like yourself."

"Good," I say proudly. "That's the whole idea." I look up and think aloud, "Wouldn't it be great if we knew which dating hardiness zones men did best in? You know, like, 'This thirty-five-year-old male has some past dating damage and will wither outdoors: dating hardiness five. However, the specimen thrives indoors with proper watering and a steady diet of sex and watching sports on television.'"

Seema furrows her brow and shakes her head. "What? What are you babbling about?"

"Dating hardiness zones. Then some men could come with a warning: this thirty-three–year-old is a toxic weed, best dealt with by spraying repellent directly in his face."

Seema ignores my joke. Through my computer, I can see her pacing around our living room back home like a caged cheetah. She prefers it when she can control my life, and when I don't do things such as go halfway around the world for part two of a booty call, then go back around the world the other way to buy a plant. (Go figure.)

Or put all my stuff in storage without leaving her a key. Seema inhales a deep breath, then exhales. Calmer now she asks, "Okay. So, where did you move?"

"I haven't yet. All of my stuff is in storage."

Even from three thousand miles away, I can see her suppress a conniption. Another deep breath, then she asks, "Less than a month before your job starts, but I suppose you know what you're doing. So when's your flight back? I'll come pick you up."

"I don't know yet," I say, wondering how long I can evade that question. "Did you know only one week of fifty-five-degree temperatures will damage the plant? Well, that explains why the trees like Maui so much: so far the only thing I've encountered here that's under fifty-five degrees has rum in it."

Another inhaled breath from Seema, then a loud exhaled sigh. She calmly asks me, "Do you want me to book your ticket? I can do that while we're talking. When are you thinking of coming back? Next week?"

"I don't know. . . . Speaking of rum"—I hold up my drink, which looks like a white Slurpee mixed with a red Slurpee—"you have got to try one of these. It's called a Lava Flow. It's a blender drink with rum, strawberries, and coconut."

"Because you know you're going to need to find an apartment before school starts, and that will take awhile. You can't afford to just plop yourself down in the Oakwood apartments or Park La Brea because you don't feel like looking."

"I know that."

"And school starts early this year, and with your prep days, you need to be back by—"

"Seema. Stop," I command. "I know I have to be back soon, I'm not an idiot. But I have to figure this out on my terms, not yours. And even if—"

As I'm talking, through my screen I see Scott walk in behind her, carrying a small, white paper bag. "I'm back," he tells her, interrupting me. "Turns out we didn't need to get these through the pharmacy though. As long as the over-the-counter ones have enough fol—"

Seema's eyes widen before she whips her head around to quickly alert him, "I'm skyping with Mel."

Scott smiles and walks up to the camera. "Hey, Mel. Congratulations on moving out. I apologize for my wife pouncing on you, as I'm sure she has."

"No problem. I can handle anyone from three thousand miles away," I say, getting a better look at the white bag to see it came from our local pharmacy. "What's in the bag? Did you get sick in Africa?"

"Don't change the subject," Seema snaps, slowly moving her hand toward the bag, then pushing it out of camera range.

Okay, she's being weird. I try to remember what Scott said: "Over-the-counter ones with enough fol . . ." *Fol: fall, fall guy, follies . . .*

"I was poisoned by a snake, if that's what you mean," Scott answers me. "But I'm fine."

My mind races: *Follicular . . . is that a word? Follicle . . . what is that . . . hair follicles.* "Are you losing your hair?" I ask Scott.

"Yes," Seema says with complete authority, while Scott carelessly runs a hand through his hair and says, "No. Nothing like that."

She shoots him a look.

Think, Mel: follicles. Let's see . . . follicles can also mean ovarian . . .

"Folic acid!" I yell triumphantly. "You needed over-the-counter pills with folic acid. Which means . . ." I stop. Wait . . . "Holy shit!" I blurt out. "You're pregnant?"

"What? No!"

"You're glowing!" I say accusingly.

"I am not."

I point at my screen. "And your face is a little puffy."

"I just got off a plane. I'm retaining water."

"So, what are you? Like, three months along?"

"Six weeks! Jeez. I'm barely late, and I'm already puffy?"

I cannot suppress a smirk. "Gotcha."

Silence. I watch Seema and Scott engage in one of those married-people conversations that's all done with silent looks.

"I'm going to leave you two to hash this out," Scott says, smiling and walking out of sight. Then I hear him say, "You better be back in time for the next baby shower."

"I will be," I promise.

"Good. I hope to get the Maserati charm."

I allow a minute for him to get out of the room. Then I ask in all seriousness, "How do you feel? Any nausea?"

Seema is calmer now. "Not yet. It's still really early on."

"Do you want a boy or a girl?"

"I just don't want a nine-pound foot."

Typical Seema answer. "Is Scott happy?"

"Over the moon. He wants to look at three-bedroom houses in the suburbs."

"Scott?!" I exclaim, shocked. "In the suburbs?"

"I know my husband well enough to know we'll drive half an hour out of the city, and he'll start breaking out into a rash. But it's fun to dream and look at places."

"So, see, it's good I moved out. Now you're free to move on to act two: the James years."

Seema sighs. "The baby isn't coming for months. You need to get home and get back to your real life."

I take a deep breath and prepare to stand up for myself. "Not now I don't."

"Seriously, I can help you. I can start perusing Craigslist for rentals—"

"Seema, just stop," I say warningly.

"Just give me a return date. You're being ridiculous."

"Well, I'd rather be ridiculous than boring!" I yell at her angrily.

Seema looks startled. I lower my voice, but I'm still angry. "Jesus Christ! I have mapped out everything in my life based on what I thought I wanted at eighteen. And to what end? Do you want to know how being ridiculous feels? It's extraordinary! It gives you the courage to grab a cab and chase down a groom on a runaway horse. It makes you fly to Paris on a whim. It allows you to spend your birthday in Italy with a former *Esquire* model. And it gets you excited to learn about a plant you've never heard of."

I can tell Seema wants to counter what I'm saying, but as she opens her mouth to respond, I beat her to it. "I need to figure out what's going to make me happy in my life. Long term. And I need to do it on my own. And it may wind up being totally ridiculous, and not how I thought it was going to look at all. It may blow up in my face. But I need to do it. I need to be ridiculous right now."

Seema nods her head. "Okay," she says quietly.

"Thank you."

"You know I—"

"I know," I answer, before she gets all emotional. "And I appreciate that. Now get some sleep. You're resting for two now."

"All right. I love you."

"I love you too."

"Call me soon?"

"Yup. Or you call me," I say.

And we hang up.

I take another sip of the Lava Flow. I do like it, even though it's starting to taste a little too much like a Popsicle. I wonder if anyone makes Hawaiian wine?

There's a loud knock on the door, and Ashley pops her head into the office. "Jeff wants to know if you still remember how to bartend."

Eep. "Remembering implies there was a time when I knew how to do it."

"He said you used to do it in college."

"Oh, God, at his fraternity parties. Not for real."

My phone beeps a text. I look down to see Jeff has written:

You'll wing it. Get your butt in here.

"Saturdays are normally bad," Ashley tells me. "But there are only three of us, and we just had a wedding party of sixteen come in. We passed 'slammed' about ten minutes ago. Can you help?"

"I can try."

"Awesome." As Ashley walks back out, I can hear her yell to Jeff, "She'll do it!"

I grab my umbrella drink and head on out.

FORTY

The moment I walk out of Jeff's office to survey the overflowing crowd, I know I'm in over my head. But I'm just the extra help, I assure myself, so anything I do will be seen as a bonus.

As I jump behind the bar, Jeff quickly leans in to me and says in a low voice, "Just keep track of the drinks you pour, and I'll handle the register. Remember, these are mostly honeymooners, so ask them about their wedding."

"Done," I say confidently, even though I have absolutely no confidence in this situation.

I walk to the left side of the bar, where a tanned Adonis in a yellow silk Hawaiian shirt has just sat down with his cute new wife. I throw two cocktail napkins in front of them, one for each drink, then bust out with a cheerful "Aloha! Welcome to the Male 'Ana! What can I get you guys?"

While the girl peruses the cocktail menu, her husband asks, "What beers do you have on tap?"

"We have several," I say, motioning to a row of beer taps behind me and quickly scanning what we have as I say with (completely made up) authority, "Most of them are produced locally. What are you into? An IPA, a porter . . ."

"Actually, I like lagers," he says, squinting to look at the signs on the taps, "but I'm not seeing one."

I turn quickly to reread the taps, then turn back to him as if this were old hat. "We have a great lager from the Maui Brewing Company. It's called Bikini Blonde. Very clean, very fresh." How do I know we have a great lager? Because if Jeff picked it, it is by definition "great." How do I know it's clean and fresh? It's a freaking lager.

"Awesome. I'll take that."

Men are easy. "Perfect," I say to him sunnily as I grab a pint glass, pull the tap, and pour. As I hand the groom his beer, I look over at his perfectly toned and tanned new wife.

"I want to get one of the drinks you're famous for," she says as she studies our drinks menu as if there were going to be a quiz later. "What do you have that's potent, but not too tropical?"

Not too tropical in the middle of a tiki bar? Sigh. Okay, she's probably had her fill of mai tais and is tired of rum. So we go vodka. And nothing with pineapple, guava or passion fruit. I read her menu upside down and quickly choose one.

"I think you'd like our Kipona Aloha, which in Hawaiian means 'deep love.' It has strawberries, basil, a little bit of lime, and vodka, shaken, not stirred, and served in our souvenir heart glass."

"Let me give you a taste," Jeff says to her, magically appearing next to me, and effortlessly handing her a squinch glass of the concoction (I noticed earlier he always pours what's left in the blender into small glasses for tasting). Then he walks away to help another couple.

I smile as I watch her take a taste. Her face lights up, "Oh my God, that's so good! I'll have one of those."

"You got it," I say with deceptive cheeriness as I carefully layer strawberries and basil into a pint glass, then cover the solids with plenty of lime and vodka. I throw a shaker over the glass and give my arms a workout. "So how long are you guys in town for?"

Time flew. I spend the next eight hours listening to honeymooners tell me about their weddings, their proposals, their crazy aunt Ednas, and their wildly romantic honeymoons.

Weird. But despite being single, I loved being surrounded by that feeling of optimism that everything was going to turn out perfectly.

I have to say—I did occasionally roll my eyes.

Like when one newlywed asked me, "What do you have that's purple?" I thought to myself, *Are you painting with it or drinking it?*

But I didn't miss a beat. I cheerfully told her, "Hau 'Oli," probably botching the Hawaiian pronunciation within an inch of its life. "It means 'happiness.'"

When she and her husband ordered that, I grabbed the cocktail shaker and yelled to Jeff, "How do I make a Perfect Happiness?"

"Much like life, Perfect Happiness always includes a healthy shot of Malibu rum." Then he taught me how to make the drink right in front of the customers: coconut rum, triple sec, blue curaçao, and cranberry juice, shaken with ice and poured into a glass that looks like a laughing Buddha.

Four other signature drinks were on the menu, and by the end of the night I rocked those bitches! There was the Hapai, which was supposed to be good luck for pregnancy and fertility.

"Aren't all drinks for pregnancy and fertility?" I asked Jeff aloud, and got a good laugh.

Then we had the Honi, the Hawaiian word for "kiss." That one was red and promised romance. The Pomaika'i brought good luck. Ola was for your health (although if you're having a drink with five shots of hard liquor in it, I'm not sure how healthy you'll be feeling the next morning).

And I learned how to make all of them.

I spent that night in an exhausting, adrenaline-filled learning frenzy! I learned everything from the proper way to shake a cocktail (I had the pint glass over the stainless-steel canister part down, but I was shaking wrong), to how to tap a beer keg, to which red wineglass goes with cabernet, versus pinot noir, versus merlot. I even learned how to make the perfect lemon twist.

Ah . . . learning. It had been so long since I had been out of my element and clueless that I had forgotten how exciting it was to do something I didn't think I could do. Something I had power over, that I could immediately see I was doing badly, or doing well.

For the first time in I don't know how long, I was excited to be working.

By the time I lie down in Jeff's guest room at 4:00 A.M. and stare out the window at pitch-blackness, I realize just how worn-out I am. I can feel my biceps starting to stiffen up. I am definitely going to need a long shower in the morning, and my mind is still reeling, trying to figure out the Micros computer system the bar uses, with all its different-colored buttons and screens representing different drinks and liquors.

I close my eyes, feeling the sting that comes when you've been up too long, and take a deep breath, trying to get my shoulders to relax.

What a night.

I really hope I can talk him into letting me bartend again.

· · ·

The following morning, I awaken to sunshine streaming right into my eyes. I squint from the glare, then look over at the alarm clock on the nightstand: 10:15.

We didn't get out of the bar until around three, and I didn't get into bed until four. And I'd barely slept in the days leading up to landing here.

So by my calculations, I should be dead right now.

I glance out my window, at what was pitch-black the night before, and have to adjust my eyes to the brightness of both the sun and the colors. Jeff's house rests on a hill, so from my room, I can see nothing but bright green palm trees, white and yellow flowers, and a few roofs of neighboring houses. Wow—and this is only the guest room.

I climb out of bed and put my feet down on his polished hardwood floors. Then I go to my suitcase and rummage around for a T-shirt, my UCLA workout shorts, and my running shoes.

Jeff won't miss me—he'll be asleep until at least noon. I take the spare key he gave me and write him a note, which I tack on his refrigerator.

Gorgeous morning.

Gone running.

Might never stop. ☺

And for the first time in over a year, I run for miles.

FORTY-ONE

You see things differently when you're in a new place—you notice details that haven't registered in a while at home. My run (or should I say, my run, followed by walk, followed by run—it has been awhile) was glorious in that I happily soaked up what to the locals is mundane.

I delighted in everything I looked at, just in Jeff's neighborhood. People coming out of their houses to get the Sunday paper (who knew people walked out to get an actual paper in this day and age), families dressed for church or a beach day piling into the car, the kids laughing and happy and not even realizing they're growing up in the prettiest place on earth.

I jog down to the beach, completely empty even though it is a magnificently beautiful day. I watch a woman sip her coffee in a paper cup while walking her golden retriever. Another woman, with a stroller, jogs up to her and gives her a big hug. A woman walks out of the grocery store, carrying her canvas bags filled with food. Older men play chess at a table near the beach.

I keep running.

When I walk back into the house (or should I say stumble back into the house; I may have overdone it), I am greeted with the wonderful scents of coffee and bacon.

"Good morning, sunshine!" Jeff cheerfully greets me from his kitchen while scrambling eggs with a rubber whisk. "How do you like your eggs?"

"In a brownie."

"Scrambled it is!" he says cheerfully as he scrapes the eggs out of a Calphalon frying pan and into a large serving bowl. "Wait until you try these eggs. They come from chickens down the street who, I'm sure, Leilani wants to run over. Unfortunately, the bacon is not from a local producer. Pork is huge here, and we cannot seem to raise enough pigs on this island for everyone to snack on. But it does come from a smokehouse in the Midwest that is quite good."

"Sounds amazing," I say, walking toward the kitchen. Jeff's house has an open floor plan combining a large living room, dining room, and gourmet kitchen. And from every one of those areas you can see the ocean through gleamingly clean, floor-to-ceiling windows that showcase palm trees waving in the breeze in front of a wall of blue water. This is the first time I've been able to see Jeff's house in the daytime, with all of the curtains open, and his view on full display. "Holy crap. You have an amazing view of the ocean."

"It's Hawaii. There are Denny's here with amazing views of the ocean. I have freshly brewed Kona coffee in the thermos, there's Danish on the table, and your bacon and eggs will be ready momentarily."

Jeff brings the bowl of eggs and a plate piled high with bacon to the table, already set for two people, complete with cloth napkins. "Breakfast is served."

"Your house is perfect," I say as I sit down and pour myself coffee. "I'm almost afraid to touch anything."

"Please. You should see this place after I've thrown a party," Jeff says as he takes a seat. "Last June, I woke up to a duck waddling around my living room."

"And by 'duck' you mean . . . ?"

"I mean an actual duck. Get your mind out of the gutter." He hands me an envelope. "Your winnings, sir."

I take the envelope, confused. "What are you talking about?"

"You know, from *Casablanca*? Louie says, 'I'm shocked to find gambling'? 'Your winnings, sir.'"

"I know what movie you mean. I meant what winnings?"

"Your tips from last night."

I try to hand him back the envelope. "I can't accept this. I was just helping out."

"No, no. We have a rule: everything goes into the tip jar, everyone gets an equal cut. No exceptions."

"You're letting me stay here, and you bought my airplane ticket. Yesterday was the least I can do."

"Take it. We each cleared over five hundred dollars last night. Use it to book a massage or something."

"I can't accept . . ." I'm not sure I meant to snap back the envelope so quickly as I ask, "Wait—five hundred dollars for one night?! Is that normal?"

Jeff's face lights up. "Seeeee . . . Now you're thinking about it. Is it normal? Hmm. For a Saturday night, yes. But I assure you, we don't do that well on Tuesdays, and it's why I don't even bother being open on Sundays or Mondays."

"Can I go back on Tuesday?" I ask, still staring at my wad of cash.

"You won't make that kind of money. Saturdays are our big night."

"That's okay. I had fun. I want to do it again."

He shrugs. "Okay, that'll give me more time to find someone permanent." He takes a bite of bacon. "In the meantime, since the bar is closed today, I figure we'd go snorkeling and have a picnic lunch at Kapalua Bay, followed by cocktails and a tiki-torch ceremony at the Westin in Ka'anapali, and then on to dinner somewhere fun."

My eyes light up. "A tiki-torch ceremony? Like a real one?"

"No, like a fake hotel one. But it's like a luau: if you're in Hawaii, you gotta go at least once. Come on. Chop, chop."

Within ten minutes, I have wolfed down my breakfast, taken a shower, thrown on a swimsuit, and packed clothes for later in the evening.

We then head up the coast.

FORTY-TWO

After a lovely forty-minute drive up the Honoapiilani Highway (pronounced Hah-noe-ah-pee-ee-lah-nee. Doesn't that sound much more exotic and fun than the San Diego Freeway or the Union Turnpike?), we get to the town of Lahaina, and Jeff pulls his car into the Foodland parking lot. "This, my dear, is Foodland—the island's neighborhood grocery store. There's also one in Kihei that's open twenty-four hours a day, so if you need dental floss at three A.M., you're set."

We walk through the parking lot in what in any other part of the country I would consider hot and muggy weather and into the delight of crisp, cool air-conditioning.

Jeff grabs a plastic, green basket, and we could be walking through any supermarket chain on the mainland—save for all of the sunscreen, masks, and snorkel gear on display near aisle three. We make our way to the seafood section, where I see a large sign on the wall behind the counter that says HAWAII'S HOME FOR POKE.

I turn to Jeff. "What's poke?" I ask, making the *e* silent.

Jeff grins at me. "Actually, it's pronounced *poh-kee*, and it is one of *the* Hawaiian delicacies you must eat while you're in Maui."

I check out all of the varieties of poke through the deli's glass. There are bright red chunks of fish that don't seem to have sauce, brownish-pink chunks with a light brown coating and herbs, white chunks swimming in some sort of marinade, and about a million others, all displayed in sparkling stainless-steel trays. "Looks like raw fish."

"There's some cooked stuff. But mostly it's raw fish marinated in soy sauce and anything from wasabi to seaweed to tomatoes. Poke is a Hawaiian staple. There are a million kinds, and it's all fresh. And poke doesn't just refer to raw fish. Poke is a Hawaiian verb that means 'to section, slice, or cut.' So it can refer to anything that is sliced or cut, including edamame."

A middle-aged gentleman sporting the name tag JOE walks up to us and cheerfully says, "Hi, folks. What can I get for you today?"

"We'd like half a pound of your ahi, a half pound of the salmon, plus let me get half a pound of the garlic soybean poke and . . ." Jeff turns to me. "Do you like fermented black beans?"

I involuntarily make a face. Jeff laughs. "Okay, I'll take that as a no." He turns back to Joe. "Let's just do half a pound of shrimp ceviche." Then he turns back to me. "Plus, I have a sauvignon blanc to go with all this that's going to make you so happy, you might buy a silver wine charm for your bracelet."

Moments later, we have plastic containers of various types of fish and are heading toward the produce section. "I know it's a cliché, but we're getting a pineapple. Oh, and I forgot . . ." He takes my hand and walks me over to aisle four, the canned section. "Check this out."

In front of me is a wall of Spam. All kinds of Spam: classic Spam, lite Spam, Spam with less sodium, something called Spam spread. "Ew . . ."

"Don't say that. The stuff is pretty popular on the island."

"Not enough sauvignon blanc in the world . . . ," I insist, shaking my head.

A few minutes later, we are back in Jeff's car and heading to Kapalua Bay, which is a sheltered white-sand beach near the Ritz-Carlton hotel. We have to wait a few minutes for a space in the small parking lot off to the side.

Once parked, we pull out beach bags filled with various snorkeling gear Jeff has acquired over the years (masks, flippers, and snorkel tubes) and one large picnic basket.

I cannot yet see the beach as we get out of our car, walk past some public restrooms and through a rocky tunnel, but then the path opens up to palm trees and gloriously sparkling water.

As we walk along the light sand beach, Jeff asks, "Have you ever snorkeled before?"

"Other than in a pool when I was ten, I have not."

"This is the perfect place to do it because the water is so calm. See how there's a reef on each side?" Jeff points to a reef to our left, and I can see it begins a C-shaped cove with a reef on either side of the bay to keep the waves from coming in, ensuring that the water stays calm and clear.

I inhale a deep, cleansing breath, and revel in the salt smell. "Very peaceful."

"Yes. The fish think so too. The other benefit of this place is you can just walk out into the water. Some places, like Molokini Crater, you have to take a boat to get to. Here, you can grab your mask and snorkel tube, walk out into the water, swim past the breakers, and, boom, fish everywhere."

We pick a spot in the middle of soft sand and put our stuff down. Jeff pulls a pair of blue flippers out of the bag and throws them to me. "If you want to go even further out, you can use these."

"Flippers!" I say, my face lighting up. I carefully put them on my feet, then walk around to test them out as Jeff lays out large beach towels for us to sit on.

"How do I know if they are the right size?" I ask as I carefully lift my knees up and down, admiring my new shoes.

"What is it about women that they always want to walk around in their flippers? It's not a strappy high heel. It's a flipper—one size fits all."

He has a point. I do look kind of silly walking in my flippers. It's like walking to the ice-skating rink in your skates—you can't look graceful. "Do these flippers make my butt look big?" I joke.

To my surprise, the beach is not very crowded, and it's also very quiet.

I pull a mask from the bag, along with a snorkel tube. "So what do I do now?"

"Defog your mask, and go to town." Jeff pulls a small bottle of "defogger" out of a bag and tosses it to me. "Only use a drop or two."

"Right," I say confidently. I open up the bottle . . .

Then stare at it.

Jeff is pulling various gear and sunscreen out around us and hasn't noticed me yet.

Finally I look at him. "Let's play a game where we pretend I'm the stupid tourist."

He smiles. "You don't know how to defog a mask?"

"I didn't even know *defog* was a word."

He laughs, takes my mask, puts a drop of goop from the bottle on the inside of the mask, and rubs it in. Then he does the same with the other side, then hands me the mask. "Go to town."

As Jeff prepares the picnic (including pouring himself a glass of wine from a plastic decanter), I stand there, confused as to what to do next. "So I'm just going to walk out there," I say, pointing to the water in front of us, not five feet away, "and there will be fish?"

"No. You want to walk over to the north end of the beach and snorkel around the rocks. There's more fish at the reef. The water's calmer, so it's clearer, plus sometimes there are turtles."

"Me? Aren't you coming?"

"With my fear of sharks? God no."

"You have a fear of sharks?"

"Yes."

"And yet you moved to Hawaii?"

"Don't sound so *Jaws IV* about it. We have land in Hawaii." He pulls out a colorful hardback book entitled *Fish of Hawaii*. "You want to take a look at this before you start? It shows you what a humuhumunukunukuapua'a looks like. Did you know that that used to be Hawaii's state fish?"

I look back at the water, confused. "Are there a lot of sharks out there?"

"You mean ones that eat snorkelers? No." He opens the book. "Oh, parrot fish! Those are good too."

"You're actually going to read a book about fish rather than see them for yourself?" I ask incredulously.

"What can I say? It is the delightful quirkiness that is me," he says, returning to his large book and leafing through the pages.

I cross my arms and lean on one hip, trying to give him my best look of pity.

Jeff takes a sip of wine from his pool-safe wineglass, unfazed. He knows I'm trying to make a point, but refuses to look up from his book.

"Oh, come on!" I plead. "If there is one thing I have learned in the past few weeks, it's to stop reading about life and get off your ass and start experiencing it! You have an entire other world less than ten feet away, and you're just going to let it slip away from you because of fear."

Jeff looks up. "That was the plan, yes."

"You can't make life decisions based on fear," I say firmly.

Jeff sighs. "Fine." He puts down the book and pulls a mask and tube from his bag. "But if you see a shark near me, punch it in the nose."

I look at him blankly. "Wait, is that a thing?"

"Actually, it is. It disconcerts the shark."

"Well, it would certainly disconcert me."

Jeff defogs his mask, and the two of us walk to the north end of the beach to snorkel along the rocky reef. I carry my flippers and put them on just before we wade our way in. Once we are waist-deep in the water, Jeff tells me to put on my mask, put the tube in my mouth, and lean into the water.

Immediately after sticking my head in, I see some bright yellow fish with stripes flit past. These I would find out later are called butterfly fish. A bright blue fish then swims right past me. I wade farther into the water to see a school of silvery fish with large yellow and white stripes going across their sides. I fall into a floating position at the surface of the water and use my flippers to propel myself into deeper water, hoping to see a Nemo fish (called a clown fish—they're orange), some blue parrot fishes, or maybe a humuhumunukunukuapua'a, which are multicolored, and I think look as if they're wearing yellow lipstick.

Just as I start watching a superthin silver fish race through the water, I hear a horrific scream.

I throw down my legs on the sand and turn around toward the sound. Jeff is wading back onto shore quickly, his tube out of his mouth, his mask up.

"What happened?" I yell to him as I race back to land.

"Don't know! I hurt my foot!' Jeff yells.

By the time I get back to shore, Jeff is sitting at the water's edge, holding on to his foot, which is covered in blood.

My eyes go wide. "Jesus."

The top of Jeff's foot is split open, and blood pours out everywhere.

"It's fine," Jeff insists tensely. "Just hurts like a son of a bitch. But I'm fine."

"That looks like you're going to need stitches."

"I said I'm fine."

"You're bleeding a lot."

"I'm not going to ruin a perfectly good day cooped up in an emergency room," Jeff snaps.

A very handsome dark-haired man in swim trunks rushes up to us. "I'm a paramedic. Can I help?"

"No," Jeff begins angrily, turning to him. "Everything's . . ." Jeff's gaydar goes off at the sight of this gorgeous guy, and his voice immediately softens. "Fine. Absolutely fine."

The paramedic looks worried. "You seem to be bleeding rather profusely. Mind if I take a look at it?"

Jeff waves him off. "It's nothing. Throw a little salt in it, I'll be good to go."

The man visibly winces at Jeff's suggestion. "I wouldn't recommend that," he says, kneeling on the sand to get a better look at Jeff's bloody stump. "It looks like the top of your foot scraped against some coral. I can see there's still a piece lodged in there."

"Really? Oh. I was looking out over the water and thought I saw a fin. I panicked and tripped over a rock at the reef. Maybe I hit the coral then."

"That's probably what happened. I'm going to try and pull the coral out and see if we can't get you cleaned up."

"Pull away . . . um . . ."

"Brian."

"Pull away, Brian."

Brian points to a towel and a beach bag a few feet from us. "I have a clean towel in my bag. Let me go grab it."

"Okay, Brian," Jeff says, pleasantly smiling at his new love.

The second Brian is out of hearing range, Jeff's smile disappears. He takes my hand, looks at me with all kinds of seriousness and urgency, and whispers to me, "Invite him with us to the torch-lighting ceremony."

"How can you even think about sex at a time like this?" I whisper back.

Jeff shakes his head. "It's like we've never met."

Brian the paramedic returns, holding a bright white towel that is about to look like a crime scene and a small spray can of what I assume is Neosporin. "All right. Now what's going to happen is I'm going to pull out the coral, then immediately put pressure on the wound with this towel. Be prepared for a sting."

Jeff's smile returns. "No problem. And, Brian, thank you so much for your help. I'm Jeff. This is my friend Mel. She's visiting from Los Angeles, and I thought it would be fun to take her snorkeling, then to a torch lighting at the—oh, son of a bitch, damn, fuck, motherfucker!"

"Sorry, sir. It's out now. Let me get you cleaned up."

Brian the paramedic sprays some disinfectant onto Jeff's foot, and I swear Jeff's going to leap off the sand and stay levitated a good five feet.

"Are you all right?" I ask him.

"I've had better moments," Jeff tells me through gritted teeth.

Then he asks Brian, "Do you like sushi, because there's this won-derful place in Kihei"—Jeff continues in a rapid, pained voice—"ow, that hurts! Ow, ow, fuck! Ow! Brian, are you free for dinner?!"

Even in hideous pain, Jeff can still try to make a love connec-tion. You gotta admire that kind of chutzpah.

"I love sushi," Brian says to Jeff, smiling, then turns to me. "He's going to need stitches. There's an urgent care in Lahaina that's open, if you can drive him. Otherwise I can call an ambu-lance and have him sent to the emergency room."

Jeff waves him off. "Oh, I'll be fine. So are you seeing anyone, Brian?"

I watch a shy smile creep across Brian's face, "No, Jeff, I'm not. And you're not going to be fine until after you get some stitches."

Brian helps Jeff hobble on one foot to Jeff's car, while I quickly pack up our stuff on the beach. By the time I get to the car, I can hear them making a date for tomorrow night. I shake my head, in awe at Jeff's uncanny ability to always make lemonade from lem-ons (or in this case, Bloody Marys from blood).

Soon I am driving Jeff to the urgent care center in Lahaina, which is a large town on the western side of the island between Kihei and Ka'anapali filled with restaurants, shops, and people whose friends have not caused them to need minor surgery.

I park the car and have Jeff lean against me as we hobble into the clinic. Within ten minutes, we are in Patient Room One, wait-ing for the doctor on call.

As Jeff texts Brian back and forth from his seat in the middle of the room, I examine his bloody foot. "I should have never made you go into the water with me. I am so, so sorry."

"No one makes me do anything. And I'm fine." Jeff continues texting madly on his phone. "Besides, for all you know, my mis-adventure could lead to a marriage.

I shake my head, guilt ridden. "Your foot's getting worse, and you have so much adrenaline pumping through you right now, you don't realize how much pain you're going to be in tonight."

"I have a man who looks like Clark Kent without the glasses agreeing to have dinner with me. Life really doesn't get any better than that."

I blink a few times, deciphering his description. "You do realize you just described Superman, right?"

"Let's hope so," Jeff deadpans as he reads a text from his phone. He looks up at me. "Hey, do you think you could make yourself scarce tomorrow night?"

The doctor walks in, wearing a white lab coat, reading from a clipboard. "Good afternoon, Mr. Greco, I'm Dr. Cameron—"

"Airport guy!" I blurt out.

Suddenly, I feel sick. My gut is starting to clench, the way it did when I was fifteen years old, standing next to my high school crush's locker so we could accidentally on purpose run into each other.

Airport guy looks up from his clipboard. First, he looks surprised, then his face lights up. "Hey—it's my buddy from the bar. Mel, right?"

He remembered my name! Charming airport guy remembered my name.

Jeff tosses his phone down, much more interested in this new turn of events. He turns to me. "What kind of buddy?" he asks, his voice dripping with innuendo.

"Stop it," I say quickly under my breath. "Yes," I answer in a normal voice to airport guy. I'm struggling to remember his name. Damn it! It's something French. "Um . . ."

"Ben."

"Ben! Yes, of course. Benoit."

"Benoit," Jeff repeats seductively, eyeing me mischievously.

I bug out my eyes at him, signaling for him to shut up. Fortunately he takes the hint.

"What are you doing in Maui?" Ben and I both ask each other simultaneously.

"I live here./I'm visiting," we answer together.

"But I thought you lived in New York," I say.

"No. I have business there. But you live in LA, right?"

"I do."

"Wow," Ben says. "And yet, here you are. In my office."

I nod slowly, still a bit flabbergasted. "Here I am. In your office. That could be our six-word memoir."

Ben nods. "Huh. Sooo . . . How did Paris go?"

"Good," I say, then quickly change my story. "I mean, we broke up. But good."

"Interesting," he says, nodding.

I lean in to him, looking for clarification. "Interesting how?"

Before he can answer, Jeff jokes, "Interesting in that he's so fascinated with you at this moment, he has totally forgotten about the man with the bloody foot."

Ben turns to Jeff. "Oh. Sorry. Let's take a look at your foot."

Ben examines Jeff's foot, asks a few medical questions, then concludes, "You're definitely going to need stitches. Let's also get an X-ray just to be sure your bones are all okay."

Within a few minutes, the nurse has taken Jeff to X-ray, and Ben and I have a moment alone to talk. "So, how are you liking Maui so far?" he asks.

"Other than being in a doctor's office on my second day, it's good." I shake my head, still stunned. "Man. Had I known you were a doctor who lives in Maui, I'm not sure I would have ever let you leave the bar."

Ben laughs at my (sort of) joke.

He thinks I'm funny. Good.

Then the laughter fades, and we share an awkward moment.

Ben grasps for some conversation with a doozy. "So . . . Paris guy is done with." He nods his head toward X-ray. "Is this Maui guy?"

"What? Him? Noooo . . . No, Jeff's a friend. A platonic friend. A gay, platonic friend."

Ben nods, clearly observing me.

I nod back, trying to think of something clever to say. "So, a good-looking, single doctor. Are *you* gay?" Yeah. That was exactly the type of bon mot I was shooting for.

"Um . . . no. I'm straight. But I have friends I could introduce him to, if you're trying to set him up."

"Oh, no. Unlike me, Jeff has very few problems in that area." *Unlike me? What are you saying, Mel?* "Actually he's ditching me for a date tomorrow night, so I have nothing to do. Any recommendations?"

"That depends. Do you want to do something touristy like a luau, or just something laid-back, like checking out a great sunset?"

I want to do something with you! I am screaming in my head. *I want to do anything with you! I'll go pick up dry cleaning with you! I will happily wash a cat with you.*

"I don't know," I say diplomatically, and far more calmly than I feel. "What would you suggest?"

Ben smiles and shrugs. "I'm off at five tomorrow. Are you free for dinner?"

"I would love that," I say, suppressing the urge to giggle.

I have a date. With a gorgeous, well-traveled doctor who lives in Maui.

Kind of ridiculous. I think Marilyn would be proud.

FORTY-THREE

Several hours, five stitches, and one smoking-hot doctor's phone number later, Jeff and I are back at his place. While I make dinner, Jeff lies on his couch, his wrapped foot elevated on a pillow and an iPad in his lap, stalking my new crush for me. "Okay, he's not on Match.com, howaboutwe.com, or any of the other dating websites that serve the island," Jeff informs me, sounding as serious as a supporting character talking to Tom Cruise via headset in, well, almost any Tom Cruise movie.

"I don't want to know," I tell Jeff firmly as I chop up lettuce in the kitchen. "The last few weeks have been all about doing something different: seeing new places, meeting new people, experiencing new things. And it's making me really happy. So in light of that, I'm going to try a different way to date: no Internet stalking, no waiting by the phone, no overthinking what he says, where he takes me, or what he does. I will just live in the moment, and the relationship will unfold exactly like it's meant to."

"Wait. You mean you plan to actually go on a date to learn about the guy?" Jeff asks in mock horror. "Without any recon? Wouldn't that involve asking questions and feigning interest?"

"Shut up," I say, only slightly kidding.

"Seriously, if you want to ask questions and feign interest, become a bartender. It pays better," Jeff tells me distractedly as he reads. "Man, there are more than twenty Ben Camerons on Facebook, plus a bunch of Benjamins. And don't even get me started on the other social-media sites out there." He turns to me and asks accusingly, "Are you putting green peppers in my salad?"

"Yes, because we just met today for the first time," I answer sarcastically. "Just the yellow ones. I know."

"And no tomatoes," Jeff reminds me as he continues to read the screen. "Do you know when you google *Ben Cameron,* you get almost two hundred million results?"

"No, I don't. Because, once again, I'm not going to google-stalk."

"I'm pretty sure he's not the famous cricketer," Jeff says, almost to himself. He looks up from his iPad. *"Famous cricketer.* Sounds like an oxymoron, doesn't it? Like *lovable cat* or *good first date."* Jeff continues to read, then sighs. "Seriously, I can't find him. Do you think he's Amish?"

"No, I do not think he's Amish," I grouse. "Try Dr. Benoit Cameron." Then I catch myself. "Wait. No. Don't."

"Already on it," Jeff says happily, his fingers blurring over the keys.

"Here we go! Oooohhhh . . . fancy. Graduated from Stanford undergrad, apparently a swimmer there . . ." Jeff turns to me, smiling, "You know what they say about swimmers?"

"No, what do they say?"

"More likely to be eaten by sharks." Jeff turns back to read. "Went to med school at Columbia, followed by an ER residency in Manhattan. Just moved here last year."

"Fine. Now turn off your computer. Dinner's almost ready," I command.

As I open the refrigerator to grab dressing, my mind drifts to thoughts of Ben. I can't help it. I am actively trying to stop myself, but it's like trying to stop the ocean waves from crashing or a new *Star Wars* movie from being made. "Do you think he moved here for a girl? Wait! No! Don't answer that. I'm not doing this to myself. I will find out anything I want to know about him tomorrow. And I will not even think about him until tomorrow. Tonight, I am going to enjoy a huge salad with you, watch a little Bravo—"

"Yeah, I'm not doing that."

"—watch a little History Channel with you, then go to bed." I bring large bowls of salad into the living room and hand a bowl to Jeff. He looks confused. "Okay, why are we having salad for dinner?"

"Because I need to lose fifteen pounds by tomorrow. Eat up."

As Jeff and I dig into our salads, my phone beeps from across the room to alert me that I have a text.

We both freeze. I say nothing and continue to eat my salad.

Yes, obviously, I am wondering if it is Ben, hoping it is Ben.

But I'm not going to look.

Jeff and I eat in silence for a bit. Then he eyes me, amused. "You're not even curious?"

I make a point to shrug nonchalantly. "I'm having dinner with my friend. I'll check my phone after dinner."

I know in my heart that everything I have just said is a lie. Because my first thought is *Please be him*. "I need some more croutons." I pop off the couch and head toward the kitchen. "Can I get you anything?"

"No. I'm good," Jeff says through a full mouth.

On the way to the kitchen, I pass the phone on the counter to see that there is a God:

Hey. It's Ben Cameron. I'm getting off work in an hour.
Any chance you want to hang out tonight? (If you
have to take care of Jeff, I totally understand, and
I'll see you tomorrow.)

OhmyGodOhmyGodOhmyGod.

I grab my phone, throw all of my sanctimonious lectures out
the window, pull a Leilani, and thrust the phone into Jeff's face.
"What do you think this means? Should I go? What is 'hang out'?
He didn't say 'hang out' at the airport; he said things like 'vision
of loveliness' and 'fell in love.' What does this mean?"

Jeff pulls his head back a bit to look at the text. "Well, for one
thing, it means he's not in an airport for less than an hour with
you. When we tell you we've fallen in love on the first date, you
tend to freak out. And no man under the age of eighty should ever
utter the words *vision of loveliness* aloud. Makes it sound like he
still puts on his socks with garters."

"Good point," I am forced to admit. I look at the text again. "I
think I should let him miss me a little. Conjure up a little mystery."

Jeff pats me on the shoulder. He sounds a bit surprised as he
says, "Good for you."

"Wait." I point to Jeff. "Except, how long am I here for? A
week? Two weeks? Why miss out on an opportunity to see him?
I'm not playing the long game here, I'm playing the short game.
Hence . . ."

"Hence?"

"Hence," I repeat firmly, "I should go."

Jeff narrows his eyes. "Well . . . I guess there's something to be
said—"

"Then again," I refute, "why would I want to make this easy

for him? I mean, really, isn't a girl's favorite part of the relationship the beginning? When the guy's trying hard?"

"Actually, I think a girl's favorite moment of the relationship is
right after she gets engaged. But by then she's caught, which
would mean your argument . . ."

I bug my eyes out at him.

"Sorry," Jeff apologizes. "You don't even really need me here in
the room for this, do you?"

Jeff's phone beeps a text. I look over his shoulder and see it is
Brian:

> Do you want me to come over and look in on the
> patient?

Jeff immediately types back . . .

> I would love that. I'm sending Mel off on a date with a
> cute doctor.

"Wait! What?" I exclaim.

"Look, you know you're going to go out with him. Now, you
can either bore me for the next twenty minutes listening to you
argue with yourself, or you can jump right in, say yes, and spend
that extra time taking a shower and shaving your legs. Your call."

I'm sure my mouth looks like a straight horizontal line as I
stare at him, assembling in my head an unbelievably strong and
witty comeback from an independent woman who doesn't need a
man.

Instead, I begin texting back to Ben as I ask Jeff, "You have
razors in the guest bathroom, right?"

"Remember not to overthink it," Jeff jokes as I head toward the guest room.

"Again, shut up."

Well over twenty minutes later, I am showered, shaved, spritzed with perfume, and completely made up to look as if I have no makeup on.

I also have nothing to wear. Or at least nothing that says, *Oh, are you here? You caught me completely unawares. I just happen to look this fantastic all the time, and without any effort on my part whatsoever. This just happens.*

I stare at the clothes in my still-packed suitcase and wish I had time to hit the mall. I yell from my room to the living room, "I need you to help me pick something to wear. And by that, I mean I have nothing to wear."

"Sometimes I prefer my dates that way," Jeff yells back.

Within minutes, I walk out of my room wearing a beautiful, little black dress I bought in Paris.

"Wrong!" Jeff, still working on his iPad, declares from the couch without even looking over at me.

"You haven't even looked at it yet."

"I know you well enough to know your first attempt always tries too hard." He turns around to see me. "I see I'm still batting a thousand."

"This is a beautiful dress," I insist, suppressing the urge to stomp my foot like a toddler.

"For cooler weather and a nicer restaurant, yes. But you are in the tropics on a Sunday night with a guy who just asked you out less than an hour ago. Assume you're going for fish tacos and dress accordingly."

I sigh, turn around, and head back to my room. Eventually, I settle on a sand-colored denim miniskirt, and a dark blue silk Hawaiian shirt that I borrow from Jeff's guest closet. (I'm not even going to ask why he has an assortment of expensive Hawaiian shirts in his guest closet.)

After getting Jeff's approval, I spend twenty minutes doing exciting things such as reapplying deodorant and fluffing out my hair. Finally, I reappear to Jeff proudly, throwing up my arms and announcing, "Ta-da!"

Once again, he doesn't look up from his work. "Change the shoes."

I let my shoulders slump as I turn back to my room to change out of four-inch heels and into some sparkly, flat sandals.

"There are condoms in my nightstand!" Jeff yells to me.

"I'm not bringing condoms," I tell him firmly. "I'm not having sex."

"No judgment. But in the last few months you have been a bit of a—"

"I'm done catting around," I declare as I emerge from my room. "I'm sick of the aftermath. If he really likes me, he will drop me off at the end of the night, give me a quick kiss good-night, then ask me out again. If he doesn't like me, he will drop me off, lie and say he'll call me, and I'll never hear from him again. Either way, it's a million times easier to wait by the phone if you haven't done the walk of shame."

"A million times easier?" Jeff repeats doubtfully.

"Fine. Four times easier. My point is, it's less likely to drive a girl to a Sara Lee cheesecake and a bottle of pinot for dinner."

Jeff winces. "Why wouldn't you at least go for a prosecco?"

"That's what you took from my theory? A poor wine pairing?"

Jeff shrugs just as his doorbell rings.

"He's here!" I whisper urgently, racing up to Jeff in panic. "Go answer the door."

"Doofus, your doctor boyfriend put me on bed rest. I'm not supposed to get up."

"He's not my boyfriend, and if I answer the door, I'll look too eager."

"And if you don't answer the door, you'll look like an asshole."

"Oh. Right. Crap."

I walk to the door, take a deep breath, and open it.

Ben stands in the doorway, holding a potted money-tree plant.

"Wow! Most charming thing ever." I take the money tree and quickly put it in Jeff's dining room. "All right, we'll leave you alone. Don't wait up!"

"Don't come home too early," Jeff says in a bright voice. "Where are you taking her? Fish tacos?"

"Ah! Brilliant!" Ben says, his face lighting up. "I was still debating. But you mean the place with the surfboards—"

"Yeah," Jeff interrupts, "and that tree near the outside . . ."

Ben nods. "Plus it's open—"

"Till ten on Sundays. Exactly. And they won't kick you out if you stay late. Although for drinks after dinner—"

"Life's a Beach. I'm way ahead of you," Ben interrupts. "So, originally, I was thinking—"

Jeff puts out the palm of his hand. "Let me stop you right there. Trying too hard. Take her there—"

"The third time we go out. You're right. What do you think about tomorrow?"

"Well, we were supposed to go to the Black Rock torch lighting today. Maybe tomorrow?"

Ben nods, impressed. "Good plan."

I cross my arms. "I'm sorry. Am I getting in the way here?"

Ben looks confused. "No."

Jeff smiles at me. "Actually, *you* are," he says, gesturing to Brian, now standing in the front doorway. "Get out."

I blow Jeff a kiss, which he pretends to catch and bring to his heart.

Then I push Ben out the door.

Forty-four

Jeff nailed it when he suggested that Ben take me to a fish-taco restaurant. I'm guessing it's one of the only casual restaurants in Kihei open late on a Sunday night. There are no waiters, you order at the counter, the tables are made to look like surfboards, and the restaurant is brightly lit. Very.

Not a romantic atmosphere by any stretch of the imagination, but maybe Jeff's onto something. I've been on a zillion first dates where we're both trying too hard, and I wound up spending more time worrying about what to order, what to say, and how to dress than I did about whether I even liked the guy. Maybe it's time for a first date where I get to eat messy-eating food with my hands and get to say whatever pops into my mind.

"These tacos are amazing," Ben assures me once our food comes. "Along with all the regular stuff you find in tacos, they also put coleslaw made with buttermilk in the middle. And all of the fish here is superfresh."

I bite into my taco, accidentally dripping taco filling and cole-slaw sauce all over my bright blue plate. The ahi tuna tastes insane. "Wow," I say through a full mouth. After I chew and swallow,

I tell him, "Man, that's good. Star-Kist and ahi should not even get to share the same last name."

"So much of the flavor has to do with how fresh everything is," Ben says, swiping his taco in sauce that dripped onto his plate. "Particularly the fish. I'm telling you, the first few weeks I was here, I ate fish three times a day."

"So what inspired you to move here?" I ask as I pop a delicious french fry into my mouth. "The food?"

"Oh, that. The weather. A few other things. Long, boring story with notes of self-righteousness."

"'Notes of self-righteousness.' Sounds intriguing."

"It's not, I promise. Besides, I'd rather talk about you. So what happened in Paris?" Ben asks as he opens his second taco and pours Tabasco sauce on it. "Did you get all the sex you want?"

"Does anyone ever get all the sex they want?" I joke.

Ben makes a joke of motioning to an imaginary waiter. "Check."

I laugh, then bring the conversation back to him. "So, did you go to medical school out here?" I ask, even though, thanks to Jeff, I already know the answer.

"No. Went to Columbia, then stayed in New York for my residency."

"Did you know anyone who lived here before you moved?"

"Yes and no. I actually have a friend from medical school who practices in Honolulu. She invited me out here after I left my wife. Oahu wasn't quite the right fit for me, not sure why. Maui felt more like home."

"You were married?" I blurt out. (Note to self: google-stalk and facebook-stalk the crap out of that nugget of information later this evening.)

Ben shakes his head. "Yes, and I don't want to bore you with that story. It's not exactly good first-date material."

"What *is* good first-date material?"

"Politics, religion, future," he jokes. "And my love of ComicCon. That always gets the hot girls excited."

"But not exes?" I probe, trying to sound as light as possible. "Because I am fascinated to know what idiot woman could have let you go."

He takes a second, probably to debate what to share with me. "Have you ever been married?" he asks thoughtfully.

"No."

"Well, my experience is, when recounting what happened, you both end up looking like crazy people, clueless people, losers and assholes. Who's playing which role kind of depends upon the day and the fight. Soooo . . ." He shrugs and tries to force a smile. "I kind of hope we can talk about something else."

"Okay. . . . So what brought you here?"

"My friend Randi invited me to stay with her in Honolulu during my separation. I just got on a plane and never looked back."

I can't help myself—my jealousy rears its ugly head. "So, you didn't fly across the world for sex with Randi?"

He chuckles. "With Randi? No. She was my roommate in med school. She's pretty, but there was always something about her that was more like a sister. Anyway, so I go to see her and stay with her family. She's an ER doc too, and she doesn't do call. She only works four twelve-hour shifts a week—no seventy-hour work-weeks. She has a toddler and a baby and a husband who works a nine-to-five job in local advertising.

"It took me all of one day to see she was happy. And I wasn't. There was so much I hated about both my job and my life. I hated the constant adrenaline I needed to keep up with an emergency room in Manhattan. What was exciting at twenty-six can be exhausting at thirty-two."

"I feel that way about dating," I joke. Well, sort of joke.

"Yeah, me too. Anyway, so I was walking on the beach in Waikiki, playing with Randi's kids, and as I tossed her giggling toddler up in the air for the fifth time, I realized that I don't have to be the person I set out to be when I was a kid. When I was ten, I thought Bo from *The Dukes of Hazzard* was cool—what the heck did I know? I immediately started to make job inquiries and applied for a medical license in Hawaii. Eventually, I found an urgent care in Lahaina looking for someone."

I realize I've been nodding the entire time he's been talking, "Wow. You actually followed your midlife dream. Good for you." I take another bite of fish taco. Culinary-orgasm good. "So, any regrets? Miss anything?"

"I'll admit, I do miss the money." He motions out the window toward the town, pitch-black and mostly asleep on this peaceful Sunday night. "But I love the million-dollar weather." He takes another bite of food. "So, what about you? What's your life story?"

"Not done writing it. Check back with me in thirty years," I say, smiling, as I eat a french fry.

"How long are you here for?"

"I don't know. How long can you be charming for?"

"If I said the rest of your life, would that be overkill?"

"If you say the rest of my life, I will camp out at your doorstep and facebook your mother," I answer without missing a beat.

He laughs. And not one of those polite first-date laughs—a genuine guffaw.

Excellent.

For the rest of the meal, we talk about the usual first-date stuff: where we grew up, how many brothers and sisters we have, our majors in college, etc. We talked about books, movies, and our favorite bands.

And we laughed. We laughed all night. He told one story about his family dog that had me laughing so hard, I nearly fell over, and my sides hurt.

After dinner, instead of going to a bar, we walked across the main street in town and took a long walk on a pitch-black beach.

I love the sound of pounding ocean waves. The tide must have been coming in because all I could hear was ocean—no people, no cars, nothing but that Zen sound that makes me want to close my eyes and float.

Ben and I walk for a while in silence. I feel the way I did when I was fifteen, and a German transfer student named Horst walked along a beach with me, and I kept trying to figure out how to get him to hold my hand. Everything felt new and hopeful back then. That same feeling washes over me now.

"Are you cold?" Ben asks.

"Maybe a little," I admit. We had taken off our shoes, and all I was wearing was a short-sleeved shirt and a miniskirt. So, yes, I was freezing.

"I'm sorry—I forgot to bring my jacket. Do you want to go back to the car?"

"No, no. I'm fine," I lie.

"You sure?"

"I'm sure."

He stops to face me. "No, you're not."

Kiss me, kiss me, kiss me, kiss me, I think to myself, hoping he'll be able to read my mind.

"Do you want to go someplace warmer? Maybe get some coffee?"

I decide to go for broke. "Or we could go to my place for a while."

A weird look crosses Ben's face. "You know what? I have a long drive back and have to be at work in the morning. Can I take a rain check?"

Wait, what? "Oh. Sure," I say, vaguely startled. Wasn't this date going well? Have I been going on so many bad dates I don't know what a good one even looks like anymore? "We're still seeing each other tomorrow, right?"

"Oh, yeah. I think that Black Rock idea will be fun." He rubs my shoulders with his hands. "Let's get you home."

We head back to the car. He doesn't kiss me. As much as I am tempted to, I don't lean in to kiss him either. I have decided that, at least for tonight, I am going to be the woman who is being pursued. Or not pursued, or whatever this is.

Once we're at his car, Ben pulls out a jacket from his backseat and wraps it around me. Then we hug.

And that's all we do.

All right, I'll admit on the drive home, I am ridiculously tempted to lean over and kiss him. But instead, I lean back and try to wait.

We get back to Jeff's house. His living room light is off, but his porch light is on.

As Ben walks me to the doorstep, we see that Jeff has put the money tree Ben brought just outside the front door.

Taped to one of the branches is a note from Jeff:

Why, will you look at that?! A money tree! Right here on our date! Why, I'll bet if I kissed her in front of that tree, she would find it incredibly romantic! Romance-novel romantic! Bore-her-gay-best-friend-with-the-details-twelve-times-over-breakfast romantic!

"Oh my God!" I say, horrified and covering my face.

Ben, on the other hand, can't stop laughing. "You know what I love about him? It's the subtlety."

"I am *so* sorry. I can't believe he did that."

"Well, it's a nice thought. I'll see you tomorrow," he says, still smiling.

And he kisses me . . . on the cheek.

Yes, on the cheek.

Say what now?

"Pick you up around six?" he asks me cheerfully.

"Perfect," I lie, trying to keep my voice from catching a bit.

"Great," he says happily. Then he turns around to leave.

I watch as he walks to his convertible. As he opens his door and climbs in, he yells to me, "Does your key work?"

"Huh?" I look down at my key. "Oh, hold on. Let me check."

I easily slide my key into the lock and turn it to the right just as Ben says, "Good, because I couldn't leave until I knew you were safe inside."

Damn, I guess I did that too fast then. "No, we're good," I say awkwardly, and force an even more awkward smile and a wave.

Ben waves back, then closes his door, turns on the car, and pulls away just as I walk into the house.

Okay, seriously, what was that all about?

Why would a guy who has told me he's not gay ask me out two nights in a row, then kiss me on the cheek at the end of the night?

I flip on the living-room light and cover my eyes. "Okay, first of all, I'm sorry if I'm interrupting. And second of all, I'm going to fucking kill you, but not until you give me advice."

It's so quiet in here I'm pretty sure I hear crickets. I open my eyes to see neither Jeff nor Brian is here. What is here is a silver champagne bucket on the kitchen counter with a bottle of Mumm's chilling and a note telling me, *Brian and I decided to go out. Enjoy!*

I angrily yank the champagne out of the bucket and put it back in the fridge. Then I rummage through his freezer to find something with a lot of cream. I pull out a fifty-six-ounce tub of Roselani ice cream and read the label, "Haupia." I peel off the lid and smell coconut. That'll do. I grab a spoon and the carton and head for my room.

Minutes later, I have changed into shorty pajamas, eaten a good third of the tub, and am sitting in bed, google-stalking Ben on my notebook computer. Other than for some doctor stuff, and a picture of him at a swim meet in high school, I hit a dead end. I do manage to track down his Facebook page, but all it says is that he is a male living in Hawaii and that to get any more information I will have to friend him.

I click off his Facebook page to see that Nic has just updated her Facebook status with *The cost of prom night on average is $1,139 per attendee, or $2,278 per couple. Seems more romantic to just fly to Paris for the night, but maybe I'm old.*

She's up. Huzzah! I quickly write to her:

You have no idea how much I miss you right now. What are you doing up?

Then I wait for a response. Less than two minutes later, my cell phone booms Elton John singing "The Bitch Is Back."

I smile and pick up immediately. "I should never have let you choose your own ringtone."

"Ah, but you're smiling, aren't you?"

"I am. How is the baby?"

"He's delicious. Although I am doing lap number million and six around the living room, trying to get him to sleep. How is Maui?"

I sigh loudly. "It's perfect other than I have a guy problem."

"Already?" Nic asks in surprise. "You've been there minutes."

"I know. Remember that guy, Ben, I met at the bar in JFK?

"You met a guy at a bar in JFK? Like the airport?"

"Okay, let me start over. So there's this guy . . ." I quickly fill Nic in on all of the Ben details, ending with tonight's date and peck on the cheek. "So, what do you think?"

"Hmm," Nic thinks aloud. "Girlfriend?"

"No, I don't think so. He did recently go through a divorce though."

"That could mean he has a harem of rebound women lurking about. Gay?"

"Did I mention Jeff was his patient?" I ask dryly.

"Fair enough. Plus, who's closeted these days?" Nic thinks a moment, then throws out some doozies. "On some kind of anti-depressants and can't get it up? Maybe on heart medication and doesn't want to get superexcited? Über-Christian?"

"Okay, if any of these are true, I don't want to go on the second date."

Nic whispers, "Oh, JJ's asleep. Hold on." While she's off the phone, I put a lid on the ice cream, bring it back to the freezer, then fall down the rabbit hole of the Internet. Clicking on the hotel with the torch-lighting ceremony brings me to a site selling previously owned time-shares in Maui, which leads me to a real estate site, which lists year-round rentals on everything from studio apartments to multimillion-dollar estates. By the time Nic has come back, I'm already on to my next subject in my head.

"He's divorced," Nic continues from before. "Does he have kids he had to get home to? Maybe he's not ready to tell you about them yet?"

"What do you think of my taking a sabbatical from my teaching job?" I ask, admittedly rather out of the blue.

"What?" she blurts out.

As I read a post about a one-bedroom in Kihei near Jeff, I tell her, "It's just that I'm looking at these rentals in Maui, and if you're here for more than a month, they can be almost reasonable."

"Minneapolis reasonable or Los Angeles reasonable?"

"Probably San Francisco reasonable, but that's not my point. I'm not tied down by a man yet, my family's all over the country, my job will wait for me, if I haven't already been laid off. Why not move here for a year?"

"Because your family is in LA. We're your family."

"Yes, you are and I love you. But . . . I don't know. I mean, it's weird that this guy didn't kiss me good-night. But it's been less than an hour, and I'm already thinking about other things. The old me would be completely obsessing about him until he picked me up tomorrow night, at which time I would have tried to find a way to kiss him just to make myself feel better. The new me is thinking, *I have no furniture. I could rent a studio" apartment, get a futon and a money tree, and eat tacos every night.*"

Nic is quiet on the other end.

"Nic?"

"Wow. Sorry. Just surprised. Are you serious?"

Am I serious? Right now, I don't know. But I love the possibility that I could be. That tonight, if I wanted to, everything could change. "You know what? I'm just babbling. Throwing out ideas. I didn't mean anything by it." Then I change the subject. "So I'm done obsessing for tonight. Talk to me about you. How are you? How are the girls? What camps are they in? How's Jason? How tired are you from the baby?"

"The girls are both in paleontology camp this week. And Jason has actually been driving them in the mornings without the need to snooze seven times . . ."

We spend the next hour talking the way we used to in college. She gave me every detail of her day-to-day fabulous life, and I listened intently and laughed a lot at the way she described things. And unlike sometimes in my past, I am not even the tiniest bit jealous.

Because the moment I realized it was in my power to rent an apartment in the most beautiful place in the world, it no longer mattered that she had hit most of life's milestones before I did. I am just hitting different ones. And at my own pace. So while one woman's milestone might be *Get married,* it turns out one of mine is *I'm going to go look at an apartment tomorrow. All by myself.*

All by myself is a great milestone.

FORTY-FIVE

The next morning, I wake up around 9:00 A.M., grab an old Go-Go's T-shirt from Jeff's guest closet, throw on shorts, stretch, and go for a run through town.

Kihei is different on a weekday. The vibe is different. I won't say it's fast paced, it's not, but people have gone to work, and the stores are all open. Everything—the scenery, the smells, the sounds—it all feels colorful and warm. I have fun running past regular things that somehow look different—better!—here in paradise: a preschool with kids happily climbing a multicolored, plastic jungle gym and gleefully chasing each other across the bright green lawn. Teenagers walking in and out of the grocery store. A mom with a jogging stroller chatting with another mom who's baby is in a BabyBjörn. I jog past a beach where I almost run smack into the middle of a series of chess tournaments between pairs of senior citizens. Finally, I end up at a mom-and-pop bakery and pick up a couple of chocolate croissants.

I come home, make coffee, then quietly knock on Jeff's door. "Are you alone?" I whisper cautiously.

"Why are you whispering?" Jeff asks in a normal voice. "If I am alone, you would need to speak up to wake me up, and if I'm not alone, you'll wake up Brian anyway."

"Sorry. Are you decent?"

"Sadly, yes," Jeff says through the door.

"Meaning you're alone."

"Indeed. Come on in."

I walk in, carrying a breakfast tray with a croissant, cup of coffee, small glass of juice, and his painkillers for the day. Jeff is wearing a beat-up AC/DC concert T-shirt that was ancient back when he wore it in college, and some plaid pajama bottoms. His face lights up as he sits up in bed. "Oh, nice." He grabs the painkillers the moment the tray is in swiping distance.

As Jeff pops the pills with some juice, I ask, "How do you feel?"

"Like I'm never going to walk again without limping. I'll be fine though. So, did you do the walk of shame?"

"No!" I say, offended. "I was home by ten. He kissed me good-bye. On the cheek."

"Ooohhhh. Ouch."

"I know, right? No thanks to you, by the way. What was up with those notes?"

"Crap. I thought I was being cute. Sorry."

"Yeah, dude. Seriously," I say, climbing into bed next to Jeff. "But you can make it up to me by allowing the obligatory 'What the fuck is he thinking?' questions."

"Shoot."

"He kissed me on the cheek, yet he is taking me out again tonight. Thoughts?"

"In no particular order: My note screwed him up, and he thought I could be in the living room listening in. Or he met you when you were flying to meet another dude, who he worries you're still stuck on. Or he's just mind-fucking you, and he's hoping you will have taken it personally and be all over him tonight to prove your sexual worth as a female."

"Huh. All of those are decent. I'm impressed. Okay, next question: Do they have malls in Maui?"

"Malls?" Jeff repeats in a nondescript redneck accent. "You mean those highfalutin places where they sell T-shirts and cologne?"

"I need to get a new outfit for tonight. Just answer the question."

"There's one in Kahului. Built with tons of beige and off-white stone. It looks like it could be in any suburb in Phoenix."

"Perfect," I say, my face lighting up. "I also want to buy a University of Hawaii T-shirt to go running in. Where would they sell those?"

"We have this newfangled place called Costco that should have them."

"Is that also in Kahului?"

Jeff smiles. "Look at you, sounding like a native."

"I've been practicing," I tell him proudly. "You can pretty much sound everything out, provided you say each vowel. Check it. *Hoo . . . moo . . . huh . . .* wait. No. *Hoo . . . mmmoooooo . . .*"

"*HOO-moo-HOO-moo-NOO-koo-NOO-koo-AH-poo-AH-ah,*" Jeff says, the behemoth word effortlessly rolling off his tongue.

"See, like that!" I say, clapping once, then pointing at him. "That's the fish, right?"

"It is indeed the fish."

"Wanna go run errands with me?"

"Although I love the joie de vivre with which you ask, I want to stay on bed rest. Would you mind picking up socks for me at Costco? I'll pay you back. Oh, and Tide."

"I would love to," I say, bouncing off his bed to get ready. "Give me ten minutes to shower, and I'll be your girl Friday this lovely Monday." As I walk out of Jeff's room, I happily announce, "And, Brian, you can come out of the closet! Your car's still parked out front!"

As Brian sheepishly walks out, Jeff asks, "Couldn't you have just said, 'You can stop hiding'?"

I turn to Jeff on my way out and shake my head while I answer cheerfully, "You know, I really couldn't."

Forty-six

> I bought a money tree to put on my balcony. Want to
>   come see it tonight?

Ben texts me while I'm in the shower.

Hm. After last night, I am torn between happily thinking,
Oh my God! He's inviting me to his apartment. I'm in! and irrita-
bly thinking, *Oh my Gawd . . . He's inviting me to his apartment.
I'm out.*

To get a little clarification, I write:

> Stop being so cute.

Thank God for texting, as I'm not sure which version of me
would have surfaced when I asked that. Ben writes back:

> I'm actually serious. I have today off, and if there is a
>   shot in hell you're coming over after dinner, I will
>   spend the day cleaning.

Hm. Doesn't exactly sound like a guy who plans to kiss me on the cheek later, does it?

I used to hate texting. I thought it encouraged a complete lack of communication with fellow human beings because we don't speak to each other, and therefore we can't hear each other's intonations. All we do is type. Everyone in their own little worlds typing away, correcting themselves before they send out a sentence, making themselves look as perfect as possible, and not even vaguely real.

Of course, when one is in the throes of the first few dates, looking perfect is the goal. So while I still think texting is bad for society, I think it's working out quite nicely for me right now.

I walk out of the guest room in my day clothes, seeing Jeff reclining on the couch, going through his DVR list. "Where's Brian?"

"Had to go to work. Now why would I have recorded NASCAR?"

"You thought that one guy with the hair was cute," I remind him as I walk up to the couch. "Ben just texted to ask if I plan to see his place tonight. Ostensibly to know if he has to clean up his apartment. What should I write back?"

"What do you want to write back?"

"Do you have a tongue? I wouldn't know after last night," I say dryly.

Jeff considers that. "A bit crude, but it has a certain charm to it. Give me your phone."

I hand over the phone and Jeff quickly reads our texts, then types back:

Honestly, I'm not sure. Turns out I have to work for Jeff tomorrow night at Male 'Ana, so I may have to make it an early night.

"Do I have to work for you at Male 'Ana tomorrow night?"

"Oh, you picked up on that. Good," Jeff says, grinning. He picks up a pile of Hawaiian shirts. "Is that okay?"

"My God. I'd love that. I had so much fun working Saturday."

"Excellent. Because bartending requires being on your feet for eight hours. And I can barely hobble around for five minutes right now."

My phone beeps another text.

> Can I pick you up at 5? There might be a little traffic getting back up here for the torch lighting.

I show Jeff the text. "What do you think? Straightforward response back, or flirty? Oh, maybe mysterious!"

Jeff grabs my phone, types, and sends:

> Come on, baby. Light my fire.

I exhale a loud sigh and shake my head. "He's going to know I didn't write that. I'm not cool enough to write that."

"Sure you are. You are whatever you decide to be."

My phone beeps.

> Is that Mel or Jeff? Sounds more like Jeff.

I take my phone back. "You've been cut off."

FORTY-SEVEN

Here's something I never thought I'd say: My errand day was fantastic. I ate Spam for lunch! I had never eaten Spam, but in Hawaii it is considered a local dish, and I knew it couldn't possibly be as bad as poi, so I had it rolled in sushi and it was . . . well, okay, it didn't taste as bad as the escargot I had in Paris, anyway. The point was I tried it! I did something new!

I bought a bright purple lei at Costco because they sell them there *every day*! At the mall, I learned that some people spend $300 on an ugly Hawaiian shirt, and seriously, what is up with that? I bought a new perfume that smells like flowers. I have worn the same perfume since I was fifteen—for me, this was big. I ate something called Tiger's Blood shave ice, which is actually just a red-berry-flavored snow cone and has nothing to do with Charlie Sheen. I also looked at an apartment.

Just to look, I'm not going to do anything stupid. But something about going by myself to see a new place was intoxicating. I got to decide if I wanted to live with beige carpet, and I didn't have to wander the rooms secretly wondering what my roommate thought of it, or how it was affecting the mood of my boyfriend.

The only opinion I needed was mine. And I am good at sharing my opinion with myself.

Although sometimes I have been guilty of arguing with myself. Usually, it is because I am very good at presenting both sides of a case.

The latest case: Ben.

I spent much of the afternoon rehearsing in my head how the end of the evening would go. He could flirt with me all he wanted, be as charming as he was at the airport, and as handsome as he was last night, but if he didn't kiss me at the end of the night, I was moving on. Just going to put my key in the front door lock and not look back.

I am such a hypocrite.

The second I opened the door at five o'clock, I knew my lips and my brain would be arguing for the rest of the evening.

The man was gorgeous. Just his eyes made me want to buy a poster of him to put over my bed. His look was casual, yet appeared effortless: a simple button-down shirt with dark jeans. Hair that looks as if he quickly put a comb through it—maybe. Shoulders that I want to wrap my arms around forever.

But I suppressed the urge to invite him to my bedroom, said a quick good-bye to Jeff, who was on his best behavior, and began our date.

On the way to his car, Ben gently takes my hand in his and says, "You look very nice."

I look down at our hands. Okay, this is a date. "Thank you. So do you."

He walks me to my side of the car and opens my door. "Thank you," I say again, a little surprised at the chivalry. I mean, ever since car-door locks unlocked automatically, has any man done this?

Ben waits until I get in, closes my door, then walks around to his side.

I love it when men open the door for me. I don't know if we're allowed to be postfeminist, but to me it's a lovely courtesy. "So, did you clean your apartment today?" I ask brightly.

"I did. Although I know you have to get home early, so if you don't see it tonight, that's cool."

Um . . . okay. Not a date then?

We begin our drive up to Ka'anapali, which is normally about forty-five minutes away. Ben, like many people in Maui, drives a convertible. He asks if it's okay to put the top down, and I wholeheartedly say yes. The conversation flows naturally, as does my hair in the warm ocean breezes.

About half an hour in, we get caught in traffic. Ben slows down to a crawl and sighs. "I'm sorry about that. I forgot it was rush hour."

"This is rush hour?" I ask, turning my head to see the glittery ocean on one side of us and trees and greenery on the other, rather than a minivan filled with kids and a weary mom on one side of me, and an asshole in a BMW on the other.

Ben leans over, takes my hand. "So how was errand day?"

"Amazing," I tell him excitedly. "It was so mundane, yet so cool all at once. At one point, I went to the dry cleaner's for Jeff, and it was right next to a nursery, which smelled phenomenal, so I just walked over and got lost in rows and rows of flowers. Blooms I've never seen before. And I never do that at home. I can't even tell you if we have a nursery in Hollywood, much less what kinds of flowers it sells. Then I went to this place for shave ice, which I learned was pronounced *shave* ice, not *shaved* ice. And it had this supersoft feel to it, and there were all these cool flavors I could put on it. Forget cherry and grape. How about tamarind and li hing mui?"

"Li hing mui?" Ben repeats, surprised. "You had salted plum?"

"Actually, no. I had Tiger's Blood and Wedding Cake. But the point was, I *could* have had a snow cone made with li hing mui. It's like all of these opportunities are everywhere, just begging me to experience life differently. And they're not only at the nursery or a shave ice place. They're at Foodland! They're at Costco! I mean, who knew Costco could be fun?"

"Any man who wants a good deal on a new seventy-inch-screen TV?" Ben jokes.

I shake my head. "What is it about men and TVs?"

He shrugs. "I don't know. But they make me happy."

I laugh. "You know the best thing I bought at Costco? A University of Hawaii T-shirt. I've never wanted a T-shirt from anyone but my alma mater, but this one looked so cool. And I thought to myself, 'That will be great for running.' And I realized I'm actually looking forward to my run tomorrow morning. I'm not doing it because it's good for my health or because it'll help me lose weight. I just want to run and see more sights. I'm telling you, I haven't been this exhilarated in years."

"So, have you thought about staying?"

"You mean permanently?" I ask, a little startled by his question. I mean, I had looked at an apartment, but that was kind of just for fun.

"Why not? You just said you're more exhilarated than you've been in years. Have you thought about staying, and keeping that feeling?"

As traffic begins to clear, and Ben revs his engine, I take a moment to really consider moving. Is there a way that I can stay? Do they need teachers here in Maui?

Ben kisses my hand lightly, then takes his hand back to continue driving, "I'm sorry. I didn't mean to freak you out. It's just that listening to you reminds me of myself last year. I know exactly what you mean about the excitement, about how something as routine as walking around takes on a new feeling. That's why I moved here. Everything is familiar, yet different. When I came, it completely got rid of my weltschmerz."

"You didn't freak me out at all. As a matter of fact you've got my brain going in five hundred different directions right now." As I watch us pass a small beach where a family grills on a public barbecue, I finally admit, "Non sequitur: I'm not a doctor. Is weltschmerz a breathing problem?"

"No. Weltschmerz is . . ." Ben wracks his brain. "Hmmm. I think the Germans call it 'world-weariness,' but to me it's more like the sadness you feel about your real life versus your ideal life. Like . . . real life was fine, but there was no ideal life left to pursue. When I moved here, I got rid of that feeling. I felt excited about things again. I wanted to move forward again."

"That's exactly how I'm feeling right now. Although I am level-headed enough to know this could just be that I'm having a great time on vacation." As our car makes its way through Lahaina, we both lose ourselves in our own thoughts for a bit. As we pass the street where Ben works, I ask him, "So when did you realize this was home?"

Ben smiles to himself, possibly laughing at a private joke. Then he shakes his head. "Never mind. It's stupid."

I smile, intrigued. "Wow. Look at that smile on your face. When was it?"

Ben continues to smile. "Okay, but you have to promise you won't think this is lame."

With my index finger, I draw an imaginary X over my chest. "Cross my heart and hope to visit you in urgent care."

Ben debates another second, then relents. "Okay. My mom was

always into Christmas, and she'd always force us to go to this tree farm and pick our own tree, then haul it back home for fifty miles. Plus, she'd buy us each an ornament every year, so when we grew up, we'd have all these ornaments she hoped would have sentimental value. In college, it drove me nuts that on my first night back, I couldn't see my friends because she'd make my sister and me go pick out a tree, then lug it into the house, take forever putting it up, pull out ornaments, etc. My first wife was never into Christmas, so we never had to put up a tree, which was fine by me. And then we broke up, and I rethought life, and . . ."

I watch him for a minute and wait. Nothing. "And what?" I finally ask.

"And when I was thinking about moving here, and I had the job offer, I went to look at a condo. And I walked in and immediately thought, *The tree goes there*."

He's silent after that.

I think that might be the cutest thing I've ever heard. But that's not what I say. Instead I say, "You know, I think I do want to see your condo tonight. I need to see where you put your tree."

FORTY-EIGHT

Soon, we are at the Sheraton Maui, which has a torch-lighting ceremony a little before sunset. A man in authentic Hawaiian garb runs around the property lighting torches, climbs onto a cliff called Black Rock, lights a final torch, then dives off.

It's a complete tourist trap, and I am loving it.

Ben and I share *pupus,* which is the Hawaiian word for "appetizer." Ben starts us off with the furikake-seared ahi. "Furikake is this dry condiment from Japan that everyone puts on rice over here," he explains. "It's crunchy, with sesame seeds and seaweed and some other stuff. Very good." He then orders us some Kalua pork sliders, and Hawaiian beef pipi kaula flatbread.

As much as I love Hawaiian drinks, I'm already tired of them, so I order a glass of sauvignon blanc. Ben gets a local beer. Again, the conversation is easy. Unfortunately, Ben is not—he has not held my hand since we got here, nor has he tried to kiss me. This, despite how almost every couple here seems to make me want to scream, *Get a room!* And its being a hotel, they probably have one and should stop making me feel bad about myself.

I do happily eat away my feelings, taking a messy bite of the pork slider. "This is fantastic," I gush. "Although I'm not tasting the Kahlúa."

Ben laughs. "No, it's not Kahlúa, the drink. It's *Kalua*—no *h*— and it's a town in up-country that has a lot of farms. The restaurants here try to go as local as possible."

"See, just sitting around stuffing my face, I learned something new. How cool is that?"

Ben pops a slice of rare ahi into his mouth. "It's very cool. So, how long do you plan to stay?"

I try to dodge the question a bit. "You mean tonight or in Hawaii?"

Ben shrugs. "Both I guess."

"Well, as for tonight, I do have to work for Jeff tomorrow, but he isn't starting me until three, so I can be out late. As for Hawaii"— I shrug—"I actually don't know. A week, maybe two?"

Ben purses his lips and nods in mock seriousness. "Two weeks is better. You should stay for two weeks. Or three."

"Maybe four," I continue the joke.

"You could quit your job and stay a month."

"I could see that Christmas tree you were talking about," I say, knowing this is just kidding around, wishful thinking. "So, what is Christmas here like? Do you have Christmas tree lots, or do people just decorate palm trees?"

Ben laughs. "A little of both actually. I have definitely seen decorated palm trees. But there is an actual Christmas-tree farm in Kula, which is up-country, but not to be confused with Kalua. Kula's where I got my tree last year."

"A Christmas-tree farm in Maui. Wow. There is actually a person in the world who gets to live on a Christmas-tree farm *and* in Hawaii. If they live near a cupcake bakery, they've hit life's trifecta."

Ben smiles appreciatively and takes a sip of his beer. "True. Although for all you know, one day this woman with the charmed life went to a bridal shower, pulled a silver charm out of her friend's cake, and left it all to work at the Rock and Roll Hall of Fame in Cleveland."

I finish another pork slider, then laugh and say with my mouth full, "If she did, *cherchez l'homme*."

Ben furrows his brow. "I'm not sure if most guys would like to think that they could inspire such a change in a woman's life. Most of us would be terrified of that."

"Huh. I wouldn't be terrified at all. I'd love to think that I could inspire someone to change their life."

"Really?" Ben asks, tilting his head, staring deep into my eyes and looking intrigued.

Well, now I'm uncomfortable. "I don't know. Possibly," I say, trying to sound casual.

Ben keeps staring at me intently. I would like to hide now.

On to more comfortable subjects. "So Christmas . . . tell me more!"

Ben leans in toward me and almost whispers, "I have a better idea."

And he kisses me.

Yes! Finally!

We kiss for a few moments, then I shyly pull away from him, allowing him to see me smile and blush.

Just then, the waitress comes by to see if we'd like another round, but Ben says no and asks for the check. When she leaves, he gently takes my hands in his and smiles. "Okay, you've got a couple of choices here. I could take you to Banyan Tree, which is a five-star restaurant in Kapalua with a filet mignon and seared foie gras that I think would convince you to stay until New Year's."

"Okay, that sounds amazing."

"Or, if you wanted to stay a little more fun and casual, I could take you to Duke's Beach House, which has loads of tiki torches and these crab-and—"

"—macadamia-nut wontons. I love those! You have a Duke's here?"

"Wait. How do you know Duke's?"

"My friend got married at the one in Malibu."

"Really? Did she have a cake pull?"

"Thank God, no. I choose Duke's—"

"Wait. One more choice. This last place is very romantic, right on the ocean, and the chef will make you whatever you want. Provided we stop at the grocery store on our way over."

I giggle. I don't mean to, but I actually giggle. "Hm. What's the chef's specialty?"

Ben leans in to kiss me again. This time, we make out long enough to be one of those couples where I want to yell, *Get a room!*

Eventually, we come up for air. I smile bashfully again, then lean in, kiss him lightly on the lips, and say, "I think I'd like to try that last place."

"Excellent choice, madam."

Turns out Ben didn't need to cook until morning.

FORTY-NINE

I awake to the sound of ocean waves crashing against the sand. I open my eyes. *Ouch. Jesus, it's bright in here.* I blink a few times to adjust, then look over to the other side of the bed.

It's empty.

Fortunately, I smell bacon, so I am okay with that. "Do you have a shirt I can borrow?" I yell out toward the kitchen.

"I like what you're wearing now!" Ben yells back.

"Seriously, I will start rummaging through your dresser."

I think I hear a laugh. "Second drawer for the shirts. Closet if you want to wear one of my button-ups and be sexy as hell."

That would be trying too hard, I decide. (Although I do give it a moment's thought. But am I that girl? No, I just don't have the confidence to pull that off.) I shimmy into my underwear from the night before, pull out a New York Mets T-shirt from his drawer, slip it on, then walk out of his bedroom to the kitchen, where Ben is standing at his stove cooking bacon, and wearing nothing but boxers.

Yum. I mean that on so many levels.

I also see the rest of his condo in the light of day for the first time. Ben lives right on the beach. Like, *right on* the beach. Which means all I can see from his floor-to-ceiling windows is the island of Lanai on one side, the island of Molokai on the other, and nothing but ocean in between. It is stunning.

"Wow," I nearly gasp. "Last night, I didn't realize quite how close to the ocean you were."

"Yeah, the view is what sold me on the place." He turns to me. "Although right now I'm happy to say it's only the second-prettiest sight here."

I smile, walk up to Ben, and wrap my arms around his almost-naked waist. "That smells great. What time is it?"

"Eight. I couldn't sleep, and I didn't want to wake you."

I give him a dubious look. He smiles and corrects himself, "Well, okay, after waking you at five, I wanted to give you a break." He kisses me lightly, then whispers, "I missed you."

"I missed you too," I say, grinning like an idiot. I know Ben has Tuesday off, so I ask him, "Do you want to do anything before I have to get back to Jeff's?"

"I have some thoughts," he says seductively, and pulls me into another kiss.

We take so long kissing, the bacon burns.

Soon Ben is putting the overcooked bacon and eggs onto plates while I pour coffee (and learn he takes milk, no sugar), and soon we are sitting at the glass table on his balcony having breakfast, with the Pacific Ocean less than ten feet away, and a money tree he bought yesterday next to my feet.

I close my eyes, inhale a deep breath of salty air, and exhale contentedly. "This feels great," I say, totally relaxed, and wondering what Zen officially feels like.

"Good," Ben begins, his tone suddenly a little strained. "So,

I need to tell you something. But you have to promise me you won't freak out."

I pop open my eyes. Of course he does. "Oh, crap. You have a girlfriend, don't you?"

Ben points at me and gives me a triumphant "No!"

I glare at him and continue to guess. "Fuck buddy?"

"No."

"Kids? Fake medical license? Wanted for fraud in seven states?"

"Wow, you've dated some losers," he jokes.

I decide to go with a glare in response.

Ben takes a deep breath. "Okay, it's not that bad. It's just that . . . um . . . the reason why I was in New York wasn't just to see my parents. It was also to see my wife."

My jaw drops ever so slightly. You know how some animals, when they get scared, neither run nor fight, they just play dead? Just call me Ms. Six Feet Under.

Ben continues nervously, his words coming out in starts and stops. "We were planning to file divorce paperwork when I was there, but then she said she wanted to wait a little longer."

I think I'm still glaring. Mostly, I'm not moving.

Ben keeps filling the silence. "We got married spur of the moment a few years ago; she was the sex I went across the country for. We broke up six months later, and I moved here. But by then she was applying for her green card, she's Italian."

Oh my God, am I really hearing this?

"But it wasn't a green-card thing. I swear. She already had a work visa. She's a model."

Fan-fucking-tastic.

"I was in New York for the final two-year green-card interview, and she said she wanted to be the one to file for divorce, but then her boyfriend broke up with her, and she thought maybe we should just stay married and then she'd have a place to stay in Hawaii if she ever modeled here again, and I should have told you last night, but you were so beautiful and I'm really not a dick even though I'm hearing myself talk and I realize I sound like one, and please say something."

He stops. I stare at him. All I can get out is "How is a wife not a fuck buddy?"

"Clearly you've never been married before," he jokes.

I throw down my napkin and angrily kick back my chair. "Jesus, I'm out of here."

Ben follows me through his living room, and into his bedroom. "You haven't let me finish. It's not a real marriage."

"They never are," I deadpan.

"No. This one's not. I really am getting divorced."

I cross my arms. "Did you have sex with her when you were in New York?"

Ben looks up and squints his eyes, which is my answer right there.

"I can't believe I slept with you," I spit out, angrily throwing off his shirt so I can change back into last night's clothes.

Ben gently puts his hand on my shoulder. "Can we just talk?"

I pull my shoulder away and turn around as quickly as a snake about to strike. "If you touch me again," I say with preternatural calm, "you will be in urgent care as a patient. That I promise you."

Ben puts up the palms of his hands in surrender. He sits on the bed quietly, waiting for me to get dressed, at which time I assume he'll take me home.

I assume wrong.

"Hey, wait a minute!" Ben blurts out. "I just realized something: I had not met you the last time I slept with her, which was before I left New York, when you didn't even exist to me yet. I met you in the bar after I said good-bye to her and got into a cab. You, on the other hand, have slept with at least one guy since we met— the guy you flew halfway around the world to have sex with. So, if anything, *I* should be the one mad at *you* right now, not the other way around."

I take a moment to consider his point. It does seem to have some validity.

Which I absolutely refuse to acknowledge. "I had sex with him. I didn't marry him!"

"And I haven't married or had sex with anyone since I met you," Ben argues. "Therefore, you should be apologizing to *me*."

I furrow my brow, confounded that he could make such a stupid argument. "In the first place, you have not been able to legally marry someone since you met me because . . . Let's see, why is that? . . . Oh, yeah . . . because you're *already married!* And how do I know you haven't had sex with anyone since we met?"

"I just told you. And technically I have not lied to you since we met."

I am going to need Botox after this conversation. "Technically?"

Ben takes a deep breath and shrugs self-consciously, "Well, in a few minutes, you'll probably think to argue that my not telling you about my marriage was a lie of omission, so I figured I'd nip that in the bud."

I throw my arms up in the air in exasperation and walk out of the room.

Of course Ben follows me. "You know, really, if you think about it, if this is the worst fight we ever have—"

"Oh, this is the worst fight we're ever going to have," I assure him. "Because I'm never seeing you again."

"Hold on," Ben continues, his voice calm. "Listen. I like you. You're only here for a few weeks, and my wife is an ocean and a continent away. I could have easily hidden my marriage. I didn't. I told you the truth. I will continue to tell you the truth. Ask me anything you want. And, at the end of the conversation, if you want to leave, I'll take you home."

Ben and I stare at each other for several moments, both saying nothing.

The weird thing is, my gut tells me he's a decent guy. He's right, he could have hidden this from me, but he didn't. And I really would like to see him again while I'm still in town. Finally I ask, "When are you planning to file for divorce?"

I watch his breath catch. He pauses, debates an answer. Finally he admits, "I have no idea."

I raise an eyebrow at him. "So you'll take me home now?"

Ben sighs and nods slightly. "Yup."

When Ben drove me home, the silence was deafening. When he pulled up to Jeff's driveway, I took a moment to get out of the car. In my mind, I was desperately trying to find a way for this to work out. I kept trying to think of what he could say to keep me there, something about Christmas trees or money trees or "Fell in love for an hour" six-word memoirs. But I knew nothing could fix this.

I remember when Nic was pregnant, she said she would rack her brain for hours on end, trying to figure out a way for her baby to come out without a huge head sliding through a small hole, presumably stretching and tearing and ripping to shreds everything in its path, or having her stomach and its layers upon layers of muscle and fat slit open with a knife to pull the baby out. No matter how much she tried to find a solution, the facts were what they were, and in the end it was going to be painful.

Just like this.

"I know you're really mad right now," Ben begins. "But if you can think of a way I can make it up to you, let me know."

I turn to him as I open my car door. "I've got a better idea. If *you* can think of a way to make it up to me, let me know." And then I walk out of his car and out of his life.

The moment I unlock the door and walk into Jeff's house, I start to feel better. Even if I am greeted with a gleeful "Slut!" from my disabled roommate watching TV on the couch.

"He's married," I angrily tell him as I throw my stuff down at his door and head over to him for a much-needed hug.

"Aw . . . sweetie."

"He's a fuckhead," I state unequivocally. "We will never speak of this dark day again." I gently sit next to Jeff and put my head lightly on his chest. "How's your foot?"

"Better actually. You know, you've had a hard night. Why don't you get some rest. I can probably hobble around the bar okay."

"Absolutely not. You're still injured. Besides, I could use the distraction."

"Of a bunch of happily married newlyweds?'

"No. Of learning how to be a bartender. I had fun Saturday. And I'm not going to let one bad date ruin my vacation." I stand up. "Give me an hour. I need to get in a quick run and a shower, then we'll head out."

Jeff nods approvingly. "Good for you. Moving forward like that. So you're feeling empowered?"

"Oh, God, no. Not even vaguely. I feel like eating a pound of chocolate-chip cookie dough and washing it down with two bottles of chardonnay while watching hours upon hours of reality shows. But I'm going for a run instead."

As I head to my room to change into running clothes, I hear

Jeff say, "That's my girl. Oh, by the way, an apartment manager called me this morning, wanted to know how long you've worked at my bar."

I stop in my tracks. "Damn." I wince and turn to Jeff. "I'm sorry, I just didn't want to give him my school in Los Angeles. I wanted to look local."

"I told him the truth. I said you've been with me for years."

I wait for a barrage of questions or, worse, a lecture. Instead, Jeff blows me a kiss and goes back to his program.

I love him for that.

FIFTY

Later, the two of us head to Male 'Ana for a lesson in bartending.

Jeff is seated behind the bar in a chair, trying not to let his foot bother him, while I am standing behind the bar, waiting to be inspired by his tutelage.

Jeff picks up the soda gun from his end of the bar while I stare at the one in my hand. "As you know from Saturday," Jeff begins, "this is your soda gun, which shoots out Pepsi, Diet Pepsi, 7UP, ginger ale, orange juice, soda water, tonic water, and plain water."

I'm already feeling overwhelmed. "Looks complicated," I am forced to admit, seeing the letters L, C, T, Q, G, and O on six different buttons, in addition to two larger buttons marked SODA and WATER, and mildly panicking.

"So was Coulomb's law constant the first time you saw it, but I'll bet you mastered that."

"I love a man who can use Coulomb's law constant in a bar," I flirt.

Jeff smiles at me. "Okay, L stands for lemon-lime soda, which in our case is 7UP; C should mean Coke, but we use Pepsi here."

"So why don't you get a button that says P?"

Jeff smiles brightly. "Why did Albert Ghiorso name the ninty-ninth element einsteinium instead of marilyn monroeium?"

I think about the question for a moment. I'm embarrassed to have to admit, "I don't know."

"Which is the same as my answer to your P question," he says, shrugging. "I have no idea."

He goes through the rest of the buttons, and soon it's as easy as the Pythagorean theorem.

So began my not-quite-one hour of unofficial bartender training. I learned some interesting stuff during those fifty-eight minutes, such as that calling the liquor *well, call,* and *top-shelf* works better because the terms *cheap-ass, doable,* and *trying too hard* never quite took off, and that chatting up customers is the main trick to getting good tips and good word of mouth.

Jeff ends his lecture with "Remember, if a customer is here drinking alone, ask if everything is okay without being too nosy. And always remember, our main clientele is the shiny-ring set. So ask them about everything wedding related."

"Shiny-ring? You mean the newlyweds?"

"Yeah. I started calling them the shiny-ring set when I realized none of their rings had been dinged up yet, there's no patina. Anyway, most bartenders have to deal with slightly depressed clients who want to get drunk and tell you all about their problems. Here, most of our clients want to tell you about how he proposed, what she wore to the wedding, the worst wedding gift they got, and maybe give a funny anecdote about his new mother-in-law's twenty–four-year-old boyfriend."

I nod. "Got it. Like being a bridesmaid all over again."

"Kind of, yes. Except, in this case, you're genuinely happy for them. Just remember, we're not really selling cocktails, we're selling dreams. These people just got married, they're thinking about how perfect their lives are going to be, how many children they'll have, cuddling up at Christmastime to a roaring fire, moving to a new home. And whatever the dream is, we get to be a part of that. So it's actually pretty cool."

"Okay," I say, smiling, although the idea of cuddling up at Christmastime makes me a little sad at this moment.

"Why the look? Are you sure you're up to doing this today?"

At that, my shoulders tense up in outrage. "I've known the guy for a total of about thirty-six hours. If I'm not fine, something's wrong with me."

Jeff jokes, "And by that you mean you're not fine."

I smile and say lightly, "And something's wrong with me. Yes."

Jeff smiles. "I like your style."

In that moment I realize, "You know, I'm starting to like my style too."

Because for the first time in my life, I am not obsessing over this breakup. I'm not wondering what I did wrong, not worrying about if I was too fat for him, or not smart enough for him, or not successful enough for him. That's beta-dog thinking: How will the other dogs in the pack feel? Let me adjust how I feel accordingly.

No. I'm going alpha the whole way and only care about how I feel.

Leilani charges in, a woman on a mission. "Why is it all men are the same?"

"We're not," Jeff assures her. "The ones you're choosing are always the same."

"Seriously, what is wrong with men?" she says, tossing her phone and purse on the bar, grabbing an apron, and tying it around her waist.

"Honey, customers start coming in only half an hour," Jeff gently reminds her. "We don't have that kind of time. Just tell me what happened."

She lifts up her phone for Jeff to read. He visibly winces. "Oh, swing and a miss."

"Can I see?" I timidly ask.

Leilani shows me her screen. It's the classic three words that rile up any woman (well, at least when she's sober):

Hey, you up?

I shake my head. "And not even an 'MFVodka.' That bastard and his booty call."

"Wha—? No. That's not the problem. Look at the time."

I read. "He wrote it at ten thirty in the morning," I say, confused about her outrage.

"I know!" Leilani spits out. "What the hell kind of booty call starts at ten thirty in the morning?! What, do I have to feed you bagels first?"

Jeff and I look at each other. "Would you like to break it to her?" I ask him.

Jeff shakes his head. "Probably won't do any good, but, Leilani, sweetie." Jeff puts one hand on each of her shoulders and looks deep into her eyes. "Sharks are a real problem. Men propositioning you in bathrooms can be a real problem."

"Can be?" I ask.

Jeff turns to me and jokes, "So many of them end up being senators. Gross." Then he turns back to look into Leilani's eyes and enunciate every word. "Men texting you at ten thirty in the morning is not a real problem."

Leilani's jaw drops. "You take that back."

"If you want to talk to a woman with real problems, Mel just found out her guy is married. So let's dial it back a notch."

Leilani's eyes widen. "Oh my God. Should I get the bat?"

Jeff rolls his eyes.

I blink a few times. "For what exactly?"

She shrugs, looks at me as if the answer were obvious. "We tell his wife, give her the bat, and point to his car."

"Ummm . . . while that is very sweet of you, let's keep that in our back pocket for now."

"Okay. But I have your back. You're Jeff's ohana, you're my ohana. Got it?"

"Got it," I say, surprisingly verklempt at the sentiment.

Leilani looks at the phone one more time, sighs, and puts it in her purse. "I should have never MFVed." She heads back to the storeroom to restock the red and white wine just as Ashley comes charging in.

"I'm sorry I'm late. I had to swerve to avoid missing a—"

"Stop," Jeff says. "Please, darling, do not say deer, chicken, or goat to me one more time."

"Doughnut shop," Ashley says, smiling and holding up a big pink cardboard box. "I just had that psychic feeling that one of us was grappling with a problem and would need doughnuts today."

I decide to be touched that Ashley would be so attuned to my soul, rather than think the obvious—there are three women here today. Of course one of us would need a doughnut.

FIFTY-ONE

I spend Tuesday night ever so slightly out of my comfort zone. Which is perfect.

I think most of us are happiest when we're ever so slightly out of our comfort zone. Being out of your comfort zone means you're experiencing something new, and we don't often get that as adults.

When we're children, we experience newness all the time: the first time we walk, the first time we see a balloon, the moment we finally master riding a two-wheeler. All of it is new to us, and each experience brings with it a fresh wave of happiness. And sometimes optimism too. The first time a baby talks in full words and gets his or her point across to Mommy or Daddy, what a feeling of joy that must create. How much more power and control did we all suddenly have in our world at that moment. Can an adult even imagine that feeling? Maybe that's why children laugh so much more than adults do, appear so much more gleeful all the time—they're still experiencing all of these firsts.

And we still have a few firsts as teenagers, not as many, but they're there. I vividly remember the happiness I felt after I passed my driver's test, and the drive to the grocery store that night, all by myself, to pick up a pound of butter and some baking potatoes for my mom. I felt alive. Anything was possible.

And I remember the butterflies I felt my first day teaching, being secretly terrified of the students, writing my name on the board, giving my first lecture. By fifth period, I was floating on a cloud as I happily paced around the room, perfectly explaining my first lesson, and giving the kids a math riddle about dots versus lines.

Of course, every girl remembers the first time she made out with a boy she really liked. The first kiss might not have gone as planned (braces can be deadly), and I've yet to hear a good story about the loss of someone's virginity. But the first time that guy whom you've been dreaming about—soooo cute, too cute to ever possibly like you back—does like you, then kisses you for the first time . . . Ah, if I close my eyes, I can still sort of remember that feeling.

It's no wonder women spend most of their twenties chasing men, dieting for men, dressing for men, undressing for men. We spend those years chasing the high of that first kiss.

How often do we get those moments by the time we're in our thirties? The bike riding, the driving test, the first dream job, the first dream boy? It's hard to keep finding firsts. Maybe one of the reasons these newlyweds come in here so happy is simply because they've never been married before. The beautiful girl sipping her champagne cocktail gets to use the word *husband* for the first time in her life. That is pretty damn exciting. And it's one of the last firsts she may get in her life.

And now, completely despite myself, I have stumbled upon a new first. I won't say that tonight I mastered the Micros computer, with all its buttons and drinks, but I am definitely on the way to making it my bitch. And I have quickly become a pro at shaking up the cocktails, pouring the wine in the right glasses, and chatting with the customers. (It didn't hurt that I taped cheat sheets throughout the bar to remind me which cocktails contain rum versus vodka, or that you have to tilt the glass slightly when you pour a beer from the tap.)

Even cleanup was fun. Jeff has janitors who come in and do the real scut work, but we still need to bus tables, wash out glasses, and disinfect sinks. During that hour, Leilani hooked up her iPod to Jeff's portable speaker system, and played every happy, silly dancing song from KC and the Sunshine Band's "Boogie Shoes" to Macklemore's "Thrift Shop." Whistling while you work is good; polishing glasses while rapping to the eighties is golden.

By the time I crawled into bed at three in the morning, I was exhausted and a little sore.

It was glorious.

I don't remember the last time I slept so soundly.

FIFTY-TWO

The following morning, I sleep in until almost eleven. When I wake up, I check my phone, and as I listen to a voice mail, everything in my life suddenly becomes clear.

I climb out of bed, then do my usual run, followed by a trip to the local bakery. I stare at the glass cases of delectable pastries for ten minutes before finally selecting a lilikoi Danish for Jeff and a boule for me. Then I go to the market and buy bacon.

I figure the question I have for Jeff requires that I butter him up with bacon grease and a buttery Danish.

I get home, cook him breakfast, then, carrying a tray piled with bacon, Danish, and coffee, I knock on his door. "Wakie wakie!" I say in a clear, loud voice.

"Is it time for cakie?" Jeff jokes.

I open the door. "No, but it is time for bacon," I tell him, smiling.

Jeff turns his head slightly, eyeing me suspiciously. "You cooked? What's going on?"

"Nothing's going on," I assure him as I bring the tray to his bed and place it over his lap. "I figure you should still rest your foot for another day or two. Plus, bacon goes very well with pain meds."

"Okay, seriously, what's up? Did Ben text you last night? Did you sneak off this morning to see him?"

"No," I say, repressing the urge to be insulted and cheerfully unfolding Jeff's napkin and handing it to him. "Why would you assume this has anything to do with a guy?"

"Because you have that weird look on your face that you get when you're hiding something."

"What look?"

"You know the look."

"There's no look."

"Fine, there's no look," Jeff repeats dubiously. "So what then? You're getting depressed about being thirty-three, and you'd like me to be your sperm donor if neither of us finds—"

"Why would you go there?" I ask, exasperated.

"Honey, you'd be surprised how many female friends have my sperm on hold for their thirty-seventh birthdays."

"I actually would not, you're a genetic catch. But that's not what I want to talk to you about." I take a deep breath, then give him my news. "The apartment manager called me this morning. I got the studio. I'm signing the lease today."

Jeff looks stunned. I take his silence as an invitation to continue. "It's small, but it's really beautiful. There's a view of the ocean from my living-room-slash-bedroom. Nothing as spectacular as yours, but it's pretty amazing. And there's a pool in the complex with a Jacuzzi, and the beach is only a few blocks away. It's perfect."

Jeff shakes his head. "Mel—"

I put out my hand. "Stop. I have played in my head everything you can possibly say. Everything Nic and Seema and my mom could say: 'This is insane.' 'You're confusing vacation with reality.' 'You don't know anybody here.'"

Jeff gives me another one: "You don't change your life based on three days."

"Why not? The first time I saw UCLA was on a college tour. I was there for less than three hours. And yet I went, and it was the best decision of my life. And do you know why I went?"

Jeff shakes his head.

"I felt like I belonged. After only three hours I knew that was where I was supposed to be. And I went. And I met you and Seema and Nic and you were my family, and everything I have ever loved in my grown-up life in some way came from that decision. And now, you're right, I haven't been here long. But I have that same feeling in my gut. This is where I'm supposed to be right now. This is where I belong."

Jeff watches me in silence. I wait for a response. Finally he takes a bite of bacon, nods, and quietly says, "Okay."

"Seriously?" I say, suspicious. "No lectures about how I haven't thought this through? No gentle guidance, explaining to me all of the logical reasons why I shouldn't do this? No sermons about actions having consequences?"

Jeff shrugs. "I was never the sermon type."

I immediately pull Jeff into a hug. "Thank you, thank you, thank you!" I say, relieved. "You have no idea how much I love you right now."

"You do know you could just stay here though, right? I mean, the guest room is empty."

"I know. And I love you for that too. But I've never lived by myself before. I think I need to do that right now. I do have one minor favor to ask you though."

"Anything."

"I want to work for you," I say quickly. Then I speak a mile a minute so I can get my whole argument out before Jeff says no. "I loved bartending. I had the best time Saturday night, and then again yesterday. It was the most fun I've had working in years. I loved talking to people about their weddings! It was invigorating! It was hopeful! I'm telling you, I felt eighteen again."

Jeff looks mildly horrified. "Would you want to be eighteen again? Wait, weren't you dating *me* when you were eighteen?"

"Okay, fine. Twenty-one, then. The thing is, I want to take a sabbatical from teaching for a year. Just for a year. I want to learn how to make Kipona Alohas properly. I want to say *Kipona Aloha* in my everyday life. And *kipa hou mai* and *pomaika'i* and *mahalo* and that fish with the ridiculously long name."

"*HOO-moo-HOO-moo-NOO-koo-NOO-koo-AH-poo-AH-ah.*"

"*HOO-moo-HOO-moo-NOO-koo-NOO-koo-AH-poo-AH-ah,*" I repeat effortlessly.

Jeff nods approvingly.

I pantomime raising the roof, proud of myself.

Jeff shakes his head, so I stop.

"You can't work for the next few days anyway, right?"

"Um . . . well, it's going to be tricky."

"Then let me be your bartender this week. If you hate me, I'll quit. If I hate it, I'll quit. Otherwise, I can replace that bartender who left."

Jeff appears to be considering the idea. I put the palms of my hands together as if I were about to pray. Then I give him my big puppy eyes and beg, "Please, please, please . . ."

He seems worried about me. "Are you sure you're not doing this because of a dude?"

"No! That's the best part. For the first time in years, maybe since I went to a different college than my high school boyfriend, it's not about a guy! Ben may know where his Christmas tree is going, and I might secretly be tempted to see it, but I now know where *my* Christmas tree is going. And I can't wait to say *Mele Kalikimaka* on my own!" I tell Jeff proudly.

Jeff furrows his brow. "I have no idea what that means."

"It means 'Merry Christmas.' "

"No, I know that part. I mean, I don't understand what you're talking about with the Christmas trees—"

"You don't have to," I interrupt. "In my head, it makes perfect sense. My point is, I don't need a man. I need to be excited to get up in the morning." I put my hands back together and beg once again. "Just please let me do this. It may be an incredibly stupid idea, and I might fall on my ass. But at least I'm not going to be doing it because I think it's going to put me on a path that will one day make me happy. I'm doing it because it will make me happy right now."

Jeff inhales a deep breath. "Okay."

"Really?" I say, surprised. "But I have a whole speech planned out."

"Of course you do. You're you. The truth is, I'd love to have you here. I like having someone around who is excited to go to the dry cleaner's."

"Yay!" I say, practically pouncing on him again. I begin kissing him on the cheek over and over. "Thank you, thank you, thank you!"

"Just promise me one thing?"

"Anything."

"Don't tell Seema or Nic about this until you're absolutely sure. I don't want to be seen as the Pied Piper."

"You got it!"

I bounced around Jeff's house until around three, when I got a text from Ben:

> You left your charm bracelet here. Can I stop by and drop it off sometime?

Sigh. Of course I did. Why wouldn't I have?
Or, more concisely, shitdamnfuckhellsonofabitch.

FIFTY-THREE

I decide not to answer Ben's text for at least twenty-four hours.

Which probably means I'll be lucky if I get through to the morning, but it's a start. Progress—not perfection. The old Mel would have jumped in a car to retrieve the bracelet *tout suite*, then probably lost control and slept with a married guy. The new Mel has decided that, while I do need to get my bracelet back, I have lots of options here on how to do it: everything from sending Jeff to retrieve it to sending Leilani and her bat. Or I could ambush Ben at work and demand it back in a place where I can threaten to cause a scene if he doesn't hand it over immediately and let me walk out of his life forever.

Therefore, I decide to take a day, or maybe even two, before I write back.

Jeff is staying home for one last night of recovery, which allows Leilani, Ashley, and me to see how we work as a team on a weeknight. As we prep for the night—unpacking and polishing souvenir glasses for people to take home, wiping down tables, restocking liquor of all sorts—we discuss the married-man problem.

"You gotta cut bait," Leilani declares. "Men don't leave their wives."

"I disagree," Ashley counters. "He's already said they're separated, the rest is just semantics."

"I don't think he ever actually said they were separated," I admit.

I get a victorious "Hah!" from Leilani, just as Ashley mutters, "Rats."

"Although he did say she has a boyfriend in New York," I continue.

Ashley points to Leilani and yells, "Hah!"—as Leilani asserts, "He's lying."

"How do you know he's lying?" I ask.

"Were his lips moving?" Leilani asks as she wipes down a table.

Ashley shakes her head. "So he has to go through some paperwork. All men have a changing of the guard. None of them like to be alone. If they did, they'd be women."

Leilani stops and stares at her, then looks to me. I shrug, then say to Ashley, "Okay, we give up. What's a changing of the guard?"

"You know how at Buckingham Palace the queen has these uniformed guards who have to frown all the time?"

"Um . . . I guess."

"Well, at eleven A.M. every morning, there's this whole ceremony where the New Guard marches over to the palace to replace the Old Guard. There's music, and the captains of both the New Guard and the Old Guard exchange the palace keys, and, like, both guards make a show of arms. You know, what's interesting is they're all actual soldiers, many having served overseas—"

Leilani makes a show of yawning. "Yeah, 177. We get it, you finished college early, and you know a lot of trivia. Get to the point."

"The point is, every morning at Buckingham Palace there is a certain amount of time when both guards are there at the same time. Ben is your palace. You are the New Guard. You just need to get the keys from his wife."

"You mean steal the keys," Leilani retorts.

Ashley brings a box of small drink menus framed in black metal stands to Leilani. "You know what your problem is? You think men are supposed to live up to some romanticized ideal, and if they can't live up to it, they should be thrown away. That's fine when you're twenty-four and look the way you do. But what about when you're thirty-three and—"

"Please don't finish that thought," I beg insistently.

Ashley places the box down at Leilani's table, then heads back to me. "My point is, older men have more baggage, but less drama. Give him a chance."

Leilani begins placing the framed drink-menu stands on each table. "You do not know what you're talking about. He's a loser who's best left lost."

"Excuse me . . . are you getting a PhD in romantic psychology?" Ashley challenges.

Leilani counters with "When was the last time you were on a date?"

"I am choosing not to date right now so that I can focus on my music, my dissertation, and my sleep. But believe me, I know more than you. You needn't be a chicken to judge an egg."

Leilani shakes her head. "Babe, I love you. But what is it with you and chickens?"

Leilani walks out to the tables on the garden patio to place a drink-menu stand in the center of each table, while Ashley heads to the stockroom.

I can't help but follow Ashley. "Um . . . I have some follow-up questions. What does 177 mean?"

"Oh." Ashley waves me off. "Technically, that's my IQ. But we all know those tests are just a bunch of shenanigans. Leilani likes to call me that when she thinks I'm sounding stupid."

Ashley lifts a case of cabernet sauvignon from a corner and heads out the door. I grab a case of pinot grigio and race after her to the racks behind the bar where we keep the wine. "And how are you working on a PhD when you're only twenty-two?"

"Oh, that," Ashley says, clearly embarrassed. "I skipped two grades, so I went to college at sixteen, had a bunch of AP credits, so I finished at nineteen, did the master's thing, and now other than my thesis I'm done with my PhD."

"Wow," I blurt out, a little stunned. "You're going to be Dr. Ashley soon?"

"Well, first I have to finish my thesis. That's actually why I'm working here. I'm disproving the myth of the meet cute."

"I'm sorry. The what now?"

"The 'meet cute,'" Ashley repeats. She opens her box and begins pulling out bottles of red. "When civilizations stopped arranging marriages, women assumed the burden of attracting, marrying, then mating with men. The concept of romance was born in order to facilitate this process. And part of the romance mythology is the core belief that we each have one soul mate, who we are destined to find through no preplanning of our own, because that is our fate. It follows that once we find that person, we immediately know that they are our soul mate, and vice versa, and that there are no real obstacles to overcome. The theory is, because your soul mate is your destiny, everything should be smooth sailing. Academically, I can prove that's complete bullshit."

"I thought you were here for your music."

"I am. But you'd be surprised how unpopular punk rock can

KEEP CALM AND CARRY A BIG DRINK   { 355 }

be to tourists. I was once compared to a cat being romanced by a pit bull."

"I meant that as a compliment!" Leilani yells from outside.

"And I took it as one!" Ashley yells back. She then says to me, "But it's not everyone's cup of tea. I'm playing next Monday night at a coffeehouse in Kula, if you're free."

FIFTY-FOUR

By ten o'clock, the evening is in full swing. I'm rocking the bar, Leilani is a superstar waitress, handling all of the tables both inside and outside the bar, and Ashley is easily keeping us stocked up with everything, while also helping me pour beers and wine. I'm having my usual good time learning about people's weddings and learning what not to do at my own (one couple got married in matching Wookie costumes by a Darth Vader reverend. What about this says romance?), what not to do on my honeymoon (one newly married couple were waiting by the bar's front door right at opening to escape the seven children they brought with them, all of whom are staying at the Grand Wailea and currently eating room service under the guidance of not one, but two, babysitters. I suspect the parents will be here until closing).

Ben has written me a few texts throughout the night, beginning with a bit of mystery:

You have every right to still be pissed. But can you meet
me for a drink? I'll bring by not only your bracelet,
but a little surprise.

Surprise? What kind of a surprise? Why do people always sound so mysterious when they want you to call back?

All right, I have only so much willpower. I can't help myself—there was still so much more I wanted to say/yell. I write back:

I'm working for Jeff tonight. Won't be able to do anything for a while.

I proudly decide to be just as mysterious as him. *A while* can mean anything.

But I can't help myself. I then type:

So what's the surprise?

Ben writes back within a minute:

After I got home from dropping you off, I called her and
told her all about you. See, now you have to see me.

How do you figure?

Come on. Aren't you the tiniest bit curious how the
conversation went?

I am strong and silent for about one hour. Then a couple tells me the story of how they met. They were both hiking at Lands End in San Francisco, and she was tired and sat down, and he shared his water bottle with her and introduced himself and . . . Okay, so I weaken. I quickly pull my iPhone from my pocket to covertly text:

Maybe.

"What are you doing?" Leilani asks rather harshly as she walks up to the bar.

"I can't help it," I whine, flipping my phone around to show her his texts. "What if this guy is my soul mate?"

"Then you'll be wife number two, who he will proceed to cheat on with soon-to-be wife number three."

Ashley walks behind the bar carrying two large bottles of replacement rum. "When? The minute she lives a million miles away from him?" Ashley argues. "This Italian-model wife of his could have chosen to move with him to paradise; she stayed in New York. The marriage is over. Time for the band to play."

Okay, I may have been boring them with details throughout the course of the evening. But isn't one of the benefits of having girlfriends that you can bore them with details of your travails with men? (Now that I think about it, I'm blessed that I already have girlfriends here I can bore.)

"What is wrong with my saying that Mel deserves better?" Leilani asks Ashley as she walks behind the bar to join us.

"What is wrong with my saying Mel deserves happiness? And the only way she is going to get it is to get realistic?" Ashley asks.

"Realistic happiness," Leilani snorts. "That is a contradiction in terms right up there with 'hip-hop royalty.'"

Ashley crosses her arms and squints at Leilani. Then a thought seems to percolate in Miss 177. I wait a few seconds until it bubbles over. "I think I know how I can prove my point," Ashley decides. "What say you to a little wager?"

The way Leilani is standing, girl fighting pose, you'd think she was about to ask Ashley if she wanted to dance, bitch. "Name it," Leilani dares.

Ashley turns to me. "Mel, what made you change your mind and write back just now?"

Ugh. I hate being on the spot. "Ummm . . . ," I begin timidly, then I tilt my head toward the couple I just served. "They told me the story of how they met: he shared his water with her on a hike, and he immediately knew that she was the woman he was going to marry right then and there."

Judging from her wicked smile, you'd think Ashley was about to be a pit bull violating a cat. She makes a show of slowly rubbing her hands together. "Perfect." She turns to Leilani, "If I can prove to you that the first three couples we ask did not have the wildly romantic courtship they tell everyone they did, but are still happily married, Mel gets to text Ben back and say she will see him tomorrow. What do you say?"

Leilani appears nonplussed. "You're going to ask a bunch of disgustingly over-the-moon newlyweds to admit they have problems?"

"No. I'm going to ask them to admit they had some hiccups when they first started dating."

Leilani seems dubious, but game. "And if I win?"

"If you win, I'll run over a chicken."

I gasp. Ashley immediately recants, "Okay, I won't run over a chicken. But I will buy you chicken for lunch."

Leilani grunts. "No, you won't."

"You're right, I won't," Ashley admits. "But if you win, Mel won't call or text him. Do we have a deal?"

Leilani looks over at me. Pushover that I am, I nod pleadingly. She nods as well.

"Excellent," Ashley chirps. She walks over to the couple I have just served and smiles as she asks, "So, Mel tells me you guys have a really wonderful story of how you met. What are you guys drinking?"

"I'm having the Ho'omaika'i 'ana," the wife tells her, taking a sip of her drink with a straw. "And my husband's having the Ku'u Lei."

"Fab." Ashley turns to Leilani. "Can you whip up a batch of those two?" Leilani nods and begins her mixology as Ashley tells the couple, "We would love to give you guys a refill, on the house, if you can answer two questions for us to settle a bet."

The husband laughs nervously while the wife giggles. They exchange a look, then he says, "Shoot."

"How did you guys meet?" Ashley asks them.

I watch as the wife tells Ashley the same story they told me before: a cold, foggy day at a forest on the edge of San Francisco, she rested, he shared a water bottle, the rest was fate.

"That is amazing," Ashley says happily as Leilani hands her the drinks. "Now, would you mind telling me how you guys really met?"

Crap. They looked stunned. Jeff is about to get his first one-star review, and it's all my fault.

Ashley continues, "Don't be shy, we're all friends here. I'm just trying to make a point. None of us really have a 'meet cute.' We all have the story we have to tell our friends when we introduce him over dinner for the first time. So, how did you guys really meet?"

A smile creeps onto the bride's face. She smacks her groom on the arm and bursts out laughing. He laughs too. Finally he asks, "Have you ever heard of the dating website howaboutwe?"

Turns out, they first met online. They talked for a few weeks, he finally suggested going hiking at Lands End, and that's how they eventually had their "meet cute." She did get tired and he did share his water bottle with her, but that's not the point.

Ashley also got the girl to confess that at the time she was "in a complicated relationship with someone else" that she "was trying to get out of."

Okay, she wasn't getting out of a marriage, but close enough.

As their story ends, a handsome *GQ* model (I'm guessing) asks Ashley, "Free drinks! Can we get in on that?"

"Absolutely!" Ashley assures, him, walking over to the gorgeous couple. "Way you told your grandma you met?"

The blond, new wife giggles as she says, "I saw him in a library and followed him out to a coffeehouse, where I introduced my-self."

"Awesome. Real way?"

"Met her over beer pong," he admits. "I was on a date with her roommate at the time."

"We have a winner!" Ashley says, turning to Leilani. "Leilani, be a poodle and set them up."

"But I really did see him at the library," blond wife insists. "I was stunned when Jodi showed up with him the next week at our favorite bar."

"And that's the beauty of the meet cute: it's always based on a sliver of reality, just like all good lies," Ashley tells the blonde warmly. Then Ashley turns around. "Okay, I need one more. Mel—you pick."

"No. Not fair," Leilani protests. "She could rig the couple."

"How do you *rig* a couple?" Ashley asks.

"I don't know. But if you're going to prove your point, the last one has to be fated, not someone she can pick. So . . . the next couple who comes into this bar. All or nothing."

"I just won two."

"Aren't you sure of yourself?"

"Of course."

"Then all or nothing—the next couple to walk in."

Ashley gives a quick nod. Let the games begin. For the next minute, the three of us stare intently at the front door. I can almost hear the sound track from one of those cheesy Western movies where the man in black and the sheriff in white walk to the middle of the dirt road bisecting the town, face each other, and fire their guns.

Finally, a couple walks in and heads straight for two empty seats at the bar.

They're in my station, so I walk up, throw down two cocktail napkins in front of them, and say, "Aloha, I'm Mel. Welcome to Male 'Ana. What can I get you?"

The woman's face lights up. "Hey! I'm Mel too. That's easy. What would you recommend, Mel?"

Not knowing what that coincidence is supposed to mean, I look over nervously at Ashley and Leilani, who are frozen in place, staring at the couple.

The looks on their faces reminds me I'm being ridiculous. I turn back to the couple and ask, "Do you like strawberries? Because we have a fantastic drink with strawberries, basil, and vodka called the Kipona Aloha, which means 'deep love' in Hawaiian. It's served in a heart glass that you get to take home."

"Sure. That sounds great. Two Kipona Alohas," Mel tells me.

I smile. "Be right back."

As I walk away to get berries to put in a glass, Leilani and Ashley race up to me. "Ask them," Ashley demands urgently.

"Okay, we look psychotic right now. Both of you go back to work. I'll ask her when the time is right."

Leilani walks out from behind the bar to the lanai to take more drink orders while Ashley whispers to me, "But what if it's fate?"

"Then it will be fate just as much in ten minutes as it will be now. Go."

As Ashley heads back to the storage area, I throw some strawberries and basil into a pint glass, then return to the couple. As I muddle the basil in with the berries, I tell them, "You came at a great time. We have a fantastic game going on right now, and the prize is a complimentary first round of drinks."

"Wow," the man says to me. "Cool. So what's the game?"

"How did you two meet?"

The couple exchange a look, complete with knowing smiles and amorous, silent promises. "I met her in a bakery," the man tells me as he flirts with his wife.

The woman continues, "Ben works for the best bakery in Cleveland. I was picking up a chocolate cake for a bridal shower. We were doing this weird fortune-telling thing called a cake pull—"

"—where you have to pull charms out of the cake," I say, my heart jumping into my throat.

She points to me. "Oh my God, yeah. My friend was getting married, and she wanted us to rig the cake with these charms. Long story. Anyway, so I walk into the bakery, and there's this amazing-looking man at the front counter—"

"Hold on," I say, putting my hand out, my palm toward her. "Real quick. What charm did you end up getting?"

I knew she pulled the money tree even before she told me. I knew the bride had tried to rig the cake and it didn't work. I knew that nothing I asked would really matter at that moment, but I had to finish Ashley's challenge. So after I heard all of the details of the meet cute I asked the inevitable: "So how did you two really meet?"

Again, they exchange looks, but this time they both appear confused. "We met in a bakery," Mel repeats.

So Leilani won the bet after all. So, as promised, I won't text Ben again.

But haven't the rules changed here? I mean, the two of them

are named Ben and Mel, and they met right before a cake pull, where she pulled a money tree.

Damn. Seriously, what are the odds? Shouldn't that be some sort of signal from the universe?

But that was really how they met. They really were soul mates, fated during our romantic era to be with one another after a meet cute, without any major obstacles in their path, destined to be happy forever.

Not until two Kipona Alohas, one Pomaika'i, three beers, and one bathroom break (Mel's) later that I learned one more thing about fate.

That, sometimes, it needs a little nudge.

Once Mel is in the bathroom and out of hearing range, Ben leans in to me and asks, "Can you keep a secret?"

This might be my favorite part of the job. I lean in, smile, and whisper conspiratorially, "Always."

He darts a glance toward the women's restroom and, deciding the coast is clear, tells me under his breath, "We really met at a bar."

Intrigued, I lean in closer. "Oh, yeah?"

He smiles and nods. "Her bachelorette party. I suggested she buy a cake from me for her shower and gave her my card. *She* was the bride, not her friend." Ben leans back and takes a sip of his beer. "I'm sure that makes me sound like an asshole. But let me tell you, I knew after five minutes of talking to that woman that she was getting married because she thought that was what she was supposed to do, not because it's what she wanted to do. Now I'm from the Midwest—I think you have to do what you're supposed to most of the time: I get up at three in the morning to be at the bakery by four. I pay my mortgage on the first of every month. I visit my grandma at her retirement home every other Sunday.

And that's all good. But we all have enough supposed-to's in life. Who you marry should never be one of them."

I smile. "Thanks, Ben. Your story means more to me than you know."

Mel happily bounces back to us and hops on her barstool. "What did I miss?" she asks Ben cheerfully.

Ben smiles at his bride. "Well, I'm guessing that Mel here has this guy on her mind. And I can't tell if she's torn because she thinks she's supposed to be with him, or if it's because she thinks she's supposed to stay away from him. Either way, her heart has already told her what to do. Now she's got to have the strength to do it." He winks at me. "So, are you going to go get your cake?"

A smile creeps onto my face, and everything suddenly becomes clear. "You know, Ben, I am."

FIFTY-FIVE

About ten minutes after my conversation with Newlywed Ben, during a quick break, I head into the back room to text Married Ben.

> Did you get married because you wanted to, or because you felt like you were supposed to?

Ben takes about fifteen minutes before he writes back:

> A combination of the two I guess. I was of a certain age—it's expected. So, do I get to see you?

I read and reread his text several times. Finally I type back:

> Do you want to meet me at Male 'Ana a little after closing? Say around 1?

> I can do that. But are you sure you don't want to come to my place? More privacy to yell at me. ☺

> I'm done yelling. You either thought about me after JFK
> or you didn't. Bring the bracelet.

At midnight, we closed up, and by one o'clock we were all cleaned up and ready to head out.

Leilani stayed with me while I waited.

By 12:55, I felt as if I was going to throw up. "I need a drink," I say, grabbing a beer pint and getting ready to pour.

"Uh-uh," Leilani says, pulling the pint glass out of my hand and filling it with Diet Pepsi. "You need to be fully present for this."

I take a deep breath, then a nervous sip of soda. "What about a Valium? Would that be poor form?"

"See, I knew there was a reason you liked me. Free drugs," I hear Ben joke.

I turn around, and he is standing by the door, looking amazing in a simple T-shirt and blue jeans.

I feel as if I'm about to faint and fall back ever so slightly to feel Leilani catch me and prop me back up. "Hey," I say.

Yup—witty as ever with my openings.

"Hey," he replies. Then he nervously tells me, "You look good."

"Thanks."

The two of us stare at each other for what seems like seven years.

"Okay, well, I hate to miss out on all this witty repartee, but I got an MFV I'm late for." Leilani grabs her purse, then rubs my shoulder. "You good?"

I nod once decisively.

"All rightie. I'm a phone call away if you need anything." She walks toward the door to leave, but can't help but kindly suggest to Ben, "You be nice. I'm kama'aina. I can have five Brigham Young football players here in twenty minutes."

Ben is unfazed by the threat. "I will keep that under advisement."

"Good. And if it turns out she chooses you, I'm having a little shindig at my apartment next Sunday. You two should come by."

And she's out the door.

"I suppose I deserved that," Ben tells me as he walks toward the bar. "So, how have you been?"

"I've been fine. So what did your ex say?" I blurt out.

"Wow. Jumping right in, I guess," Ben says, shaking his head once quickly.

"I'm sorry," I tell him nervously. Why won't these butterflies go away? "Can I get you a drink?"

"Sure. Can I have a beer?"

"No problem," I say, pouring him the same Maui Brewing Company IPA he drank during the torch-lighting ceremony.

"You remembered," Ben says as I hand him his glass.

"I remember a lot of stuff," I say, trying to sound light. "Such as . . . and I'm just throwing out a random example . . . how you told your wife about me—"

"Ex-wife."

"—ex-wife about me and you wanted to tell me all about the conversation."

"I'm not sure that's quite how I put it." I pull out my phone and show him his text. "Or, that's exactly how I put it." Ben takes a nervous sip of beer. "Okay, before I tell you about that, I have something to tell you, but you have to promise—"

"Oh, for God's sake."

He chuckles. "No, no. It's a good thing. Ever since we met, I've been thinking about you. A lot. I had just come from Isabella's apartment, and I knew it was over, like *over* over, and I was just sitting at the airport bar feeling sorry for myself, and then here comes this cute girl, and she was cute and funny and self-deprecating and it must have taken me twenty minutes even to say hi. And then it was easy. And I liked this girl. But of course she was on her way to Paris to be with the love of her life—"

"He was so not the love of my life."

"Well, I had known you an hour. Although I will say, all the way to LA I kept thinking, 'That relationship wasn't going well, you could have taken him. Why didn't you at least get her number, you idiot?' And then you walked into urgent care and . . .'" Ben looks down at the bar, unsure of what to say next. "Well, in a six-word memoir, 'Don't ever let her leave again.'"

I squint at him, smiling. "Do men really say things like that?"

Ben shakes his head and exhales a deep breath. "You know, we really don't. It doesn't become us. I'm already ready to kick my own ass right now."

I run around the bar and give him a big kiss.

We kiss for a while, and the butterflies dissolve. "I thought about you too," I admit.

Ben smirks. "Good."

"Shut up. Okay, what happened with Isabella? Did she yell?"

"No," Ben says in a cryptic way. "I told her I'd met someone, and she wasn't mad at all. Which it turns out makes sense because she's back with her boyfriend, and they're now engaged."

My eyes bulge out, my chin drops, and my mouth falls open. Ben points to me. "Yeah, that's pretty much how I reacted. She invited me to the wedding, but that's a little too 'we can still be friends' for my taste. But no yelling. The whole conversation, I kept bracing for the other shoe to drop. Or, more likely, to get thrown at my head. But, no, nothing. It's over. We're cool. On to the next."

"Wow," I say, a little stunned. "So, you really are getting divorced."

"Yeah. She filed the paperwork with the State of New York today, and I should be served any day now."

I smile and joke, "Can I do it?"

"Ha-ha," Ben deadpans. "Anyway, that means I'm now free to date whoever I want for as long as you want. So, how much longer are you in town for?"

Which is my cue to say, "Okay, I need to tell you something. But you have to promise me you won't freak out."

EPILOGUE

One year later

You know the best part of a destination wedding? No cake charms!

I'm kidding of course. The best part is you can throw the whole thing together in less than a month, and if you do it through a fabulous five-star resort, very little planning is involved.

On the anniversary of the day we met back at JFK airport, Ben proposed at a sacred Hawaiian burial site called Dragon's Teeth in Kapalua, which is a dramatic collection of jagged rocks overlooking the Pacific. We decided to marry on the anniversary of our first kiss.

We immediately called a resort in Wailea, then our friends and family. The whole process took about an hour.

It was a small wedding, fewer than thirty people. Our theme was "no runaway brides or grooms." Actually, Ben and I did have our own little mantra for the wedding: If you're not relaxed right now, change what you're doing. Today, it's someone else's problem.

I refused to let Nic and Seema throw me a bridal shower—arguing that I had had enough of those to last a lifetime. We also didn't bother with a gift registry. As far as I was concerned, I had everything I could ever want or need. Instead, we asked guests who wanted to give gifts to donate to Math Rocks!—a college scholarship fund I created for women who wanted to major in mathematics. (Turns out, I still have some excitement about math after all.)

Jeff threw our rehearsal dinner at Male 'Ana and had it catered with all of my favorite Hawaiian foods I'd discovered in the past year: Kalua pork, furikake-crusted calamari, and of course lots of poke! We also had fresh pineapple and guava, vanilla and lilikoi cupcakes, and so many honeymoon cocktails that we used all of the cabs on the island for a brief few minutes sending guests home.

The next day, I got the gift that I had waited for my entire life: to be the bride. My dress was a beautiful white, sleeveless gown I picked up at a consignment shop in Kahului. I wore a white-orchid lei and fresh flowers in my hair instead of a veil.

Nic was my maid of honor, and Seema was my bridesmaid, just as we had planned in college. I let them choose their own bridal-party gowns. (As I have said before, sometimes it pays to be the beta dog. No eight-hour trips to the bridal salon! No arguments over the benefits of satin over taffeta! No headaches and blurred vision trying to see if there is a difference between amethyst and lilac!) Nic looked spectacular in a dark purple, sleeveless sheath gown from Pea in the Pod. Yup, Pea in the Pod. She was once again pregnant, although fortunately only five months along, so we didn't worry about her water breaking or anything else going wrong at this wedding. Seema wore a lavender, sleeveless, V-neck chiffon dress with ruching from Suzy Chin. One wore flats, one wore sky-high heels. They could not have matched less.

They were perfect.

We held the ceremony a little bit before sunset, in front of the

sparkly Pacific Ocean. Instead of flowers, we had the gazebo decorated with money trees. Jeff officiated. Ben's sister was his best
woman, his best friend from college his groomsman. We had one
ring bearer, Jason Jr., and six (count 'em, six!) flower girls: Ben's two
nieces from Los Angeles, Nic's stepdaughters, Malika and Megan,
and Seema and Scott's twin girls, Bindu and Jyotsna.

It is now just after the ceremony, as light turns to dusk, and as
waiters hand out flutes of champagne, our guests get to watch our
own private torch-lighting ceremony. (Which basically just con-
sisted of us ordering a dozen torches to be lit by one of the hotel
employees. But I am loving it!)

Dinner is an amazing five-course feast featuring local cheeses,
fresh fish, locally grown beef, and the most famous dessert in the
world: wedding cake.

Our cake is nothing fancy, just a standard three-layered, white-
frosted confection with purple orchids decorating the top. On the
bottom and middle layers, however, is something a little different:
purple satin cake-charm ribbons poke out, hinting at a treat inside.

"You didn't," Seema says in disbelief when she sees the cake
being wheeled out into our reception area.

"I did!" I proudly tell her. "And, Nic, in honor of you, I rigged it!"

"Really?" she asks, intrigued. "Which one's mine? You have no
bride and groom on top of the cake: How do you know who gets
what? Are you the first one to pull?"

"Relax. It will all work out the way it's supposed to."

I walk up to Ben, who begins a toast. "I'd like to ask everyone
to gather around our cake for a moment."

Our guests do as they are told, and Ben explains, "A little over
a year ago today, I met the most beautiful, amazing, funny woman
in the world. And in a bar, no less!"

Laughter from the group.

Ben looks at me and smiles. "At a bridal shower for a friend, this amazing woman pulled a silver charm from a cake, similar to the cake you're looking at now. The charm was called a money tree, and my bride"—Ben turns to me as he realizes for the first time— "no, my *wife* . . . didn't quite know what it meant. Nonetheless, the charm led her on a spiritual journey, which led her to Hawaii, which led her to me."

I look at my . . . oh, my goodness, it's *husband,* isn't it? . . . smile and give him a quick kiss. Then I turn to our guests. "I need everyone to put their finger through a loop and pull. Whatever charm you get should tell you your future."

"But how do we know—" Nic begins.

"Just pick one. It'll all work out the way it's supposed to," I assure her.

Everyone pulls, laughs, and starts comparing their charms. The kids immediately begin licking off the ganache filling around their charms.

"Wait, are they all money trees?" Seema asks, amused.

"They are!" I answer.

At which time, Ben holds up his glass and makes a toast: "May you complete all of your journeys and find all of their charms."